The
Champagne Crush

The Champagne Crush

A Romance Novel

CAROLINE O'CONNELL

SPARKPRESS

Published in 2025 by
SparkPress, an imprint of The Stable Book Group

32 Court Street, Suite 2109
Brooklyn, NY 11201
https://shewritespress.com

Library of Congress Control Number: 2025909821
Print ISBN: 978-1-68463-334-0
eISBN: 978-1-68463-335-7

Interior design and typeset by Katherine Lloyd, The DESK

Printed in the United States

TO

Mom and Dad

Like myriad champagne bubbles aging
in the bottle for years, people's hidden agendas
and true selves burst open when the pressure is released,
creating long-lasting ripples.

Chapter One

New York—January

The celebratory sound of corks popping stilled conversation in the room. High above Manhattan's snow-covered streets, tuxedo-clad waiters picked up silver trays brimming with crystal champagne flutes and began serving the assembled guests. A glimmer of late-afternoon sun streaked through the conference room's floor-to-ceiling windowpanes, illuminating thousands of tiny bubbles floating their way to the surface of each glass.

"Ladies and gentlemen, I'd like to propose a toast." Chris McDermott, president of Winston & Wright, raised his flute. His six-two frame and deep voice commanded attention. "I am pleased to introduce this special preview tasting of our most important creation to date."

Gazing at the effervescence in his glass, Chris nodded toward the dapper Frenchman standing next to him. "We are indebted to you, Jean. Your winemaking talent has brought us one step closer to our dream." He tipped his flute toward Jean. "Here's to stellar reviews for our *cuvée de prestige* when it's launched at Vinexpo in June."

Sounds of clinking glasses were followed by murmurs of appreciation as investors and top executives took their first sips and savored the complex flavors. They breathed a collective sigh of relief. Many had a considerable stake in the success of the company's first premium sparkling wine.

Well-wishers clustered around Chris and Jean to offer congratulations. Everyone was in a festive mood. Or so it seemed.

A half hour later, the crowd started to disburse. Chris glanced at the door as a distinguished-looking older man walked in.

Chris grabbed a remaining flute and offered it to him. "Glad you're back. How was the trip?"

James Winston, founder and chairman of Winston & Wright, loosened his tie. "Had a productive meeting at Trianon. Left Charles-de-Gaulle two hours late—typical." He regarded the bubbles, took a sip, and let it savor in his mouth. "Jean outdid himself. Our French partners should be pleased." He set the glass down. "Sorry I missed the tasting. How did it go?"

"A big hit. Looks like our investment is paying off."

"I should hope so," James said. "We have a lot riding on this." He stepped to the side, away from the others. "By the way, I heard in France that Relais & Châteaux plans to announce a contest featuring French champagnes and California sparkling wines. If so, we should consider entering our new *cuvée*."

Chris was wary of subjecting their *cuvée* to another hurdle, especially a contest. He preferred to leave the verdict to wine critics who knew what they were doing. He sidestepped. "I'll see if it comes up in Napa this weekend."

"Speaking of Napa, I know you've got a lot on your plate, but I'd like you to do me a favor." James pulled a file out of his briefcase. "There's a family friend working the event this weekend, and I want to offer her a job through the launch to beef up our publicity outreach beyond wine circles." He handed a paper to

Chris. "She has celebrity connections and some PR experience at a top firm in LA. I thought it could fit in with our efforts to create media buzz."

Chris glanced at the résumé and his blood pressure started to rise. It listed work on lavish movie premieres and celebrity profiles in entertainment magazines. "We don't have the budget for glitzy Hollywood parties." He shook his head. "Gee Jim, you know how much stress we're under. I don't have time to babysit a novice."

"See your point. But our outside firm is corporate. We need to pull out all the stops—add some pizzazz. I'd like to give her a try."

Chris realized James wasn't going to let him off the hook. "Okay. You're the boss. But if she becomes a burden, we'll have to cut the experiment short."

"That's your call," James agreed. "Thanks for handling this."

Chris glanced at his watch: almost six o'clock. He still had to finalize his presentation for the conference panel and get a few hours of sleep before his early flight in the morning. James's idea of *pizzazz* looked like one big headache to him.

Across the country in Napa, a grandfather clock chimed fifteen times, barely heard above the commotion in the Winston Resort dining room. The staff was in high gear, moving furniture, vacuuming rugs, and polishing silver and china in preparation for the kickoff of the California Sparkling Wine Producers' tenth annual conference.

Amid the hubbub, a striking woman with emerald-green eyes and honey-blonde hair clipped and arranged long-stemmed roses in an array of colors in antique porcelain vases, a scene reminiscent of a Renoir painting. Catherine Reynolds loved being surrounded by flowers: the colors, the scents, the textures.

She mused on their silhouettes and realized a rose motif would be a good addition to the sketch she was mocking up for her application to the Cornell Hospitality Intensive. Catherine's hopes were pinned on earning admission to their exclusive certificate program so she could finally gain steady employment and start supporting herself at twenty-eight without running to her parents.

This short-term job had been a godsend. Catherine was grateful her former boss at Kerner Public Relations had recommended her to his friend Tom, the resort director, who'd hired her two months ago. Her mandate: to coordinate holiday festivities and the event this weekend. To help with logistics for the three-day conference, Catherine had brought in her former assistant at Kerner, Claire Darnat, so they'd have two sets of hands setting up the workshops, field trips, and parties.

Claire picked up the latest vase to place on a serving table. "*Elles sont très belles*," she complimented.

"*Merci* Claire," Catherine said, thankful the older Frenchwoman had been willing to join her for this temporary gig.

A loud crash in the kitchen caught Catherine's attention. The head cook ran in. "That new pastry chef and I are going to come to blows," he said, waving his arms. "She wants to tie up one of my ovens for two hours with her fancy desserts."

"That's my fault." Catherine was glad she wouldn't have to deal with this temperamental chef much longer. "I suggested Anna try napoleons, my grandmother's special recipe. We'll bake something simpler tomorrow."

"That's better," he huffed and retreated through the swinging doors.

Catherine grabbed a handful of extra roses and placed them in a pitcher. She turned to Claire. "After I stop by the kitchen, I'm going to run these over to Robert's bungalow."

Claire frowned. "Shouldn't he be bringing you the flowers?"

"He's stressed about the big brass coming this weekend. I want to cheer him up." She sniffed the roses and wished she felt a stronger attraction to him. Her past had taught her to be wary when it came to men.

She'd met Robert Kenyon, a handsome Brit, her first day on the job. He'd seen her in the resort office and immediately asked her out. Initially she resisted, since they worked at the same small company. Eventually, his dry wit and persistence wore her down. It became clear why he was an effective sales manager when he didn't take no for an answer.

Before she'd left to spend the Christmas holiday with her family in Paris, she'd relented, and they went on their first date. The last three weeks he'd poured on the charm, wining and dining her, pressing his pursuit. She'd held off on becoming intimate. He was pushing for a weekend getaway after the conference when her job wrapped up. She hadn't given him an answer yet, but she had splurged on a sexy new outfit in case they took that trip to Carmel.

Stepping out the kitchen back door, Catherine took a garden path past a row of elm trees and a tranquil pond. Some staffers, like Robert, were offered long-term accommodations in private bungalow cottages near the main building. As she approached his porch, she heard him grunting, then a woman's voice shouting his name and urging him on. Sounds of their bodies slamming together were unmistakable.

She walked up the steps. The door had been left ajar. *Maybe in their haste.* She grimaced. Debating a split second, she pushed it open and walked in, as they both screamed their release. She slammed the door shut and Robert looked up, startled.

Their eyes locked. "What are you doing here?" he said.

"I brought these to surprise you." Catherine held out the flowers to ward off the sight in front of her.

He pulled futilely at the sheets. "For heaven's sake, could you give us some privacy—we'll discuss this later."

"There's nothing further to discuss," she said. "Thanks for the lesson in male morality."

In a couple of long strides, she reached the bed. She pulled out a yellow rose and threw it at him. "This stands for infidelity, you jerk." Then she took a step closer. "What the heck, here's the whole bunch." She tipped the pitcher and poured its contents, ice water and all, onto his naked back. He groaned a different tune as she walked out.

A reminder that I'm a terrible judge of men.

Chapter Two

Napa—124 days to Winston cuveé *launch*

Late January in Napa is normally rainy and cold, but this Friday afternoon was crisp and clear and unseasonably warm. Chris McDermott gazed at the passing vineyards as their driver turned onto Napa's Highway 121, known as Carneros Highway. His traveling companion, Sean Dunlavy, Winston's sales director, was buried in charts on his laptop. Barren vines staked in rows stretched as far as the eye could see, their grapes dormant this time of year.

It felt good to be home. Chris was a country boy at heart. He and his two younger brothers had grown up in bucolic surroundings on the McDermott ranch in Rutherford, not far from Carneros. He had fond memories of his childhood, except for the early morning chores. After high school, he'd landed a football scholarship to Stanford and went on to seek fame, fortune, and his MBA at Harvard.

The fortune part progressed faster than expected when he made astute stock investments at his first job out of college on Wall Street, garnering almost $2 million. Three years later, through a mutual acquaintance, James recruited him to assume the position of president of Winston & Wright. Chris opted to invest most of his money in the company. He believed in putting it all on the line and wanted to be an equity stakeholder before they implemented their expansion plans overseas.

That investment added to his stress level right now. Chris needed to ensure a successful launch at Vinexpo to get his stake back, plus a bonus, to use for his family's nascent winery in Rutherford. His dad and brothers were depending on him. He planned to join them in five years when he turned forty.

The car passed a signpost announcing Winston Resort & Winery and turned onto a stone-paved drive framed by mature eucalyptus trees. At the entrance, a long line of uniformed parking attendants was on full alert greeting guests.

"Looks like Tom is running interference out front," Sean said.

Chris stepped out and clasped hands with Tom Banbury, director of operations. "Good to see you. Things must be pretty busy."

"That's an understatement," Tom said. "With conference guests, plus other visitors, we're at full capacity."

Tom directed two bellhops to take their bags. "Why don't you two check in, and I'll meet you back here in a half hour for a tour of the improvements at the winery."

"Sounds good," Chris said.

Fifteen minutes later, Chris returned to the lobby and decided to look around while he waited for the others. Winston & Wright, also called "Winston" since Alan Wright was a silent partner, was one of the few wineries awarded a building exemption to construct a resort adjacent to their winery operation. Napa Valley had become a popular destination for weekend getaways and special occasions, prompting a big demand for upscale accommodations and gourmet restaurants. Local officials had limited development, so most resorts couldn't offer proximity to a winery.

A sense of nostalgia swept over Chris as he strolled through the lobby. At first, he thought it was the comfort of the setting, which reminded him of the McDermott ranch. The Provençal decor featured terracotta tile floors, enhanced by colorful area rugs. Tall earthenware pots held large floral arrangements and added another splash of color. Comfortable leather chairs with cushions in Mediterranean blue and white were placed in quiet corners, inviting guests to curl up with a glass of wine.

Nope, that's not it.

It was the scent of chocolate chip scones wafting from the kitchen, just like his mom used to bake.

After a few quick strides through the empty dining room, he pushed open swinging doors that led into a gleaming chrome-surfaced kitchen. All was spotless except for a large table where two women baked furiously, immersed in their work. Each wore a large white apron and matching hat, which offered little protection from the flour that covered every exposed inch of their bodies.

The scones on the counter looked delicious. Chris's mouth watered. He had to have one. A woman with blonde hair in a tight bun pulled a sheet pan out of the oven and spotted him. "I'm sorry, sir. The kitchen is off limits to guests."

Not reading the signals, Chris tried to charm his way into a scone. "I don't mean to intrude, but those scones smell like the ones my mom used to bake." He gave her one of his engaging smiles. "Could I try one?"

"They're too hot, and we're busy. They'll be out later." She shook her head and went back to stirring a wooden spoon in a large bowl of batter. "You'll just have to wait."

Chris wondered why she was so obstinate. He felt like a scolded child. "Forget it," he growled, then stalked off.

He was still fuming when he reached the foyer where Sean waited. "What happened to you?" Sean asked. "You look steamed."

"I just got chastised by a spinsterish cook for invading the kitchen," Chris said.

Sean laughed. "Guess you've been in New York too long and lost your country-boy charm."

The two men walked out the main entrance and met Tom coming up a side path. "I'm glad we have a few minutes to meet before the kickoff," Tom said.

When the Winston Resort was conceived, it had been designed to highlight the agricultural connection. Buildings were arranged in a semicircle and featured large bay windows to bring in natural light and offer sweeping views of the vineyards below. Courtyards with well-tended gardens and wrought-iron benches connected the buildings and were used for outdoor concerts and parties.

At the end of the path, the men approached a sprawling two-story structure. The exterior resembled the rustic style of the nearby resort, but inside those similarities ceased. This was a modern, state-of-the-art production facility for turning grapes into sparkling wine.

Tom led them to an area near the loading dock. "Let's start with our new tank press." At Winston, the grape clusters went into the juice press, stem and all. Chris knew some wineries took the step of destemming before the juice press, but this was rough on the grapes. Winston chose a gentle pressing to extract the juice then discarded the skins and leftover stem pulp. Tom demonstrated how it worked. "Obviously, we won't be getting any real use until the harvest in September."

They moved on to a second-floor observation post, where the men had an overview of the operation for the initial stages of the process. Large stainless-steel tanks, connected on top by a grid of crisscrossed pipes, received the juice from the press for the first fermentation. The tanks were clearly labeled to indicate which of the three grape varieties was inside. In this stage, yeast converted the sugars in the grape juice to alcohol and carbon dioxide, while any leftover sediment settled to the bottom.

Chris was pleased with the operation. "Can't believe it's been seven years since Jean finalized the blend for our first prestige label. A long haul from the vineyard to final product." He knew they were fortunate that a renowned winemaker created the unique blend, known as a *cuvée*, of the three still wines.

Sean tapped his sales charts. "Jean's reputation caused our presales to soar, plenty of pent-up demand to taste what he's come up with."

"Speaking of the launch," Chris addressed Tom, "how are we doing locating enough jeroboams to use for Vinexpo in Bordeaux?" Jeroboams held the equivalent of four normal bottles. Chris thought their immense size was unwieldy. But he was overruled in favor of the drama and wow factor for the big reveal.

"I'll admit, we had to hustle when the decision was made to use those large bottles," Tom said. "The Trianon folks were able to send them over from France, so we're all set for that final transfer stage."

"Thanks, Tom." Chris pulled out his phone to check messages. "I know you and Sean have sales and distribution issues to go over, and I've got some calls to make. I'll see you tonight."

The resort's outdoor lights flickered on as dusk faded into night. At a vanity in her upstairs guest room in the main building,

Catherine applied the finishing touches of her pale pink lipstick and sprayed Chanel's Allure perfume on her pulse points. The scent reminded her of shopping trips with Grandma Reynolds and lifted her spirits. A boost she could use right now.

Reeling from Robert's betrayal, she hoped to avoid a scene with him over the weekend. How humiliating. At least the shock didn't bring on one of her panic attacks, a worry that always lay close to the surface. When they occurred, she couldn't control the shortness of breath, dizziness, and sometimes actual fainting spells.

She took a sip from a glass of Winston's latest rosé sparkling she'd been drinking to calm her nerves and fortify her courage and tilted it toward the mirror. "Showtime."

Catherine's first stop was the kitchen, a place where she always felt at home. Busy waiters prepared trays of warm hors d'oeuvres chosen to compliment the flavors in the sparkling wines. She sampled a few to make sure the pastry shells were crispy, not soggy, and the lobster skewers were tender, not overcooked.

The headwaiter gazed in her direction and spoke softly to the server next to him. "We're going to have to do double duty as bodyguards to protect our fair princess from male admirers."

Catherine smiled inwardly at the overheard compliment but didn't acknowledge it. She wore an Yves Saint Laurent midnight-blue cashmere fitted suit that hugged her body, accenting her slim figure. The cropped jacket cinched at her waist, and the tight skirt fell just below her knees. Not the easiest to walk in, especially in three-inch Ferragamo heels, but it created the desired effect.

Grabbing her phone and small clutch, Catherine went to the end of a nearby hallway where she found Tom Banbury and Doug Barr, president of the California Sparkling Wine Producers, greeting arrivals at the door to the banquet room.

"You did a great job transforming this place," Tom said. "I hardly recognize it."

"Thanks. The staff was a big help." Catherine had honed this skill from growing up in consulates and attending receptions. Her American father was a diplomat in France. Her French mother instilled in her an innate taste and knack for creating environments. Catherine's dream was to develop this talent and eventually run her own resort.

The conference committee had decided to kick off the weekend with an evening reception. Since January weather was too cold to have it outside, Catherine had been assigned the task of converting the large space into an intimate club. Instead of normal overhead lighting, area spotlights and tall white candles on pedestals illuminated small seating groups simply adorned by large bouquets of exotic flowers. Tables for each sparkling wine company were decorated with silver linen tablecloths and champagne flutes stacked into small pyramids, a balancing technique Catherine picked up one summer in her youth. Dramatic and evocative.

"Looks like we're off to a good start," Tom said. "One more thing. Chris McDermott, our president, is here from New York and wants to speak with you."

Catherine couldn't imagine what that was about unless it was a message from James. She hadn't revealed to Tom that the chairman was a family friend. "I'd be grateful if you'd make him feel welcome," Tom added.

"Of course." Catherine wasn't looking forward to charming a gray-haired corporate stuffed shirt, but she owed Tom that much. She excused herself to finish checking on the arrangements.

All the prestigious wineries were represented, including Moët's Domaine Chandon, Mumm Napa, Schramsberg, Taittinger's Domaine Carneros, Roederer Estate, and others. Conference attendees seemed in high spirits as they greeted each other and sampled the sparkling wines from each house.

Chris and Sean strode in a few minutes later, and the women in the room took collective notice. It looked like Hollywood had come to Napa. Tall, trim, and pressed in what appeared to be Armani suits, tailored white shirts, and silk designer ties, the men were an eyeful for those accustomed to the casual style that was the norm in Napa. The admirer only needed to decide if she preferred Sean's sandy-brown hair and good-ole-southern-boy sexy brown eyes to Chris's handsome dark-Irish looks, complemented by piercing blue eyes. Even the casual observer could see neither was wearing a wedding ring. Engines revved and the chase was about to commence.

After extricating themselves from the ladies, Chris said, "Let's try the sparkles." They made their way to the Schramsberg table to taste their new Blanc de Blancs.

While Chris jotted notes on a small card he carried for these occasions, Sean seemed to drift into a reverie. "Now, there is a vision of enchantment, a striking beauty."

Without looking up, Chris said, "I think the bubbles are going to your head, my friend. Maybe we'll have to—" He stopped midsentence when he saw who Sean was referring to. "I don't believe it. She looks kind of like the woman from the kitchen this afternoon."

"You can't mean the spinsterish chef," Sean scoffed. "Do you need glasses? That woman is beautiful."

"She looks different when the flour is washed off her face and she's not wrapped in an apron. Perhaps she has an evil twin."

Sean clinked his glass against Chris's. "I'm glad you've ruined your chances so I have a clear field to press my pursuit."

"What makes you think she's available?" Chris countered. "In my experience, women like that are always taken"—he shook his head—"or too high maintenance."

Tom approached and noticed the men's gaze. "I see you've spotted Catherine Reynolds."

"She's Catherine Reynolds?" Chris sputtered. "The consultant? I saw that woman baking in the kitchen, under a cloud of flour. Unless she has a twin?"

"Nope, she's an original. Let's go over and I'll introduce you." Tom led the way.

Sean cast Chris a winning grin and punched him in the arm.

Chris nudged Sean back with his elbow and said softly, "You know James asked me to offer her a job. If she takes it, we frown on employees fraternizing."

"She looks like a goddess," Sean said. "I'll take the heat. I think I have an instant crush on her."

"Don't say I didn't warn you," Chris said. "Hopefully, she'll decline the job."

Tom reached Catherine and gestured to the men. "Catherine, I'd like you to meet two people from our corporate office in New York: Chris McDermott, president of Winston & Wright, and Sean Dunlavy, the sales director."

Chris sensed her embarrassment at their earlier encounter. He knew he felt the same way. Time to make amends.

"It's a pleasure to meet you," Chris said, extending his hand. "I think I saw your twin baking up a storm this afternoon." She gave him a grateful look, and he held her hand a few seconds longer than necessary.

Sean cleared his throat, breaking up their gaze. "Miss Reynolds," he said, "you look lovely tonight."

"Thank you," she murmured.

"I have something I'd like to discuss with you," Chris said. "Are you free for breakfast tomorrow?"

"Yes, we could meet at eight in the café."

"I'll see you then."

Chapter Three

Napa—123 days to Winston cuvée *launch*

Like other top lodgings in Napa Valley, the Winston Resort spared no expense in matching good taste with elegance and comfort. The rooms were luxuriously appointed to pamper guests, including high-thread-count linens and goose-down comforters. Even those amenities didn't aide Catherine's slumber. She'd slept fitfully. She couldn't shake the shock of Robert's deception: his naked body entwined with a young woman she recognized from the winery's internship program. He'd tried to talk it over later, but she couldn't face his excuses.

Her immediate problem was entertaining an executive-type over breakfast. She had no idea what he wanted. She reminded herself of the Girl Scout motto her best friend, Vanessa, recited constantly: "Be prepared—for anything." Catherine's battle armor was to look as put together as possible and not show her emotions. It worked . . . most of the time.

She arrived at the Soleil Café early, hoping to score a quick espresso before her meeting. She needed her caffeine fix. No such luck. Chris was already waiting at a prime table in the glass-enclosed patio overlooking the vineyards. Catherine preferred this cozy garden room to the resort's formal restaurant. Early sunlight shimmered off the grape motif on the pale-yellow Limoges china, set atop linen placemats in a matching design.

Chris looked up from his phone and waved. *Uh oh.* His smile was seductive. He stood up to pull out her chair. "I'm sorry we got off on the wrong foot yesterday," he said.

"Apology accepted," Catherine said, grateful they could move past the kitchen encounter. While they regarded menus, Catherine stole another glance at Chris. He really was quite handsome. The blue sports jacket brought out the blue of his eyes.

The waiter materialized and took their orders. Then Chris got down to business. "You may have heard about the new prestige sparkling we're launching in June."

"Yes, Tom mentioned it," Catherine said.

"We're looking to hire a publicity manager, someone to increase our participation in high profile events and gain coverage in mainstream media outlets." Chris averted his gaze. "James Winston asked me to offer you the position."

Catherine's couldn't mask the surprise on her face. "That's unexpected."

Their drink orders arrived. Hers, an extra-shot cappuccino with soy milk; his, a regular coffee, black. Catherine took a sip and sighed. Chris looked at her quizzically. "Need my java jolt first thing," she said.

She had blocked out the next few months to study for the Cornell entrance exam and finish her designs for the application, so this was a nonstarter. She took another sip to stall and consider her response. They'd already gotten off on the wrong foot; she didn't want to give him an abrupt dismissal. "What's the job description?" she asked.

"To be honest, it's not very defined yet," Chris said. "We have an outside firm, but they're corporate, ads in the wine press, stuff like that. James thinks we should pursue more lifestyle and entertainment press, add some glitz." He frowned at that last remark, which told Catherine all she needed to know about his thoughts on the subject. This job had "difficult" written all over it. He seemed reluctant to make the hire, and the stated goal was amorphous. Good thing she had other plans.

In addition, this was a serious job with high stakes; she had no training in corporate public relations. At Kerner, she'd been hired to help stage parties for press coverage. It was easy to get media hits when you had A-list celebrities involved.

"It would entail working out of our New York office," Chris continued, as he sprinkled salt on his scrambled eggs. "Though the winery operation is in Napa, James based the headquarters in New York. He plans to expand overseas, and we have a partner in France, so New York makes more sense."

Catherine finished a bite of her toast and figured she'd better stop him there before he suspected she was leading him on. "Thank you so much for considering me for this job. I appreciate your taking the time to explain it to me, but this doesn't fit into my plans right now." She didn't feel the need to elaborate.

Chris nodded. "I understand."

She was relieved he didn't press her for more explanation and wondered if he was glad she didn't accept the position. He didn't appear upset she'd declined. She glanced at her phone. "I've got to leave in a few minutes to do a final run-through of the room setup for the first panel."

"Of course." Chris signaled the waiter to bring their check.

As they stood up to leave, she extended her hand. "Thanks again for taking the time to speak with me." When they shook, she felt a jolt of attraction. *Where did that come from?*

Catherine went straight to the banquet room and found Claire at the sign-in table where attendees picked up their badges. The room had been transformed into a large meeting space and conveyed a different vibe from the party atmosphere of the night before. Conference schedules were placed on each chair, and a gourmet coffee station near the entrance did brisk business.

The tenth annual meeting of California Sparkling Wine Producers had an ambitious agenda. Owners and operators of California sparkling wineries formed the association to promote their products as a group. Each year they met to address issues affecting their reputation and sales. This year's theme was Appellations and Labeling.

Tom Banbury welcomed the eighty participants to the Winston Resort and introduced Doug Barr.

Doug stepped up to the podium. "Good morning. There is one last-minute announcement to share with you. Relais & Châteaux has decided to sponsor a contest among its members to choose sparkling wines to be featured in their properties next year, in two categories—French champagne and California sparkling wine."

Hands started to raise for questions, but Doug ignored them and continued. "In order to qualify for the contest, you must compete in the Plaza Blind Tasting at our New York gala in early April and receive a medal—gold, silver, or bronze. Good luck to all of you who choose to participate. Will be a great opportunity to showcase our California sparkling wines."

Then Doug straightened his notes but never glanced down as he ticked off the key issues for the weekend.

Catherine and Claire stood at the back of the room during Doug's kickoff. Catherine was a big fan of Relais & Châteaux properties. She hoped James's company fared well in the competition and felt a twinge of regret she wouldn't be around to help.

"What did Chris want to meet with you about?" Claire asked.

"Believe it or not, he offered me a job," Catherine said. "He seemed reluctant about it, though."

"How did that come up?"

"James is behind this. He's chairman of the company and a close family friend," Catherine said. "In any event, I need to focus on my application to Cornell."

"Then you declined," Claire said.

"Yes, I just said it wasn't a good time."

"Too bad." Claire beamed. "That young president seems like a catch."

"No matchmaking. I'll admit he's appealing, but I'm off the market right now." The women turned their attention back to the podium.

After lunch, everyone met at the resort entrance to board Mercedes-Benz buses for the afternoon field trip, a winery tour. Chris was glad to see they were getting back to basics. Tours fostered an appreciation for the time and effort that went into each bottle and were the first step in creating loyal customers. That outreach extended to invitations from wineries to tasting events, concerts, and even themed cruises.

Domaine Chandon was chosen to host the tour because it was nearby in Yountville and the operation was large enough to accommodate their group. It was also the first sparkling winery in northern California built by a French champagne company,

Moët & Chandon, in the early 1970s. Mumm, Taittinger, and Roederer had followed suit, each investing millions of dollars to purchase prime acreage and build state-of-the-art facilities.

Chris and Sean were among the last people to board the third bus. It was half empty, but they grabbed seats in the back row so they could speak without being overheard. Sean gestured to Catherine, who sat at the front of the bus. "Is she taking the job?"

"Nope," Chris said. "Think she realized she'd be in over her head."

"Sorry to hear it," Sean said. "I still might try to get her number."

Chris directed his gaze toward Catherine, who was in an animated conversation with a slight, dark-haired man who appeared to be a close acquaintance. "Looks like she prefers a certain stuck-up Frenchman." Chris couldn't fathom how Catherine could enjoy Patrick Tournelle's company. He was such a snob. "Wonder why he's attending," he said. "Tournelle is a French champagne company."

"Didn't you hear? They recently bought a small sparkling winery in Sonoma."

"Wonder what his end game is." Chris had had a few encounters with Patrick Tournelle at industry events in New York and always left with the impression he considered California sparkling second rate to French champagne. Granted the products were different, but the top California sparklings were excellent quality in their own right.

"Do you think he got an early heads-up on the Relais competition?" Chris asked. "Maybe he's working some angle there."

Sean shrugged. "Have no idea. Assume we'll be entering."

"Oh yes," Chris said. "Another hurdle for us to navigate. We'll need to place in the blind tasting to be taken seriously as a prestige label."

The bus passed the entrance gate to Domaine Chandon, drove past lushly landscaped grounds, and pulled up to the main building. A guide met their group.

"Welcome to Domaine Chandon." The guide explained he'd be taking them on a custom tour that covered aspects of the public tour but also areas normally off limits to guests. "Since our process is proprietary, we ask that you don't take photos. Feel free to ask questions as we go. Please follow me."

The guide led the group to an enclosed courtyard. "We'll start with the grapes. As you can see, the vines are dormant right now. The first new buds will break in March." Signs indicated the sample grapes staked in three separate sections: pinot noir, pinot meunier, and chardonnay. "We normally use the traditional three-grape varietals in blending our sparkling wine. When we conduct tours later in the year, we invite guests to taste the grapes."

Chris liked the hands-on approach. "It always starts with the grapes" was his mantra.

He noticed Patrick stayed close by Catherine's side as the guide took them through the grape pressing and first fermentation of the juice. Domaine Chandon's operation was on a much larger scale than Winston's. The stainless-steel tanks were immense.

Like all companies that adhered to the *méthode champenoise*, Domaine Chandon transferred the blended still wine into bottles for the second fermentation, where the effervescence was created. The guide led them into a cellar-like storage space. It warmed Chris's heart to see row upon row of bottles, stacked horizontally, undergoing their second fermentation. It was orderly and symmetrical and to him a work of art, part of a process that had been followed for centuries.

What was relatively new was the large *gyropalette* in the next room, and that caused a stir among the group. Patrick raised his hand. "At our champagne house in Épernay, we still use *remueurs* to turn the bottles each day. We feel this contraption detracts from the history and purity of the process."

"To elaborate for our guests who aren't steeped in the mechanics of the operation," the guide responded, "a process called riddling involves turning every bottle, each day, ever so slightly, to coax the remaining sediment down to the bottle stem for removal."

He walked over to the *gyropalette*. It resembled a giant box tilted on its axis. "*Remueurs* are highly skilled, and it's time-intensive labor. Many houses are automating that process with these machines."

Chris felt the need to chime in. "I respect the skill of riddlers, rotating up to fifty thousand bottles per day, but unfortunately that's a dying art."

Patrick appeared ready to debate the point further, but the guide motioned the group to keep moving and ushered them into an adjoining building. He raised his arms in an expansive gesture. "We're at the last stage."

The group faced a large assembly line with a conveyor belt to hang bottles, upside down and single file. "When the winemaker determines it is time for the disgorgement, each bottle is dropped neck down in a cold brine solution to freeze the remaining sediment," the guide explained. He picked up a bottle to demonstrate. "When the machine removes the temporary cap, the frozen sediment comes shooting out, and a dosage of reserve wine is added to round out the flavor and determine the level of sweetness." The group spread out to look at the machine. "After that, the final cork and foil cap are attached. *Et voilà*."

Good ending. Chris joined in the applause for the presentation. He was impressed with the quality of the tour.

"I'm sure you'll all agree that the finale of any tour should be a tasting." The guide led them back to the main building.

Domaine Chandon's bar overlooked rolling lawns dotted by hundred-year-old oak trees. A crush of people from the earlier groups had already begun mingling.

Normally, at the conclusion of a tour, visitors were offered a "tasting flight," consisting of a sampling of different wines to compare flavors. This group was too large, so waiters carried trays featuring Domaine Chandon's premium sparkling, étoile Tête de Cuvée.

Chris took a few sips and let the wine linger in his mouth. "This is good." He gestured to his glass. "They're impressing us with their best stuff."

"Yes, they're strong competitors." Sean grabbed his glass. "I'm going to mingle and see if I can pick up any gossip."

Chris guessed Sean would go in search of Catherine. He spotted her on the nearby terrace speaking to a short bespectacled man wearing a plaid bow tie. She caught his eye and waved him over. "Chris, do you know Ken Barnett? He's a columnist at *Wine Spectator*."

"Nice to meet you." Ken held out his hand and the men shook. "Hear you have a new prestige label launching at Vinexpo."

"Yes, we do," Chris said. He was pleased Ken had heard about the launch and made a mental note to follow up.

"So, how do you two know each other?" Chris asked.

"Believe it or not, we met at cooking school in Paris, years ago." Ken shook his head. "She was a twenty-year-old model taking a pastry class, and I was a late-twenties nerd in the wine program. Somehow we clicked." He smiled. "Well, I've gotta run. Catch up with you later, Cat." Ken gave her a quick hug and headed toward a group by the door.

Chris turned to her. "Cat?"

"Yes." She pursed her lips. "It's a nickname I picked up years ago and haven't been able to shake."

"It suits you." He caught himself gazing at her and snapped out of it. "I need to call the office before we board our bus."

"Sure," Catherine said. "See you later."

Chris hated to admit it, but he was intrigued. Catherine Reynolds was an attractive puzzle he couldn't figure out. Good thing she wasn't coming to work for him.

Chapter Four

Napa—122 days to Winston cuveé *launch*

Catherine's sleeping companion nuzzled her neck. She rolled over. "*Bonjour chérie. As-tu bien dormi?*" A calico cat pawed at the covers and elongated beside her. Catherine glanced at her antique travel clock: 7:00 a.m. She'd been restless and hadn't fallen asleep until late, an all-too-familiar occurrence.

She extended her arms, mimicking her cat's outstretched paws, and got out of bed. Time to catch the sun's early light. Catherine pulled on a cashmere peignoir that matched her rose-colored silk pajamas and opened double French doors leading to a small balcony. She braced herself against the cold morning air and moved closer to the outside railing.

Catherine loved Napa Valley. It was such a contrast to the urban sophistication of her youth spent in Paris and Geneva. The pace was more relaxed here. She could take runs in the vineyard each morning. Instead of car horns blaring and planes flying overhead, she heard birds chirping and crows cawing. She felt closer to nature's elements and the natural rhythm of life.

In the field below, workers inspected dormant vines. One of the men, who stood taller than the others, turned around. It was

Chris McDermott. *Boy, that guy sure is hands-on*. She wondered what he was doing out in the vineyard. At this hour. He looked dangerously handsome in faded jeans and a work shirt.

Chris looked up in her direction and caught her gaze. He smiled and waved. She realized, belatedly, that she was visible to others: tangled hair, no makeup, in her robe! She blushed, waved back, and rushed inside, embarrassed he'd caught her in a state of dishabille.

Mon Dieu. She'd become so casual here. Mother would be shocked.

Catherine's phone rang. As if reading her mind, her mother was calling from Paris.

"Hi Mom. I don't have much time now. Need to get ready for the conference."

"Hello, Catherine. This will only take a few minutes." Her stern tone scared Catherine. "I received a message from your accountant. Your bills are exceeding the monthly draw we agreed on." Catherine's heart sped up.

"The latest credit card statement has a $2,000 clothing expense. This is exorbitant and has gone on far too long," her mother said. "We've told you repeatedly you need to learn to budget. That time has come. We're cutting you off. You're old enough to figure out how to manage on your own."

Catherine was devastated but too proud to beg. "I have to run. I'll talk to you later." This was the worst timing. She'd been planning to ask her parents for more money the next few months, so she could devote all her time to completing the Cornell application and studying for the entrance exam.

She had to regroup, pronto. Then she remembered James's job offer. It was a lifeline she needed to grab. If it was still available. It was also a big gamble, since she had no experience in corporate PR and the position seemed precarious. She didn't have any other options. She'd have to make time for her Cornell prep on weekends.

Catherine wondered what Chris would think when she announced she'd changed her mind and would like to accept the job. She certainly couldn't tell him the reason.

Chris was having trouble reconciling the temptress on the balcony he'd admired a few hours ago—*like a scene from* Romeo and Juliet, he groaned—with the cool sophisticate at the back of the banquet room.

Notepad in hand, Catherine stood next to Claire by the coffee station, formal demeanor back in place, hair in one of those stylish buns she seemed good at. She wore a camel-colored conservative suit with damn provocative high heels that enhanced her sexy legs.

That woman is a chameleon. Earlier this morning she'd looked like a model for elegant lingerie; now she resembled that woman's ice-princess twin, still beautiful but much less approachable. Chris was becoming reluctantly more attracted by the hour.

"How'd it go with the workers this morning?" Sean asked.

"Normal concerns about salary and their job security," Chris said. "They've heard rumors about automating more of the plant."

"Wonder where that came from?"

"No idea. Maybe other wineries are trying to poach our trained cellar workers," Chris said.

Sean took a sip of coffee. "I'll see if Robert has any insights. He's sales but interfaces with winery supervisors."

"Good idea." Chris left to join the panel members taking their seats up front.

Doug Barr called the room to order and introduced the topic for the morning session, "Appellations and Labeling," key points outlined on a large projection screen next to him.

"Obviously, we won't resolve all these issues today." Doug gestured to the chart. "Many of them are beyond our control individually. We do have the power to tackle these areas as a group, particularly in influencing better legislation for accurate labeling and respect for specific appellation areas."

You can say that again. It was insane for mediocre sparkling wine fermented in vats, not bottles, to be labeled champagne. So misleading to consumers. Chris was proud of what they were doing at Winston to create a top-tier sparkling that could compete with champagnes from France.

Over the next two hours, there was a substantive strategy session and lively discussion. Specific committees were assigned to work further and report back in a few months.

APPELLATIONS & LABELING

"**Traditional Method**" on label: Sparkling wine created outside the Champagne region of France that uses the same *Méthode Traditionnelle* of second fermentation in the bottle.

"**Aging Information**" on label: How long has the sparkling wine aged? (Release after more than 1.5 years for normal blends, or at least 3–7 years for premium and vintage-year sparkling.) Should labels indicate how long the bottle has "rested" after disgorgement before its release?

"**Appellation**" on label: Napa, and its environs like Carneros, are gaining recognition and respect for the unique characteristics and high quality of the grapes grown there. Work with sparkling wine producers and regulators to recognize and determine specific geographic areas in California that warrant an "Appellation" and ensure growers are abiding by that distinction (and not saying grapes from the Central Valley are Napa just because they're shipped to Napa wineries for fermenting and production).

During the question-and-answer session at the end, Patrick Tournelle spoke up. "I need to take issue with the goal to have California sparkling compete directly with French champagne." He looked around the room. "We French are proud of the quality and unique flavor of our champagne and rightfully consider it a superior product to sparkling wines from other countries. In addition to the unique growing conditions, we've been making champagne for centuries and have reserve wine from many decades to use in blending our *cuvées* for finesse and complexity."

Chris raised his hand. "I'd like to respond to that." Doug gave him the floor. "We don't dispute the important legacy of French champagne. Many of us are partnered with French firms. We're just saying give California sparkling a chance. In blind tastings, some of our labels have beaten less stellar French champagnes." Chris looked pointedly at Patrick. "Plus, our bottles are more affordable, so you don't have to wait for a special occasion to splurge." Chris figured Patrick's French pride would demand the last word, and he was right.

"*Oui*, our company just acquired a subsidiary in Sonoma," Patrick said. "But that is for our US customers. We don't mislead ourselves into thinking we're selling Porsches when they're Fords. The French people will not be fooled by slick American marketing. They know the difference."

"I hope we come up with a slick marketing campaign," another panelist quipped. The audience laughed, diffusing the tension in the room. Chris felt his Irish temper about to kick in. Patrick Tournelle's snobbery rubbed him the wrong way. Good thing they were wrapping up.

"Well, it's an interesting debate," Doug concluded, "and one we'll be able to continue when our group meets in New York. The final category in the Plaza Blind Tasting will face off California sparkling against French champagne." He thanked the panelists and reminded everyone that the closing lunch would begin in thirty minutes on the outdoor terrace.

As the room cleared out, Catherine approached Chris. "Do you have a minute?" she asked.

"Sure," Chris said. He directed her to a quiet spot. "What's on your mind?"

"I was wondering if the job we discussed is still available." She chewed her lip. "If so, I would like to accept."

That was about the last thing Chris expected to hear. This seesaw back and forth wasn't a good omen for the future. At the least, she was one flighty chick. But he promised James he'd extend the offer, so he had no choice.

"Yes, it is," Chris said. "Might I ask what changed your mind?"

"After thinking it over, I realized I acted hastily." She fiddled with her files. "I think I can contribute to the launch effort."

"Okay, we'll give it a try." Chris's reluctance increased by the minute. "We'll go over most of the details when you get to New York. Our marketing director left, so you'll be reporting to me. I'll admit this is not my area of expertise." His brow furrowed. "James said you have some PR experience?" He left the question hanging in the air.

"I worked for an entertainment firm in LA. Kerner, have you heard of it?" Catherine asked.

He shook his head. "No, I don't travel in those circles. What types of things did you do?"

"Helped with events, parties, lined up celebs . . ."

"Guess that's a start. Are you familiar with the champagne business?"

"Not the inner workings. I know the French champagnes and some of the families who run them."

"We'll need to bring you up to speed on other aspects. Our main job is to have a flawless launch at Vinexpo in June. Our backers' financial investment in the company is in jeopardy if that fails." *Including my life savings.* "The salary is modest by New York standards, but there will be generous bonuses after the launch . . . assuming we're successful."

"Thank you for the opportunity," Catherine said.

"Since you're now part of the team, why don't you join us for dinner tonight?"

"That would be nice," she said.

Catherine walked into the French Laundry in the company of three attractive men. The dining room bustled this Saturday night. It was one of the top-rated restaurants in the country with a limited number of tables; conference attendees booked reservations months in advance to experience Thomas Keller's flagship eatery and enjoy the Michelin three-star experience.

Chris, Sean, and Tom looked handsome in their tailored suits and pressed shirts. They'd forgone ties, which were not required in the dress code. Catherine had changed into a black knee-length Dior dress, dabbed perfume on her pulse points, and applied a luscious coral Chanel lipstick to complete her makeover.

After checking their coats, the maître d' led them to a corner table. Catherine appreciated the warm decor, including remnants of the building's original wood timbers and river rock walls, from its earliest incarnation as a saloon, constructed by a Scottish stonemason a century ago. Sean maneuvered to pull out Catherine's chair, but the maître d' got there first.

Chris suggested they start with a bottle of champagne from their French partner Trianon. The flutes were served, and Sean raised his glass. "To the successful launch of our *cuvée de prestige* and a special welcome to Miss Reynolds." Sean gave Catherine an engaging smile and touched his glass to hers.

"Looks like we're going to have to leash him in," Chris murmured to Tom. Catherine's sharp hearing caught his remark, but she kept her face impassive—as she did when she heard Tom whisper back, "She seems to have that effect on any eligible bachelor who enters her vicinity . . . beware."

Sean looked over. "What are you two discussing?"

"Tom was congratulating us on luring Catherine to New York," Chris said.

The waiter described that evening's special *prix fixe* menu: nine small courses prepared with the freshest foods from the market that day and vegetables and herbs from the restaurant's garden. Catherine was eager to savor Keller's latest creations. She knew him through her family connections in Paris and their friendship with Guy Savoy, one of Keller's mentors. She sampled one of the rolls, still warm from the oven, mouthwatering.

To accompany the meal, Tom chose a pinot noir from a boutique Napa label, Hollywood & Vine.

"I hear the Winston marketing director left," Tom said.

"Yes, Sam wanted to get out of Manhattan, find a slower pace to raise their kids," Chris said. "The board decided to hold off replacing him for now. Much of that work is being handled by our outside firm, the Lexington Group."

"Some of us in-house would have preferred to have been given a shot at that position," Sean said. Chris didn't respond, and Catherine hoped that tension wouldn't affect her job.

The first course of Chesapeake Bay softshell crab was placed on the table.

"Mmm, this is delicious," Chris said between bites. "Justifies the exorbitant prices."

Sensing an implied criticism, Catherine came to her friend's defense. "Thomas Keller is a perfectionist. It's very costly to find the best ingredients and devote painstaking hours to create each dish."

"James said you know many French chefs," Chris said as he mopped up the sauce with his brioche.

"I grew up in Paris and my parents entertained a lot. It's a world I'm familiar with," she said.

Sean poured more champagne in her glass. "I'm sure you'll be a great addition to the team."

When the next course of Silver Queen corn pudding and grated truffles arrived, Chris steered the conversation to winery operations with Tom. They discussed the logistics of making sure bottles were in stores in time for the rollout. The timing for disgorging, the final process of removing sediment and affixing the permanent cork, needed to be synchronized. Most of the normal bottles had already been disgorged and were "resting" for six months to be ready in June.

From their conversation, Catherine learned jeroboams were complicated. Because they held the equivalent of four regular-size bottles, the disgorging needed to be done by hand, closer to the release date.

"Assume you've got the facilities lined up for the jeroboam disgorgement in late April," Chris said.

"Yes, and we've told everyone the use of this large bottle for the launch is strictly confidential," Tom said.

"Good. We want that wow factor at the party in Bordeaux. It will be a showstopper when we saber the first bottle," Chris said.

Catherine loved the concept. Sounded dramatic.

While the group indulged in a decadent dessert of Valrhona bitter chocolate soufflé with apricot marmalade, the waiter proposed after-dinner drinks.

"If you don't mind, I'd like to call it a night," Chris said. "I've got an early flight tomorrow."

The waiter brought their bill. Catherine knew it had to run close to $2,000 for four people. Chris didn't mention the price tag when he put his credit card on the silver tray. She liked a man who paid the tab with no fuss. She assumed it was covered by a company expense account.

"Glad you were able to get a table," Sean said to Tom. "I'll be asking their sommelier to place an order for our new prestige label and will mention the gastronomic meal we enjoyed tonight. That always helps."

At the coat counter, Chris reached for Catherine's cashmere wrap and held it for her. It seemed his hand lingered a fraction longer than necessary on her shoulder before he murmured, "See you soon in New York."

Chapter Five

New York—116 days to Winston cuvée *launch*

The plane touched down at JFK late Friday afternoon. Catherine scooped up her belongings and the animal carrier under the seat. "Soleil, sweetheart, *nous sommes ici.*" The sleepy calico opened her hazel eyes, yawned, and let out a plaintive meow. "Yes pumpkin, we're back to make our mark in the Big Apple."

A driver from Winston's car service stood at the security checkpoint holding a sign with Catherine's name. He escorted her out to a nearby town car and stowed the luggage. She sank into the back seat, pulling Soleil onto her lap. Might as well enjoy the ride. No more limos; she was on a tight budget.

Manhattan felt like a second home to Catherine. Since childhood, her family had traveled to New York from Paris a few times a year. They had usually stayed at the Plaza, convenient for activities with her dad: trips to the Central Park Zoo in summer and ice skating at Rockefeller Center in winter. Her mother, a consummate shopper, had fostered Catherine's expensive taste on their visits to Bergdorf Goodman and the original Saks Fifth Avenue store.

Her father was raised in Manhattan and the family estate in the Hamptons, where Grandma Reynolds still lived. Catherine's fondest memories were museum days with Gran. The Metropolitan Museum of Art was an immense treasure trove, so they focused on one area each visit: European paintings or Greek and Roman sculpture. As Catherine got older, the Frick Collection became her favorite for the manageable size, prized collection of English portraits and Turner seascapes, and peaceful inner courtyard.

The driver took the route into the city via the Long Island Expressway. When they approached the Midtown Tunnel, the island of Manhattan loomed. Catherine never tired of the awesome sight of all those skyscrapers clumped together: the United Nations Headquarters, the Empire State Building, and the iconic Chrysler Building with its Art Deco terraced crown. She marveled at the power they represented. New York City. Considered the center of the universe by its residents.

Traffic was heavy, as usual, so Catherine had plenty of time to reacquaint herself with the city's high-octane energy. Well-dressed men and women spilled out of office lobbies onto sidewalks to brave the rush-hour stampede home. Elegant designer showrooms were closing for the day, and trendy restaurants and bars were opening their doors for the evening parade. A far cry from the rural calm of Napa.

On Madison Avenue, they drove uptown past small boutiques, sidewalk cafés, art galleries, and florist shops, reminiscent of Catherine's favorite neighborhoods in Paris. When living in New York, this was the *quartier* she preferred.

The town car turned the corner and pulled up to a three-story brownstone. Catherine jumped out to ring the bell. The driver started unloading her eight suitcases and boxes, muttering about women not knowing how to travel light.

A striking Black woman opened the door, waved wildly, and came down the steps to embrace her. "Hello girlfriend. Welcome back to civilization. I'm sooo glad you're here." While the driver was dealing with the luggage, Vanessa bent to pick up Soleil's carrier. "Let's get you settled, Miss Sunshine."

Catherine knew Winston's payment to the driver included gratuity, but she gave him an additional tip, partly in thanks for lugging her suitcases up one flight of stairs.

After they got everything inside, Vanessa pulled out two champagne glasses from open shelves in the kitchen. "Let's have some sparkles, and I'll take you on a tour of our digs."

"Let's see how well stocked you are." Catherine opened the refrigerator. "Only French champagne, nothing from California?"

"I haven't figured those out yet. It's easier to go with the French labels we grew up with. What would you like?"

"Let's splurge on Dom Ruinart. Reminds me of our private tour of their cellar in Champagne." Catherine had been fascinated by the beauty of Dom Ruinart's two-thousand-year-old underground caves, dug out centuries earlier by Romans mining the chalk and renowned for the vaulted ceilings. The guide had explained how the depth and chalky walls naturally maintained the cool climate needed to store the bottles.

Vanessa removed the foil cap and popped the cork. "I, for one, am celebrating our reunion. New York hasn't been the same since you left, and your antiques will be a definite improvement to my flea market bargains."

They clinked glasses and Catherine took her first sip. "Grandma Reynolds is having her driver bring my stuff this weekend."

The long friendship of Vanessa Alexander and Catherine Reynolds had begun at boarding school in their teens.

Notre-Dame de Grâce: L'École des Femmes, on the outskirts of Geneva, Switzerland, attracted pampered girls from many countries. Even then, Catherine and Vanessa had stood out from the crowd. Vanessa's beautiful café au lait skin, five-nine statuesque frame, pale blue eyes, and husky voice were a striking contrast to Catherine's smaller five-seven lean build, shoulder-length honey-blonde hair, and mesmerizing green eyes.

Although their families and upbringing were very different—Vanessa's boisterous and affectionate and Catherine's formal and reserved—the girls could not be closer if they were sisters. Neither had siblings.

Vanessa's parents had met in San Francisco. Her father, an aspiring Black jazz musician, pursued her mother, a blonde, blue-eyed hippie from Marin County who made jewelry and dabbled in art. It was infatuation at first sight. Both families had reservations about the match but love prevailed. They waited to start a family until his jazz career took off, so they were in their mid-thirties when Vanessa was born.

After graduating from Notre-Dame de Grâce, Vanessa and Catherine had enrolled at the Sorbonne in Paris but didn't make it past the first year. Their connections and striking looks landed them lucrative modeling contracts. They preferred the glamorous lifestyle of travel and photo shoots to the grind of papers and tests at the university.

Not tall enough to be a serious model, Catherine had tried other jobs, eventually landing on public relations and event planning. She'd done that the past couple of years but lacked serious training. She was counting on the instruction and certificate from Cornell to pursue her real passion: managing her own resort.

Vanessa did occasional modeling assignments when the money was good, but now her music career was taking off.

Catherine lifted her champagne flute to offer a toast. "To best friends and new beginnings. Tell me about the gig you landed."

"It's a big break." Vanessa's eyes lit up. "A hip jazz club needed a quick replacement singer and my agent got me in."

"That's great." Catherine was thrilled for her friend.

"Three nights a week and pays pretty well. Thankfully, this apartment is rent-stabilized. Let's figure out where your stuff will go."

Vanessa led Catherine on a tour of the prewar apartment. Catherine loved the ten-feet-high ceilings and hardwood floors. They each had bedrooms with large windows facing the street and adjoining bathrooms with retro clawfoot tubs.

The dining room had been converted to an office space they could share. Vanessa favored the cozy breakfast nook, adjoining the kitchen, for her meals. If they wanted to host dinner parties, they could entertain in the living room, where the focal point was a large brick fireplace, flanked by white bookshelves on both sides.

After changing into comfortable leggings, the best friends lounged on large pillows in front of a roaring fire, finishing off the bottle of Ruinart and devouring a pizza. Soleil curled up nearby, soaking up the warmth.

"This is pretty spacious for New York," Catherine noted, looking around. "Except for the nonexistent closet space. Good thing I have an armoire"—she pulled Soleil closer and gave her a pet—"but it won't hold all my clothes." Catherine was an inveterate shopper, part of the reason she was in major debt.

"You'll need some of those chic outfits for your new job," Vanessa said between bites. "Should be an interesting change from Kerner."

"Actually, it's a lifesaver. I need the money," Catherine said.

Vanessa looked perplexed. "What about the money from your parents?"

"I'm now officially poor." Catherine twisted her ring. "My mom hit the roof when I maxed out my last credit card. I'm cut off completely."

"That's harsh."

"I feel stranded," Catherine admitted. "I have no savings and was planning to use the next few months to study for my Cornell entrance exam. Will have to squeeze that in on weekends."

"At least you have this new job to cover your bills."

"We'll see. I'm afraid it's tenuous. My boss didn't seem enthusiastic about hiring me."

"Speaking of men, what happened with that guy at the winery you were seeing?"

"Robert was not the answer to my dreams. In fact, it was another crash and burn." Catherine grimaced. "I caught him cheating."

"What a heel," Vanessa hissed.

"With a girl barely over eighteen. It was so humiliating."

"Did it trigger a panic attack?"

Catherine shook her head. "Surprisingly, no." She'd been prone to panic attacks—shortness of breath, faintness, even passing out—since a traumatic experience in her teens. Vanessa was one of the few people who knew about what Catherine viewed as a debilitating weakness.

"He made a feeble attempt to talk it over," Catherine said. "That's about the last thing I want to do . . . give him a chance to blame it on me."

Vanessa put her arm around Catherine's shoulder. "We'll figure it out. We've both got exciting new jobs."

"Yes, but yours seems to be more of a sure thing." Catherine prayed she was up to the challenge ahead.

Monday morning arrived quickly. Catherine and Vanessa had spent a hectic weekend arranging her furniture in the apartment. Catherine dressed with special care in a dark-brown Lanvin skirt suit and Roger Vivier heels. She styled her long hair stick straight and applied light makeup, enough to enhance without overdoing it. She kept the jewelry simple: diamond stud earrings and an antique Cartier watch that complemented her heirloom ring.

Joining the crush of people approaching the landmark Seagram Building on Park Avenue, Catherine looked up and admired the modernist bronze-and-glass structure, designed by Mies van der Rohe in the 1950s.

For good luck, she carried a slim leather portfolio Grandma Reynolds had sent on Saturday with her boxes. The note read: "This belonged to your grandfather. He bought it in Florence on our honeymoon. He would have been so pleased to know you were using it for your new job at his friend's company."

Grateful that she was a few minutes early, Catherine took the elevator to the twentieth floor, resolutely drew in a breath, and stepped out. The receptionist took her name and said the chairman wanted to meet with her first thing. She stole a quick glance around, taking in the sleek lines and modern decor. The office suite exuded power and masculinity.

In preparation for her new job, Catherine had read up on the company history over the weekend. Compared with other sparkling wine producers, Winston & Wright was relatively new to the scene, established ten years earlier by James Winston and Alan Wright. They were both successful investment bankers who amassed sizable fortunes from their work on mergers and acquisitions—*like Grandpa*, she reminded herself. That's how they'd all become close friends.

James's passion was champagne. It started as a hobby, along with fine wines, cigars, and vintage cars. While on a golfing trip to Napa, he'd learned about a prime vineyard and winery recently put up for sale. He persuaded Alan to join him as co-owner, and they took the plunge. Alan remained a silent partner, serving on the board and playing the role of chief advisor.

Catherine was ushered into James's office. He was on the phone and gestured for her to take a seat facing his desk. He finished the call and stood to greet her. "Welcome, my dear." He walked around and gave her a light hug. "Glad you accepted the job."

"I'm very grateful you thought of me," she said. Catherine was pleased to see him looking fit. In his mid-sixties, James Winston had enviable thick silver hair and knowing blue eyes, and he wore expensive suits perfectly fitted to his tall frame. Grandma Reynolds had told Catherine his dress shirts came from "one of those custom tailors in London."

He sat back down. "We've assembled quite a team for this launch, and your entrée into society circles and experience with high-profile events will be a strong addition." He paused, then added, "And selfishly, having you here is like family, someone I can trust."

Catherine laughed. "I'm thrilled for the opportunity, but you're making it sound like the Mafia. This business can't be that cutthroat."

"You know I tend to be intense," he said. "But it is competitive, and we are ruffling some feathers." He clasped his hands on the desk. "We've heard rumblings that we could be subjected to a smear campaign, or worse. I'd like you to keep your eyes and ears open and let me know what you hear, even if it seems innocuous."

"Of course, you have my loyalty." Catherine wondered what she was getting herself into. "This business is new to me—"

"Precisely, which is why it wouldn't be out of the ordinary for you to be inquisitive. Also, let's keep this between the two of us for now."

"I always wanted to play Mata Hari," Catherine quipped. She couldn't resist teasing him. Even though she now worked for James's company, their families were close and spent many summer holidays together. "I hope you have a dashing guy for me to pry secrets from."

There was a rap on the door, and Chris stuck his head in. "Oh hi, thought you were alone," he said in James's direction. "Your secretary's away. Don't want to interrupt your meeting."

James and Catherine grinned at each other, and she whispered, "That's not who I had in mind." In fact, Chris McDermott was on her list of men to avoid. She'd seen the way women flocked to him at the opening-night party in Napa, and she strove to avoid that "female magnet" type.

"Hold on. I'm just welcoming Catherine." James held out his arm to gesture Chris back. "I'm sure you two have lots to discuss to bring her up to speed."

"Yes, I thought we'd meet over lunch." Chris glanced toward Catherine to see if she agreed. "I've got meetings all morning."

"That sounds fine," she said.

After the door shut, James regarded her. "Just out of curiosity, why doesn't Chris fit the 'dashing guy' description?"

"Let's just say we didn't hit it off when we first met. I have a feeling we approach things differently."

"Very diplomatic answer . . . which Chris isn't, sometimes. Hopefully, you can both adapt."

"Seriously, are there any people I should be checking out?" Catherine sought clarity about this addition to her job description.

"I'm not sure yet. Let me look into things a bit further." James stood up as she prepared to leave.

"Thanks again for giving me this chance." Catherine smiled. "I'll try to make you proud."

"I'm sure you will," he said.

As a sought-after bachelor in New York, Chris was accustomed to escorting attractive women to trendy restaurants. Catherine seemed to cause more of a stir than most. Doors were whisked open, heads turned, men stared in open admiration. Most surprising to him was that she seemed oblivious to the commotion, or maybe she just took it in stride.

The maître d' welcomed Chris, who was a regular at Daniel. When he saw Catherine, his face lit up. "Mademoiselle Reynolds, what a pleasant surprise. *Et vos parents. Vont-ils bien*?"

"*Oui, merci. Ils vivent toujours à Paris*. I just moved to New York for my new job at Winston." She gestured to Chris.

"Congratulations. You'll be their secret weapon. I shall send you both a glass of champagne to celebrate."

Guess the lady's got connections, Chris admitted to himself en route to their table.

They were seated in mahogany high-back chairs with coral leather padding, a splash of color in contrast to the subdued earth tones of the walls.

"My parents were regulars at Le Cirque," Catherine explained, "when Daniel was head chef there, his first job in New York. He came from generations of chefs in Lyon and apprenticed at top kitchens in France for his training."

"I admire his entrepreneurial spirit," Chris said. "Now Daniel Boulud has a dining empire." Chris hoped his family's winery ambitions had a measure of that success reaching their goals.

While they regarded menus, a waiter materialized with a bottle of Veuve Clicquot and two crystal champagne flutes on a tray. He showed Chris the bottle and poured the sparkling liquid into their flutes, leaving room at the top of each glass for the bouquet to fully release.

"What a thoughtful gesture," Catherine said. "How do restaurants decide which complimentary champagne they'll serve?" She took a sip. Chris was momentarily mesmerized by her red lips.

He set his glass down and snapped back to the topic. "Now you're entering the marketing realm. One would think a house champagne is chosen because it's a superior product. But it has a lot to do with relationships and getting a deal on the cost. Veuve Clicquot is a quality French champagne at a fair price, so in this case they made a wise pick."

Chris held his glass higher to get a better view. "You can tell they just uncorked the bottle from the number of bubbles streaming up." He favored a newly opened, well-chilled champagne. This was good stuff. "One of our aims is to convince restaurants to offer Winston's sparkling."

"The competition sounds fierce," she said.

"I won't lie. It requires time to build those relationships. We're always striving to strengthen our connections with chefs and sommeliers. That's part of Sean's job, but we all cultivate our contacts. Why don't you make up a list of chefs you could help pursue, and we'll go over that with Sean."

"I'm looking forward to renewing old ties," Catherine said. "How about the price? Is it reasonable?"

"We try to be. Winery costs are high, so our profit margins don't give us much room to negotiate." Chris explained that Winston had a good reputation in the industry, but they needed to reach out to a wider audience of people who favored still wine, or even beer, over sparkling.

"In my circles everyone drinks champagne," Catherine said. "Isn't that a stretch to target beer drinkers?" She looked dubious.

"I'm a beer drinker," he said, daring her to react.

Their lunch plates were served, sparing her further comment. Chris was ravenous. He'd ordered roasted Canadian chicken with Swiss chard tortellini, and it smelled delicious.

Between mouthfuls, Chris reiterated Catherine's job parameters: increased media visibility and participation in special events. "Jim says you've got good PR contacts. To be honest, I'm not very familiar with publicity—my focus is on crunching the numbers. Our outside firm, the Lexington Agency, will have some ideas."

Catherine finished a bite of her tuna Niçoise salad and put her fork down. "I have a meeting there tomorrow. What have they been doing?"

"Our account rep, Robin Bronstein, will bring you up to speed. They're focusing on traditional events and a limited advertising campaign. We're behind on finalizing a marketing theme for the *cuvée*. Haven't settled on anything,"—he paused and made air quotes—"'sexy' enough yet." He frowned, wondering if she could see he wasn't enthusiastic about dealing with this aspect. "See what Robin has come up with when you speak with her."

He set his glass down. "You'll be reporting to me," he reminded her. "I know effectiveness is hard to measure, but your mandate includes booking at least one national media hit per month. And we do a ninety-day review for all hires."

Catherine nodded and jotted down notes on a lined pad.

The hour flew by. The waiter placed dessert menus on the table. They both declined, and Chris asked for the check.

"Do you have any questions for me?" Chris asked.

"Yes, you mentioned I'd have an assistant. I'd like to bring Claire in for that position. We work well together, and she's willing to relocate to New York."

"That should be okay," Chris said. It seemed pretty cheeky to him. Catherine got the job as a favor from James, and now she was asking for her handpicked assistant. "If Claire's willing to come in at that salary and human resources signs off."

"I appreciate it." Catherine reached for her purse.

They walked outside. "I need to run a few errands before I head back," she said. "Thanks for lunch."

"You're welcome." Chris decided to walk back and enjoy the beautiful day. He wondered if Catherine would last more than a week or two. She seemed in way over her head. He was surprised Claire would be willing to take a flyer on the job. *Wonder if Claire realizes how precarious it is*?

Chapter Six

New York—106 days to Winston cuvée *launch*

As it turned out, Claire did accept the job offer. She told Catherine her sister had been urging her to move to Manhattan. Claire was widowed and her younger sister newly divorced, so they planned to share living expenses and explore the city together—when Claire had free time, that is.

Claire started work a week after Catherine's first day on the job. "Your office is set up already. Impressive." She sat in an upholstered Queen Anne chair facing Catherine's desk.

"Helped to get hand-me-downs from my grandma." Elizabeth Reynolds had insisted on giving her granddaughter an antique furniture set that included a small maple desk with curved legs, matching bookshelves, two chairs, and a side table. It filled the space, technically a window office, albeit a very small one. Manhattan real estate was exorbitant, and Catherine was a junior executive.

Catherine had adorned the walls with a framed set of grape botanicals picked up at a poster shop and a watercolor of the south of France, painted by a friend from her school days. Photos of Grandma Reynolds and Soleil were prominently displayed on the table behind her desk next to a vase filled with white freesias.

Beneath the cozy exterior, Catherine's files were compulsively organized and color-coded—a throwback to her regimented boarding school days. Winston provided a laptop computer and a mobile phone for work-related calls, but Catherine remained old-school in her ways. She took out her notepad. "It's really good to have you here—a partner amid the jungle."

"You mean the New York jungle or the workers in the office?" Claire asked.

"The corporate jungle, I'm afraid." Catherine sighed. "I get the distinct impression people don't want me to succeed. I met with Robin at the Lexington Agency, and she seemed defensive they brought me on."

"Not surprising. Probably trying to protect her turf," Claire said.

"She implied there was no need for my services, that everything was fine. I finally got a list of the events so far, and it looks skimpy. Plus, they aren't using celebs." Catherine frowned. "She said Chris preferred it that way."

"You'd think they'd welcome your help. Maybe this Robin person doesn't want to share the credit if things go well," Claire said.

Catherine took a sip of her coffee. "Which brings me to my second problem. Chris is my direct boss, and he's overseeing my ninety-day review. If he's not with the program on using celebrities and adding glitz, then my efforts will fail."

"That seems narrow-minded," Claire said. "We'll just have to prove him wrong."

Or go down in a blaze of glory trying, Catherine vowed to herself. She handed Claire a list. "Here are the industry events Lexington scheduled so far. It's all traditional stuff."

Claire took a quick read of the page. "It does look uninspired."

"I'm going to call some friends in Hollywood." Catherine pulled out her chestnut-brown file for projects and upcoming events. "Maybe we can connect with something splashy out there . . . tie in with the Oscars."

"Good idea, but that's coming up soon. The date got pushed to mid-March, so that gives us a slim chance." Claire indicated how slim by holding her thumb and forefinger a quarter inch apart. "We'll have to move at lightning speed."

"You're not kidding. I feel like I'm playing catch-up. Let's draw up a list of possible events." Catherine tapped a pen against her file. She felt the pressure of her looming presentation to the Winston board of directors next week. Chris had sprung that on her a few days ago.

The women mapped out a draft list of things to do. "Let's keep this to ourselves until we've filled in the details," Catherine said. "I don't know if I have any allies, except for James and Sean."

"Sure thing."

"I'll ask a few friends outside the company for advice," Catherine said. "In the meantime, I have to prepare for a status meeting with Chris and Sean tomorrow."

Tuesday morning, cappuccino in hand, Catherine sat down at the conference table and placed her notepad and hot-pink priority file in front of her. She'd endured teasing about her color-coded files but remained determined to maintain her personal style among the prevailing male-dominated culture. Case in point: She could hear Chris and Sean coming down the hall talking about last night's Knicks game.

The two men walked in and Sean gave her a big smile. "Morning, Miss Reynolds," he drawled. "You're looking lovely today." He pulled out a chair next to her and sat down.

"*Merci*, Mr. Dunlavy," Catherine bantered back, enjoying the compliment but not taking it seriously. She knew the company frowned on office flirtations. That had been covered in her human resources orientation.

"Does that signify something special?" Sean pointed to Catherine's hot-pink file.

"Yes. This is for priority pending."

"I'm glad seeing us is at the top of your list," he said, then backed off when Chris cleared his throat.

All business, Chris began. "I asked Sean to join us to coordinate how bottles are allocated and to ensure the sales and publicity events stay within our budget."

Sean turned to Catherine. "Just so you know, we have a limited number of the new *cuvée* bottles to use before the launch, but we have plenty of stock of our current rosé—"

"It's still a premium bottle," Chris interrupted. "Retails for forty bucks. We can't go overboard offering that without a guaranteed return."

"I'll need most of the *cuvée* bottles for preview tastings," Sean said. "But I could spare a few, if you line up celebs for early buzz."

"Thanks," Catherine said. "I'm working on that. Might be able to get actors to post photos with the bottle on social media."

"That would be great," Sean said. "Keep in mind, the *cuvée* bottles aren't ready yet; we're still waiting on the label."

"Once somebody finally comes up with the name," Chris grumbled. "Can't understand why that's taking so long."

Chris's phone buzzed and he glanced down to check a message, making it clear to Catherine that Chris was not engrossed in this meeting. She got the impression he'd rather be anywhere else.

Sean gave her an encouraging nod, so Catherine proceeded. "A long shot I'm pursuing is the Academy Awards, coming up soon. There's always a media frenzy covering the lead-up parties. I'm pitching venue hosts to feature Winston sparkling."

"If that comes through, I'd like to invite a few of our southern California buyers," Sean said. "They'd appreciate mingling at a star-studded bash."

Chris frowned. "I have to admit, James is keener on this celebrity stuff. I don't see the benefit. Think our energy is better spent on traditional avenues of reaching customers—tastings, restaurant parties. Do we have any cultural events lined up?"

Catherine had figured Chris would have that reaction from what Robin told her. She handed them each a one-page sheet. "Here's the list Lexington is working on." She pointed to a column. "This shows what events we're committed to after the launch in Bordeaux in early June. Then we'll have the official US launch in Napa and tasting events in other cities." She sipped her cappuccino while the men perused the list.

Chris glanced at his watch and gathered his papers. "Sorry I have to cut this short. Need to hop on a conference call in a few minutes. We'll regroup next week."

He turned to Sean. "Thanks for joining us." Then he addressed Catherine. "Feel free to drop by my office with any ideas to kick around."

"All right," Catherine said. Though she didn't plan to. Why would she want to brainstorm ideas for him to shoot down? Most employers would be grateful for her celebrity contacts.

Sean hung back to walk Catherine to her office. "Don't listen to him," Sean said. "He's never liked glitz and doesn't understand how it can be used to add cachet. I think you're a great addition to the team." He lowered his voice when they got to her door. "How 'bout that dinner I've been trying to get you to take with me?"

"It's tempting, but I've been so busy learning this job . . ." Catherine had a brainstorm. "I'm going to my roommate's jazz club on Saturday night. If you're free, we could catch her show and grab a bite then."

"As long as it's dark and private, and I have you all to myself." He gazed at her with sexy brown eyes.

"It will definitely be dark, but not exactly private—lots of people packed at small tables in a tight space." *Thank goodness.* Not the complication she sought right now. She found Sean extremely attractive but intuited that he spelled trouble, and anyway it was a nonstarter since they worked together.

"It's on my calendar," Sean declared as he opened her office door and made a sweeping gesture with his arm.

Three days later, Chris was counting on an early morning racquetball session with his good friend, Will Frost, a tall fit Brit, to work off stress. Will was a member of the Racquet & Tennis Club, conveniently located across Park Avenue from the Winston office.

During his last year at Harvard, Chris had snagged a plum summer internship at a Wall Street firm where Will was already a rising star. Will spotted Chris's natural talent for finding investment opportunities and seeded him $100,000 to invest in stocks. The original amount doubled quickly. Chris paid it back with interest, and they continued to invest together, eventually earning $2 million in profit apiece.

Will was on the board of Winston & Wright and had introduced Chris to James Winston three years ago. James hired Chris to be company president, saying Chris had the right combination of skills: familiarity with the wine industry, MBA from Harvard, knowledge of making companies profitable, and the talent to recruit outside investors.

At the time, Chris negotiated to buy a percentage of the company for $1.5 million, keeping the remainder of his stock profits in a rainy-day fund for his family. The expectation was that his investment in Winston would multiply tenfold and provide the capital to build up his family's winery in Napa. That's where his heart lay.

The men greeted each other and headed for the locker room to drop off their garment bags. They'd use the spa-like showers afterward and go straight to work.

They started batting the ball around. Chris hit harder than usual.

"Looks like you need to blow off steam," Will said. "Is everything okay at the office?"

"We're submitting the new *cuvée* for the Plaza Blind Tasting," Chris said. "I think it's a gamble."

"You have a point," Will said. "If it's not rated highly, that will set us back. Why take the risk?"

"You know James's motto, 'Go big or go home.' He feels we're ready for the challenge and wants to make a splash. I'm concerned that since it's before the June launch, the bottles won't have the full six months' post-disgorgement, which could affect the taste." Chris leaned on his racket. "Will you back me at the board meeting next week?"

His friend shook his head. "I'll need to hear all sides first."

Not the answer Chris was hoping for. A blind tasting had so many variables. What if the bottles had "cork taint" or some other unforeseen problem? It gave him heartburn thinking about it.

They started play, well matched. The rallies ran for minutes, both working up a sweat. No surprise they tied, one game apiece. Will managed to squeak out the tiebreaker.

After picking up their gear, they headed to the breakfast bar for a healthy shake.

"How's it going with that new publicity hire?" Will asked.

"Don't remind me," Chris groaned. "So far, she's one big headache." Since their meeting with Sean, Catherine had rebuffed his attempts to be a sounding board. He had no idea what she was up to and feared she and her assistant were hatching up a scheme that would backfire. They huddled in her office long hours each day, dreaming up God knows what.

"I'm afraid she's going to blow the budget on a useless celebrity bash," Chris said.

"We can't have that," Will said. "Our balance sheet has to sync up with what we promised Chamath."

Chris knew too well how important their new investor Chamath Patel was to the company's growth. "Agreed," he said.

The men headed off to the showers.

Will grinned and clapped Chris on the back. "Good luck with your new hire."

Across the street, the lady in question arrived at the office, armed for battle in her tailored suit and signature high heels, carrying her leather portfolio and morning cappuccino.

Claire looked up when Catherine walked in. "Hi boss. We got a call from Liza at Kerner." Claire handed her the message slip. "She wanted to give us a heads-up that the champagne sponsor for Wolfgang Puck's pre-Oscar party at Spago dropped out. They're looking for a replacement asap."

"Lucky us," Catherine said. She was feeling under a lot of pressure to deliver something big from her contacts, and this was it. If she could close the deal. "I need to hop on this right away." She and Claire both knew that on this primo celebrity level, she was competing against many other publicists.

Fortunately, Catherine had a longstanding relationship with

Wolfgang that went way back. Her grandparents were regulars at his first restaurant in LA, when he was head chef at Ma Maison on Melrose. One of the original celebrity hangouts, it was owned and run by famed restaurateur Patrick Terrail, a gregarious Frenchman. In the 1980s, Wolfgang struck off on his own and launched Spago, originally above the Sunset Strip and relocated later to Beverly Hills. Eventually, he branched out and opened other restaurants and even created a line of gourmet fast food. When Catherine was growing up, her parents took her to Spago on their trips to LA, and Wolfgang even stayed at their home in Paris.

Time to play the family connection card and see if she could snag that opportunity for Winston. She glanced at her watch. *Too early now.* She'd have to wait a couple hours before she called.

"Do you know if Sean's here?" Catherine asked. "I want to talk to him about the bottles."

Claire nodded. "I saw him in his office. Chris isn't in yet."

"Perfect. I don't want to give Chris a chance to shoot me down. Sean seems to be on my side."

Catherine headed over to Sean's office and rapped on the door.

"Morning." Sean looked happy to see her. "How can I help you?"

Catherine walked in and sat down. "Just heard that Spago needs a champagne sponsor for their pre-Oscar party. I know it's too early to introduce our new prestige *cuvée*. Do we have another top-quality bottle available?"

"Sure. That's a great get. We can use the rosé sparkling. We have enough cases in the Napa warehouse. I'll put a hold on them."

"Thanks so much," Catherine said.

"We need to get Chris to sign off on the expense," Sean reminded her, "since we'd be offering them gratis in exchange for the publicity."

"He seems reluctant to go the celebrity route," she said. "Can we wait until the board meeting next week to bring it up? Hopefully, they'll like the proposal, and it will be a fait accompli."

"Okay. You're a clever woman, Miss Reynolds. By the way, what time should I pick you up tomorrow night?"

"How about eight?"

"Can't wait," Sean said.

By late afternoon, Catherine reached Wolfgang and sold him on the proposal. He liked the idea of showcasing an up-and-coming California brand that had ties to a French company and was happy to support her in her new job. She was thrilled to justify James's decision to hire her.

There was sure to be a crushing media blitz: Oscar nominees in the top categories were invited, and many of them attended this annual party. Just the ticket to create buzz for Winston and fulfill a national press requirement.

Catherine had one small problem. Wolfgang insisted on finalizing the contract immediately. That meant she needed a signature. He said it should delineate how many bottles, the normal liability disclaimers (including injury from bottles, which she thought was a long shot), and reiterate that Spago made no guarantee of press coverage in return.

Sean agreed to check a draft, so she took the document she'd marked up to the copy machine to duplicate. While she pulled copies out of the tray, she overheard some of the secretaries talking from the other side of a tall partition next to the coffee station.

"I think Catherine Reynolds is so beautiful, like a princess," one of them gushed.

"I wonder where she buys those designer suits and that jewelry . . . the Cartier Trinity ring she wears every day is amazing," another chimed in.

"Oh, I don't know. She seems stuck up to me." Catherine recognized the voice of Chris's secretary, Delores. "Always keeps to herself."

Catherine had heard similar criticism before. In this instance, it didn't faze her. Her goal was to keep her job until she received the launch bonus, not to make friends with the secretaries.

"You're just jealous because your boss is obviously taken with her," the first voice responded. "He never used to leave his office, and now he checks in on her like a homing pigeon."

"You're wrong. He's worried about her messing up and making his life more difficult. I overheard him on the phone, and he said—and I quote—'James has done it this time. He's saddled me with a jet-set rich dilettante, and I'll have to make the best of it unless she quits or gets fired.'"

Not waiting to hear more, Catherine paled and rushed back to her office. *So that's what he thinks of me.* No wonder he wasn't receptive to her ideas. She shut her door, sank into the chair, and put her head in her hands. *Now what am I going to do*?

Catherine didn't want to give Chris a chance to nix the Spago deal. She'd have to go out on a limb and sign the contract herself. If she wasn't successful selling the idea to the board next week, she'd have to deal with the fallout. And quite possibly get fired for insubordination. A big risk, but one she felt she needed to take.

Chapter Seven

New York—99 days to Winston cuvée *launch*

Saturday morning dawned crisp and clear. Good walking weather. Catherine wanted to go back to bed and burrow under the covers, but Vanessa insisted Catherine join her for a power walk, said it would clear her head.

They dressed quickly and headed south on Fifth Avenue, alongside Central Park, dodging joggers and dog walkers also out early. Catherine wore designer black stretch walking pants with a matching zip-up jacket. Never sweatpants. Catherine wouldn't be seen in public wearing them. Her mother taught her it was unseemly to parade around in pajamas—notwithstanding that balcony scene with Chris in Napa.

Keeping up with Vanessa's brisk pace, Catherine reviewed her predicament. The revelation from Chris's secretary floored her. He wanted her to fail. Before that deflating news, she was starting to believe she could justify James's faith in her. Landing the Spago event was a coup that would thrill most clients. She needed to prevail at the board meeting—and keep her job.

At 57th Street, they walked east one long block then north up Madison Avenue, past some of their favorite designer boutiques, to their destination. Sant Ambroeus, a Milanese café on Madison at 78th Street, was their favorite morning hangout. Catherine loved the charming atmosphere, the display cases of mouthwatering tarts and cakes, and the scent of coffee beans grinding nearby. Close to heaven. A boost Catherine needed at the moment.

They placed coffee orders at the long granite counter near the front door and chose fresh-baked pastries—a cornetto, Italian crescent pastry filled with cream, for Catherine, and a chocolate biscotti for Vanessa.

A small table freed up, so they grabbed it, and Vanessa started in. "I wonder if those snippy secretaries were gossiping knowing you could overhear. Women can be vindictive when they're jealous."

"I don't think they realized I was listening. Didn't sound that way." Catherine took a sip of her coffee, the house specialty: an espresso with thick hot chocolate, milk froth, and a dollop of whipped cream.

"I can't believe Chris is so hung up on your upbringing and connections," Vanessa said. "So what if it's quote-unquote 'jet set'? He should realize that's an asset."

"I was just starting to feel I had a handle on things. And now this." Catherine cradled the warm mug in her hands for comfort. "Not to mention, I need press hits from the Spago event to meet my monthly media requirement. Bet Chris would nix the agreement just to prevent me from reaching my quota."

"You could go to James," Vanessa suggested.

"I don't want to drag him into this. He already took a chance by asking Chris to hire me. This is one fight I'll have to wage on my own. At least I know where I stand, and I won't be fooled if Chris seems supportive."

Catherine took another bite of her cornetto and had a flashback to her first taste of the Italian pastry, standing at the barista counter at famed Caffé Gilli in Florence. Okay, admittedly, she had a well-heeled upbringing. She'd seen the world.

Vanessa snapped her out of it. "Tell me about this dashing date you're bringing to the club tonight."

"You know I'm taking a break from men. This is being social with a coworker. And besides, company policy frowns on fraternizing," Catherine said.

"What's he like?" Vanessa dipped the last piece of biscotti in her cappuccino.

Catherine put her mug down. "He's a good guy. Been very supportive and helpful. You might like him. He's handsome and southern-gentleman sexy. Unlike Chris, he's cosmopolitan. Spent time in France, at Pommery Champagne."

"How's his French?" Vanessa asked.

"Passable . . ."

"*D'accord*, I'll be sure not to revert to French, like we do so people won't know what we're saying."

"*Bonne idée*," Catherine said. They both grinned.

Catherine insisted on paying the bill. It was the least she could do since Vanessa gave her a break on their shared rent.

The waitress returned a few minutes later with a frown on her face. "I'm sorry . . . your card is declined," she said.

"Are you sure?" Catherine asked.

"Yes, and I'm being instructed by Visa to confiscate it."

Catherine was mortified. Embarrassing situations like this didn't happen to her. She had to get a handle on her finances. This was a stark reminder she had to hang on to her job. Her accountant kept leaving messages to arrange a meeting. She needed to stop procrastinating. In the meantime, she'd use cash for this expense.

Vanessa gave Catherine a hug around the shoulders as they walked out. "Thanks for treating me." When they reached the sidewalk, Vanessa's eyes lit up. "Let's pick up some exotic tulips at the shop down the street. This one's on me."

Catherine appreciated her friend trying to cheer her up. Vanessa knew she loved creating arrangements of fresh-cut flowers. It rejuvenated her. They often sought out early-morning flower markets in whatever city they were in and wandered among narrow aisles of colorful birds of paradise from Hawaii, long-stemmed tulips from the Netherlands, and exotic orchids from the Far East.

While in boarding school, they'd picked delicate white edelweiss flowers on their hikes and pressed them between pages of poetry books to dry, before slipping them into love letters to their weekly heartthrobs at the nearby boys' school. The edelweiss wildflowers were symbolic of purity and innocence. The girls learned later that it was illegal to pick them in Switzerland.

"What beautiful flowers do we want to get this morning?" Vanessa wondered out loud as they walked into the florist. A riot of colors and fragrant smells assaulted their senses. "I was thinking tulips," she said, "but these blue and yellow irises would be perfect in our kitchen—"

"—and they symbolize friendship." Catherine completed her friend's thought. "I'll get white freesias for my desk." Even though she felt their symbolic meaning—trust—was in short supply at her office, they were her favorite flowers.

Catherine raised a hand to her mouth and tried to hide her smirk.

"I know that look." Vanessa eyed her sternly. "What are you up to?"

"Nothing," Catherine said. "I was thinking it would be a friendly gesture if I got a bouquet for Chris, say these yellow carnations." She leaned over and plucked a bunch of one-dozen carnations, dripping water out of the bucket.

Vanessa laughed. "For disdain. Shame on you. He'll never know."

"In fact, he'll assume I'm in the dark about his intentions to sabotage my job, which is fine with me," Catherine said.

After Vanessa paid for their purchases, Catherine linked arms with her friend. They walked outside holding bundles of flowers wrapped in cones of butcher paper. "Thanks for the outing. I needed it," Catherine said.

"What are friends for? I'm looking forward to meeting your escort tonight. Maybe one of us should explore that possibility further."

Although relatively new on the New York nightlife scene, Smoke was making a name for itself. The jazz club and supper lounge, located on Broadway at 106th, had a distinguished past. It used to be the space for Augie's Jazz Bar, an institution for decades. Normally, the club featured jazz quartets and occasional guest vocalists. Recently, the owners decided to add an up-and-coming singer to accompany their house band to appeal to couples out for a romantic evening.

This Saturday night it seemed Sean Dunlavy was taking that romantic evening suggestion to heart. Catherine couldn't remember the last time a guy pulled out all the stops to impress her so much. Even Robert hadn't gone this far. Sean arrived at her apartment door with a dozen long-stemmed white roses. After petting Soleil and admiring her maroon cocktail dress, he whisked her outside to the waiting limo he'd hired for the evening. Of course, he insisted on opening every door.

The intimate club was dimly lit and packed with a hip crowd of models, artsy types, and successful young professionals. Catherine and Sean were seated side by side on a plush red velvet banquette facing the stage. Sean demonstrated that he, like Catherine, had expensive taste when he ordered a bottle of Dom Pérignon for their table.

The band started playing, and the audience gave them their full attention. Catherine was thrilled her friend had landed this opportunity to pursue her dream. The owners were so pleased with Vanessa's husky voice, they'd offered her a six-month contract. Performances were selling out each night; the club only accommodated fifty guests per seating.

Vanessa started singing the Stevie Wonder classic, "Knocks Me Off My Feet." Her dad had played with Stevie years ago, and this was Vanessa's favorite song to perform. Sean stood up and held out his hand. "Miss Reynolds, I believe this dance is mine."

On a postage stamp–size dance floor, they started moving in time to the music. Catherine thought about the message in the lyrics: a love so strong it made you weak and knocked you off your feet. *When have I had that? Never.*

Sean pulled her closer. "Do you know how long I've wanted to hold you in my arms? Since the first moment I laid eyes on you."

Catherine felt a mild panic attack coming on. She focused on inhaling deep breaths to calm her nerves. A trauma in her teens had made her skittish when guys came on to her too fast, like Sean was doing. He didn't seem to notice her distress. Another signal he wasn't the right guy for her.

Fortunately, the next song was faster. Catherine pulled away and breathed a sigh of relief. Thank goodness for Kool & the Gang's "Celebration." Vanessa dedicated it to a couple celebrating their twenty-fifth wedding anniversary. The disco-era tune cooled Sean off, and they went back to the table.

When the band took a break, Catherine encouraged Sean to talk about himself. It didn't take much prompting. Like Catherine, he'd had a privileged upbringing: attending private schools and spending holidays at exclusive resorts. They compared their favorite ski runs in the French Alps. He was most animated talking about his college summers abroad exploring Europe, and the final two summers interning at wineries in France, conducting tours in English, which led to a sales job at Pommery Champagne in Épernay.

Catherine hoped to pick up some pointers on dealing with Chris, so she steered the conversation to work. Sean was less enthusiastic on that front. "Honestly, things are so crazy right now with the launch, I'm not sure what advice to give, except to keep your head down and be open to other options," he said. "If there are any hiccups with the launch, things could go south fast."

That was an eye-opener for Catherine. She appreciated the heads-up but couldn't see how it helped her situation. She didn't have other job offers lined up. She wondered if Sean did.

Their dinners arrived: seared salmon for her and barbecue ribs for him. The band's break was over and Vanessa started her regular set of French songs made popular by Patricia Kass, so they settled in to enjoy her sultry voice. This was a club where guests came to appreciate the music rather than talk over the musicians. Vanessa's vocals combined with the riffs by the saxophone player were earning loud applause at the end of every song, leading to a standing ovation at the end. Vanessa walked off and waved to Catherine, mouthing she'd join them shortly.

Catherine knew she had to halt Sean's pursuit and level with him. "Sean, you're a great guy, and I'm very much enjoying this evening—"

"—but," he interrupted, acknowledging he sensed a dismissal coming.

"I don't want to be misleading. I'm taking a break from relationships for a while."

He leaned in. "How long a while?"

"This job is more than I bargained for, and I can't jeopardize that by dating someone in the company. I need to put all my energy into it until the launch," she said.

"I can bide my time."

"I wouldn't do that, Sean." She tried to compliment her way out of the predicament. "It wouldn't be fair to deprive other women of your magnetic company."

On cue, Vanessa appeared at their table. "Hello, you two. This conversation looks intense. Mind if I join?"

"Don't be silly. We've been waiting for you," Catherine chided. She made the introductions while Sean jumped up and pulled out Vanessa's chair. He served Vanessa a glass of champagne and saluted her with his flute. "You're a big hit. I'm sure I'm the envy of every man in this room with the beauty and talent at this table."

"Quite the flatterer," Vanessa teased. "So, what were you two engrossed in?"

"Oh, just the travails at work and how consuming it is," Catherine said.

Vanessa faced Sean. "I keep telling her all work and no play keeps the guys away."

"I couldn't agree more, and what a shame it is," he said. They both laughed.

Over dessert and the rest of the bottle of champagne, they compared their favorite haunts in New York.

Catherine sat back and let Sean and Vanessa dominate the conversation. He appeared to be taking Catherine's rejection in stride as he bantered with Vanessa and focused his attention on her. They were having such a lively discussion, they were one of the last groups to leave. Sean seemed reluctant to end the evening when he escorted the women back to their apartment.

❧ ❧ ❧

Monday morning, fortified with a double-shot cappuccino from Jacques Torres up the street, Catherine arrived at the Seagram Building carrying the coffee in one hand and a large tote in the other. Time to deliver those yellow carnations.

The suite was quiet at seven-thirty, only one secretary at her desk. No one in the break room, thank goodness. Catherine filled an inexpensive glass vase with water, dropped in the carnations, and placed them on Chris's desk with a note that read, "To brighten your day, Catherine." At the moment, she'd try anything to gain his support for her event proposals and was certain he wouldn't know the underlying message of the carnations. She flashed back to the last time she took flowers to a guy. *Boy did that backfire.*

That task completed, Catherine ran water into an antique crystal vase for the freesias and placed them in her office. Claire wouldn't be in for another hour, so Catherine went over her notes for the upcoming board meeting and started jotting down ideas and questions in the margins.

Things sure had changed. Yesterday, instead of shopping or hanging out with friends, like she'd normally do on a Sunday, she'd spent the day working on her Cornell application. Now, she was back at work, trying to support herself. Aside from needing the income, it was becoming a point of pride to prove Chris wrong and warrant the trust James placed in her.

As she hummed a song from Saturday night, it suddenly hit her. Why not use "Celebration" for the theme of the new *cuvée de prestige*? We serve champagne to celebrate special occasions. Even when we drink it at other times, it puts us in the mood to celebrate.

Time passed quickly as her pen flew across the page. She felt a rush of creativity similar to when she sketched a new design. In her absorbed state, she didn't notice Chris enter her office, until he rapped on the open door. She looked up, startled.

"Good morning. You're in early," he said. "Thank you for the flowers." He had a goofy grin on his face.

If only he knew. "You're welcome," she said. So he wouldn't read too much into the situation, she added, "They were offering two for the price of one. I got them with my freesias." She pointed to the vase holding a cluster of delicate white blooms.

"How about lunch today?" he asked. Once again, Chris was clueless he was in hostile territory.

"Thanks, but I'll be working through lunch," she said. "I've still got lots to prepare for my presentation to the board tomorrow."

Chris persisted. "Anything you want to discuss or bounce around before the meeting?"

"So far, I'm okay. I'll let you know." She could tell Chris was miffed. She knew she was walking a thin line. She shouldn't alienate him further, but she certainly wasn't going to give him any information to use against her, either.

Claire arrived, which cut the conversation short. Chris looked annoyed as he left.

"Looks like you've been busy." Claire glanced at Catherine's notes. "Did you work all weekend?"

"Took a break to go to Van's club on Saturday night." Catherine smiled. "Even took a dashing date—"

"Guessing Sean or Chris—"

"Definitely not Chris. Took Sean. Wait 'til you hear what I found out." Catherine filled her in on what she'd overheard from Chris's secretary on Friday. "The nerve of that guy asking me to lunch when he's sabotaging me behind my back."

"I can't believe he's so quick to judge," Claire said. "He didn't give you a chance."

Catherine tapped her pen on the notepad. "One of Van's songs gave me an idea for the *cuvée* theme."

"Don't keep me in suspense."

"What do you think about 'Celebration'?"

The Frenchwoman's eyes lit up. "I think it sounds *magnifique*. Gives us a lot of angles to pursue. How do you propose presenting it to the company brass?"

"I'm not sure. I report to Chris, so I should take it to him. But it's clear he's not in my corner. I want to hold off and present it at the board meeting tomorrow where I have allies." Catherine knew James would be receptive, and another family friend, David Saunders, was on the board. His son, David Junior, was a few years older than Catherine; they'd all spent summers together with James's family and her grandparents on Long Island.

"That could get you in more trouble with him," Claire said.

"Possibly," Catherine said, "but we're all submitting proposals and James will be there to lend support." James had asked her to give the presentation rather than having Chris give her update. James said she would bring more sizzle.

To bring that sizzle to life, Catherine and Claire brainstormed the rest of the day. They distilled the talking points for display on a poster board:

Suggested Tagline—Celebrate: You Deserve It!

Tie in with special occasions (weddings, birthdays, college graduations).

Use celebrity connections.

They had flip charts. They had drawings. They even had music, if the occasion called for it: related songs by Kool & the Gang and Madonna. They still needed to finalize the rest of Catherine's presentation on proposed events, so they ordered in sushi and prepared to put in another late night.

Chapter Eight

New York—95 days to Winston cuvée *launch*

Showtime. Catherine repeated her mantra as she made final preparations for her presentation to the board of directors. She and Claire had finished the graphics at eleven the night before, so she'd managed five hours sleep before returning to the office. She covered her mouth to stifle a yawn.

Her nerves were frazzled. She'd taken a big risk agreeing to provide bottles for the Spago party and putting her signature on the contract without authorization. In her defense, she'd given Sean a heads-up and he was supportive, albeit off the record.

What if they didn't like her proposals? Catherine had been purposefully vague in the reports she'd submitted to Chris, so he wouldn't shoot down her ideas before they were fully considered. Clearly, they approached things differently. She hoped James and the other board members would see the value in celebrity tie-ins and endorse the theme she came up with for the *cuvée.*

Elbows on the desk, she reviewed her notes one last time. A wayward tendril of hair slipped from behind her ear. Her long tresses were pulled back off her face in a twisted French chignon. She'd chosen to dress conservatively in her rust-colored

Dior suit with fitted skirt that fell below her knees. If only she could make a strong, convincing delivery.

The board handled other business for an hour before James's secretary called her to join them. Catherine had been in the conference room for small meetings. This time all sixteen chairs were occupied and the room crackled with energy. She glanced at the numbers on the whiteboard. It appeared they had been going over financial figures.

James sat at the head of the table near the door. He walked over to greet her, gestured to the group and said, "Catherine Reynolds is here to give a presentation on marketing events we're considering. Sean Dunlavy, our sales director, is joining us for this portion of the meeting." He proceeded to briefly introduce each board member. Besides James's partner, Alan Wright, and Chris, there were two representatives from their French partner: Yves Bertrand, CEO, and Jean Boyer, chief winemaker of Trianon.

The rest were outside directors, top executives at other companies, mainly finance and banking, where James started his career. A few stood out. Will Frost, a tall drink of water in Catherine's estimation; she'd heard he was half British. David Saunders smiled and acknowledged her with a nod. She was pleased to see some diversity: two women from investment firms, an African American former basketball-player-turned-entrepreneur, and a telecom CEO from Mexico.

James had assembled quite a group. She knew they were exploring expansion plans overseas, assuming the launch was successful. That's where she came in. Celebrity buzz. Free media. She disliked the term. It wasn't free per se; it took a lot of energy to capture media attention.

Time to dive in. She was concerned her youth might be a drawback to being taken seriously. Sean gave her an encouraging smile, and she knew James was rooting for her. She set up her posters on the easel. Then she took a deep breath, looked briefly at James for moral support, and started taking them through her strategy.

First, she reviewed events Lexington had lined up for mid-June after the launch in Bordeaux, including restaurant tastings and cosponsorships at New York cultural events that might draw press. "Since Vinexpo is for the trade," she continued, "Lexington set up a US launch event at the Winston Resort. Details haven't been ironed out yet."

Then she explained a number of ways to build excitement via celebrity tie-ins, from participating in charity fundraisers to tying in with movie premieres and TV-show wrap parties.

"To get pre-buzz, there are a few events we can pursue." Catherine flipped to the next poster, titled "Tie-in with Academy Awards." "Wolfgang Puck agreed to showcase Winston's latest rosé sparkling at a pre-Oscar party he's hosting at his flagship restaurant, Spago, in Beverly Hills. It will have a crush of celebrities and widespread media coverage."

A flurry of questions ensued, mainly about the costs involved.

Chris spoke up for the first time. "Let me go on record as saying I'm not convinced an event at Spago will move the needle enough to justify the expense and man hours. Do our customers really care what these celebrities drink? Plus, there's no guarantee we'll get press mentions."

"Quite the contrary, I think," David Saunders said. "It seems to me the national pastime is following celebs' every move and then emulating their lifestyle choices."

"Eventually, we'll be looking at establishing relationships with some of these household names to enhance our brand," James said. "This could be the first step."

"There are other issues," Chris countered. "Since it's too early to offer the *cuvée de prestige,* do we feel it's worth the investment to showcase our rosé sparkling? Can we spare the bottles?"

Sean jumped in to endorse Catherine's plan. He said not only could he pull the rosé bottles from his sales allocation, but it would be a good opportunity to woo southern California buyers if he could get a handful of invitations for them to attend.

James motioned to Catherine. "We'll discuss this among ourselves and make a decision at the end of the meeting. Do you have anything else for us?"

"One last thing." She stepped back over to the easel. "I've come up with a possible theme name for the *cuvée*." The room stilled. She had their rapt attention. "Given that champagne's primary purpose is for celebrating events, large and small, why not simply 'Celebration'?" Catherine flipped the page to the poster she and Claire had crafted listing the key selling points.

"Why not indeed," James said. "It's simple yet carries an aura of anticipation. I like it."

"That tagline"—Sean pointed to the poster—"'Celebrate: You Deserve It,' fits perfectly with our sales campaign."

"I drafted a mock promo." Catherine revealed the last page. It displayed a drawing of a tilted champagne bottle. "CELEBRATION" in all caps was etched in large gold foil letters on the rectangular label. Multicolored fireworks streamed out from the top of the bottle. "The fireworks coming out of the bottle mimic the energy of the cork popping and the bubbles shooting out," she said.

"That's a good rendering," Will said. "Did you do it?"

"Yes, I studied design," she said, pleased at the compliment. She gathered her materials.

"Thank you, my dear." James stood and escorted her to the door. "You've given us a lot to consider. Chris will meet with you later to discuss next steps."

Catherine figured that was a subtle rebuke to communicate more with Chris. Soon she'd learn what fireworks she had to contend with, assuming she still had a job.

After Catherine's presentation, the board took a ten-minute break and reconvened. There were a number of issues to decide. Chris was concerned the votes wouldn't go his way—and he was right.

First, they voted on which Winston sparkling to enter in the Plaza Blind Tasting next month. Chris argued that although their new *cuvée de prestige* was excellent, it hadn't been market-tested outside the company. He lobbied for the recently released Winston rosé that was already receiving top ratings from wine critics. He emphasized that if they entered the *cuvée* and it didn't place at minimum in the lowest bronze category, that could damage its reputation and affect the success of the launch.

James was gung-ho to enter the *cuvée* and convinced all but Will Frost, who supported his friend Chris, to vote in favor.

After procedural votes on financial matters, James brought up Catherine's proposals. Chris reiterated his opposition to participating in the Spago event on the grounds that it was too costly. That vote was closer, but James wholeheartedly endorsed the plan, and Catherine's pitch won the day. On the use of "Celebration" as the theme for the new *cuvée*, they were all in agreement. Chris had to admit he gave Catherine credit on this one. It was a good concept. He just wished she'd run it by him first.

While people filed out, James pulled Chris aside. "Appears you're coming down awfully hard on Catherine's ideas," James said. "Is something going on there?"

Chris shook his head. "Not that I'm aware of. Aside from the fact that I'm afraid her celebrity proposals are going to blow our limited budget, and I can't get her to clue me in on what she's up to. Most of the time I'm in the dark . . ."

James frowned. "My secretary relayed some gossip. Seems your secretary has been spreading rumors that you weren't happy hiring Catherine and view her as a jet-set-spoiled-dilettante."

Chris dragged a hand through his hair. "I had no idea Delores could be so vindictive." He paused. "She must have overheard a private phone conversation with my dad right after Catherine started here. I was just blowing off steam. It was never meant to be repeated."

"You need to straighten this out," James said. "We don't need any distractions."

"Of course," Chris said. In addition to dealing with Catherine, he planned to have a serious talk with his secretary. If he caught a whiff of her recounting his future conversations, she'd be out the door in a flash. His trust was difficult to earn. Once violated, he cut his losses quickly. The men parted ways.

Chris stopped by Catherine's office. "Have a minute?" he asked.

"Sure." Catherine started tapping her pen furiously on the desk. He got the impression he made her uncomfortable. *Good.*

He walked in and sat down. "The board liked your ideas. Spago is a go. And we're running the 'Celebration' theme by the advertising agency before a final decision." He put his hand on her desk. "That was some presentation. Let's meet tomorrow after lunch to discuss where we go from here. Say around three o'clock."

She glanced at her calendar. "All right. I'm available then."

"Fine. Come by my office." He got up to leave, started to say something else, then just nodded and left.

The next afternoon Chris sent his secretary on an errand to avoid any friction when Catherine arrived at his office. He left the door ajar. She walked in five minutes early. Their eyes caught. *Damn she looks good.* Chris stood up and put on his jacket.

"Grab your coat, Miss Reynolds. We're going out," he said.

"Where?" Catherine looked startled.

"It's a surprise." *My turn to be unpredictable.*

They stopped by her office, and he helped her put on a long brown coat, which felt buttery soft—*probably cashmere*, he thought. *Why is my subconscious looking for opportunities to get my hands on this woman? Better tamp that down.*

She wrapped a matching scarf around her neck, and Claire gave them a quizzical look as they departed.

Chris sensed Catherine wasn't fond of surprises. *That's tough.* He maintained his silence in the elevator and led the way out of the building to the town car waiting on Park Avenue.

He held open her door and instructed the driver to take them to Central Park. "Sometimes I like to get out of the office for fresh air—clears the mind," he said.

"You know, I'm not wearing my walking shoes," she cautioned.

No kidding. Her three-inch stiletto heels set off her calves and that slim-fitting dress very nicely. He was content to keep her guessing during their short drive, the least he could do to repay her for keeping him in the dark on her marketing proposals.

They passed through Grand Army Plaza, located at the southeast corner of Central Park. The driver pulled up to the curb next to the park entrance marked "Scholars' Gate" and hopped out to open Catherine's door.

Chris got out on the other side and walked over to the horse carriages nearby. He greeted one of the drivers. "Hello, Seamus. How is Swagsational today?"

"He's chipper. Seems happy to see you," Seamus said.

Chris reached up to pet the horse's mane and offered him cut-up apple from a plastic bag in his pocket. "Hey boy, how are you doing?" The horse nudged his hand and whinnied.

"Let's take a spin." Chris held out his arm to assist Catherine into the carriage. She looked startled, like she was about to object, then accepted his help.

Seamus climbed onto his seat and turned to Chris. "Your usual route, sir?"

"Yes, Seamus, thank you." Chris made sure Catherine was bundled up in warm blankets.

Seamus flicked the reins and they were off. It was cold, but sunny, and they had the path to themselves.

Chris decided to clear the air right away. "I found out my secretary was engaging in office gossip and wanted to set things straight." Catherine frowned. *Okay, she probably did hear about it.*

"Yes, I heard something."

"I'm sorry," he said. "I never meant for any comments I made blowing off steam to be repeated. I'll admit to some initial reservations due to your lack of experience, but you've worked hard, and I apologize for my bias."

Catherine seemed to relax and soften before his eyes. "I appreciate that," she said. "This is a new arena for me, so I'll make mistakes . . ."

"You seem to be holding your own, so far. In fact"—Chris paused—"the advertising firm raved about your proposal to use 'Celebration' as the theme for the *cuvée*."

Catherine's eyes lit up.

"That means you can start mocking up corresponding slogans and pitch ideas," he said.

Seamus pulled over to the side. "Would you two like some hot chocolate?"

"Great idea," Chris said.

Seamus handed the thermos and Styrofoam cups to Chris, who served Catherine then poured a cup for himself.

"Hot and delicious," Catherine said. "This hits the spot."

Chris took a sip and agreed. To his amazement, he was really enjoying this outing. The brisk air was invigorating. There was light snow on the ground near elm trees that had lost their leaves, looking barren and ethereal in the winter light. Quite magical.

Bringing himself back to the task at hand, Chris had one more point to make. "I do need to be kept apprised of all future projects you're hatching," he said.

"Okay." She nodded. "Fresh start." She tilted her head, eyeing him coolly. "Does that mean you'll support all my proposals?"

Wow, she plays hardball. "You drive a tough bargain," Chris said. "We'll have to see about that."

He held out his hand to shake hers and didn't release hers right away. Felt too good holding her hand.

While the horses clip-clopped along, he told Catherine what brought him to the park. Manhattan had such a hectic pace he made it a point to get outside in a natural setting for perspective. At home, in Napa, he was accustomed to surveying their ranch on horseback with his dad.

The carriage passed an ice-skating rink doing brisk business—kids bundled up, hanging on to their parents' arms while learning to skate. "I used to come here with my dad," Catherine said.

Chris could picture it: an enchanting little girl with pigtails, wearing a fashionable ice-skating skirt over matching leggings, looking up adoringly at her dad.

"When you fed the apple to the horse, it reminded me of a story my dad told me when we watched horse carriages ride past," she said. "Have you heard how New York became referred to as the Big Apple?"

"Nope. Don't know that one," Chris said.

"The story goes . . . in the 1920s, horse races in New York earned the top money. Horses up for a big prize purse were promised a 'big apple' from their trainers if they won," she said. "Jazz musicians picked up the reference and used 'Big Apple' for higher paying gigs in New York. Guess it stuck."

"Thanks for enlightening me." *She's pretty adorable when she lets her guard down. No wonder she had the board members eating out of her hand.* Even his tough-to-please friend Will seemed taken with her.

This was a wholly different side of Catherine. She was becoming more appealing to him by the minute. Her femininity wreaked havoc on his senses. She seemed so delicate and smelled like the fresh flowers in her office. The carriage returned to Fifth Avenue sooner than Chris would have liked.

Two days later, Catherine and Vanessa were in a cab on their way to a trendsetting art gallery in SoHo.

"Okay, start dishing," Vanessa said. "Haven't talked since you came in swooning after your meeting with your boss Wednesday. Been dying of curiosity."

Where to start. Catherine was trying to puzzle it out herself. The outing had felt like a date by the end.

"Chris McDermott is full of surprises," she began. "He heard about the rumors his secretary spread and apologized. Said he wanted to start over. Clean slate."

"Do you believe him?"

"I'm not sure. I still don't think he feels I'm up to the job. And we definitely disagree on using celebs. But I give him an A for creative outings." Catherine pulled out her compact and checked her lipstick, stalling for her punch line.

"I thought he was a stuffed shirt type," Vanessa said.

"So did I until he took me on a carriage ride through Central Park." Catherine grinned from ear to ear.

Vanessa's eyes widened. "He did what? Isn't that a bit corny?"

"I know it's for tourists, but it was kind of endearing. And"—Catherine shrugged—"it felt so removed, like we could have been in one of our favorite European cities, except for the occasional screaming cabby." She snapped her compact shut. "I'm afraid my icy cool may be in danger of melting. I think he's interested . . ."

"Hey, wait a minute. That doesn't sound like the best idea." Vanessa waved her hands in front of Catherine's face for emphasis. "Earth to Cat. Don't forget he's your boss."

"You're right. Keeping my job is the number one priority." Catherine pulled out her wallet to pay the driver, in cash. This was a work expense.

Tonight, *Vogue* magazine was hosting a Moët & Chandon champagne reception to introduce a hip French jewelry designer. Catherine and Vanessa knew *Vogue*'s editor from their modeling days, so they received invitations to many of the parties. A nice perk.

Catherine wanted to observe how a prestigious champagne house used a cultural event to promote their product, and she needed to network with the press covering it for future Winston events.

They pulled up to the entrance, and the women moved from the quiet tête-à-tête in the cab to the frenetic atmosphere of paparazzi camera flashbulbs popping amid a crowd of passersby on the sidewalk gawking at the arrivals.

The gallery showcased up-and-coming artists in different mediums, in this case necklace art pieces. Normally, Catherine's expensive taste ran to Cartier and Bulgari jewelry, not affordable on her present limited budget. In her modeling days, she'd learned how to mix it up with *faux bijoux* that were colorful and clunky to offset the classic jewels worn every day, or the special occasion family heirlooms borrowed from a safe-deposit box.

The minimalist gallery space was a fitting backdrop to the chicly dressed beautiful people admiring each other and the art and jewelry on display. Waiters circulated trays of Moët's Brut Impérial and light canapés. Catherine and Vanessa never ate at these soirées—could smudge your lipstick, or even worse, have onion in the ingredients.

They grabbed flutes of champagne off a passing tray and clinked glasses before taking their first sips. "Mmm, good," Catherine said. She realized her palate for premium champagne was becoming more refined.

The purpose of these events was to garner press mentions, instill goodwill among top clients, and generate sales. From the looks of the women drooling over the necklaces, that final goal appeared to be in sight.

Vanessa moved toward the jewelry display. Catherine touched her shoulder. "I'm going to circulate and see what press is here." Champagne flute in hand, she went in search of journalists covering the event.

She recognized editors from the *New York Times* and national entertainment magazines. She told them about her new job, and they exchanged business cards. Catherine knew these contacts wouldn't help until she came up with an actual event for them to cover. She needed a media placement in the next few weeks to meet her monthly quota.

She spotted an old acquaintance, Jacqueline Collart, a mid-forties Frenchwoman she'd met in Paris through their mutual friend Patrick Tournelle. They'd never been close; Catherine sensed she felt competitive with other women.

Of course, none of this chilliness was evident when they greeted each other. It was "kiss kiss" pecks on both cheeks and "*vous êtes très chic ce soir.*" Jacqueline was not a natural beauty, but she exuded style; she wore chic outfits, had her dark hair cut fashionably short, and always sported a tan, even in winter.

Jacqueline had started out in public relations for French chefs in Paris and New York. Eventually, she landed a job at *New York News*, writing the "All About Wine" column. Catherine noticed that she shortened her first name to Jacqui on her business card. *Maybe she thinks that sounds more chic.*

"I didn't know you were living in New York," she said.

"I moved here at the beginning of the month for my new PR job at Winston & Wright." Catherine handed her a business card.

"Congratulations. How did you snag that?"

Catherine ignored the subtle slight that she wasn't qualified, although that could prove to be true in the end. Instead, she extolled the virtues of Winston's new *cuvée de prestige* hoping to interest Jacqui in writing a feature, or at least a mention, in her wine column.

"Vanessa's singing career is taking off," Catherine said. "She's lead singer at Smoke on the weekends." From the look on Jacqueline's face, Catherine had the impression she'd expected the former models to fade into the woodwork rather than land enviable jobs.

"We'll have to get together for lunch sometime," Jacqui said.

"Yes, that would be nice. See you soon."

Vanessa waved Catherine over to the jewelry display. "Cat, this is Remy Camoin, *joaillier extraordinaire*." Vanessa turned to him. "My friend, Catherine Reynolds."

"*Bonsoir madame*," Remy said. He bowed slightly, raised Catherine's hand to his lips, and brushed them over her knuckles, the French gesture of kissing a woman's hand on greeting. *Old-fashioned*, Catherine thought, *for a young man in his thirties.*

He wore the uniform of artist types: black jacket over an untucked white linen shirt and designer black jeans, which set off his jet-black hair. No tie. A good-looking man.

With Catherine's prompting, Remy shared his artistic journey. He'd attended École des Beaux Arts in Paris then established a workshop in Limoges constructing necklaces using French artisans not normally associated with fine jewelry. He'd hired local ceramicists to transform his sketches into delicate porcelain shapes in vibrant hues. To fasten them together, he employed seamstresses trained in the art of sewing ribbon and lace for haute couture garments. Each piece was one of a kind, crafted by hand.

Vanessa leaned closer and whispered in Catherine's ear, "Isn't he divine? I'm so excited about the backup singer gig at the Academy Awards my agent got for me that I mentioned it, and Remy offered to lend me one of his signature pieces to wear." It went without saying, the Oscars broadcast was an enviable audience for any designer, reaching millions of television viewers around the world—from the red-carpet interviews beforehand to the actual show itself.

Vanessa tried on a few necklaces and immediately became the center of attention, a role she wore effortlessly.

"Do you like this one?" Vanessa turned to her friend and held up a long necklace of sapphire-blue porcelain stars in various sizes, strung together by a thin black velvet cord intricately knotted.

"It's perfect," Catherine said. "The blue will pop your eyes and the stars fit the Hollywood theme." Catherine reached over to view it more closely.

"What an amazing ring," Remy said, pointing to Catherine's finger. "May I examine it?" He held his hand out in expectation.

Reluctantly taking it off, Catherine kept close watch while he turned it over in his hand.

"A vintage Cartier Trinity," he said, admiring the three interlocking bands of gold. "Appears to be the traditional white gold for friendship, yellow gold for fidelity, and rose gold for love."

"That's right," Catherine said.

"But it looks unique," Remy continued. "The diamonds and emeralds on the gold bands are exquisite."

"Also true," Catherine said. "One of a kind, created for my French great-*grand-mère*."

"I assume you have it insured," he said.

"To steal it, they'd have to pry it off her hand," Vanessa intervened. "I've only seen her take it off to have it polished."

On that cue, Remy returned the ring to Catherine, who put it back on her finger and rubbed it with her opposing thumb. She felt incomplete without it on her hand.

Vanessa glanced at her watch. "I've got to scoot."

"Let us know if you want to pick up the necklace or have it delivered," Remy's assistant said, "and we'll make the arrangements."

"Thanks so much," Vanessa said. "I'll work out my dress, probably something slinky with a plunging neckline."

Catherine needed to return to the office to finish a report, so the cabbie dropped her off and continued on with Vanessa, who had a rare Friday night off.

The Seagram Building was quiet. The guard waved a friendly hello and moved the log-in book toward her. She signed in and checked her phone to enter the time: 8:40 p.m. In her former life, she'd be going to dinner or a party at this hour.

She used her keycard to activate the elevator and got off at the twentieth floor. The same keycard opened the suite door. The office was dark and desolate. Everyone had gone home.

Catherine turned on an overhead light, went to her office, and got to work. She opened her kelly-green folder for pending reports and took out her notes in four areas: new ideas, pending projects, completed, and budget.

She desperately needed a national hit. Catherine reviewed her pitches to television programs and figured it might be a good time to catch her friend Sue Hamilton, host of a popular TV news magazine show. It was almost six in Los Angeles; Sue picked up on the first ring.

"Hi Cat," Sue said. "Emma tells me you have a new job." Sue's younger sister, Emma, was a classmate of Catherine and Vanessa at the Swiss boarding school. Sue attended the same school a few years earlier.

"That's right," Catherine said. "I'm doing publicity for a Napa sparkling wine company. Thought you might want to do a profile on the handsome mid-thirties president for your 'Executives to Watch' segment." Catherine knew her friend was attracted to good-looking business types. This was like dangling catnip.

Sue bit hook, line, and sinker. Turns out they'd just had a cancellation, so Sue was keen to find a replacement guest to fill their taping in a few days. She was sold on the idea of her television crew filming a location shoot at Chris's family ranch in Napa. Then they'd do a more formal interview with Chris at the Winston office in New York.

Catherine assured Sue that Chris was articulate and photogenic, known as "camera ready," an important consideration for television. When they hung up, she emailed Chris's photo, bio, and suggested talking points to Sue for the segment.

Exhilarated after the call, Catherine needed to get Chris to sign off right away. She debated calling him this late on a Friday night. He might be on a hot date. She decided to send an interoffice email.

Five minutes later, he called. "Got your message," he said. "You're working late. Where are you? The office?"

"Yes," she said. "Trying to get through my to-do list. Sorry to bother you, but this is urgent."

"No problem, I'm just pouring over spreadsheets in my home office. Guess we're both working late on a Friday night."

"I've lined up an interview with ABC-TV next week," she said. "They want to shoot at your family ranch in Napa and later here in New York. It's a profile to highlight the launch."

There was a pause on the other end of the line. "I thought we agreed James would be the spokesperson. He's the founder and chairman."

"I appreciate that, but the reporter wants someone younger, more relatable. She's an old friend, said she'd give us positive coverage."

"Okay, you've twisted my arm," Chris said. "I'll go out a day early and get some work done with Tom at the winery. Assume you'll be there to monitor the interview?"

"Yes, I'll fly in the night before." She had to scramble to put everything into place.

"Be careful when you're at the office by yourself at night," Chris cautioned. "Have one of the security guys escort you out for a cab."

"Okay, I will." She liked this protective side of Chris.

After they hung up, Catherine raised her right fist in a victory gesture. This interview should meet her national media quota for the first month. She could breathe a momentary sigh of relief.

Chapter Nine

Napa—89 days to Celebration launch

Chris felt good to be back in the saddle, even if the reason for the trip was a television interview he dreaded. Their ranch spread out before them, Chris and his dad toured the perimeter of the property on horseback. The sun rose over the Vaca Mountains to the east, waking up rows of vines stretched across the valley floor. Dairy cattle grazed in a pasture near a large red barn. Closer to the one-lane highway stood a wood-frame ranch house with red trim and window flower boxes brimming with white geraniums.

Richard McDermott pulled his horse to a stop alongside Chris. "Well son, can't say I'm not surprised you let someone talk you into doing an interview here at the ranch. You've always guarded your privacy." He tipped his cowboy hat. "She must be pretty persuasive."

"What makes you think it's a she?" Chris eyed his father.

"Just a hunch." They regarded each other, and as usual, Chris blinked first. They both grinned.

"Yeah, she is pretty persuasive, and I'm not sure what I'm going to do about it," Chris said. "I invited Catherine to stay over in the guesthouse tonight." He justified the gesture by telling himself it would save the company money on a pricey Napa hotel, but who was he kidding.

His dad picked up on the direction Chris's mind veered. "Good. Seems to me it's about time you consider getting serious with someone."

"Whoa," Chris said. "We haven't even been on a date yet. And I'm her boss, at least through the launch."

"Well, speed things up. The ranch hasn't been the same since your mother passed away, and I'd like some grandkids to spoil."

Chris warmed to the idea of his kids running around the ranch, causing trouble like he and his brothers used to do, and being spoiled by their grandpa. He might need to move up his imaginary timeline on when to settle down—if the right woman came along.

Pulling him out of his reverie, his dad changed topics. "What needs to be done to prepare for this hotshot reporter?"

On steadier ground, Chris said, "They'll arrive in an hour with the crew. We'll probably film by the corral, and they want some shots of the property. Maura's all set to serve coffee and muffins."

"Too bad your brothers aren't here to get their handsome mugs on TV, too."

Chris's twin brothers, Michael and Edward, were graduate students in the agriculture program at UC Davis. Even though they were twelve years younger, all three McDermott brothers were very close.

They rode back to the barn in companionable silence, anticipating Maura's hearty breakfast: usually omelets with a variety of fillings, flaky buns straight from the oven, and fresh fruit. At the stables, they were greeted by a large golden retriever, tail wagging furiously. "Hello, Cubby." Chris gave him a scratch behind the ears.

The men brushed down the horses, washed up, and went into the kitchen, drawn by the smells of freshly ground coffee and frying bacon. Maura clucked over the family like a mother hen. They were grateful for her devotion, even if they chided her about it from time to time. She had come over from Ireland as a young woman seeking employment and a chance to start a life in America. She'd signed on as the McDermott's housekeeper twenty years ago, a role that became indispensable when Anne McDermott fell ill and passed away. After serving the men at the breakfast table, she went about her chores.

Over bites of scrambled eggs, the men reviewed the latest plans for their nascent family winery. Richard's parents had bought the ranch with a small inheritance back in the 1950s and established a thriving dairy farm. An only child, Richard took over the business after graduating from college. Early on he'd had the foresight to understand winemaking was becoming a lucrative industry in the valley. He gradually started converting acreage to vineyards and cut back on the dairy operation. They mainly grew Cabernet grapes, which Rutherford was known for, and sold them to midsize wineries that depended on independent growers to supplement their own harvests. It was a profitable business but hadn't made them rich by any means.

Chris and his brothers had committed to eventually join their father in the family business. They wanted to expand, buy more land, and build their own winery to make a decent profit and ensure a legacy for the family. That required millions of dollars. Richard had put some money aside, and they could take out a small loan. But they were counting on Chris's investment in Winston growing exponentially after his launch bonus.

Chris knew he would be a better asset to the McDermott winery if he got real-world experience first, and he'd enjoyed stretching his wings in the corporate world. He figured by the time he reached forty he'd have the knowledge and contacts to put the McDermott winery on the map.

Right now, a more immediate task loomed.

Catherine pulled up to the McDermott ranch house as Sue and the film crew were getting out of their cars. Arriving in San Francisco late the previous night, Catherine had stayed in a motel by the airport, which meant she'd needed to leave very early to make it to Napa for the 9:00 a.m. shoot. She stifled a yawn. *Hope they're serving strong coffee.*

She parked and joined them on the porch. Sue's version of country attire consisted of tight black jeans tucked into knee-high Ferragamo boots and a low-cut, clingy red top. *She must be freezing in this chilly weather.* Sue's long chestnut hair was styled straight, and full makeup added star power to her beautiful face.

Thankful she didn't have to glam it up for the camera, Catherine wore a tailored pantsuit and comfortable walking shoes, hair pulled back in a ponytail. She greeted Sue and the women shared a light hug.

"Good to see you," Sue said.

"You too," Catherine replied. "I'm glad we could make this work."

A slightly plump older woman opened the front door. "Hello everyone. I'm Maura. Come on in." She ushered them into the living room. In addition to Sue, there were two cameramen, a sound guy, and the director. The atmosphere inside changed from relaxed to frenzied in the space of a few seconds.

Chris walked over to the group. Catherine spoke first. "Chris, I'd like you to meet my friend and *Newsline* host, Sue Hamilton."

Sue reached out to shake Chris's hand. "Thanks for agreeing to do this on short notice."

"Sure. My publicist is very persuasive," he said.

While Sue spoke to the crew, Chris pulled Catherine aside. "Thanks for making the trip. I'm glad you're here." She felt a new warmth from him and wondered if it had to do with being on his turf. Whatever it was, she liked this side of him.

Chris waved his father over to meet them. Then the crew introduced themselves, and Richard offered to show them around to scout locations. Catherine noticed that on their way out the guys managed to grab muffins that smelled like they had just come out of the oven.

"Is there someplace we can go over the script?" Sue asked.

Chris threw a questioning glance in Catherine's direction. "I didn't realize there was a script."

"Welcome to television," Sue said. "It's not as spontaneous as it looks."

Chris ushered them into the dining room. They sat down at a large oak table with high-back cane chairs. Maura placed a fresh carafe of steaming coffee on the sideboard under a window facing a vegetable garden.

Sue handed out a two-page, double-spaced topic breakdown for the Q&A. "I jotted down some key points, and we can modify as we go, keeping in mind that the whole segment runs only eight minutes. Much of what we shoot will end up on the editing room floor."

"Anyone else want coffee?" Catherine asked as she went to the sideboard.

"I'll take a cup black, thanks," Sue said.

While they perused the breakdown, Catherine poured the coffees and added cream to hers. She took her first sip. It was strong and delicious. She grabbed one of the cranberry-walnut muffins and made a mental note to ask Maura for the recipe.

Sue began by asking Chris what attracted him to the job at Winston & Wright as opposed to some other executive position. He explained he was drawn to the company's potential for growth, and the Winston philosophy aligned with his values—demand top quality, seek out the latest technology, and share the joie de vivre.

"Those tenets are exemplified in our first prestige blend, which we're launching in June," Chris segued. "We used grapes from a vintage year, the wines were expertly blended by a world-class winemaker, and we allowed the wine to age longer—seven years to be exact—to bring out the full flavor. The joie de vivre will be when people taste it for themselves."

Sue laughed. "Very well said."

As the conversation progressed, it became evident to Catherine that her friend seemed to have more than a business interest in Chris McDermott. She leaned in close, asked personal questions about how he spent his time in New York, and kept touching his arm. Miffed at her friend's flirtatiousness, Catherine sighed in relief when the director returned with the crew. "Okay folks, we're ready for the shoot," he said. "Let's start outside by the corral."

The corral was across the paved driveway next to a red barn. Two horses were saddled up and tied to a railing.

Catherine stood near the director behind a cameraman. Richard and Maura stood off to one side to observe Chris's first television performance.

When everyone was in place, the cameraman yelled, "Rolling." Sue faced the cameras and began. "Hello, this is Sue Hamilton reporting from Napa Valley, California. We're here for *Newsline*'s series on 'Executives to Watch.' Today we're talking with Chris McDermott, president of Winston & Wright's Sparkling Winery. This is Chris's family ranch in nearby Rutherford and, as you can see, he grew up in bucolic surroundings." One camera panned the property and followed Sue as she stepped over to join Chris, who leaned against the corral. He looked like one of those sexy models in a Levi's ad in his faded blue jeans and cowboy boots.

"Thanks for letting us invade your private paradise," Sue said.

"It's my pleasure, Sue. Welcome to the McDermott ranch." He leaned over to shake her hand.

Catherine watched, fascinated, as Sue wove her magic and got Chris to share childhood memories. He talked about early morning chores milking cows, attending a one-room schoolhouse where kids in all the grades knew each other, and playing sports with his brothers. A far different world from Catherine's girlhood living in embassies and attending boarding school. Toward the end, Chris answered questions about his career and role at Winston.

As they had prearranged, Chris offered to take Sue on a riding tour of the property. A cameraman would follow along to film background footage for Sue's voiceover. *This is going well.*

"One last question." Sue smiled. "What are the qualities you're looking for in the woman you'll bring home to the McDermott ranch someday?"

Chris glanced at Catherine, who gave him a helpless shrug. "Well, Miss Hamilton, that day is far off." He paused. "But you come awfully close—bright, beautiful, interested in what I have to say, and occasionally full of surprises." He wrapped his arm around her shoulder. "And now shall we see if the property meets with your approval?" Sue appeared smitten as they mounted the horses and rode off, camera in tow.

That's great television, Catherine acknowledged—good visuals and snappy dialogue. She wondered if Chris liked Sue's flirtatious banter. She realized she wouldn't be happy if his interest took a turn in Sue's direction. She knew Sue would find him attractive. She hadn't figured she'd feel the same way. Chris wasn't normally her type. She couldn't act on it, anyway, since keeping her job was paramount.

An hour later, Sue and the crew wrapped up and prepared to head over to the Winston Winery to shoot background footage. Catherine left with them to observe the filming and meet with Tom afterward.

Late in the afternoon, Catherine returned to the McDermott ranch. After unpacking a few things in the guesthouse and handling urgent email, she went to see if she could make herself useful before dinner.

She walked up a brick path past the vegetable garden and heard Maura humming an Irish ballad through the kitchen screen door. Maura looked up as Catherine walked in and gave her a welcoming smile. "Hello, dearie. Have you come to be put to work?"

"Yes, I have. How did you know?" Catherine asked.

"Well, everyone pitches in around here, and rumor has it you know your way around the kitchen." Maura went back to chopping carrots and adding them to a stock simmering on the stove.

"I enjoy cooking. It relaxes me," Catherine admitted, pleased to hear Chris had been talking about her.

"I'm making a fig tart for dessert and want to bake something for tomorrow morning." Maura wiped her hands on her apron and walked around the cooking island to pull out flour and sugar. "What do you recommend?"

Catherine had a flash of whimsy. "How about chocolate chip scones? I know a killer recipe."

"That works." Maura pulled out a baking sheet. "They're Chris's favorite."

Catherine kept her knowledge of that to herself. She set to work laying out the ingredients and preparing the dough.

"Your friend Sue seems quite taken with Chris," Maura said. "Hope her show puts him in a good light."

"He seemed to enjoy her attention," Catherine said.

"Don't let that lighthearted banter fool you." Maura waved her knife. "That's his defensive shield when women come on to him a bit too strong. He's old school, like his dad. He likes to do the pursuing."

Catherine couldn't resist digging further. "He never mentions any serious girlfriends from his past . . ."

"That's because there haven't been many. I've known that man since he was a teenager. He forms strong attachments that don't come along very often." Maura stirred the pot. "His mother died of breast cancer five years ago, God rest her soul." Maura kissed her fingers and crossed her heart. "He's still mourning that loss. They were very close."

"I'm sorry to hear it." Catherine had disagreements with her mom but couldn't imagine losing her, especially so young.

The women continued to work side by side and started comparing recipes. Catherine felt right at home. The timer went off to indicate the scones were done. She pulled the sheet pan out and put it on the stove to cool.

Chris walked in at that moment. "My, those scones smell good. Did you know they're my favorite?" he teased.

"I had no idea," she lied, although she remembered all too well their first encounter when she kicked him out of the

Winston Resort kitchen. "They're just out of the oven, so I should let them cool for a few minutes."

"I think I can handle the heat." He gave her a scorching look as he reached for a scone.

Maura slapped his hand. "No special treatment just because you were a big TV star today, mister. They have to cool, and dinner will be ready in a few minutes."

"All right, I can be patient." He left to join his father in the living room.

While Chris and his brothers were growing up, the McDermott family had sat down to dinner together every night, catching up on the day and discussing current events and local valley news. When they got older, they met for drinks in the living room and waited until Maura announced dinner was ready.

Chris liked this tradition and vowed to continue it when he had a family. *Wonder where that train of thought is coming from.* Maybe Miss Hamilton's questions about the little lady he'd bring home. It certainly wouldn't be her, not his type. Even though she seemed keen on throwing her hat in the ring.

His dad had already opened their favorite cabernet to let it breathe. Chris walked over to the granite bar and poured the cab into two long-stemmed, wide-brimmed Bordeaux-style wineglasses and took one over to his father, who was standing in front of the large stone fireplace. They both wore faded jeans, cowboy boots, and crisply starched plaid shirts. That was the extent of dressing for dinner on this ranch. Chris clinked his glass with his dad's. "To a good crop and successful harvest this year."

The kitchen door swung open and Catherine walked in. She'd changed for dinner into black skinny jeans and a caramel

V-neck sweater that accented her honey-blonde hair, which she wore down. Chris couldn't help staring. *Now that's my type. She looks delectable.*

He went behind the bar to pour her a drink. "What is your pleasure, Miss Reynolds?"

"I'll have what you're drinking." She stepped over to join him.

"Excellent choice." He held the bottle for her to inspect then poured wine into her glass.

"I don't know that label. Kenmare Cabernet." Catherine swirled the wine in the glass, put her nose over the rim to sniff, and took her first sip. "This is good. Is it a local wine?"

"I'm glad you approve. You're one of the select few to sample the first cabernet sauvignon from the McDermotts' new wine label, Kenmare—my mother's maiden name and a town in Ireland where our family is from."

She took another sip. "You mentioned a family wine. I didn't know you were this far along. Is it sold anywhere?"

"Not yet." Chris explained how anyone could produce a custom wine with their own label by buying grapes from quality growers, renting winery equipment, and using an experienced winemaker. Chris and his dad knew the valley well, so they were able to choose the best grapes and oversee the process themselves.

The last five years they'd been using grapes solely grown on their property. Since they intended to build their own winery, these bottles were a preview they'd been sharing with local restaurants and distributors.

"This reminds me of wines I've tasted in Bordeaux," Catherine said.

"Yes, wines labeled Bordeaux are usually a blend of cabernet sauvignon and merlot," he said. "We'll see how they compare when we're in Bordeaux for Vinexpo."

Maura appeared at the door. "Dinner's on."

"Sounds good. I'm famished," his dad said.

They carried their wineglasses into the dining room. His dad pulled out Maura's chair next to him and sat at the head of the table. Chris pulled out a chair for Catherine on the other side of his father and sat next to her.

"Everything smells delicious," Catherine said.

"Thanks, dearie." Maura passed the platter of chicken marsala with parmesan risotto for Catherine to serve herself first.

Chris noticed how close the two women seemed to have become in just one day. In this setting, Catherine seemed more relaxed. It appealed to him. Chris topped off their wine while his dad filled water glasses from the pitcher on the table.

"This roasted asparagus looks so fresh," Catherine said.

"I found it at the farmers market yesterday," Maura said.

With Catherine's interested prodding, the conversation at dinner continued with Chris and his father explaining their plans for the McDermott winery.

When they were finishing the fig tart dessert with freshly whipped cream from their dairy, his dad leaned over to Chris. "Why don't you show Catherine our current operation? It's not much yet, but she'll be able to say she saw a world class winery in its early stages." He stood up and grabbed his plate. "I'll help Maura clear the dishes. You two can take off."

Chris didn't need prompting. He was feeling inexplicably drawn to Catherine. The temperature outside dropped quickly, so he bundled her up in one of his warm leather jackets. It was three sizes too big, which only made her look more adorable.

They stepped onto a moonlit path and walked a short distance to the temporary winery: an aluminum-sided structure that held rudimentary winemaking equipment next to cases of empty bottles. A walk-in cooler held samples of the wines they'd already produced laid horizontally on racks. On the far end of the room, a partial wall separated the "office"—an old metal desk, a long table with office equipment and a computer, one file cabinet, shelves brimming with books and magazines, and a large bulletin board with articles and graphs clipped on it.

"I know it doesn't look like much yet," Chris said. "But it's the genesis of our dream. My dad and I have been working toward this moment for many years, the chance to create our own family wine."

He held out his hand. "Let's go sit outside. It's such a clear night, we should be able to see the stars."

They sat on hay bales near the barn, and he wrapped his arm around her shoulders to keep her warm. He pointed up to the sky. "Most nights you can see the constellations and major stars, unless there's cloud cover." He pulled her closer. "There's Venus . . ."

"Named after the Roman goddess of love and beauty . . ." Catherine chimed in.

Seems the beauty is right here, sitting next to me. "How about you, Catherine Reynolds? What are your dreams?"

She tucked her hands into the jacket pockets. "Unlike you, my dreams have changed over time. When Vanessa and I were teenagers, we went into modeling." She made a face. "It's not as glamorous as people think. Now, I'd like to pursue a career in the hospitality sector." She sighed. "Still working that out."

"I'm sorry I doubted you in the beginning. I think you're a wonderful asset to the company." *And to my life.*

He stood up and silently offered his hand, pulling her up to face him. An owl hooted nearby, momentarily jarring him from his intent to steal a kiss. He took a deep breath and gazed into her upturned face. Her long-lashed eyes blinked as she looked into his questioningly.

"We'd better get going." He turned her around and draped his arm over her shoulders as they walked back. When they reached the guest cottage, he gave her a warm hug and walked off. *She's too appealing. I'm falling fast.*

Catherine woke early to the sound of a rooster crowing. She pondered the events of the night before. Talk about getting swept up in the moment. Chris had taken her stargazing, for heaven's sake. Could it get more romantic? Good thing he put the brakes on or she might have succumbed—and that wasn't a good idea.

The sun was coming up and she wanted to get some much-needed exercise. After donning running shorts and putting her hair in a ponytail, she set off down the road.

Catherine ran effortlessly due to her lean athletic build. It felt good to breathe in clear, fresh air, stretch her legs, and get her pulse up.

Early morning rays shimmered off dew on the vines. Birds chirped and swooped in search of breakfast. Catherine felt like a free spirit as she got farther away from the buildings and bustle of the ranch. *This is pretty idyllic.* Grounded in life's natural rhythms, yet close to a major city. She wanted to linger but had to get ready to drive to San Francisco for her flight back.

Catherine showered and packed quickly. She just had time for a quick coffee and chat with Maura, who she sought out in the kitchen. Maura was rinsing dishes while humming along to Vivaldi's *La Primavera* playing on the radio.

"Good morning," Catherine said. "That's one of my favorite concertos."

Maura smiled. "We may be out in the country, but we still enjoy our culture. Richard takes me to San Francisco to hear the symphony each season."

"Sounds like a great balance. The serenity and beauty of the country with a cosmopolitan city nearby."

"That's it. I only wish Napa Valley hadn't become so popular and expensive. The winery expansion is going to cost the McDermotts a pretty penny. Did Chris give you the grand tour?"

Catherine blushed as she recalled the grand tour he'd almost started to make of her body. She turned to pour a cup of coffee and collect her thoughts. "Yes, he's very passionate about it."

"That figures," Maura said. "The McDermotts are passionate men—dark Irish, you know."

"Wonder if one can get singed from being in close proximity," Catherine said softly.

"I doubt it," Maura said. "They're very honorable and careful about others' feelings, after their own loss. I think that's why they're wary about forming attachments in the first place."

Catherine was grateful to Maura for being so open with her. "Thank you for your gracious hospitality. You've made me feel right at home."

"It's been my pleasure. Chris is lucky to have you on his team."

"That is kind of you to say, but I still have a lot to prove. Need to get going, but I'll keep in touch." Then Catherine did something out of character with a new acquaintance and gave the older woman a brief hug.

Chris walked in at that moment. "Good morning, ladies. Do I get a hug, too?"

"That all depends," Maura said. "You might start by carrying this young woman's bags out to her car."

"Leaving? So soon?" He looked disappointed.

"Yes, have to dash to the airport," Catherine said. "Maura, I'll send those recipes I promised."

After Chris loaded her bags into the trunk, he met Catherine on the driver's side. "This TV shoot was a good idea, Miss Reynolds. I hope you have some other field trips planned."

"As a matter of fact, I do," she said. "The Academy Awards are coming up soon. Means we'll have to go to LA."

"I can hardly wait," he murmured as he placed his arms on either side of her body against the car. *Like two teenagers*, she reflected. He leaned in and claimed his hug.

Chapter Ten

New York—84 days to Celebration launch

Catherine walked into the Peninsula Hotel on Fifth Avenue for her early-morning appointment. She'd been back in New York three days and was still recovering from jet lag. On international trips, she took prescription sleeping pills, but for shorter flights she made her body tough it out and adapt naturally. Waking up at the crack of dawn to arrive by 7:30 a.m. didn't help. This corporate work wasn't for sissies.

James Winston was seated at a corner table reading the *New York Times*. When she approached, he stood up to pull out her chair.

"Good morning, Jim. It's great to see you," she said.

The Peninsula was one of Catherine's favorite hotels. She knew James had a standing reservation at Clement; he said he enjoyed the camaraderie with other regulars, titans of business. The intimate interconnected rooms of the restaurant were elegantly furnished: white linen tablecloths, fine silver and china, and, importantly, tables spaced far enough apart for privacy.

"Thanks for meeting me early," James said. "I figured we could speak freely, away from the office, no interruptions."

"My pleasure." Catherine put the napkin in her lap. "This is a lovely restaurant."

The waiter arrived to take her order. Without looking at the menu, she rattled off her no-fuss breakfast: cappuccino, one egg over easy, and toast with jam.

"They have my usual order." James took a sip of water.

Catherine pulled a sky-blue file out of her tote and put it on the table.

"I heard rumors you color-code your files," James said. "What does blue signify?"

"It's my file for meeting notes," Catherine said.

"Glad to see you're keeping to your methods." James smiled. "How did the TV shoot in Napa go?"

"Very well. Although Chris seemed reluctant to be the center of attention, he's a good spokesperson." Her cappuccino arrived in a delicate china cup. She put in a half spoon of sugar and stirred. Finally, some caffeine.

"Yes, he can be very effective," James said.

At many things. The tenderness of Chris's goodbye hug by her car undid her. She'd melted into his body while he held her close. She was in danger of falling for her boss—a big red flag.

"Any other news from Napa?" James inquired.

"Yes." Catherine snapped her attention back to the task at hand. She relayed what she'd learned from the pastry chef, Anna, at the Winston Resort. Anna's boyfriend, Javier, worked in the winery. He told Anna a few corks were unintentionally popping off magnums. He was worried he'd get blamed for the spillage.

"It's probably nothing," she said.

"It's normal to lose a few bottles," James said. "I'll check with Tom."

"Please keep the source confidential. I told Anna I wouldn't get her boyfriend in trouble." Catherine spread jam on her toast.

"Sure," James said. "Speaking of wineries, do you have any connections at Tournelle? Our Trianon partner heard Patrick is bad-mouthing certain champagne houses to Relais & Châteaux members in an attempt to influence the contest in his favor."

"Our families are close." *To put it mildly*. Her parents were best friends with the senior Tournelles, Patrick's parents. She knew Patrick and didn't think he would risk his reputation to gain advantage in a contest. If she did learn damaging information and passed it on to James, it could cause major problems with her parents.

"Don't put yourself in a compromising position. Just let me know if you hear anything related," James said. "And please don't mention this to Chris right now. Tom tells me he and Patrick almost came to blows during the Napa conference. I don't want him distracted about this until we know more."

The rest of the breakfast, Catherine filled James in on her media progress. The Spago party was coming up in ten days and the New York gala two weeks after that. "So far, press confirmations are high for both events," she said. "It's a matter of getting actual coverage and prominent mentions of our label."

"You've been a strong asset," James said, "as I knew you would be. With your connections and creativity, coming up with the theme for the *cuvée*, we're lucky to have you on our team." He pushed his plate away.

"Thank you." She was pleased at the compliment.

"You know this could turn into a permanent position."

Catherine felt a pang of guilt. She hadn't confided in James that she planned to leave her job right after the launch.

James glanced at his watch and signaled for the check.

"How's your grandma?" he asked. "Haven't spoken to Elizabeth in a while." Elizabeth Reynolds was James's neighbor on Long Island. When their spouses were alive, the couples had socialized regularly.

"She's in good health," Catherine said. "Seeing her after I return from LA. She's coming into the city to meet me for afternoon tea."

"Please tell her I say hello."

"Will do." Catherine took a last sip of coffee.

"Let's go," he said. "I'll give you a ride to the office."

The rest of the day passed in a blur. Catherine looked forward to a quiet, early evening at home. On the way, she picked up Chinese takeout, with an extra piece of plain broiled chicken for Soleil.

When she opened the apartment door, she was greeted by the sound of Boney James's smooth saxophone coming from speakers in the living room. Tall candles on the fireplace mantle created a warm glow. *This is more like it. Wonder what the special occasion is.*

Vanessa came out of the kitchen in a kimono, her hair wrapped up in a towel. Catherine gave her a coy look. "For me? You shouldn't have."

"I have a last-minute date with Sean tonight," Vanessa said. "We finally synced up our schedules."

Catherine was a bit surprised Sean had moved on so quickly from his pursuit of her, but she was relieved she wouldn't have to fend off his advances any longer. Her heart lay in a different direction.

"When is that, by the way?" Catherine set down her purse and gave Soleil a rub behind her ears.

Vanessa looked at the clock. "Oh my gosh, in thirty minutes. I've got to get busy."

"Think I'll make myself scarce and leave you two to your own personal journey of discovery." Catherine tilted her head. "And, of course, I'll expect a full report."

"*D'accord. Comme toujours.*"

The next morning, Catherine was impatient to hear about her best friend's hot date. She knocked lightly on Vanessa's bedroom door.

"Go away. It's early," Vanessa groaned.

"How 'bout a steaming hot cappuccino?" Catherine said through the door. "Figured I could get some gossip out of you if I plied you with gourmet caffeine."

"All right, I'm coming," Vanessa answered. She padded into the kitchen a few minutes later, wrapped in a terry robe with fuzzy slippers on her feet. "Girl, you look dressed and pressed and ready to go. Early start today?"

"TV shoot at the office," Catherine said. "At least I'm not in front of the camera."

In their cozy kitchen, Catherine finished foaming the milk and sprinkled chocolate shavings on top. "So how was your date with the devastatingly handsome Sean Dunlavy?" Catherine placed the porcelain mug and an almond biscotti on a matching plate on the bistro table in front of Vanessa.

"He took me dancing at a new salsa club in SoHo." Vanessa sipped her cappuccino. "Mmm . . . yummy."

"Sounds like fun . . . and?"

"He sure knows how to sweep a girl off her feet." Vanessa paused, looking dreamy.

Catherine snapped her fingers. "Earth to Van," she said with a laugh.

"And . . . I like him. He seems like the complete package: smart, successful, sexy, and serious about pursuing me."

"So, what else happened?"

"He opened up, shared his background. Told me about his upbringing in the South and his family, all overachievers. His dad and brother are attorneys in Raleigh." Vanessa took a bite of biscotti. "He spent time in Europe, so cosmopolitan, open-minded . . ."

"I'm glad you're having fun," Catherine said. "He seems like a good guy."

"My only worry is he's moving awfully fast. Wants to go away for a weekend." Vanessa cradled her mug. "After our first date! I'm busy at the club, and we have our LA trip coming up, so I can hold him off for a bit, let things develop."

"Good plan. Make sure he treats you right." Catherine took her mug to the sink. "I've got to dash. We have the final interview with *Newsline* this morning. I hope Sue doesn't throw herself at Chris, as she seems inclined to do."

Vanessa lifted her mug in salute. "Thanks for my wake-up. By the way, you look great."

"*Merci.* Spent extra time pulling myself together."

"It shows," Vanessa said.

Catherine didn't add that she'd made the effort because she wanted to look good for Chris, whom she hadn't seen since their tender hug in Napa. She'd styled her hair in soft curls, applied enhancing makeup around her eyes, and wore her honey-gold Dior suit with matching heels.

The television crew was setting up in the conference room when Catherine arrived at the office. The director prearranged to shoot part of a sales meeting to illustrate that aspect of the business. Afterward, Sue would conduct a final interview with Chris in his office.

Delores hovered near the door. Catherine approached and asked her when Chris was due in. "He's on his way," Delores snapped. "Hope your reporter friend gets here on time and doesn't keep him waiting."

Catherine had no idea why this woman was always curt with her. A young woman, probably early thirties, Delores wore conservative suits on her short, overweight frame and pulled her dark hair back in a severe ponytail. Either she was being overly protective, or more likely, she had a crush on her boss. *If that's the case, she'll probably be rude to Sue, too.*

At that moment, Chris and Sue got off the elevator together. Sue laughed at something he said, and they looked very chummy. "Good morning, everyone," he said.

Sean and the sales reps showed up, and there was a big commotion in the conference room as microphones were tested. Everyone took their seats. It had been agreed beforehand that Sean would run the meeting. They'd film the first half hour to get footage to edit in later. No strategic information, like specific sales targets or dollars earned, would be revealed.

Off camera, Sue and Catherine stood together in the back of the room. Sean seemed to relish the attention as he led the discussion about the company's growth in the marketplace and emphasized the sales reps' role in promoting their first *cuvée de prestige.*

They took a break, and the crew moved their equipment to Chris's office down the hall. Chris and Sue sat at the round table Chris used for meetings, circled by light shades and two cameramen.

"Chris, please speak a few words," Sue prompted, "so we can make sure your mic is working. While you're at it, why don't you share something intimate about yourself?"

"Well, Miss Hamilton, since you're a reporter, I'd be safer reciting these cue cards." The sound guy smirked and gave Chris a thumbs-up.

"We're all set," the director said. "Roll camera."

Sue started by asking Chris about the origins of Winston & Wright. He described the company's beginnings ten years earlier when James Winston and Alan Wright bought a modest property in Napa. From day one, they'd established the company philosophy: demand top quality, seek out the latest technology, and share the joie de vivre.

"On the second point, we're partnering with a research team at UC Davis to learn methods to mitigate the effects of drought," Chris said.

"Napa has been ravaged by wildfires," Sue acknowledged. "Nature can be fierce."

"Then, of course, the joie de vivre happens when you enjoy the wine," Chris said.

"After this buildup, I'm anxious to try your new sparkling," Sue said. "When will it be available?"

"Good question," Chris said. "It will be in stores mid-June, but I have a sample to share with you." Chris slid over a tray bearing two champagne flutes and a preview of Celebration. He picked up the bottle and displayed it to Sue and the camera. "As you can see, the permanent label hasn't been affixed yet. This is temporary—"

"'Celebration,'" Sue read out loud. "How clever and appropriate."

Chris removed the foil, expertly popped the cork, and poured the bubbly liquid into the glasses. He presented one to Sue. "Well, Miss Hamilton, what is your verdict?"

She lifted her flute, gazed at the bubbles, and took a sip. "Very impressive." From her expression, she could just as easily be describing what she thought of Chris. She took another sip and set the glass down.

"I'm glad you like it," Chris said. "Our winemaker, Jean Boyer, deserves much of the credit. We were fortunate to have a once-in-a-decade harvest. Then Jean worked his magic to blend the three wines and *voilà*." Chris lifted his flute and took a sip.

"Thank you for sharing your story and this special sparkling with us," Sue said.

"You'll have to tell all your friends," he said.

Sue laughed. "I think we just got the word out." She faced the camera, addressing the audience. "I invite you to share your sparkling stories on our *Newsline* social media pages." She leaned over to shake Chris's hand, and the director called it a wrap.

The crew packed up in a few minutes. Catherine was relieved the morning had gone smoothly. No hitches today. Chris took a phone call while she and Sue chatted in the corner.

"Thanks for the tip on this one, Catherine. I owe you," Sue said. "Not only will my boss be pleased with the piece—lots of good visuals from the ranch and a timely story—I've developed a new interest in sparkling wine." She glanced at Chris, who was on the phone. "Hopefully, I can get your boss to give me more instruction."

One of the first lessons Catherine had learned as a diplomat's daughter was to camouflage her feelings. She smiled in acknowledgment but felt like disavowing her friend. Sue should have checked, as friends do, before flirting with Chris. On the upside, Catherine was learning how he responded when a beautiful woman came on to him.

Chris finished his call and joined them. "Here's my card," Sue said as she handed it to him. "Feel free to call if you think of anything else."

"Thanks for the coverage," he said. "We appreciate it."

"I enjoyed this shoot. Hopefully, we can meet again," Sue said.

Chris walked her to the office door. "I'm sure Catherine will put you on the list for our parties, and you're welcome to bring a friend."

He asked Catherine to stay a minute after everyone else had left. Chris shut the door and smiled. "I missed you. Let's meet for dinner Friday night."

When she didn't respond immediately, he tilted his head and looked her in the eyes. "A working dinner."

"Okay, sure," she said. "What time?"

"How about eight? What restaurant would you like?"

"JoJo would be nice, if we can get a reservation. It's near my apartment." Catherine had been meaning to go there. This was a perfect opportunity.

"I'll see what I can do," he said.

Chris was able to secure a table and arrived early Friday night for their rendezvous. JoJo restaurant was situated in an elegant townhouse on two levels. The maître d' seated him in a cozy alcove on the upstairs level, facing the street. The rooms were light and airy, befitting the modern decor, pale parquet floors, and whitewashed brick walls—a beautiful space.

After ordering a glass of Bordeaux from Saint-Émilion, Chris reflected on his conundrum with Catherine. He felt a strong attraction to this woman and hoped the sparks in Napa were the prelude to something deeper. He'd assumed she'd be stuck up, but she was quite the opposite. Pitching in to help Maura in the kitchen. Showing interest in the McDermott winery. Stargazing and a tender embrace he didn't want to end. *Can't get much more romantic than that.*

Only caveat: She worked for him, at least temporarily. Three more months. He should be able to keep things platonic until then. If things moved too fast, he'd have to speak to James. Ugh, like asking her father for permission to date. *I'm too old for that.*

The lady in question was being ushered to the table. He stood to greet her and pulled out her chair. She looked divine. *Women must know intuitively how to drive us poor saps crazy.* She wore a sleeveless, clingy black dress that skimmed her knees and bared her back, which he got a good look at when she took her shawl off.

"What would you like to drink?" Chris asked.

Catherine glanced at the page of wines by the glass and addressed the waiter. "A glass of the sauvignon blanc from the Loire, please."

She put the menu aside and turned to Chris. "You're here early."

"Yes, good chance to check out their wine list."

The waiter returned with Catherine's wine and recited the specials. She chose the roasted black sea bass, and he ordered a cheeseburger with crispy onion rings.

Chris held up his glass. "Let's toast to new beginnings."

"Agreed, new beginnings." She clinked her glass with his and took a sip.

"Nice pick." He looked around the room. "I've been to a few of Jean-Georges's restaurants. My first time here. I like the vibe."

"It's one of my parents' favorites," she said. "Shortly after they were married in Paris, Dad was sent on a six-month stint to the United Nations. Mom had heard about Jean-Georges from friends in Strasbourg, where he's from." She took a sip of wine and continued. "This was Jean-Georges's first stand-alone restaurant. Now, he's global. Glad he kept this one. It's in my *quartier*."

Chris looked at her quizzically. "Throwing those French words at me."

"*Quartier* means neighborhood." She smiled and placed a file folder on the table.

"What's with the brown file?" he asked.

"This is my file for upcoming events to update you on press for Spago."

"Can't believe it's a week from tonight."

"Me either," she said. "Lots to do."

Their meals were served. They each took a bite.

"This is delicious," Catherine said. "Jean-Georges is known for flavorful vegetable juices and light broths. Wonder what he put in this sauce?" She took another taste.

"What got you into cooking?" Chris asked.

"Both my grandmas. It was a way to spend time with them in the kitchen. My maternal grandma is French and Grandma Reynolds is American, lives on Long Island. They both have fabulous kitchens and turn out gourmet meals." She forked a bite of sea bass and stirred it in the sauce before popping it in her mouth.

Chris became distracted by her mouth and his mind started veering in unsafe directions. He needed to focus.

"I wanted to give you a heads-up about one of the guests coming to Spago," he said. "Chamath Patel is a venture capitalist from San Francisco. He's agreed to fund our expansion overseas—assuming we have a successful launch at Vinexpo." He tapped his fingers on the table. "He's also looking at our financials. We need to show good value for money spent on events."

Catherine set her fork down. "That's sometimes difficult to measure. We can show audience numbers."

"What press are we expecting at Spago?" he asked.

She gave him a one-page report. "I'm working on national hits, like AP photos—to capture the Winston logo on the bottle. A firm in LA is coordinating entertainment media. Lots of celebs are confirmed. And I'm pitching wine press. Ken Barnett from *Wine Spectator* is coming."

"Will be nice to see him." Chris liked the guy. "Seems like a good chap."

"The best. He's trying to get his editor to commit to a full feature on Winston. He'll be at Vinexpo too." She took a sip of wine. "Is there anything we should do to impress Chamath at Spago?"

"Have everything run smoothly." He picked up an onion ring. "I'll let you know if I think of anything else."

"Thanks for filling me in. I didn't realize the stakes were so high." She closed her file.

Chris figured he'd better grab this chance to learn more about her. "You mentioned your parents," he began. "I know your dad's a diplomat. I imagine your childhood was different from my life on the range."

"Yes," she laughed. "It was. My parents met in Paris, where my dad works as a US diplomat. My mother was young and beautiful, came from a distinguished French family. It was love at first sight and a lavish wedding six months later."

"Where did you live?"

"We spent most of our time in Paris, summers with Grandma on Long Island, and for high school, I went off to boarding school in Switzerland."

"Away from your family?" Chris had trouble understanding that custom.

"Yes, mother insisted." She shrugged. "That's the way she was raised, and she wanted her only daughter to follow in those same proper footsteps. I met Vanessa there, and we've been best friends ever since."

He took a bite of his cheeseburger while Catherine paused to reflect.

"I still haven't figured out where I belong—Paris or New York or someplace quieter," she said.

He wondered how she'd feel about settling down in Napa Valley. *Be careful. She'll want sophistication, and you're a country boy at heart.*

He couldn't remember the last time he'd felt so close to a woman.

Catherine looked ready to call it a night, so he asked for the check and ordered a cab.

When they reached her brownstone, he walked her up the steps and gave her a lingering hug. "You're very intriguing, Miss Reynolds. I don't know anyone quite like you."

She opened her door and glanced back. "I'm glad you're coming to LA. The Hollywood scene seems like a different world, but many of the people are down-to-earth."

Chapter Eleven

Beverly Hills—75 days to Celebration launch

The heart of Beverly Hills boasted more beauty salons per block than any other city in the country. They catered to the large group of actresses, models, wannabes, and all the other poor women who were trying to keep up with them. Business was booming. Many clients had standing weekly appointments with their hairdressers for a blow-dry or color touch-up. At full-service salons, customers plunked down big bucks for facials with clay masks. Brows were plucked, shaped, and dyed. Legs were waxed. Simultaneous manicure/pedicures were de rigueur. It was time-consuming. It was pricey. It was survival.

Catherine had arrived in Los Angeles the night before and convinced Vanessa to join her this morning at their favorite Beverly Hills salon. Since their teens in Geneva, they'd adopted the sensibility, and even necessity, of regular salon visits. Their natural beauty and striking features made it easy for hairdressers and estheticians to work their magic, enhancing that star quality. At the moment, it was waiting to be unleashed. Both wore minimal makeup and had their hair pulled back in loose buns. They'd ordered lunch from the salon's deli counter to save time and avoid being seen in public until they'd been properly primped and preened.

"This was a good idea," Catherine sighed as her feet were massaged midway through her pedicure. She could feel the tension melting as the young aproned woman kneaded the soles of her feet and sent her nerve ends tingling.

Seated a few feet away, Vanessa unwrapped her sandwich of grilled organic vegetables on nine-grain bread. "What better way to get energized for a weekend of parties. I've been looking forward to this."

They knew the stamina required to be on and glamorous at one party, let alone two or three in as many days. One didn't just show up for these affairs. You had to look like you'd stepped off the pages of a fashion magazine. This was a marathon, not a sprint. Catherine and Vanessa were old pros at this, a skill they'd trained for.

"You're the party girl this weekend," Catherine said. "I'm only here for the Spago event tomorrow night. On Sunday, I'll be curled up at home with Soleil watching you on the telly with millions of other people around the world."

"Don't remind me," Vanessa said. "I'm starting to get butterflies about that big audience."

Catherine speared a piece of asparagus with a plastic fork as the young woman placed her feet near a fan to dry. "I think when Enrique Iglesias turns up the heat, you'll be distracted. How was your rehearsal? Is he as dreamy as he seems?"

"He's pretty seductive. All that male Latin energy, and he pours on the charm. We ran through the song a few times . . ." Vanessa's voice trailed off and she licked her lips. Catherine got the impression it wasn't from the sandwich.

"Wait until he sees me all glammed up," Vanessa continued. "That should raise our temperature to sizzling."

"Now the world will see what your friends already appreciate."

"Thanks," Vanessa said. "But remember I'm just a backup singer, not the star."

"I'm sure the camera will find you, and you are singing a partial duet." Catherine blew on her nails to speed their drying.

Vanessa looked over Catherine's shoulder. "There's someone headed this way. Looks like your appointment."

An efficient-looking woman holding a cellphone in one hand and a briefcase in the other strode over to Catherine. She seemed no-nonsense in her black pantsuit and stylish flats, dark hair pulled back in a low ponytail.

"Hi Liza, thanks for meeting me here," Catherine said. "This is my friend, Vanessa." The two women smiled in greeting.

"Glad you reached out to us for help." Liza Grant, in her early thirties, was a senior publicist at Jay Kerner Public Relations, Catherine's former employer. "Jay says hello. He'll see you tomorrow night."

"How are things at Kerner these days?" Catherine asked.

"Not the same since you left. We miss your modeling tips and tricks for pulling together a classic look," Liza said.

"On a nonexistent budget, for most of us," Vanessa added.

Liza laughed. "You could say that again." She turned to Vanessa. "You know she even prepared a rulebook we're still using."

Catherine started to change the subject, but Vanessa interjected, "Do tell."

"We named it Reynolds Rules." Liza elaborated on the advice in the small book that covered everything from wardrobe, hair, and makeup to polite deportment. In addition to encouraging each woman to highlight her best features—be that eyes, lips, or cheekbones—it emphasized creating an individual look.

"It's our bible for good taste," Liza continued, "from the classic black dress with a statement choker or antique pearls, to notes on accessorizing with colorful silk scarves and layered jewelry."

It amazed Catherine how little many of the younger women knew about high fashion and formal manners, things she took for granted. She was glad her handbook was helpful, even if it might seem a bit obsessive.

Vanessa stood up. "I'll leave you two to strategize. I'm off for my facial."

Catherine gingerly opened her hot-pink file, careful not to damage her nails. "Let's finish going over tomorrow night. How does it look at Spago?"

"Just walked over from there." Liza took a seat next to Catherine. "They agreed to put the pyramid of champagne flutes outside in the garden. Who's setting it up?"

"The Winston sales rep will handle that. Also want to make sure Spago has the ice buckets with the Winston logo."

"Yes, Wolfgang instructed his staff to put them on all the tables."

Catherine knew Wolfgang was familiar with the drill from many previous media fêtes he'd hosted. The extra-large Winston & Wright label, prominently displayed on ice buckets, would be visible in press photos.

"We're using magnums and sabering the first bottle," Catherine said. "It's so dramatic when slashed open that way, practically medieval." It was a tricky procedure. Chris had assured Catherine it was safe, but the trajectory of the bottle top was an X factor. She prayed there were no hiccups.

Catherine chewed on a parmesan chip and looked at a page in her open file. "How are we doing on celebrity confirmations?"

Liza opened her iPad. "Everyone, and I mean everyone, will be at this party. Ever since Clooney and Oprah signed on to cohost. He roped in Matt Damon and Brad Pitt. There's always a mob in town for the awards, and this has become the hot ticket."

Catherine smiled. She knew George through mutual friends in London and Italy. Would be good to see him again. He was nominated for a directing award this year. "How's the media coordination?" Catherine asked. The publicists for Kerner, Spago, and the celebrity hosts all agreed to work off a master press list.

"So far, so good," Liza said. "*People* is sending a reporter and photographer. *Entertainment Tonight* and *Extra* are sending TV crews. *Vanity Fair* and the entertainment trades will be there. And, of course, the tabloid paparazzi will be swarming the sidewalks."

"Great," Catherine said sarcastically. "We'll have to fend them off at the entrance." She wasn't looking forward to the gauntlet. "Main thing I'm working on now is getting an influential wine writer to commit to coverage, not just show up, eat the food, and ogle the beautiful women."

Liza laughed. "That's always an issue. Getting a commitment."

Catherine didn't add that she was depending on at least one national hit to meet her monthly quota. *Newsline* would count for February. She needed a hit for March.

"By the way, did you hear from Sue Hamilton at *Newsline*?" Liza asked.

"She's out of town on a shoot." Sue had sounded distressed to miss the bash. It had seemed to Catherine that she was just as upset about not seeing Chris.

The women went over the list in detail and finalized the wording of the electronic press kit to be sent to everyone.

"I think we're all set for now," Catherine said. She slipped on her flip-flops and gathered up her things. "Thanks for jumping in at the last minute. It's been a big help."

"Sure thing." Liza packed up her briefcase.

They parted outside, and Catherine took a cab to her hotel on Sunset Boulevard two miles away. Her driver went north on Rodeo Drive, past stately million-dollar homes with picture-perfect yards, to the famed salmon-pink Beverly Hills Hotel.

The Winston travel agent had managed to snag last-minute reservations for Catherine and Chris. The Dorchester Collection, which owned the hotel, was affiliated with their French partner, Trianon, so the rooms were comped. Otherwise, they would have been staying at a Motel 6 to keep within the budget, not Catherine's idea of acceptable accommodations.

The cab entered the circular drive off Sunset Boulevard and drove to the front. A handsome valet, who looked like an aspiring actor and probably was, welcomed her. Catherine walked through the ornate lobby and out the back entrance, leading to twelve acres of colorful gardens and cottages. The owners had spent a fortune refurbishing the hotel and grounds, and it showed. Fortunately, they'd preserved the old-California Spanish charm, enhanced by colorful flower beds and lush foliage.

She and Chris had adjoining bungalows reached by footpaths among the tropical paradise that flourished in the warm climate. Afternoon sun cast a warm glow on blooming birds of paradise. Unfortunately, there was no time to enjoy the famous pool, notorious for starlets lounging in bikinis during Hollywood's golden era.

Catherine entered her room and snapped a few photos to put in her "Ideas" file. Two armchairs were upholstered in plush gray velvet, a black cashmere throw draped over one. An antique mirror on the wall faced shuttered windows that overlooked the garden. The sumptuous bed linens in matching gray were topped with small black tasseled pillows.

She poured half a bottle of iced tea into a crystal glass and went to work at the lacquered table she was using as a desk.

After laying out her color-coded files, a lined pad, and pens, Catherine picked up her phone and started returning calls while she checked emails on her laptop.

The master media list was coming together, thanks to the high-profile celebs confirmed. Even jaded entertainment reporters were clamoring for an invitation. Catherine put the finishing touches on her section of the press packet: Winston & Wright's company bio and "origin story," in Hollywood-speak.

The packet also described what each partygoer would receive in their SWAG bags. At Kerner, Catherine had learned the acronym meant Stuff We All Get. The giveaways included a sample pack from George Clooney's tequila company and small gifts from Oprah's list of favorite things. Winston's contribution was a champagne-bottle stopper and a discount card for 50 percent off the purchase of a bottle of Celebration on its release in June.

Catherine lost track of time until Chris texted her. He was on his way in from LAX and wanted to meet in a half hour to grab an early bite so she could bring him up to speed on final prep.

After finalizing her notes, Catherine changed into a flowy skirt, stretch top, jacket, and flats, and reapplied perfume and lip gloss. She arrived at the Polo Lounge first and ordered a glass of chardonnay. She leaned her head back against the leather banquette, sank into the seat, and let the live piano music waft over her.

A few minutes later, a deep voice intruded from behind. "Hello, Miss Reynolds. Seems to me your boss is working you too hard. You look tired." Chris took a seat next to her.

"This flitting back and forth across the country isn't for sissies," she said. "As soon as I start to adapt to California time, I'll be headed back. How was your flight?"

"Uneventful, the best kind." Chris glanced at the menu. "I'm not looking forward to the nineteen-hour time difference when I go to Australia on Saturday."

The waiter arrived and took Chris's order for Sierra Nevada beer.

"Guess you really do like beer," Catherine said.

"Can't hide my pedestrian tastes from you forever. This started as a boutique northern California beer, so that qualifies as trendy, right?" Chris grinned.

"Sure." She smiled back and took a sip of her wine.

They both ordered the Polo Club sandwich, which substituted grilled salmon for the traditional chicken and came with homemade chips.

"So"—he glanced at her notes—"what do you have for me about tomorrow night? How's the press coverage looking?"

Now Catherine was in her element. She took him through the confirmed list while they ate. "Here is a cheat sheet." Catherine handed him a three-by-five card with the names of key reporters attending.

"What about my remarks?" Chris asked. "Or do I stand silently, emulating a Hollywood hunk?"

She looked him up and down. "You could pass." If he wanted to go there, she figured she'd kid right back.

"Seems like you've thought everything through." He crunched on a chip.

"We've tried." Catherine raised both hands and crossed her fingers. "Then there are the inevitable surprises." She thought back to diplomatic receptions she'd attended and the occasional mishaps: drinks spilled on dresses, unintentional insults, and inappropriate flirtatious remarks.

She put her wineglass down. "Spago will start serving our rosé when people arrive at six. The magnum sabering is scheduled for a half hour later. We should be wrapped up by seven thirty."

"Perfect," Chris said. "I have a dinner meeting after with Chamath across the street."

Catherine covered her mouth to stifle a yawn. It had been a long day.

"I don't need any more hints. You're tired." Chris waved down their bill and charged it to his room. They took the garden path, and he wrapped his arm around her shoulders as they walked up the steps to their bungalows. Catherine liked the feel of that. If she wasn't careful, she'd develop a crush on this guy.

"Adjoining rooms was a good idea. Very convenient." Chris gave her an enveloping hug and opened her door. "Sleep tight." And he was off.

Chris was having trouble keeping his eyes off the two gorgeous women in the back of the limo with him. *This Hollywood stuff is over the top.* Catherine had insisted they arrive in style at Spago. A cab would have done the job just fine. Heck, it was five minutes away. *Smoke and mirrors*, he reminded himself.

While he was getting dressed, Chris had heard the ladies giggling through the adjoining wall to Catherine's bungalow. He'd guessed they were getting all dolled up. Mission accomplished—they looked spectacular. They'd met on the porch, and Catherine introduced him to her friend. Vanessa shook his hand firmly and looked him straight in the eye. Seemed she was checking him out to see if he met with her approval.

Vanessa was beautiful in her own right, but he wasn't the slightest bit interested in anyone other than his enticing employee. They both wore mini-length, body-hugging party dresses, Catherine in all black and Vanessa in all white, probably made by famous designers. He wondered if the sparkly jewelry they wore around their necks and dangling from their ears was real.

When their limo driver pulled up to the curb near the entrance to Spago, photographers already mobbed the sidewalk, even though the party didn't start for another half hour. A valet attendant opened the door. Chris got out and offered his arm to Catherine. The moment the first pointy toe of her high heel hit the ground, flashbulbs started popping. *Going to be some evening*, he groaned inwardly. He turned to assist Vanessa from the limo, and photographers started shouting her name, encouraging her to look in their direction. Vanessa smiled and waved. *These women are pros.*

Catherine and Vanessa paused for a few photos then glided up the temporarily installed red carpet. The trio was met by a woman at the entrance, iPad in hand, checking off press arrivals. Catherine introduced Liza Grant to Chris. He thanked her for Kerner's help at the last minute.

Bodyguards were out in full force to discourage crashers and keep wayward paparazzi out of the restaurant. One needed a verifiable embossed invitation for this exclusive event.

Inside, Wolfgang greeted Catherine and Vanessa with kisses on each cheek. "*Guten Tag*, ladies."

"Wolfgang," Catherine said, "I'd like to present Chris McDermott, president of Winston & Wright." She drew Chris over, her hand on his arm. He liked the possessive feel of that.

"Nice to meet you," Chris said as he shook Wolfgang's hand. "We really appreciate your featuring our rosé tonight."

"Glad it worked out," Wolfgang said. "The sabering should be quite dramatic, which this crowd will appreciate."

Chris had only executed the sabering a half-dozen times; he was anxious for it to go off without a hitch. It required a good knife with a sharp blade and the skill to connect at the right spot below the rim of the bottle for maximum impact. The velocity and direction of the severed bottle top was another concern.

"Your sales rep is on the patio, putting the final touches on the pyramid of glasses," Wolfgang said. "Great visual."

"Thanks," Chris said. "I'll go take a look."

A few days earlier, Sean had pulled Chris aside and told him Robert Kenyon had substituted himself to staff the event rather than the local LA rep. Chris had been annoyed Robert pulled rank and made it clear to Sean there was no money in their tight budget to cover Robert's travel from Napa. Sean had assured him Robert wouldn't bill Winston for the expense.

Stepping onto the patio, Chris admired the setting—potted palms, twinkling lights, soft music, and the center of attention, a linen-draped table with a tall pyramid of champagne flutes.

Robert greeted him when he approached. "Looks like quite the posh bash."

"I hope it's worth the effort," Chris said. "Are all the bottles prepped?"

"Yes, the wine steward has everything at the correct temp. The magnums for the pyramid are behind the bar."

"Let's head over there. I'd like to check the saber and make a few practice swings," Chris said. "Don't want to leave any room for error."

Fifteen minutes later, after Chris felt they'd prepared as much as they could, he set off in search of Catherine. Guests were streaming in, including many stunning starlets whose faces Chris recognized. It appeared most of Hollywood had shown up to honor the nominees and partake in the excellent food and wine.

Chris headed toward the entrance to find the only woman who interested him in an intimate conversation with George Clooney. All these desirable women, and his girl was the one hanging out with Clooney. Chris had read that every woman over the age of twenty-five thought George Clooney was still one of the "sexiest men alive," as he'd been dubbed by *People* magazine numerous times. He had to admit the guy exuded star power.

Catherine smiled when he approached and introduced them. "We were discussing the sabering," she said. "George offered to participate in the tower pour after the sabering."

"That's great," Chris said. "Thanks for pitching in."

"Sure, happy to help," George said. "I'm a big fan of the bubbly—even when it's sprayed at sporting events."

"Well, we won't be doing that tonight. Too many fancy gowns," Chris said, and both men laughed.

George left to take care of his cohost duties. By this time, the party was in full swing. Wolfgang's *équipe* was in high gear. Everything sparkled—fine china platters piled high with gourmet appetizers, crystal champagne flutes served by tuxedoed waiters, and of course the dazzling guests. Glittering diamonds and expensive custom jewelry set off shimmering gowns baring lots of skin. This truly was a crowd of beautiful people.

Chris was pleased to see a familiar face: Ken Barnett from *Wine Spectator*. They struck up a conversation as Catherine stepped away to speak to a photographer.

"That was quite a coup getting Winston featured at this event," Ken said.

"All Catherine's doing," Chris said.

"She's a gem. You're lucky to have her on your team." Ken lifted his champagne flute and took a sip. "Looking forward to the medieval saber demo."

"This crowd likes entertainment," Chris said. He glanced in Catherine's direction. "Looks like I'm being beckoned by the lady."

"Go ahead," Ken said. "I'm going to grab a bite before the main event."

Catherine was speaking to John Warner, heir apparent to a conglomerate that owned media companies. John was frequently mentioned in the press as an eligible bachelor and arbiter of taste in New York society. Chris recognized him because he owned a financial publication. They'd never met. Chris didn't travel in those circles and couldn't compete with Warner's jet-set lifestyle, if that's what Catherine was looking for.

When Chris approached, she spoke first. "John, I'd like you to meet Chris McDermott, president of Winston & Wright. Chris, this is John Warner."

"I read *Warner Financial Times*," Chris said. "It's well researched."

"That's good to hear," John said. "I think we have a friend in common. Will Frost."

"Will's on our board," Chris said. "He also torments me on the racquetball court."

John laughed. "I've played with Will. He's competitive. I'm at the same club. We'll have to team up against him sometime."

"That would be fun, bring him down a peg." Chris relished the chance to score a victory over his best friend. They agreed to meet up in New York before John got pulled away by another guest.

"I'm glad you two hit it off," Catherine said. "He's an old friend. I'm hoping to get coverage in his paper."

"I didn't expect to like him, but he seems like a genuine guy."

"I believe you're a snob, Christopher McDermott. What is it exactly?"

"I've had experience with people born into their positions. Many have an air of entitlement. He seems different."

"I'm glad you're willing to make an exception in John's case." Catherine bit her lip, as if trying to hide a frown. "He's a good guy."

Chris spotted Chamath Patel walking in and waved him over. "Glad you could make it," Chris said. He introduced him to Catherine.

Waiters circulated through the crowd, ringing bells to usher guests toward the patio for the ceremony. The three of them made their way to a small riser with a standing microphone, next to the pyramid of glasses on the table.

The crowd quieted and Wolfgang began. "Good evening, everyone. Welcome to Spago's sparkling salute to this year's Oscar nominees." He named the nominees in attendance to enthusiastic applause. "Our cohost, George Clooney, has a few words."

"I'll keep it very short," George said. "To the other nominees, may the best man—or woman—win, hopefully all the entrants from our movie." That drew guffaws. "The theme of this year's Academy Awards is Preserving Our Planet, so I encourage you all to donate to those nonprofit groups the Academy singled out." He looked at his pals Brad Pitt and Matt Damon and joked, "Especially those penny-pinchers Brad and Matt." More laughter.

Wolfgang leaned into the mic. "I'd also like to thank Chris McDermott, president of Winston & Wright, for providing the sparkles." He gestured for Chris to step up and speak.

Not accustomed to being the center of attention in a group of famous faces, Chris squared his shoulders and began. "On behalf of Winston & Wright, I want to thank Wolfgang for hosting this special event to celebrate the Oscar nominees. We wish you all good luck. Speaking of celebrating, we'll be launching our first prestige sparkling in June. Its name is 'Celebration.'" He glanced at Catherine, who nodded approvingly. "Knowing how you all like drama and flair, I'll be opening the first magnum tonight the old-fashioned way, with a saber." The crowd sighed.

Robert removed the foil and wire cap from the bottle and handed the magnum to Chris. Chris pulled the saber out of its scabbard, making a clanging noise, held the magnum in his left hand, and swung the saber against the seam of the bottle where it met the rim. In one smooth motion, he sliced off the top of the bottle, including the cork, and the wine began spilling out. Loud clapping erupted from the audience.

Chris quickly pulled the bottle upright and handed it to George Clooney, who moved to the pyramid, held it over the top glass, and started pouring. The wine overflowed, cascading into the glasses below.

Robert picked up the next magnum, peeled off the foil, and started to untwist the wire cap. Suddenly, the cap and cork shot out of the bottle with a loud pop, crashing into a tray of empty glasses nearby. The bubbly liquid sprayed out, splashing a few people next to the pyramid.

There was stunned silence. Then Wolfgang recovered. "Well, that's some fireworks to liven things up!" He turned to Chris. "What do you do for an encore?"

"Nothing, I hope," Chris said.

"Maybe the champagne gods are punishing me for saying I like to spray bottles," Clooney quipped.

"No harm done," Wolfgang said. He signaled the waiters to start passing silver trays of crystal flutes already filled with Winston's rosé, and the party resumed.

Chris tried to quell his anger. He couldn't believe it. They were so careful to execute the sabering properly, then the second bottle blew its top. Luckily, no one was hurt, but it could have toppled the pyramid of glasses. *What a mess.*

Robert opened more bottles—holding a towel over the wire cap and cork as he removed them. Why hadn't he used a towel on the bottle that popped? That was standard procedure. Maybe he'd been too busy ogling the starlets.

The crowd gathered around to get a closer look at the pyramid and the silver scabbard that held the saber. When the final flutes were served, Chris pulled Robert aside. "What the hell happened? Were the bottles stored properly?"

"Of course," Robert said. "They were shipped carefully, and the steward assured me they were kept at the correct temp."

Ken Barnett came over, glass in hand, and interrupted them, sparing Robert more grilling from Chris. Ken congratulated Chris on stealing the show, then added, "My guess is you blokes rigged that bit of drama with the bottle. Very clever, actually. You've got everyone buzzing about it. Don't suppose you'd fill me in on how you did it."

Chris wasn't up for banter. "When we figure it out, you'll be the first to know." This wasn't the kind of attention he sought.

"I bet Catherine could put a clever spin on this," Ken said as she joined them.

"Looks like things have calmed down," Catherine said. "I spoke to Wolfgang and assured him Winston would replace the flutes. Thankfully, no other harm was done. Not the kind of press we're looking for."

Chris's main concern was damage control with Chamath, who was in a conversation with John Warner at the far end of the patio. "I'm going to check on Chamath," Chris said. "Catch you two later."

John held up his flute in salute when Chris approached. "This is good stuff," he said. "Liked the sabering and the pyramid. Did you figure out what happened with the bottle?"

"Not yet." Chris took a sip from his glass. At least they were showcasing a very good rosé sparkling tonight.

"Clooney's known for pulling pranks. Wouldn't be surprised if he had a hand in this," John said.

Chris looked at Chamath to gauge his reaction, the only one that mattered to him.

"No harm done. You just don't want to make a habit of having snafus," Chamath said. "More than one becomes a problem."

"Agreed," Chris said. *Message received.* Things had to run perfectly from now on.

John excused himself and headed over to talk to Vanessa. *Good. Pursue her, not the other roommate.*

"By the way," Chamath said, "figured out why your PR woman, Catherine, looks familiar. I know her dad. Saw her photo on his desk."

That surprised Chris. "Doesn't he live in Paris?"

"Yes. John Reynolds helped me navigate the French bureaucracy—believe me, it's antiquated—when I was negotiating a deal to buy a French tech company. Had dinner with him and his lovely wife in Paris."

Speaking of family connections, maybe he'd hit a sore spot with Catherine when he was railing about silver spoon upbringings.

A waiter came by with a tray of mini lobster pizzas. Chamath took one with a cocktail napkin and ate the appetizer in two bites. "This is delicious. I know we're going for dinner soon, but I'm going to grab another. Let's meet at the entrance in twenty minutes."

That worked for Chris. He wanted to spend a few minutes with Catherine. He wouldn't see her again before he left for his ten-day trip to Australia. He was departing at the crack of dawn.

Chapter Twelve

New York—71 days to Celebration launch

Recovering from her second quick trip to California, Catherine opted to work from home Monday morning before a meeting at Lexington. Sipping her first coffee of the day, she reviewed press coverage on her laptop in the breakfast nook. Soleil curled up nearby on a cushioned seat under the window.

A quick online search revealed many articles about the Oscars weekend that included coverage of the Spago party Friday night. "Once again, Wolfgang Puck bests the other Academy hosts," *Variety*'s movie editor wrote. "A-list celebs and saber rattling—literally, swinging an archaic sword against a magnum of champagne to remove the bottle top. Splashy and dramatic."

The Associated Press photographer had captured a memorable photo of George Clooney pouring the first magnum over the pyramid of champagne flutes, Chris and Wolfgang on either side of him and the extra-large Winston logo on the ice bucket at the base of the pyramid clearly visible. "Clooney Sparkles," the caption read. Clooney's production company had won big in numerous categories on Sunday night, so this iconic image became the top shared photo from the Oscars. Every major news outlet, print and television, ran the AP photo. A homerun.

Catherine felt validated. She'd gone out on a limb securing the deal with Wolfgang before the Winston brass approved it, and the gamble paid off. The AP photo would be seen by millions, a big boost to their brand recognition.

The only snarky comment about the bottle fiasco came from the *LA Times* entertainment reporter: "Bottle snafu at Spago—cork pops off unintentionally and barely misses well-heeled guests." Fortunately, there was no photo of the cork crashing into the tray of glasses. Chris had been irate about the mishap and implied to Catherine that Robert was to blame for improper handling of the bottle—a nuance that was lost on her.

She wasn't surprised Robert had pulled rank to staff the party. When she'd worked at the Winston Resort, she'd observed him ingratiating himself with influential types. Maybe that's why he'd pursued her in the first place. He'd approached as she was leaving the party and made an attempt to "reconcile and be friends." When she rebuffed the overture, he couldn't resist a parting shot. "You're an entitled ice queen," he'd snapped. The rebuke hit close to home. She'd faced similar criticism in the past and it hurt. An example of how dating someone at work could backfire.

Soleil roused from her nap and padded over for a pet. Catherine massaged behind the cat's ears and was rewarded with a deep purr. After a final sip of coffee and a bite of toast, she finished her initial report on the Spago coverage. She scooped her files into the leather portfolio and headed out for her meeting.

She splurged on a cab instead of taking the subway, not her favorite mode of transportation. She couldn't believe it had come to the point where a short cab ride was a luxury.

Lexington's swanky offices in Rockefeller Center encompassed a large suite in the midtown Manhattan building. The department that handled Winston & Wright was part of a much bigger marketing company that ran national and international advertising campaigns.

Catherine declined coffee offered by the receptionist and was ushered into a conference room. A pitcher of ice water and glasses sat on a sideboard against the wall. The account rep, Robin, along with her assistant, Julie, walked in and took seats on the other side of the long mahogany table.

"Congratulations on the great coverage this weekend," Julie said. "That AP photo went everywhere."

"Thanks," Catherine said. From previous meetings, Catherine grasped that Julie was more supportive than her boss, although they were both from the same mold: efficient, driven, eyes glued to their phone screens. They donned high heels to enhance their petite statures and wore stylish suits in dark colors. Catherine guessed they were in their mid-thirties. They generated lots of reports and kept a strict eye on the budget and retainer they were billing Winston.

"We're compiling a list of all the hits from our clipping service," Julie continued. "It will be in our weekly report."

Not buying into Catherine's victory lap, Robin opened her file. "Now on to our next event, the gala at the Plaza Hotel in two weeks. We'll be running point on that." She passed Catherine a copy of the agenda.

"Let's review the tick tock for the evening," Robin said. "The Plaza Blind Tasting will be at four p.m. for invited guests in the Edwardian Room. General arrivals at five-thirty p.m. for the reception in the Terrace Room, and dinner guests will be invited into the Grand Ballroom at seven p.m."

The fundraiser was an expensive ticket: $250 to attend the champagne reception and $750 to attend the reception and gala dinner. Plus, guests would shell out more money to bid on the prized bottles auctioned off after the dinner. This year's beneficiary was the UC Davis Sparkling Winemaking Program.

"Good news," Catherine said. "I reached Trevor Jones. He's willing to forego his speaking fee to be auctioneer." She'd called in favors to track down the popular late-night host through mutual friends in Switzerland, where his father lived.

"That's great!" Julie said. "He's hilarious. That should liven things up."

Catherine opened her chestnut-brown folder for upcoming events. "How many complimentary tickets have we allocated for the press?"

"Twelve seats at the dinner," Robin said. "We can invite more to the reception beforehand." The Plaza had agreed to reduce their normal per-person dinner fee to the nonprofit rate, which still ran over $100 per head to cover the food, service, and ballroom expenses. Participating sparkling producers were donating the wine.

Many New York notables in entertainment and business were attending. Not as star-studded as Spago, but still press-worthy.

"I'd like four media tickets." Catherine ticked them off on her fingers. "*Wine Spectator*, *Newsline*, Jacqueline Collart at *New York News*, and the director of the documentary crew filming the event."

"We can accommodate that," Robin said. "Tell me about the documentary."

"Netflix signed a deal with the California Sparkling Wine Producers to cosponsor a one-hour doc on California sparkling," Catherine said. "They're mainly filming in California but are traveling to New York to get footage of this event."

"Are the sparkling and champagne houses okay with the evening being filmed?" Robin asked.

"Yes, we have an agreement with the doc producer that we

have first look at all footage and can veto anything that looks confidential to any of the houses," Catherine said. "The director, Kevin Block, lined up his crew to film the whole event, starting with the blind tasting. He'll be a guest at dinner, but his crew will continue filming throughout the evening."

Julie pulled a diagram out of her file. "Here's a rough seating chart." The handout showed a floor plan of the ballroom. Tables of ten filled most of the large space between the tall pillars lining each side. "The band equipment will be on the back of the stage."

"Speaking of music," Catherine said, "I confirmed Vanessa Alexander to sing with the band after the auction."

"I'll add that to the press release," Julie said. "Saw her perform at the Oscars. She's got a great voice and that star quality."

"Who is deciding which tables to seat the press folks at?" Catherine asked.

"I thought we'd put them together." Robin glanced at her phone as if indicating impatience.

"I believe it's much better if they're interspersed at tables hosted by champagne houses. More personal, builds relationships," Catherine said.

"That's a lot of work matching them up and getting permission from each company," Robin said.

"I'll work on that," Catherine said.

"Just to clarify, we're taking credit in our April report for the press coverage at the event, since we're coordinating the evening." Robin set her pen down.

This was a big surprise to Catherine. She'd assumed it would be shared credit given that she was assisting with the coordination. She didn't see any harm in them both listing the media coverage in their reports. She'd been counting on the gala to meet her April media placement requirement.

She had only one other card to play. "I think I should get credit for 'All About Wine' since Jacqueline is my contact." In a call after the *Vogue* party, Jacqueline had promised Catherine she'd include Winston in her gala write-up.

"Sure, if you insist." Robin exuded annoyance. She shuffled her papers, indicating an end to the meeting. "We have our marching orders."

Two days later, Catherine had a date with her grandma for afternoon tea at Bergdorf Goodman. Just the break she needed.

From childhood, Catherine had delighted in teatime with Gran. She remembered wearing her favorite party dress, black patent leather Mary Janes, pink ruffled socks, and a matching pink bow in her hair. She'd sip hot chocolate with marshmallows on top. They'd be served egg salad sandwiches on white bread, no crust, cut in quarters, followed by warm chocolate chip cookies, fresh from the oven. Her mouth watered thinking about it.

It was a beautiful day, so she decided to walk from the office. She wore a midcalf skirt and comfortable one-inch sandals. Stepping out of the Seagram Building, she strolled three long blocks west to Fifth Avenue and five short blocks up to 57th Street.

Located in the heart of Manhattan, Bergdorf Goodman was her favorite department store in the city. It reminded her of Bon Marché in Paris, another venerable institution frequented by elegant older women and their daughters. Bergdorf carried a beautifully curated selection of clothes by top designers. Catherine briefly admired the artistic window displays facing the sidewalk, swung open the door, walked past the perfume and cosmetics counters, and took the escalator to the seventh floor.

"Hello dear." Elizabeth Reynolds was waiting at the entrance to the restaurant. She looked a decade younger than her seventy-six years in a chic gray pantsuit that complemented her blue eyes and silver-white hair, cut in a stylish bob. Catherine greeted her grandma with a warm hug.

The maître d' welcomed Elizabeth by name—she was a regular customer on her shopping trips to the city—and they were led to one of the tables near windows overlooking Central Park. A hidden gem, BG resembled an intimate old-world salon with enviable views and an elegantly designed space in neutral tones with gold highlights.

"Since you haven't had time to visit your grandma, I figured I'd come into Manhattan and take you out to tea," Elizabeth said.

"Sorry I've been so busy." Catherine took a seat in the high-back chair. "This was a lovely idea."

The waiter arrived to take their order. "Let's get our usual," Elizabeth said to Catherine, who smiled in agreement.

"We'll each have the royal tea with Veuve Clicquot," Elizabeth told the waiter. "My granddaughter will have a pot of Jardin Bleu tea, and I'll have Earl Grey."

As typical, the small dining room was packed with an afternoon crowd of well-dressed ladies and the occasional out-of-place guy, sipping tea and speaking in hushed tones. Many had shopping bags from purchases in the store.

"I've been looking forward to this all week," Catherine said as their champagne flutes were served. "Reminds me of our trips here when I was a little girl."

"I'm glad you could get away from work. This is a treat for me . . . to see how my only granddaughter is doing."

Catherine took a sip of her champagne. "I haven't had a chance to thank you in person for encouraging James to hire me. I really appreciate it."

"My pleasure dear. I received your lovely thank-you note."

A waitress poured tea into their fine china cups and set the teapots nearby. Then she placed a three-tier tray of finger sandwiches, scones, and small desserts on the white linen tablecloth. "Let me know if you'd like anything else," she said.

"We're fine for now," Elizabeth said. She poured a smidgen of heavy cream in her teacup and stirred. "Is James looking out for you?"

"He's been very supportive," Catherine said. "But it's high stress and I'm learning as I go." She placed a cucumber-and-cream-cheese sandwich on her plate. "The timing couldn't have been better. I desperately need the job. I'm broke." She held her hands out palms up.

Elizabeth set her teacup down. "I thought your parents were pulling from your trust until your career took off."

"They were, but Mom cut me off in January, said I was going through my draw too fast."

Elizabeth's late husband had left $250,000 in his will for Catherine to be held in a trust her parents controlled until Catherine turned thirty. She hadn't been paying much attention, but her mom claimed she'd gone through $100,000 over the past three years. At that rate, there wouldn't be much left when it vested.

"Oh my, I didn't hear about that." Elizabeth frowned.

"One other thing." Catherine stirred sugar in her tea while she gathered her thoughts. "I think Mom got upset at Christmas when I declined to go on a blind date with their friends' son. How antiquated is that? She wants to see me"—Catherine paused to make air quotes—"'settle down.'"

Elizabeth cut a piece off her chicken tarragon sandwich. "Your mother could be operating off her personal experience."

"What do you mean?" She had no clue what her grandma was talking about.

"I assumed your parents shared the story. They were matched up. By their parents."

"I never heard that." Catherine was astonished.

"My dear husband became close friends with your mother's father when they were students together at INSEAD, near Fontainebleau." Elizabeth took a sip of tea and continued. "When your dad went to Paris on his first work assignment, the men conspired to have their children meet."

"I heard Mom and Dad met accidentally at an embassy party."

Elizabeth smiled. "They did meet at an embassy party, but your mother had to be coerced into going under false pretenses. The fathers had to scheme to make sure your parents actually met at the party without realizing it was prearranged. It was a big affair, lots of people." She spread lemon curd on her scone. "Then the men made sure your parents ran into each other a week later at another function."

"Wow." Catherine took a bite of a chocolate-covered strawberry.

"After those machinations, nature took its course," Elizabeth said. "There was a slight age difference, your father being a few years older. But I think that normally works well."

"I heard you grandparents were friends. Just didn't put it together," Catherine said.

"Your grandpa and I were thrilled that you'd have a broader range of experiences, being half French, growing up in Europe." Elizabeth cradled her teacup. "I think you'll see it suits you well in adapting to this new global environment."

Shaking her head in amazement, Catherine finished the last sip of her champagne.

"What does your mother think you're looking for in a man?" Elizabeth asked.

"We haven't really discussed it. I guess she'd say someone who's a good provider, wants a family. Since Dad is so great, I don't think she realizes how many insincere guys are out there."

"That sounds a bit jaded for one so young. I hope you haven't had too many disappointing experiences."

Catherine shrugged. She didn't want to share the trials and tribulations of her disastrous single life.

"What are you looking for?"

"For starters, someone who cherishes me and is attractive inside and out." Catherine gazed out the window. "Recently, I'm understanding it's important to find a guy who is passionate about his goals, has a worldview." She laughed. "And then, of course, he has to be good with kids and animals."

"Those sound like good qualities. I hope you find that guy." Elizabeth reached out and patted Catherine's hand.

"Me too. But first I need to become financially independent, get a head start on my career." Catherine made a face. "My expertise is shopping, and I miss it."

"We can rectify part of that right now," Elizabeth said. "One of my favorite pastimes is spoiling my only granddaughter. Let's get you a fancy dress for that gala you mentioned. It will be my early birthday present to you."

"My birthday's not until June. Are you sure?" Catherine set her napkin on the table.

"Nothing would give me greater pleasure," Elizabeth said.

On Friday morning, Catherine acknowledged she was overdue for the inevitable reckoning with her accountant, Curt de Crinis. She'd avoided his meeting requests for weeks, blaming it on her travel and long hours at work, not keen on going over the details of her poor finances. The pep talk from her grandma earlier in the week had helped her summon the courage to face the consequences.

Curt had agreed to meet at noon so Catherine could come on her lunch break. She'd already left the office during work hours for her afternoon tea date and didn't want to give the snippy secretaries more ammunition to badmouth her.

The office of Davis Investment Advisors was in the Empire State Building. Catherine exited the subway station and looked up at the landmark art deco building. She had a flashback to the final scene in *Sleepless in Seattle*, when Meg Ryan and Tom Hanks finally united on the top observation deck. She sighed. *No romantic rendezvous for me today.*

Navigating past a swarm of tourists in the lobby and enhanced security checkpoints for the elevators, Catherine reached the thirtieth floor. The office suite reeked of affluence: wood-paneled walls, tan leather furniture, and a three-foot-high bouquet of fresh exotic flowers. The young, attractive receptionist pointed out the Nespresso coffee machine and said Curt would be out in a few minutes.

Curt de Crinis was a junior partner at the firm. Catherine's grandmother had been a client for decades and was close friends with the founder and senior partner, Virginia Davis. Catherine had engaged Curt's services two years ago when it became clear she needed help filing her taxes and staying on top of her bills.

A nearby television was tuned to the CNBC business network, on mute with closed captions. Financial magazines, including the *Wall Street Journal* and *Warner Financial Times*, were in a neat pile on the black coffee table. Looking around, Catherine realized this was Chris's realm. He'd made his money in the stock market at a relatively young age and used his financial acumen to spearhead Winston's expansion. She couldn't even stick to a budget. They came from very different worlds.

Curt arrived and apologized for running a few minutes late. He led her back to his small office. She'd only been there a few times in person to drop off signed forms. Everything else had been handled by mail and email.

Motioning for her to take a seat, Curt sat behind his desk and got down to business. He pulled out a manila file—*no flashy color-coding there*—and opened it up. "Catherine, I'm glad you were able to come in today. As we discussed on the phone, your parents have stopped putting money into your checking account, and it's overdrawn."

He glanced at the spreadsheet in the open file. "It's great you found a job, but that income barely covers your monthly expenses." Curt tapped the file.

"In addition, there's the matter of our fee to pay your bills and handle your taxes." He took a sip of coffee out of a mug imprinted with the slogan "Brokers Rule." "I know Elizabeth Reynolds is an important client here, but my boss has insisted I can no longer handle your account until you have the means to pay our fee."

"You mean you're firing me!" Catherine said.

He grimaced. "Something like that."

This was even worse than she anticipated. Catherine was reeling. No more making waves at work and going out on a limb, as she had done signing the Spago contract before getting approval.

"I was hoping you'd advise me on how to get a loan." She fingered her Cartier ring. "I need to come up with $25,000 for a Cornell training program I'm taking in July. We're expecting bonuses in June but that's not guaranteed . . ."

He glanced at her ring. "Have you thought about hocking your jewelry, or any valuable art you might own?"

Catherine sucked in her breath. She couldn't do that. "That's a very last resort," she said. "The ring is a family heirloom."

"I'm sorry to be the bearer of bad news." Curt stood up and went to hold his office door open for her. "Hopefully, the bonus will come through." He walked her out to the reception area.

"You're not kidding," she said. "Thank you for your time." Her manners kicked in and she extended her hand to shake his.

She headed for the elevator feeling overwhelmed and embarrassed that she'd gotten to this point. As she pushed the button, she became lightheaded. *Oh no, not now.* Her breath came in short gasps. A panic attack was imminent. She was on the verge of fainting. The small crowded space in the elevator would make it worse. She barely managed to find a quiet corner in the hallway before she slumped to the floor.

When she revived, the receptionist was knelt beside her asking if she could help. Catherine was mortified she'd fallen apart in such a public place. She told the receptionist she needed to sit by herself for a few minutes to recover. She never admitted they were panic attacks, except to Vanessa.

Chapter Thirteen

New York—63 days to Celebration launch

Four days had passed since Catherine's meltdown outside her accountant's office. She was meeting Vanessa downstairs in a few minutes before a dinner appointment with Patrick Tournelle.

Over the weekend she'd dealt with her finances. For the past six months, she'd thrown all her bank and credit card statements in a box, figuring her accountant would handle things. As she'd sorted through the pile of papers on her kitchen table, she was dismayed to learn how much money she'd spent. Her mom had a point. She needed to track her spending, create a budget, and stick to it. And she desperately needed that launch bonus.

Seeing Vanessa would cheer her up. Catherine had dressed that morning for day-to-evening in a sleeveless Yves Saint Laurent dress in cocoa brown that fell above the knee, showing off her legs. She swapped out the matching jacket for a shimmery black cashmere wrap with gold threads and donned her black stiletto heels. She transferred her essentials bag from her large tote to a small clutch. Final steps: dressier jewelry and a spritz of perfume. Voilà. Party girl.

One benefit of Winston's office in the Seagram Building was the Grill and Bar on the ground floor, a convenient and classy place to host guests for lunch or dinner meetings. Vanessa stood waiting at the entrance.

Catherine gave Vanessa a warm hug. "I'm glad we could fit this in. I need my gal pal time." She envied her friend's comfortable outfit: dressy jeans set off by ankle boots, and a long cashmere sweater belted at the waist.

After ordering drinks—coffee and Bailey's for Catherine and a lemon drop for Vanessa—Catherine crossed her legs on the barstool and faced her friend. "So how goes it with the smitten Sean Dunlavy?"

Vanessa had slept away from their apartment the past three nights, so Catherine assumed Sean had swept Vanessa off her feet and into his bed. She wanted all the details. How did he break down Vanessa's resistance? She usually played a little harder to get. Did he treat her like a princess? She deserved no less.

Vanessa admitted she couldn't resist his full court press after a dry spell with men. He checked all her boxes: dashing, attentive, cosmopolitan, and a dream lover. She didn't get into graphic details; that was never their style. Catherine was happy for her friend, who seemed starry-eyed.

"I keep going back for more." Vanessa looked like the cat who slurped the cream. "I don't know if this is forever. Perfect for now. We did have the talk about dating exclusively, which he brought up. That was very gratifying. You don't want to share your guy."

"Amen," Catherine said. "What's his place like?"

"It's near the United Nations, doorman building, small park across the street. He got a good deal on the rent from a friend who was moving to Europe. Cozy kitchen. He makes me cappuccinos in the morning." Vanessa picked up a salted cashew from the small bowl on their table. "Sean says you and I are lucky to have such a close friendship. Told him a little about our school days."

"Hope you didn't give up our secret club," Catherine said.

"Oh, no. Would never divulge Les Femmes," Vanessa said.

At their boarding school, Our Lady of Grâce: L'École des Femmes outside Geneva, Catherine and Vanessa had formed a club with four other girls dubbed "Les Femmes." The liberal arts curriculum emphasizing art, music, theater, and language was more rigorous than they'd anticipated. The club provided an escape from the constant pressure of papers and tests. They pulled pranks. They flirted with boys at other schools. They went on ski vacations together. And they formed a lifelong bond of sharing and trust.

"So, how's work going?" Vanessa asked.

"Crazy busy. At least the gala is coming together." Catherine filled her friend in on notable VIPs on the guest list, and they discussed the outfits they planned to wear. It was shaping up to be one of the major events of the season.

"Any developments with Chris?"

"No, he's been in Australia for ten days. He's due back today."

Catherine's dinner appointment, Patrick Tournelle, arrived promptly at six thirty. She spotted him at the door and caught a brief frown on his face when he saw she wasn't alone. He quickly masked it with a smile and walked over.

"*Bonsoir,* ladies," Patrick said. "What a pleasure. Two beautiful women. Hello, Vanessa." He bent down and gave her a polite peck on each cheek then turned to Catherine.

"*Chérie*, very good to see you." His kiss lingered on her cheek.

The waiter appeared and Patrick ordered a bottle of Tournelle Champagne and three glasses. He turned to Vanessa. "Of course, you're invited to join us for dinner."

"Thanks," Vanessa said. "I have to dash in a few minutes. We were just having a girls' catch-up until you got here. So, what's going on with you these days?"

"Oh, boring work. In town for the gala this Saturday." Patrick nodded approvingly to the waiter as he displayed the bottle of champagne before opening it. "We just bought a winery in Sonoma."

"Guess that means you'll be in the US more often," Vanessa said.

"Yes, traveling a lot," he said. Then Patrick regaled them with gossip about the latest news in Paris, much of it about their acquaintances.

Fifteen minutes later, the restaurant hostess informed Patrick his dinner table was ready. Patrick stood to pull out Catherine's chair and addressed Vanessa. "Will I see you Saturday night?"

"I'm singing after the auction. Had to get the night off from my new cabaret gig."

"I heard something about that," Patrick said. "We'll have to arrange a night there."

Catherine wondered which one of their friends told him. She hadn't mentioned it.

As they stood to leave, Chris and Sean walked in and took seats at the far end of the bar. *He must have just arrived from the airport.* She was happy to see him and struck by how handsome and tanned he looked, probably from touring the vineyards.

As they neared that end of the bar on the way out, Catherine told herself to play it cool. She spoke first. "Hello Chris, Sean." The men nodded and Sean gave Vanessa a big grin.

"You've got quite a dedicated employee," Vanessa told Chris. "I barely see my best friend, she's working so hard."

"We value hard work and *loyalty*." Chris emphasized the last word.

Patrick responded to that salvo. "Our philosophy at Tournelle is if you're not clever enough to hang onto your assets, you don't deserve to keep them."

Chris looked irritated but said no more.

"Come on, honey," Vanessa whispered to Catherine. "We'd better get Patrick out of here before World War Three erupts."

After they were seated, Catherine turned to Patrick. "What was that all about? Are you trying to rile Chris? Don't forget he's my boss."

"Sorry, don't want to put you in a tough position. He's so . . ."—Patrick paused, searching for the words—"as you say, by the book. Rubs me the wrong way."

"Could you try to be nice to him, for me?" She had to navigate between these two.

"Anything for you, my dear." He put his hand on hers and gazed into her eyes. With another guy she might have felt sparks, but with Patrick it was comfortable familiarity, like she'd feel with an older brother.

The rest of the evening went more smoothly. Catherine enjoyed Patrick's company over the gourmet meal. He asked why she took the job. She admitted she was broke and needed the income after her parents cut her off. He looked surprised. Their parents were best friends, but he hadn't heard about it.

Catherine was gratified her precarious financial situation wasn't common knowledge among their crowd in Paris. She preferred to handle her affairs privately. She figured Patrick would respect that.

Toward the end of dinner, after polishing off most of the bottle of champagne himself, Patrick let his guard down. "Our company has big expansion plans," he said. "Sonoma is only the first step. We have a backer with deep pockets. He expects a good showing for Tournelle at the Plaza Blind Tasting, but that should be no problem."

Wow. That was putting a lot of eggs in one basket. What if Tournelle didn't do well at the blind tasting? More to the point, what was she going to do with this intel? James would find this news useful. Now that the conflict presented itself, she was reticent to take action that could cause friction with her family.

He suggested they share a crème brûlée dessert. Catherine took a few bites but had lost her appetite.

Patrick walked her out to the building lobby and moved in for an intimate embrace. Catherine gave him a brief hug and was grateful the elevator door slid open, cutting off a longer goodbye. She waved as the door closed and rode back to the office to wrap up her monthly report.

On his way to work the next morning, Chris picked up an extra shot black coffee to combat jet lag and make it through the day. He sat at his desk mustering the courage to apologize to Catherine. He blamed exhaustion for his foul mood at the Grill last night. He was so happy to lay eyes on her after his long trip, but he'd blown it when he saw her with Patrick. That guy had a way of pushing all his buttons. She shouldn't be caught in the crossfire, though. Not to mention, he wanted to pursue a relationship with her. He wasn't handling it well. Time to face the music.

Chris walked down the hall and rapped on Catherine's door. "Hi," he said as he strolled in.

"Good morning," she said. "Are you here to give me a loyalty test?"

He held up his hands. "Sorry about last night. Missed you . . . it's been ten days. Then seeing you with Patrick set me off." He ran a hand through his hair. "Will you forgive me?"

Catherine hesitated, fiddled with her files, and studied him. "Okay."

It wasn't a resounding absolution, but Chris figured he'd have to take what he could get and try to earn his way back into her good graces.

"Also, James called a meeting for eleven a.m. with the folks from Trianon. They'll want a short presentation on the gala."

She nodded.

"Second, Sue Hamilton left a message. *Newsline* is airing tonight. Will you watch it with me? Italian at my place."

Catherine looked hesitant.

"Pleeeease," Chris pleaded. "I'll send a driver to pick you up."

"Okay," Catherine said for the second time. "Since I roped you into the interview."

"Thanks." He sighed in relief.

Two hours later, Chris arrived at the conference room before the others and placed copies of his report in front of each chair. James walked in a few minutes later accompanied by Jean and Yves. The finance people showed up and sat at the far end of the table.

James took the head chair. "Welcome, everyone. We thought we'd take advantage of Yves and Jean being in town to discuss what Chris learned on his recent trip to Australia. And we'll go over the financial update we're presenting to Chamath on Monday."

Indicating the three-page document in front of each person, Chris outlined his findings. Presently, the Australian wineries were making chardonnay and pinot noir still wines. He recapped the cost and time involved to convert their operations to sparkling wine. They'd need space, equipment, and training to create the sparkling blend and proper bottle storage for the second fermentation.

"As you all know," Chris said, "securing these contracts is crucial to our deal with Chamath. I'm drawing up letters of intent to lock them in." Chris closed by saying he'd go over the winery integration in more detail with Jean and his team when he went to France the following week.

James chimed in. "I think it would be beneficial if Catherine Reynolds joined Chris on the trip to coordinate with Agnès on the Vinexpo launch party."

"Good idea," Jean said. "We're hosting a reception next week in Épernay for Relais & Châteaux members to taste our wines for their contest. She can assist with that too."

"Then it's settled," James said.

Distracted by the thought of traveling with Catherine, Chris silently thanked the gods.

James called a five-minute break. The group mingled around the coffee station and helped themselves to fresh donuts. Catherine walked in, and Chris noticed the finance guys gaping at her, mouths dropping open, full of half-chewed donut morsels.

When they spoke earlier, she'd been seated, so he hadn't seen her slim-fitting short skirt and sky-high heels. No wonder the guys were gawking.

James offered Catherine a chair next to him, and the meeting resumed.

"Catherine, thanks for joining us," James said. "Please update the group on your meeting at Lexington and plans for the gala."

Catherine placed her blue file on the table. Chris wondered what that color signified. She pulled out her notes and took them through the timing for the evening: starting with the Plaza Blind Tasting hosted by Relais & Châteaux; then a cocktail reception where the tasting results would be announced; culminating in the star-studded black-tie gala dinner and auction.

"It goes without saying, we need to do well at the blind tasting," James said. "It's the first time our new *cuvée de prestige* is being evaluated, and placing in one of the categories is a requirement for participating in the contest."

It's make or break time now, Chris thought. Everything was riding on that.

Catherine cited press coverage they anticipated and handed out seating charts for the Winston tables at the dinner. James was hosting one with board members and their French partners, and Chris was hosting the second table for guests and members of the media.

So far, the organizers had managed to keep costs to a minimum. All the proceeds were going toward the fundraising goal of $250,000 for the UC Davis Sparkling Winemaking Program.

"Speaking of fundraising," James said, "we're donating three cases of our best bottles to be auctioned off. They should fetch a decent price." He turned to Jean. "What do you think they'll bid for your prized bottle of Trianon 1952?"

"*Beaucoup, j'espère*," Jean said. "At that level, we know they're not buying it for a backyard barbecue. It's a rare, precious bottle, not available in stores."

Proper storage of these ancient bottles was key, Chris knew. They had to be impeccably preserved in a cool, dark cellar to remain drinkable. The flavors become more layered, some would say toasty. These unique bottles were collectors' items, as treasured as other valuable works of art or antiques.

"We all want to be the house whose bottle wins the highest bid," James said. "For bragging rights, and . . ."—he paused—"for the cause, of course." He glanced at his watch. "I guess that wraps things up for now. We've got our marching orders." The group started to disperse.

"One more thing," James said as he stood up. "Our illustrious president is making his starring debut on national television tonight—*Newsline* on ABC at seven. Tune in if you can." He leaned over and winked at Catherine, quietly congratulating her on setting it up. Chris was struck by the closeness between them.

Catherine found it ironic that she was working while Chris had left early to pick up takeout for their television viewing party. A reversal of roles from the "little woman" preparing dinner for her man after his long day at work.

As promised, he arranged for the Winston driver to pick her up at six-fifteen in front of the Seagram Building. Twenty minutes later, she arrived at a tall, modern building on the West Side, one block from Central Park, near the Natural History Museum. Chris buzzed the front door open and directed her to his apartment on the twelfth floor.

Catherine noted the minimalist black-and-white color scheme in the lobby and headed for the elevator. Chris stood at his open door and beckoned her in. "Thanks for agreeing to come over," he said.

Whatever Chris had selected at the neighborhood Italian restaurant smelled delicious; she detected garlic, basil, and lemon. "Mmm, smells good," she said. "What did you get?"

"Chicken fettuccine alfredo, classic Italian salad, and cannoli for dessert," he said as he took her coat.

"Sounds yummy." But not as yummy as how Chris looked in faded blue jeans. She felt overdressed but figured he'd appreciate her short skirt and heels.

"What's your pleasure?" he asked. Catherine gave him a questioning look before he added, "What would you like to drink?" She wondered if he was flirting with her.

"I'll have what you're drinking," she said. Chris reached over to show her the bottle before he poured some in her wineglass. She read the label: Domaine Carneros Palmer Chardonnay.

"Isn't that a sparkling wine company?" Catherine asked.

"Good catch," Chris said. "Yes, Domaine Carneros is mainly sparkling, but like some French champagne houses, they make a select number of still wines."

Catherine swirled the wine in her glass, sniffed, and took a sip. "It's very nice."

While Chris busied himself getting out serving bowls, Catherine looked around. The apartment had an open floor plan. A long granite counter divided the all-white kitchen and a spacious living room with windows overlooking Central Park.

The decor was spartan, although the pieces were good quality—a brown leather couch and matching chairs faced an entertainment unit with a stereo and large-screen TV.

A library alcove off the dining area looked like it served as a home office. Prominently displayed on the shelves were framed photos of his family, including one of Chris with a woman who appeared to be his mother. He was in Stanford football gear; she had a proud smile, long auburn hair, and the same startling blue eyes.

She noticed Chris had already put place settings on the coffee table in front of the couch. He walked over and put the salad and rolls on the table and turned up the volume on the remote. The *Newsline* theme music swelled. Catherine recognized the horn fanfare from composer John Williams's "Call of the Champions." Very stirring.

"Let's take a seat," Chris said. Catherine joined him on the couch.

Sue stood in the studio facing the camera. "Welcome to *Newsline*. I'm Sue Hamilton. We have an exciting lineup tonight. First my Wednesday profile and then a news report." *She looks good*, Catherine thought. Very professional in a charcoal tailored pantsuit cinched with a belt at the waist, showing off her enviable figure. Catherine knew the camera "added" a few pounds and Sue must work hard to maintain a toned body.

Catherine tipped her wineglass toward Chris. "To your successful TV debut."

They directed their eyes to the television. "This week's featured guest, Chris McDermott, is president of Winston & Wright, a relatively new company in the growing sparkling wine business in the US. We went to Napa, California, to learn more about this industry and this executive to watch."

The first segment started with an overview of the sparkling wine business, using footage the crew shot at Winston with Sue's voiceover. Then Sue appeared on screen walking through the vineyards at the Winston Winery while explaining the difference between sparkling wine and champagne from France. After showing B-roll of the winery operation inside—stainless-steel vats and bottles in their second fermentation—Sue segued to her interview with Chris at his ranch.

It seemed evident to Catherine that Sue was smitten with Chris, or else a convincing actress trying to boost television ratings. He looked very handsome, and his charisma was palpable as he parried with her during their conversation. The segment ended with Sue's question to Chris about what he looked for in a woman and his response: "Well, Miss Hamilton, you come awfully close—bright, beautiful, interested in what I have to say, and occasionally full of surprises."

On the commercial break Catherine took a sip of wine to calm her nerves. Chris spoke first. "To dispel any doubts, your friend is not my type." The oven timer went off, and he went to the kitchen and brought back a steaming bowl of pasta. He served Catherine then himself.

They ate in companionable silence for a few minutes until the show came back on. Sue introduced the second segment at the office in New York, focused on Winston's history. Catherine knew this was great coverage for the company. The piece culminated with Sue sipping a sample of the Celebration *cuvée de prestige* and saying she'd recommend it to her friends. Another homerun.

Back in the studio, Sue faced the camera. "For you ladies in the audience, not only is Chris McDermott an executive to watch, but up close in person he's also just as fascinating and appealing as any of the men featured on our 'Most Eligible Bachelors' list. So, we're officially adding him to the group." She walked over to a poster board and wrote Chris's name below a half-dozen other well-known single men, including John Warner. The show cut to break.

"What the hell," he said. "What's that all about?"

"I have no idea and I'm not happy about it. Sue said nothing to me." Catherine was indignant. Aside from the fact that Sue had sprung this with no warning, it hit her: She didn't want Chris on any eligible bachelor lists. As far as she was concerned, he was taken. By her. She was in deeper than she realized.

"It's not your fault." He put his arm around her shoulders and drew her closer. "And besides, I'm not as eligible as she thinks." He picked up the remote and turned the television off. "We've been dancing around this connection we have, and I think it's time to discuss it."

Catherine set her wineglass down and held onto the stem for support.

"Let me be crystal clear. I'm drawn to you. You're like no woman I've ever known, and I'd like to pursue a relationship." Chris reached over to hold her hand. She felt a strong *zing*, nothing like her lukewarm response when Patrick made a similar gesture.

"The catch is we need to wait until after the launch. Big money and careers are on the line. I can't jeopardize those stakes by getting distracted—and believe me, you're distracting." Chris took a sip of wine with his free hand.

"Not to mention our company policy frowns on fraternization," he said. "I wouldn't want to get you in trouble."

Catherine appreciated his concern for her job security. She reminded herself that was priority one. He was distracting, too.

Chris squeezed her hand tighter. "I'm proposing we keep things light until after Vinexpo—and then start dating and all that entails."

He gave her a seductive look, and she knew he meant intimacy, her scary area.

"I realize this is a big ask. Men seem to flock to you. Are you willing to make a secret pact that we wait for each other until after the launch to explore where this attraction takes us?"

If she was honest with herself, Catherine admitted this had been percolating between them for a while—maybe all the way back to that first weekend in Napa two months ago. They were inexplicably drawn to each other. Chris was different from other men she knew, and she found him very appealing.

"I say yes," she said, then leaned in and wrapped her arms around his neck. Chris pulled her in for a tender hug.

"In the meantime," he whispered in her ear, "I'm looking forward to being your unofficial escort at the gala, since we're hosting the table together. Should send a subtle signal I don't belong on any eligible bachelor lists."

She smiled in agreement and hugged him tighter.

Chris chuckled. "Love your enthusiasm. I guess we'll have to define the parameters a bit more. Let's say one kiss to seal the deal."

Slowly, he lowered his lips to hers. She let out a soft sigh and kissed him back.

Chapter Fourteen

New York—59 days to Celebration launch

In a cab on his way to the much-anticipated Plaza Blind Tasting, Chris was still riding high from his evening with Catherine three days earlier. He'd hoped she'd agree to the pact to start dating after the launch, but he hadn't figured on the combustion they generated when she was in his arms. She practically melted before his eyes. It was very appealing. They had sizzle in spades. *I have a big crush on this woman.*

Now he wondered if he could hold it together and be a gentleman for the next two months. It would require all his willpower. Especially since they were traveling to France together in a few days. *Better get through the weekend first*, he chided himself. He was sure she'd look delectable tonight.

He saw Catherine, surrounded by people at the press table outside the Edwardian Room, before he was immediately pulled into a conversation with James and Chamath.

"Here you are," James said.

"Would you believe this is my first blind tasting?" Chamath said.

Chris normally enjoyed these events, but tonight there was too much on the line. He and James attempted to project confidence in the outcome, but there were many variables they couldn't control—namely eight people who had their own subjective criteria for judging the wines. It was nerve-racking. If Celebration didn't win an award, they were out of the Relais & Châteaux contest.

A twenty-four-foot linen-draped table was set up near the windows overlooking Central Park. High-back chairs for the judges were placed behind the table facing the assembled guests. The room's paneled oak wainscoting and intricately trussed wooden ceiling lent an old-world air that suited the occasion.

There was a buzz in the crowd as the judges arrived and made their way to the front. Twelve houses were competing: six California sparkling and six French champagne. Each had admission tickets for staff and guests, in addition to members of the press and other guests of the California Sparkling Wine Producers—a packed turnout.

No wine was being served at this event. That would come later at the reception. There were elaborate coffee stations along the back wall. Chris poured himself a black coffee and rejoined James and Chamath.

"Did you catch the *Newsline* interview Wednesday?" James asked Chamath.

"Yes, great coverage, congrats on that," Chamath said. "Wonder if we'll have to act as bodyguards to protect this eligible bachelor from the single ladies tonight," he jested, pointing to Chris.

"Hope not." James laughed. "As far as I'm concerned, he's on his own."

The event was about to get underway, so Chris was spared more ribbing from the men.

Chris attended many wine competitions in the US and Europe. They could be long drawn-out affairs if panels were judging different types of wine from numerous countries. For this hybrid event, the organizers kept it simple. There were three categories: California sparkling wines, French champagnes (from houses that had subsidiaries in California), and the last category, French and California companies competing against each other. Chris thought that one should be the most interesting and controversial. He didn't anticipate a "Judgment in Paris" scandal, but anything could happen. Winemakers were still referencing the 1976 blind tasting in Paris, when upstart California wines bested French red and white wines, shocking the panel—and the world.

The judges—four from France and four from the US—were a mix of Master Sommeliers and wine critics chosen by *Decanter* magazine, the host for the event. Rigorous blind tasting guidelines were being adhered to. For each category, the judge would be presented with a tray of six glasses, the only labeling a small number on the base of the glass. Each had a notepad, scoresheet, and pen. To clear their palate between sips, there were glasses of water and plates of crackers. They weren't actually drinking the eighteen wines—just the normal swirl, sniff, sip, and spit.

"Didn't expect to see the spittoons," Chamath said. "Forgot they don't actually drink the wines."

Chris handed printed cards to James and Chamath. "Here are the specific entries in each category. The winners will be announced at the reception."

Trays of half-full champagne flutes were brought out, and a hush broke over the crowd as the competition commenced. After tasting each wine, the judges jotted down their notes and ratings in three categories: gold, silver, and bronze. Unlike the Olympics, there were no restrictions on how many awards could be given in each category. That was up to the judges. It all depended on the quality of the wines.

When the third and final trays of glasses were served, Chamath excused himself to check his messages. The judges had their game faces on and studiously made notes. When they wrapped up, the *Decanter* host reminded the audience the results would be announced in a half hour.

The reception was underway when Chris entered the Terrace Room.

"How'd it go?" Will asked as he approached.

"Tasting ran late," Chris said. "Seemed to run smoothly. We'll soon find out how we did." A waiter passed by with a tray of champagne flutes and both men took glasses. A sign on the tray read "Courtesy of Schramsberg Vineyards." Chris took a sip. It tasted good.

"That tux still fits," Will jibed him.

Early in his career, Will had advised Chris to invest in a custom-fitted Armani tuxedo with all the accessories: bowtie, pocket square, and cufflinks. It cost a pretty penny, but it turned out to be a mainstay of Chris's wardrobe for all the formal business and social obligations he was required to attend.

Many New York luminaries had turned out for this event: the mayor, TV personalities such as Anderson Cooper and Kelly Ripa, socialites with their investment-banker husbands, Broadway stars, and A-list actors and sports figures. While the men donned black tuxedos, the women wore shimmery full-length gowns set off by glittering jewelry.

"Let's check out what they're pouring," Chris said. Tonight, the bar setup was in the middle of the room, so guests could approach it from all sides. *Very clever*, Chris thought, *easier to access and becomes the focal point*. Participating houses chose to feature special bottles for the guests to sample. This provided potential bidders a chance to preview labels to be auctioned off later. Naturally, there were no tastings for one-of-a-kind older champagnes expected to fetch the highest bids.

Sean joined Will and Chris as they checked out the bottles on display.

"My God, she's beautiful," Chris swore softly. He swore again silently, after he realized he'd been overheard.

"Are the bubbles going to your head this time, my friend?" Sean said, reminding him of the cocktail party in Napa as he directed his attention toward the object of Chris's gaze. "I believe you're referring to my date for the evening."

Vanessa stood halfway across the room speaking to John Warner, glorious in a silver-sequined body-hugging sleeveless dress with high strappy silver heels. Her hair was stick straight, falling to her shoulders. She definitely attracted many stares.

Chris was off the hook; he'd been exclaiming about Catherine, standing behind John Warner. Stunning in a backless emerald-green gown with long sleeves and a side slit that ended above her knees, Catherine looked like she'd stepped off the pages of a fashion magazine.

Will jumped into the conversation. "Is that Catherine Reynolds next to John? Seen her at board meetings. She's definitely turned up the heat tonight. Is she taken?"

"Don't think so," Sean said. "From what I hear, Chris has her working day and night. As he keeps harping, our company frowns on employees fraternizing." Sean smiled. "Don't have that issue with my gorgeous date."

"Technically, I don't work for the company," Will said. "So no problem with me asking her out."

Just what I need, Chris thought. *Now my best friend wants to ask my girl out.*

"I'd better go reclaim my date," Sean said, "before that eligible bachelor, Warner, tries to steal her away."

Will picked up the thread and teased Chris. "You and John

Warner are in some club. How did you get that show to put you on the bachelor list?"

"Ugh, it's a nightmare," Chris said. "Not the kind of notoriety I want." Their banter was cut short when Doug Barr walked to the front of the room, accompanied by two hotel staff carrying a covered easel. That got everyone's attention.

James and Chamath joined them, and Chris gave James a telling look. They both knew what was at stake. Time for their verdict.

"Ladies and gentlemen," Doug began, "please welcome Philippe Pozzo, president of Relais & Châteaux, to announce the winners of the Plaza Blind Tasting." Chris hadn't seen Philippe before. He was impeccably dressed and appeared to be in his fifties, with salt-and-pepper hair and a gregarious grin.

"Thanks Doug," Philippe said. "All the houses that receive a gold, silver, or bronze rating are eligible to compete in the Relais & Châteaux contest to determine the featured sparkling wine for our member properties worldwide next year. *Bonne chance*."

Chris sucked in a breath. The suspense was killing him.

"We'll reveal the winners in each category separately," Philippe said. "Starting with California sparkling: gold goes to Taittinger Carneros, silver to Winston & Wright and Schramsberg, and bronze to Mumm California and Roederer California."

There were whoops and hollers as guests clinked glasses. Chris exhaled a huge sigh of relief. Their new *cuvée de prestige*, Celebration, had placed silver in a competitive category. He and James slapped each other on the back, and Chamath offered congratulatory handshakes.

Trianon was entered in the next two categories. Chris knew a successful showing from their partner would reflect well on

Winston. Trianon's winemaker, Jean Boyer, had created the blend for Celebration.

"The next category is French champagne," Philippe said. "Gold goes to Moët & Chandon and Roederer, silver to Trianon, and bronze to Mumm, Taittinger, and Tournelle." *Interesting*, Chris thought. Every submission in this category won some kind of medal—no also-rans. Since Trianon and Tournelle placed, that meant they were both eligible to compete in the Relais & Châteaux contest.

After the crowd quieted from the commotion over the results, Philippe continued. "Now on to our final and, some would say, most provocative category, French champagne head-to-head with California sparkling." Chris knew this was where sparks could fly. Patrick constantly bragged about the primacy of French champagne. *Let's see how Tournelle performs in a blind tasting against top California sparkling.*

The crowd hushed. "The gold goes to Moët France," Philippe said. "Silver to Trianon France and Schramsberg California, and bronze to Roederer California." Chris consulted his list. Tournelle France and Mumm California didn't place. He wondered how Patrick would spin that loss. Luckily, that wasn't his problem. They were victorious.

As the crowd applauded the winners, the cover was removed from the easel displaying the results. Names of the companies competing in each category were printed on the board, and the victors were handwritten in the awards columns.

CALIF SPARKLING	AWARDS	FRENCH CHAMPAGNE	AWARDS	CALIF & FRENCH	AWARDS
Schramsberg	Silver	Trianon	Silver	Schramsberg California	Silver
Mumm California	Bronze	Tournelle	Bronze	Roederer California	Bronze
Taittinger Carneros	Gold	Roederer	Gold	Mumm California	
Domaine Chandon		Moët & Chandon	Gold	Moët France	Gold
Roederer California	Bronze	Taittinger	Bronze	Trianon France	Silver
Winston & Wright	Silver	MummFrance	Bronze	Tournelle France	

Doug invited the winners to step forward by category to pose for photos. James wore the silver medal for Winston and smiled broadly as cameras clicked away. Chris was gratified they'd overcome this hurdle. They had a lot to celebrate. Their *cuvée de prestige* was aptly named.

Then it was Yves's turn to accept two silver ribbons for Trianon in the second and third categories.

Now the real work began. They needed to place first or second in the Relais & Châteaux contest.

Waiters circulated, ringing bells indicating dinner was about to commence. Chris went to find Catherine. He looked forward to playing his escort role for the evening.

The Plaza's Grand Ballroom was as sparkly as the guests, an apt venue for this star-studded affair. Large ornate chandeliers illuminated the rectangular room, framed by two rows of pillars between arched openings that led to corridors along the walls. Most of the floor space was taken up by round tables of ten draped in silvery linen cloths and adorned with floral centerpieces, fine china, and crystal stemware. At one end, a small dance floor fronted the stage.

"By the way, you look stunning," Chris told Catherine as they approached their dinner table. She smiled, and he had to stifle an urge to reach out and hold her hand.

"Thank you," she said. "You're pretty dashing in that tux." He was inordinately pleased by that compliment. They were the first to arrive at the table, so they checked the place cards.

Chris McDermott	
Ken Barnett	Catherine Reynolds
Sue Hamilton	Will Frost
Kevin Block	Vanessa Alexander
John Warner	Sean Dunlavy

Chris was starting to second-guess his decision to put Will next to Catherine. *Too late to change that now.* James hosted the older crowd at a table nearby: Chamath, Yves, Jean, and Winston board members.

"Why is David Saunders Jr. at James's table?" Catherine asked. "I know his dad is there with other board members, but he's younger. He'll be bored with that gang."

"There's some tension," Chris said. "David Junior wanted my job when James was filling the position. His dad lobbied hard, but David didn't have the right experience or temperament. They didn't take it well and have been rude to me on occasion, so I give them a wide berth."

"Corporate intrigue. Hadn't heard that story," Catherine said.

"It can get complicated," Chris admitted.

Catherine made introductions as people arrived and took their seats. Waiters hovering solicitously nearby poured the first flutes of sparkling wine.

Doug Barr stepped up to the podium and gave welcoming remarks. Then he held up his glass. "Now that the first champagne is poured, I'd like to propose a toast. To a successful evening—you know what that means, folks." Hundreds of flutes clinked in unison. "We'll start the auction after our gourmet dinner prepared by the illustrious Alain Ducasse and his *équipe*."

In keeping with the exclusivity of the event, organizers had brought famed French chef Alain Ducasse over from Paris. One of the most prolific holders of Michelin stars, Ducasse had started in Monte Carlo, moved on to Paris, then opened restaurants around the world.

Trays of mouthwatering appetizers were placed on tables to sample family-style. Catherine spooned a mini tartlet topped with caviar onto her plate and passed the tray to Will.

After serving himself, Will directed his attention across the table. "Sue, that was some *Newsline* segment this week. Are you sure Chris warrants inclusion on the 'Most Eligible Bachelors' list? Not sure he has enough sex appeal."

That generated raucous laughter and caused people from other tables to glance over with questioning looks.

Will drove the point home. "I get John Warner being on the list, but Chris?" He threw his hands out.

"Hey, don't drag me into this," John said, laughing.

"I stand by our decision," Sue said. "We've received quite a few calls asking how to reach Chris."

"About that—don't you think you could have given me a heads-up?" Chris said.

"Didn't want to give you a chance to back out," she said.

Odd, Chris thought. Delores hadn't passed on any messages from random women trying to reach him after the show. He wondered if she rebuffed their inquiries without telling him. No matter, there was only one woman who interested him. She was looking distinctly uncomfortable at the topic, so he changed gears.

Curious to hear Ken's reaction to the blind tasting results, Chris steered the conversation in that direction. Ken ticked off the categories and his opinions of the winners—and losers—and how it could affect those companies going forward. "Patrick Tournelle is not going to be happy with their showing," he said.

"I like how it levels the playing field," Chris said. "A winemaker can't BS their way to a good rating. It's based on substance, not glitz or marketing."

"Was hoping to see a few more fireworks," Ken admitted.

Ah yes, Chris reminded himself, *the press is always looking for controversy*—a pitfall to be avoided at all costs.

The plates for the main course arrived. Guests had preordered their choice of curried cod and mussels or free-range herb-roasted chicken, both served with farm-fresh vegetables. After everyone was served, Chris waited for Catherine to take the first bite before he began. The chicken was delicious, moist and flavorful. Chef Ducasse knew what he was doing. So far, this was the best meal Chris had eaten at one of these large hotel events—not an easy feat to pull off.

Catherine put her fork down and drew Kevin into the conversation. "Tell us about the documentary you're filming." *She's a good hostess*, Chris realized.

Kevin proceeded to outline the parameters for his one-hour documentary on the history of sparkling wine in California. Commissioned by Netflix as part of a series on the importance of California agriculture for the US and the world, Kevin's episode tied in the exponential growth of the sparkling industry with its glamorous image.

"Thanks to your *Newsline* piece," Kevin said, "we saw how effectively Sue explained the topic and hired her to be our narrator."

"Congrats, Sue." Catherine held up her flute in acknowledgment. "Hadn't heard that yet."

Sue nodded. "We just inked the deal, very exciting."

"Like any film, we're always looking for a good story, drama, and, of course, plenty of compelling visuals," Kevin said. "And, hopefully, consideration for awards at film festivals."

Sean gestured to the bottle in the ice bucket on the table. "One strong benefit of sparkling is the affordable price, compared to a bottle of French champagne that costs two or three times as much. Granted most sparkling wines don't have the complexity of champagne, but that's not necessary for every occasion."

Chris agreed. He was glad Sean made the point.

"Have an idea for the documentary finale," Ken said. "How about a sabering and pyramid of flutes? That was quite dramatic at the Spago party for the Oscars." A reminder Chris would like to forget. The second cork popping off and barely missing the celebrity guests was a drama he didn't want to repeat.

"All good ideas," Kevin said. "May call on some of you for on-camera interviews before we wrap."

Chris was full by the time the dessert of Valrhona chocolate mousse with whipped cream and berries was served. He devoured it anyway. He noticed Catherine hadn't eaten with the gusto of others at the table. She and Vanessa only sampled their dishes. *Must be some party protocol.*

While after-dinner coffee was offered, Doug stepped to the mic and introduced the head of the UC Davis Sparkling Winemaking Program, who thanked everyone for their support and described how the money raised would benefit their research and scholarships.

"Now it's time to end the suspense and find out how much these rare bottles are worth," Doug said. "Please welcome our celebrity auctioneer, Trevor Jones." Trevor walked onstage to loud applause. Doug piped in, "You're clapping now, but if you don't bid generously, you could be on the receiving end of his jokes." That drew guffaws. The crowd was getting rowdy after a few glasses of good wine, just the thing to bid up the prices.

Trevor took the microphone. "Good evening, folks." He went into a short monologue recapping the day's events and cracking jokes at the expense of high-profile guests. He closed with, "Let's take the plunge. We have many exceptional bottles to auction off to reach our goal. Please open your wallets and bid with abandon."

There were other things Chris wanted to pursue with abandon, starting with Catherine's bare back. Her slinky dress was killing him. Unaware of his train of thought, she was in an animated conversation with Will.

The bidding became heated, and Chris directed his attention to the stage. As each lot was auctioned off, Chris and Ken jotted down notes in the margins of their programs and bantered back and forth about the prices they were fetching. Unlike the blind tasting, this process was highly visible. Chris assumed some buyers were making winning bids for the prestige and bragging rights, as much as for the unique bottles and contribution to the cause. In this case, glitz overrode substance. He said as much to Ken—not grasping he was about to fall into the same quest to be victorious.

Pleased with the competitive bidding, Trevor congratulated the crowd on their good taste. The lots were fetching higher prices than anticipated. After forty-five minutes, one final bottle remained. "Well folks, you've risen to the occasion. The California Sparkling Wine Producers thank you," Trevor said. "And now we have a special surprise for our last bottle." The crowd drew quiet. "The high bidder on this rare Trianon 1952 vintage jeroboam will also receive a two-night stay at romantic Les Crayères in Champagne and a gourmet dinner for two in their Michelin-starred restaurant, along with a private tour of the kitchen and toast with the chef."

When Catherine stood up, Chris figured she was going to the ladies' room, so he was taken off balance by Trevor's next words. "Catherine Reynolds, representing Trianon, has agreed to join the winning bidder in a toast and to lead off the first dance of the evening." He beckoned her to the stage.

Did I say I wanted a woman full of surprises? Uh-oh. He'd be damned if anyone else was getting this prize. He was feeling awfully possessive at the moment.

They were off and running. A number of attractive men participated in the early bidding, including Chris, Patrick Tournelle, Will Frost, and even Sean Dunlavy. When the dollar figure exceeded $4,000, the bidding contest narrowed to only two: Chris and Will. Trevor chided the combatants. "Looks like we have a horse race, ladies and gentlemen. Miss Reynolds, would you care to weigh in on the contest?"

All she murmured was, "I'm glad they're supportive of the cause," which prompted twitters.

When Chris made it clear he planned to bid whatever it took, his friend Will bowed out. *Finally. Do I have to broadcast my interest any louder*?

"Fair warning," Trevor announced, indicating the bidding was about to stop, and the gavel came down. "Sold to Chris McDermott for $5,000."

Amid applause, Chris walked onto the stage, shook hands with Trevor, and enfolded Catherine in a warm embrace that sent cameras flashing. Doug Barr joined the trio to pose for photos. A waiter materialized with four glasses of champagne that they sipped while the stage was being cleared.

The band took their places. Vanessa stepped up to the microphone and started performing her signature version of "Knocks Me Off My Feet."

"I believe this dance is mine," Chris whispered in Catherine's ear, before he whisked her onto the dance floor.

"You sure know how to make a splash," Catherine said. "Hope this doesn't appear like we're fraternizing."

"All for the cause," Chris murmured, holding her possessively close. She felt so good in his arms while they moved in time to the music. Vanessa sang the refrain, and he caught the message of the song—a love so strong it made you weak.

Other couples joined them on the dance floor, and Chris steered Catherine to a less conspicuous spot in an alcove behind one of the pillars. "About that bare back," he murmured and pulled her closer in his embrace.

"I thought we were going to be low-key," she said.

"You shouldn't have worn such a provocative dress."

"I don't want this to cause a problem with my job." She looked concerned.

"Your job is safe. But you're right, we should head back."

As they made their way to the table, they were intercepted by Patrick and his dance partner.

"Hello Patrick, Jacqui," Catherine said. "Chris, this is Jacqueline Collart with *New York News*."

"Nice to meet you," Chris said.

"Congrats on your wins tonight," Patrick said.

"Thanks," Chris said, surprised by his equanimity.

"I wouldn't expect the same results when you're judged by Relais & Châteaux members," Patrick said. "They have a more discerning palate than these idiots chosen by *Decanter*."

And there it is. Patrick's true sentiments. He'd barely gotten out a "congratulations" before the digs started. Not rising to the bait, he turned to Catherine. "We need to return to our guests."

Morning sunlight streamed in through the bay window. "Mmm, smells good," Vanessa said. "You're going to have to teach me how you do this."

Catherine set the steaming cappuccino with sprinkled chocolate shavings in front of Vanessa and sat down next to her in their homey breakfast nook. She pulled Soleil onto her lap, and the cat snuggled into the fluffy white terry robe. Makeup-free, the ladies looked beautiful in the natural light.

"Your door was open last night," Vanessa said, cradling her warm mug, "and you were talking in your sleep, in French the way you do."

"Did I say anything interesting?" Catherine took a sip of her coffee.

"Just caught the name Tournelle. Patrick seemed to be in full macho mode last night. Saw him talking to you and Chris. Did he make a scene?"

"He was upset about the blind tasting. Called the judges idiots." Catherine laughed. "He doesn't hide his opinion."

Catherine wondered if his champagne's poor showing against California sparkling in the final category would affect the business deal Patrick bragged about at their dinner a few nights earlier.

"He was short with Chris, and for once, Chris took it in stride, didn't engage." Catherine dipped a chocolate biscotti in her coffee.

"Maybe that's because he won you in the auction." Vanessa raised her eyebrows in question. "He outbid everyone, and you two looked pretty cozy on the dance floor."

"We had a talk—" Catherine said coyly.

Vanessa didn't wait for her to finish. "What, and you didn't tell me?"

Catherine looked sheepish. "It was only a few days ago and you've been busy with Sean."

"So, what happened?"

"He wants to start dating after the launch in June."

"That's two months away." Vanessa held up two fingers for emphasis.

"Yes, but the company frowns on what they call 'fraternization.'" Soleil yawned, and Catherine reached down to pet her. "I have to keep my job. Besides, with my prep for Cornell, I don't have a spare minute for dating."

"Do you like him?"

"A lot."

"It's about time. I'm happy for you."

"Thanks. I'm happy too." Catherine set her cup down. "Now I've got to figure out what I'm packing for our trip in two days."

Chapter Fifteen

France—55 days to Celebration launch

Maneuvering through Charles de Gaulle airport unnerved Chris. Everyone spoke French. There were signs in English, but this was clearly a French-speaking country, and they were proud of it. He'd been to France a few times to meet with their Trianon partners but hadn't managed to pick up any of the language. At least he had an attractive interpreter. Catherine fit right in, spoke the language fluently. He tended to forget she was half French. She spoke English with no hint of a French accent.

She seemed rested after their seven-hour flight. He wished he could say the same. Thankfully, Winston flew their executives business class. The fold-out beds on the Air France plane helped accommodate his long frame, and he appreciated the hearty breakfast of scrambled eggs and bacon with flaky croissants and fruit. They both ordered freshly brewed coffee.

While they stood in line at customs, Chris noticed Catherine looked almost identical to the chic French women nearby—same elegant look: black stretch jeans, designer loafers, tailored jacket, sexy knit top, and bling. Only Catherine's striking ring wasn't on her wedding finger.

They picked up their luggage, exited the secure area, and found a tall, lanky guy with longish dark hair holding a sign that read, "Chris McDermott & Catherine Reynolds." Chris liked the sound of that. Frédéric Reglain, the Trianon marketing assistant, introduced himself and escorted them to a nearby Mercedes-Benz sedan.

"Thanks for picking us up, Frédéric," Chris said.

"No problem," he said. "I like getting out of the office. It's a beautiful drive." He loaded their bags in the trunk. "Feel free to sit in back, in case you want to doze off." After they got settled, he pulled onto the autoroute heading east; they were immediately immersed in pastoral surroundings.

Chris and Catherine took the opportunity to check messages on their phones, but he was having trouble focusing. Being in such close proximity, he was sorely tempted to wrap his arm around her.

They passed through the village of Château-Thierry amid rows of vineyards. "It's lovely," Catherine said. "Like a dreamy watercolor."

"Catherine is new to the business," Chris said to Frédéric. "Maybe you could share the history of the Champagne region."

Frédéric didn't need any encouragement. He explained that like many Champenois, people born in Champagne, he was raised on the story of the region's special soil. Around eleven million years ago, according to geologists, the area was undersea. A violent earthquake pushed up the seafloor, creating a chain of hills when the water receded. Known as the Falaises de Champagne, the hills became an ideal setting for growing champagne grapes, with topsoil rich in marine organisms and minerals lifted from the seabed floor. The steep hillsides of the *falaises* proved important in growing a hardy grape.

"What a fascinating past," Catherine said. "How much land is covered in the Champagne area?"

Frédéric pointed in the distance. "As you can see, the two most important *falaises* are the Mountain of Reims to the north and the Côte des Blancs to the south."

They took a turnoff going south. "Many of the major French champagne houses, known as Les Grandes Marques, are located in Épernay," Frédéric said. "Others are in the city of Reims, the capital of Champagne."

"A friend and I visited Dom Ruinart in Reims," Catherine said. "We were taken on a tour of the chalk caves, *crayères*. They're amazing."

"Speaking of the unique soil," Frédéric continued, "the casual visitor to Champagne doesn't realize there are miles of underground caves, originally carved out for chalk quarries in the Middle Ages. The deep layer of chalk extends one hundred feet below the surface. It's the ideal cool, dry climate to store champagne while it ages in the bottle for years."

He pulled up to a château on a hill, surrounded by vineyards. The two-story structure had a stone facade and large double windows on the ground floor that were swung open, presumably to take advantage of the sunny, mild day. "Here we are," he said. "This is Trianon's private château for guests. The housekeeper will show you to your suite. Let's meet in thirty minutes to go over to headquarters."

Rather than chase modern trends, the château kept a traditional French feel that Chris appreciated: antique furniture, parquet floors, large wall tapestries, and original oil landscapes, all timeless.

They were sharing a two-bedroom suite; each had their own well-appointed bedroom and sumptuous bath. Chris liked the accommodations. *Too bad this isn't a romantic getaway.* The shared living room had a sitting area, well-stocked kitchenette, and two antique tables that could be used as desks.

A bellhop brought in the bags. Chris quickly unpacked, freshened up, and changed from jeans into slacks, pressed shirt, and casual jacket. This wasn't Napa; these French guys were always impeccably dressed. He grabbed his briefcase with notes and spreadsheets for the afternoon's meetings and walked into the sitting area.

Catherine stood at the window taking in the view below. She'd changed into a dark-brown linen pantsuit and heels and looked fresh as a peach. He didn't know how she did it. *Must be one of her mysterious female tricks.*

Frédéric met them by the front door. "Jean figured you'd be hungry, so we'll start with a quick lunch in the private dining room." Welcome news to Chris. He was famished. They hadn't eaten since breakfast on the plane hours ago. Trianon's headquarters were a short distance away in nearby Épernay, a small picturesque town where the main street was aptly named Avenue de Champagne.

The "quick lunch" turned into a three-course affair, accompanied by excellent wine, of course. The rest of the day went by in a blur. Chris lost track of how many coffees he downed in an attempt to stay alert. Catherine spent the afternoon meeting with Agnès Poiret, Trianon's marketing director, while Chris met with Jean.

When they got back to the château, Chris suggested a nap before dinner, but Catherine vetoed that idea. "Jet Lag 101 states that you need to throw yourself into the new time zone," she said. "Naps throw off your sleep cycle. Our best bet is an early dinner and then crash, preferably with sleep aids."

"Okay, sounds good," Chris said. "But I don't have sleep aids, and I have trouble staying asleep when I'm exhausted." He grimaced.

She rolled her eyes. "Don't they teach you hotshot executives how to travel? Luckily, I have extra sleeping pills. No way can you successfully navigate a four-day trip to France unless you've got provisions."

He guessed that diplomatic upbringing and modeling experience taught valuable skills. He was learning Catherine came from the Girl Scout school of preparation.

Chris managed to tough it out a couple more hours, through an early dinner in the château salon on the ground floor. Then he blissfully conked out with the help of sleep aids from his bewitching traveling companion.

Catherine's travel alarm went off at 7:00 a.m. She stretched her arms, missing her morning wake-up routine with Soleil. Nine hours of sleep. She felt energized and ready to go. According to her phone, the temperature outside was ten degrees Celsius—that translated to fifty degrees Fahrenheit. Catherine kept both versions on her phone. Her nonmathematical brain took too long to do the conversion. She knew if it was anything better than sleet and hail, it was important to get outside for some exercise.

Chris had promised to be up bright and early, said it was part of his farm-boy roots. When Catherine checked his open bedroom door, she could hear deep breathing. She peeked inside. His large frame was sprawled diagonally across the bed. *He's the type who hogs all the sheets.* The down comforter and high-thread-count Egyptian cotton sheets were in a tangle and only partially covered his long legs and bare chest. *Guess he's not wearing much.* She admired his athletic frame. Snapping out of her reverie, she knocked lightly on the door.

"Bonjour sleepyhead. Rise and shine. Time to feed the chickens." That last phrase seemed to penetrate Chris's slumber.

He lurched up like he thought he was late for ranch chores. Took him a few seconds to get his bearings.

He broke into a grin. "I love you in that robe."

Catherine blushed a matching rose color. "When have you seen me in this robe?" Then she remembered another early morning, across an ocean and a continent, in Napa.

"When I was toiling in the fields and looked up to see a vision on the balcony."

"I'd hardly call that toiling," she said. "You were just inspecting the fields." She pulled the robe more snugly around her body. "We have new vineyards to discover this morning. We need to get some exercise. How about a run?"

"Sure. We'll see what you're made of."

Fifteen minutes later, Catherine walked into their shared living room wearing coordinated running pants and jacket with a matching visor. Chris glanced up from his stretching. "Looks like you're getting ready to shoot a commercial," he said. "Puts me to shame."

He, on the other hand, was decked out in baggy gray sweatpants, a Stanford sweatshirt, and scruffy running shoes. All of which did nothing to conceal his well-muscled body.

"Let's see if all that's for show or if you can actually keep up with me on the road," he said as they strode out to the main entrance.

"Your reputation as a jock precedes you, so I'm hoping you'll cut me some slack," she demurred, not revealing her years of long-distance running.

They went outside and Chris led the way. They jogged down a nearby country road that intersected fields of grapevines in neat rows, fastened to stakes in a Y pattern. He set a relaxed pace in apparent deference to her.

After a few minutes, Catherine picked up her stride and whizzed past Chris, leaving his mouth agape at her revved-up speed. He quickly recovered, caught up with her, and scolded, "You've been holding back on me."

Since their pace had quickened, the only sounds were their feet softly hitting the dirt path and their rhythmic exhales. Catherine liked the easy camaraderie of their shared exercise. They were both in good shape and could run for miles.

Twenty minutes later, Chris glanced at his watch. "We'd better head back." They walked the last half mile to slow down their heart rates. He took the opportunity to check out nearby vines, sprouting their first leaves of spring. He plucked a leaf and inspected it. "These are pinot noir, the predominant grape in this area." He held it out for Catherine to take a look.

Catherine respected Chris's hands-on approach to winemaking. "I've been meaning to ask you," she said. "Everyone refers to *terroir*. I know *terre* means land in French."

"In winemaking, *terroir* refers to the land and all the elements that affect it," Chris said. "Obviously, soil is key, but also the region's climate—temperature, rainfall, anything that affects the grapes' growth."

A breeze picked up. Catherine unwrapped the running jacket she'd fastened around her waist and put it back on.

"The Champagne appellation has a very specific *terroir*—the rich organic soil that Frédéric explained yesterday, a cool climate that's conducive to producing acidic grapes necessary for a second fermentation, and temperatures that aren't too extreme," he said. "Although lately, temps are getting hotter, and that's a big problem."

"Do you think the French way is becoming antiquated?"

"I would just say it's different and sets a high standard. We're making excellent sparkling in other regions around the world, but it doesn't compare to the layers of complexity of the top-quality French champagnes."

Catherine had grown up around diplomats and was learning Chris had the same tactful skill—when he wanted to use it. No wonder James tapped him to run the company.

Chris lathered up in the shower and admitted he was having difficulty keeping it strictly business in close proximity to Catherine. She was damned attractive and enticing. He was developing a new respect for her. Instead of the party girl he'd mistakenly judged her to be in the beginning, she threw herself into the work. She wasn't phoning it in.

The morning passed quickly. Their busy schedule included meetings through lunch. A cup of espresso jump-started his energy level for the afternoon. They did a quick change at the château, and Frédéric picked them up for the Relais & Châteaux reception.

"You two look very smart," Frédéric said.

"*Merci*," Catherine said. She wore a short black dress and strappy heels. Chris had changed into slacks and a sports jacket. He asked Catherine to carry his tie in her purse for their dinner later. *Very domestic.*

French members of Relais & Châteaux were meeting in Épernay that weekend, so Trianon had seized the opportunity and invited them to sample the submissions from Trianon and Winston for the contest. More than two dozen members confirmed—a good turnout.

Trianon's dining room boasted plate-glass windows overlooking nearby vineyards. Serving tables held plates of crackers and toasts for guests to snack on. This was not a "sip and spit" occasion, like the Plaza Blind Tasting. This was sip and enjoy the sparkles.

Frédéric manned a pouring station with two sets of glasses. Trianon's champagne would be served in tulip glasses that curved in at the rim and Winston's Celebration *cuvée* served in traditional champagne flutes so they could be distinguished.

As things got underway, Chris saw the wisdom of James's decision to ask Catherine to help host. She was charming the members with her grace and fluency in French. From what he could make out, many of them knew her family.

Catherine stepped over to pick up a tray of flutes. Chris noticed her wrinkling her nose. "Something smells off," she said.

Frédéric sniffed the cork from a bottle he'd just opened. "Think this cork is tainted," he said. He quickly set the bottle aside, so as not to alert their guests.

Chris went ballistic but tried to keep his poker face on. First, the cap shooting off at Spago, and now this moldy cork. Too many anomalies to be a coincidence. *This isn't paranoia.* They were being sabotaged.

At least Frédéric was circumspect; their guests didn't seem to notice anything amiss. He carefully opened the remaining Celebration bottles, and they appeared to be fine.

"We dodged a bullet," Chris said. "Luckily, no other bottles were contaminated." It would have been difficult to explain how they ran out of sparkling wine for a tasting they'd arranged.

Yves stepped in front of the windows and gave a few remarks, unaware of the drama playing out at the pouring station. Then he asked Jean to discuss how the Celebration *cuvée* was created.

Jean described the qualities of the Celebration *cuvée de prestige*, ticking off the steps—the first important decision, designating the vintage grape harvest seven years ago; then his judgment determining which percentage of still wines to blend before the *cuvée* went into bottles for the second fermentation. "*À la fin*," he concluded, "determining the dosage before the final cork."

Catherine offered flutes to stragglers who had just arrived. It was hard to gauge the members' verdict on the wines. They were polite but didn't divulge their opinions. Chris sensed their preference for French labels. Good thing US and French wines were in separate categories for the competition.

After the guests departed, Chris told Jean and Yves about the cork fiasco.

"Had no idea," Yves said. "Don't think the members noticed. That can happen occasionally. Since it was only one bottle, I don't think it was anything nefarious."

Chris hoped Yves was correct, but he had his doubts. He looked at his watch. "We have to get moving. Frédéric agreed to take us on a tour before dinner."

"See you at Les Crayères," Yves said.

Catherine rode up front with Frédéric. The short drive from Trianon to Hautvillers, a picturesque "high village," took them up a narrow, winding road barely changed for centuries. Along the route, they passed well-preserved ancient buildings, some displaying forged-iron signs from a different era. Frédéric pulled up to the Abbey of Hautvillers. The small historic church overlooked fields of vineyards in the valley below.

"For Champenois," Frédéric said, "this is considered the birthplace of champagne. Other regions were experimenting with sparkling wine, but this was the place in France, in Champagne."

He led them to a patio where an ice bucket and three flutes sat on a small table. "Let's take a moment to savor a good French champagne, while I tell the story." He pulled a bottle of Moët's Dom Pérignon out of the ice bucket and opened it. "It's appropriate to drink this champagne, since Moët & Chandon named their prestige blend after Dom Pérignon." He filled the flutes. "Let's toast."

Frédéric began. In 1668, a young Benedictine monk, Pierre Pérignon, became cellarmaster of the Abbey at Hautvillers. Dom was a title given to certain Benedictine monks, so he was called Dom Pérignon. At the time, the abbey was making still wine.

Hautvillers, in the Falaises de Champagne, has a cool northern climate. Pérignon noticed when the weather turned warm in spring some bottles of wine became effervescent. By accident, they had gone through a second fermentation, creating bubbly wine. Through trial and error, Pérignon determined that wine yeast went dormant in cold temperatures. In spring, the remaining leftover yeast initiated another fermentation, creating the bubbles.

"We're talking about a lot of bubbles," Frédéric said. He explained the bottles couldn't withstand the additional pressure. Many bottles shattered or the wood plugs popped out, causing spillage. Eventually, Dom Pérignon came up with a cork plug to hermetically seal the bottles, trapping the bubbles in.

"There were still many broken bottles," Frédéric laughed, "until they devised a way to make stronger bottles." Future champagne producers learned how to create the millions of bubbles in each bottle by adding yeast to the blended still wine for the second fermentation.

"A sip to celebrate this monk and his gift to the world." Frédéric lifted his flute. Chris thoroughly enjoyed Frédéric's description. Catherine seemed mesmerized and made a few notes.

"Pérignon devoted his life to the abbey until he died in 1715," Frédéric said. "And now, let's pay our respects." He led them into the small church to view Dom Pérignon's tombstone.

They walked back to the car in contemplative silence. Frédéric checked his phone. "We have time to drive by the church in Reims, if you'd like to see it."

"I'd love to," Catherine said. "My parents were married at Notre-Dame de Paris, a similar Gothic cathedral."

Traffic was light. They arrived in Reims, the capital of Champagne, thirty minutes later. Frédéric pulled up to the plaza in front of the cathedral. He gestured to the edifice. "This church has an important historical significance in France. Starting in the thirteenth century, it was chosen for the coronation of French kings"—he paused—"for six hundred years."

"That's a long time," Chris said.

"One of the most famous coronations was the crowning of Charles the Seventh in 1429, attended by Joan of Arc. Jeanne d'Arc, in French," he added. "Unfortunately, not long after, she was captured by the English and put to death for helping French fighters during the Hundred Years' War."

"Sad story," Catherine said. She stepped out of the car and took a few photos of the facade.

When she got back in, Frédéric drove a few miles to their destination. It was clear the main business of Reims was champagne. Markers indicating numerous champagne houses, including Taittinger and Veuve Clicquot, popped up along the route. Right before the approach to Les Crayères, they passed a sign for Pommery Champagne.

Frédéric pulled into a parking spot. "We're here." He got out of the car to see them off.

"Thank you, Frédéric, for making us feel so welcome," Chris said. "You've been a great host and guide." Chris shook his hand, and Catherine and Frédéric shared air kisses on both cheeks.

"You'll have to visit us in New York sometime," Catherine said.

"It's my dream to go to the US," Frédéric said. "*En tout cas*, I will see you in Bordeaux in June."

"Yes, in two months," Chris said.

As they walked up to the entrance, Chris stifled the urge to hold Catherine's hand. She gave him his tie and pulled out a multicolored scarf that she wrapped around her neck.

Chris admired the breathtaking classic French château set in the midst of lush parkland. Yves texted he was running late, so they opted to wait in the bar. After perusing the *carte* of champagnes by the glass, Chris chose Pommery. Appropriate, since the château was built by that family. A brochure on the table relayed the history.

Les Crayères was built for Louise Pommery, the Duchess of Polignac, in 1904. Decades later, it became a twenty-room château for guests, boasting a gourmet restaurant and luxurious rooms overlooking manicured gardens. One reviewer called it "a Versailles in miniature . . . the stuff of honeymoons and weekend-away liaisons."

Their flutes were served cold, the way he liked it. They tapped glasses before taking their first sips, very much in sync, like a couple. Chris was starting to sag after a busy day preceded by an early run, but Catherine seemed like the Energizer bunny; that is, if said rabbit wore a short slim dress showcasing killer legs, which he now knew could run like the wind.

Catherine set her glass down. "This is good champagne. Smart choice for the setting. The Pommerys built a lovely château."

"This place is pretty spectacular," he agreed, then couldn't resist adding, "I know who I want to bring here for the two-night stay I won in the auction."

She blushed slightly, which he found endearing. At that moment, their reverie was interrupted. Catherine looked startled when a well-dressed older couple entered the bar.

"The Tournelles are here," she said. "Patrick's parents."

The couple saw them and approached their table. The woman spoke first. "*Chérie*, we didn't know you were in France. Your parents didn't say anything about your coming."

"This was a last-minute business trip," Catherine said. She gave each of them a light hug, then gestured to Chris. "Let me present Christopher McDermott, president of Winston & Wright." Chris stood to shake their hands. She turned to him. "Valerie and Gérard Tournelle, family friends."

"Pleased to meet you," he said.

"Our sons will be *désolés* to miss you," Valerie said. "Patrick mentioned he saw you in New York, that you looked beautiful. *Il a raison.*"

"*Merci*," Catherine murmured.

"Dear, our guests have arrived," her husband interrupted. "Great to see you, Catherine. Hopefully, we can all get together for a family dinner your next trip."

"That would be lovely," she said, and they departed.

In answer to Chris's raised brow, she said, "They're close friends of my parents. Our families went on holidays together when I was growing up."

"I disagree with Patrick's insistence that all French champagnes are superior to sparkling from other countries," Chris said. "But I do agree with him on one point. You are ravishing." He reached out and clasped her hand under the table. He prayed he'd make it through the trip with his willpower intact.

Yves appeared at the door and waved to them. He was wearing a dark suit and red tie and carrying his briefcase. "Sorry I'm late," he said. "Meeting ran over."

"No problem," Chris said. "We were enjoying a glass of Pommery."

Yves smiled. "Ah, yes, fitting."

Chris settled the bar tab, and Yves led them to Les Crayères's gourmet restaurant, Le Parc: an elegant room, seating only sixty diners, with wood-paneled walls, high ceilings, and large windows facing the château garden.

"I'm glad you're able to experience this gastronomic delight on your trip," Yves said. "It's one of the top restaurants in Champagne."

"The bartender was telling us about the extensive champagne list." Catherine placed her handbag on the small table for that purpose next to her chair.

"*Oui*, six hundred labels," Yves said. "They claim it is unique in the world to have so many."

On cue, the sommelier approached with a twenty-six-page wine list. "Let's take a look," Yves said.

"I'm deferring to you on this selection," Chris said. "You're the expert."

Yves discussed a few points with the sommelier in French and chose a vintage 2004 Dom Ruinart. "This should complement our meal," he said. "It's a bottle I've been meaning to taste."

The waiter came to take their order. They decided on the chef's menu: four courses, one selection in each.

The sommelier reappeared with the champagne bottle, showed it to Yves, and expertly removed the cork—no loud popping noise, just a gentle *swish*. He poured a small amount for Yves to test. Yves sniffed and sipped and proclaimed, "*Excellente*."

After all three flutes were served, Chris held his aloft. "*Merci*, Yves, for your partnership and warm welcome on our trip. To the successful launch of our new prestige label."

"Hear, hear!" Yves said.

They lightly touched their glasses and sipped.

The meal began with a chef's sample of small bites, known as an *amuse-bouche*. Chris had never eaten artichoke mousse on a crisp before and loved it. The chef was known for showcasing locally sourced food, Yves told them.

"Did you get any feedback from the Relais & Châteaux members after the tasting?" Chris asked.

"No, they were playing it cool," Yves said. "I did learn a rumor. Philippe is considering combining the two categories into one." He frowned. "French against US, no holds barred."

Geez. That would pit us against Trianon. "I'm not keen on that," Chris said.

"Me either," Yves said. "Our prestige champagne is quite different."

"What makes some labels prestige versus regular champagne?" Catherine asked.

"Good question," Yves said. "Like a gourmet meal, the difference comes down to ingredients and expertise." He elaborated: Grapes grown in Champagne were rated on a scale up to one hundred. Only a fraction of the grapes received the top rating; those were delineated *Grands Crus*. "These Grands Crus grapes are used for prestige French champagne."

Their first courses were served. Yves adjusted his plate. "Also, vintage years come into play," he said. "During fall harvest, if the grape quality is exceptional, the winemaker declares a vintage year. When a bottle comes from a vintage year, all the wine blended for that champagne comes from that harvest year."

"For California sparkling," Chris chimed in, "obviously, we don't have Grands Crus grapes; it's a different soil and climate." Yves nodded. "But we do have vineyards that produce premium grapes, and some years' harvests are superior. In that instance, we blend those vintage grapes and age them longer in the bottle to create a California prestige sparkling."

Chris tucked into his wild sea bass with white asparagus. "This is sensational," he said after a few bites. He noticed Catherine was eating with gusto.

Over the rest of the meal, Chris and Yves discussed the financials they were preparing for Chamath and talked about Chris's negotiations with overseas wineries to buy their properties.

There were three presentations for dessert—a pre-dessert of white chocolate sorbet, Le Parc's signature dessert of lemon cream and caramel mousse, and finally, a plate of petit fours, followed by rich coffee. Chris opted for decaf and Catherine declined. Yves drank a straight espresso.

This was the most fun I've ever had on a business trip, Chris reflected on the cab ride back to the Trianon château. He could easily imagine traveling with Catherine as a couple, for business or pleasure.

When they got back to the suite, she seemed preoccupied and hurried off to bed.

Chris had a second wind and decided to jot down some notes on the trip while they were fresh in his mind. He changed into jeans and a sweatshirt and went to work in the sitting room.

A while later, he heard Catherine crying out. She'd left her door ajar, so he rapped lightly and pushed it open. She was whimpering in her sleep. "*Non, arrête.*" Her arms were hugging her body, and she was rocking back and forth.

Hating to see her vulnerable and upset, Chris crossed over to the bed, sat down, and stroked her arm. "It's all right, Cat. No one's hurting you. I'm here." He realized the sleeping pill had knocked her out. She wasn't waking up.

Chris held her until her whimpers subsided, and she curled into his arms. *This feels too good.* He stretched out on the bed and pulled the extra blanket over them both. He drifted off to sleep, while she lay tucked in his embrace, nestled into his body.

Chapter Sixteen

Paris—53 days to Celebration launch

"You seemed awfully comfortable in my arms last night." Chris couldn't resist teasing Catherine. They were in the back seat of a chauffeured car on their way to Paris. Catherine blushed for the second time that morning, the first being when she woke up and their bodies were entwined. She'd looked so startled.

"Do you remember what the nightmare was about?" Chris asked. "You were out cold."

She shook her head. "I've been talking in my sleep since I was a little girl. My parents traveled a lot and I had nightmares. Thanks for coming to my rescue."

"My pleasure." He draped his arm on the backrest, itching to drape it around her shoulders. "After all, James told me to take care of you." Chris considered himself a gentleman but didn't know how much longer he could deny his strong physical attraction to her.

"Good thing I speak French in my sleep."

He decided not to reveal that "No, Edward, No" was pretty clear in any language. *Wonder what caused that? Can't be good.*

They arrived in Paris, and the driver maneuvered through heavy traffic into roundabouts where cars entered from every direction and motorcycles honked incessantly. You had to know what you were doing. Chris knew a word for "traffic" in French was *circulation,* which he found amusing since traffic was practically at a standstill.

He sat back to enjoy the street scene—cafés with red awnings over sidewalk tables, ancient churches next to neighborhood parks, colorful florist shops presenting buckets that brimmed with long-stemmed roses, and smartly dressed Parisians striding purposefully to appointments.

The next two days their schedule was lighter, the only business engagement a dinner tonight with Philippe Pozzo, president of Relais & Châteaux. They were staying on in Paris tomorrow for a day of sightseeing before returning to New York on Sunday.

They pulled up to Hôtel Costes, on famed Rue Saint-Honoré, surrounded by name-brand designer boutiques. Normally, this hotel would be way beyond their budget, but Catherine knew the manager and secured a discount of 75 percent off. They followed the bellhop who carried their bags to the front desk, and Chris took in the almost bordello-like surroundings: dim lighting, gold-framed paintings, dark-hued walls. A far cry from the Hilton where Chris usually stayed.

Their two-bedroom suite wouldn't be ready until midafternoon, so Catherine suggested they grab lunch. "I have just the place. It's quintessentially Parisian," she said.

They walked down Rue Saint-Honoré, turned on Rue Royale, and arrived at Place de la Concorde. "This is the grandest intersection in Paris." Catherine pointed to the huge traffic convergence and explained the sights: the Tuileries Garden on the left, the wide Avenue des Champs-Élysées on the right, and the Seine River straight ahead.

They turned onto Rue de Rivoli, strolled past arcaded shops, and entered Angelina's Salon de Thé. "Vanessa and I used to come here almost daily when we were modeling," Catherine said.

Chris liked the art deco style: mirrored walls, gilded wood, very ornate and otherworldly. *Wouldn't find this in Napa.* The host led them to a small wooden table facing Rue de Rivoli, which gave them a good view of the brisk takeout business at Angelina's pastry counter by the front door.

A waitress in a black skirt and white apron took their order. Chris went all out. In addition to a club sandwich, he ordered a pot of Angelina's decadent hot chocolate and their signature dessert, the Mont Blanc: a concoction of French meringue, whipped cream, and chestnut vermicelli. Catherine showed more restraint; she chose quiche and salad with iced passion fruit tea.

While they sipped their drinks, Chris mulled over Yves's comment at dinner last night. If Relais & Châteaux decided to combine the contest into one mega-category—French champagne and California sparkling—they had all kinds of problems. Winston would need to compete against Trianon. More concerning, Chris feared the French members would side with a French company. This wasn't a blind tasting. They knew what bottle they were being served to judge.

"Tell me about your experience with Relais & Châteaux," he said. "Do you think they'd give our *cuvée* a fair chance, if we end up competing against French champagnes?"

"I don't know." Catherine chewed her lip. "The group is prominent in France where the association was founded. It started with lovely converted châteaux known for a warm welcome and gourmet cuisine." She looked pensive. "My mother prefers grand hotels, but I love the beauty and intimacy of their smaller properties."

Chris nodded, encouraging her to continue.

"They also have a category for gourmet restaurants," she said. "We're taking the grand tour—Les Crayères last night and Guy Savoy tonight."

"Assumed these places would be pretentious," he said, "but I'm finding they seem geared to comfort."

"That's right," Catherine said. "Each member must pass an anonymous inspection and embody the Five Cs—Courtesy, Charm, Character, Calm, and Cuisine."

She set her glass down. "Getting back to your question. I can't say for certain, but I think, yes, they'd select a French champagne over California sparkling."

If that happens, we're screwed. Chamath expects a "decent" showing, whatever that means. Competing against four other California sparkling wines in one category was doable. In a field of eleven, against French champagne . . . *not going to happen.*

Better not borrow trouble, as Maura would say. He wanted to enjoy the day with his lovely companion. "I can see you feel at home in Paris," he said. "I'm wondering why you left."

"It's a beautiful city—but not as many work opportunities as in the States. Turns out, I have a knack for event planning, fell into PR work."

"Is that what you plan to pursue?"

"Not exactly. I'm interested in resort management, bringing people together for special occasions and conferences."

"Sounds like a worthy goal," Chris said. "You know Winston will have new resorts to design and manage when we expand."

"Something to think about," she said.

Chris insisted Catherine try a taste of his Mont Blanc. She dipped her fork into the decadent dessert and took a small bite. He liked the intimacy of the gesture and their comfort with each other now, like a couple.

They strolled back to the hotel.

"I need to catch up on calls and emails," he said, wishing work didn't beckon. He'd rather sightsee with her. "What are your plans?"

"I'm going to run some errands."

"If you finish by five, why don't you swing by and show me the neighborhood?"

"Sounds like a plan."

Catherine texted Chris on her way back from a nearby salon, where she'd indulged in a quick makeover: a blow-dry and manicure. He was waiting in the hotel lobby, looking delectable. The guy knew how to wear faded jeans and a crisp white shirt. If he'd worn his cowboy boots, he'd be mistaken for a handsome country singer on tour in Paris.

Chris smiled broadly when she walked up, which gave her a warm glow. *Guess he approves of my super-straight blow-dry, swingy and chic.* Didn't look like it required thirty minutes of rigorous attention, but it did.

"You look good," Chris said. "Guessing one of your errands was at a hair salon."

"Guilty as charged," she said. "Ready for a walk in the neighborhood?"

"Sure, lead the way."

They walked to Rue de Castiglione which led to Place Vendôme. "This is one of the most iconic squares in Paris," Catherine said. "An example of neoclassical architecture—elegant townhouses, eighteenth-century stone facade, arcade on the ground floor. As we say in French, *une bonne adresse*."

They approached the center of the square. "You up for a history lesson?" she asked.

"Of course," Chris said.

She told him how Place Vendôme had been commissioned by King Louis XIV and modeled after another famous square, Place des Vosges in the Marais.

"I didn't realize it was that old," he said.

Catherine pointed to the large statue of Napoleon at the apex. "This tall column in the middle is a replica of one Napoleon had built to glorify his successful battles." She pulled out her phone to take a few photos. "Every French leader has sought to construct architectural projects, *grands travaux*, to leave their mark."

They passed the Ritz Hotel, liveried valet in front attending to well-heeled guests exiting luxury cars, and arrived at Cartier Joaillerie, her intended destination.

Catherine had fond memories of trips there as a child with her mother and nana, Countess Christine. While the adults admired the jewelry, she'd drunk hot chocolate and drawn panthers in all shapes and sizes with the colored pencils and paper they'd provided.

Entering still gave her a thrill. It was renovated to mimic an elegant salon: intimate seating on upholstered half-moon sofas, juxtaposed with fabric-covered walls. Contoured mirrors and original works of art, created to pay tribute to iconic Cartier designs, adorned the walls.

Catherine spotted the manager, Alain, who came over to greet her and gestured them to a sitting area. After offering coffee, he asked if she had anything special in mind. She pulled off her ring and held it out for him to inspect. "One of my diamonds is coming loose."

Alain placed the ring on a velvet cushion and took a look. It was a custom Cartier Trinity ring. The original Trinity ring, created in 1924, had three interlocking bands of gold: white, yellow, and rose. Catherine's ring had three gold bands, but they were fastened by a small gold panther head, set with emeralds and diamonds.

Alain turned the ring over and said, "There's an inscription, *confiance et rapport*."

"Trust and communication," Catherine translated for Chris. "Qualities my French great-grandfather felt were important in relationships."

Alain looked entranced with the ring. "*C'est magnifique*," he murmured.

"*Merci*. My great-grandfather, Count de Vogle, had this ring made for my great-grandmother. My grandmother passed it to me on my sixteenth birthday."

She started rubbing her ring finger with her thumb. The finger felt naked without the ring on it. She hated to part with it, even for twenty-four hours.

"A very special gift," Alain said. "We can have this reset and delivered to your hotel tomorrow. Why don't you look around for a few minutes while I fill out the paperwork."

Only too happy to check out Cartier's latest creations, Catherine tried on numerous earrings and bracelets and agreed with the saleslady that they did indeed look lovely on her. She was so focused on the task at hand, she didn't notice Chris pick up Alain's business card.

The stop at Cartier was an eye-opener for Chris, his first experience in a high-end luxury jewelry store. Catherine seemed in her element, which showed him how far apart their backgrounds were, but that wasn't going to stop him from pressing his pursuit of this magnificent creature.

By the time they got back to the hotel, they needed to get ready for their dinner at Guy Savoy, an acclaimed Michelin restaurant.

That meant formal attire, jackets required. Chris donned his dark-blue Armani suit with a lighter blue linen shirt and matching Ferragamo tie. *Should be able to keep up with her in these duds.*

When Catherine entered their shared sitting area, Chris tried to stop his jaw from dropping. She'd transformed her look from black jeans to a dark-blue low-cut, sleeveless evening dress that clung to her body and fell just above the knee. Her high stiletto heels brought her closer to his height and made her look even more leggy. "You look good enough to devour," he said.

"Sounds like you have an appetite," she quipped. "Guy will be pleased." She sized him up. "You don't look so bad yourself."

They grabbed a taxi in front of the hotel, and the cabbie took the same path they'd strolled in the morning. Now Chris understood Paris's moniker as the City of Light. Streetlights put off a golden hue. Well-placed spots highlighted architectural details on centuries-old buildings. Parks were lit up like fairylands. Lights at Place de la Concorde illuminated the sparkling fountains framing the ancient obelisk. The Eiffel Tower, visible in the distance, was ablaze with flashing blue light.

"Wow," Chris said. "The city looks beautiful at night." Catherine smiled and nodded.

Their driver crossed over the Seine River onto the Left Bank and pulled up to another neoclassical building with an elegant stone facade.

"This is La Monnaie de Paris, the government institute for producing coins," Catherine said. "Currently, this branch makes artistic coins and houses a museum."

Chris paid the driver and walked around to open Catherine's door. He was a gentleman—and it gave him a chance to admire her legs. He held out his hand to help her out.

"Guy's restaurant moved here a few years ago," Catherine continued. "Ideal location in Saint-Germain."

They stepped onto a rouge-colored carpet runner that led them up the stairs to the second floor, where they entered through a tall ornate door.

"*Alors, ma chérie, est-ce que je te manque*?" Chris knew the urbane man with the gregarious grin who approached them was Philippe; they had met briefly at the Plaza gala.

Catherine greeted him with a big smile and outstretched arms. "*Bien sûr Philippe. Je suis très contente de te voir.*" She gave Philippe a hug, and the men shook hands.

Chris looked around. The restaurant had a number of rooms facing the Seine River. They were seated at a table next to floor-to-ceiling windows overlooking Île de la Cité, the larger island. Notre-Dame stood majestically at its far end.

"A spectacular view," she said. "I love how Guy chose this historic building and designed the space for comfort and a sublime experience." The walls, painted a deep gray, held contemporary art. Tables, placed apart for privacy, were adorned with fine linen and sparkling china.

"Yes, the mark of a top restaurant—all your senses stimulated," Philippe said. "Not just delicious food but intimate seating, attractive decor."

After their champagne aperitif was poured, Philippe proposed a toast. "Congratulations, Chris, on luring Catherine to an American company. I always knew she'd be someone's secret weapon—with her style, upbringing, and good taste."

"Why not an American company?" Chris asked.

"Because she was raised in France, of course, and has many ties here."

The waiter arrived to discuss the specials of the day and recommended the "tasting menu" of thirteen small plates. Tempting as it sounded, Chris couldn't do justice to that much food. The others agreed, so they chose a few dishes à la carte and wine by the glass.

"So, tell me what you propose," Philippe said.

"We may have an alliance opportunity," Chris said. "Winston is planning to expand to Australia and South America by taking over existing wineries and converting them to sparkling. We could partner with Relais & Châteaux properties near those wineries for an enhanced visitor experience."

"Could be interesting," Philippe said. "You're talking about converting to sparkling wine in the traditional method?"

"Yes," Chris said. "The same method as champagne—second fermentation in the bottle, same grape varietals."

"That's something to consider," Philippe said. "I'll bring your proposal to our committee."

Their first plates arrived. Catherine had a colorful vegetable dish and Philippe chose skate with caviar. On the recommendation of the waiter, Chris started with Savoy's signature artichoke soup with truffle and parmesan, accompanied by brioche and truffle butter. Best soup he'd ever tasted.

The waiter came to the table and asked if the dishes were to their taste.

"*Merci, c'est bon*," Philippe said as he broke off a piece of bread.

During dinner Philippe and Catherine discussed news about old friends, and she got him to share his thoughts on issues that were of concern to members. He mentioned that reaching out to potential American visitors was a priority for French and Italian member properties. Chris filed that away for a possible future joint effort.

"Any feedback from the Plaza Blind Tasting?" Chris asked.

Philippe sighed. "We're receiving anonymous complaints that it was rigged, especially the final category of French against

California. Sour grapes, if you ask me." Philippe grinned. "Pun intended, as you say in American."

After a sip of wine, he continued. "Between us, I find it annoying. We're considering doubling down. Changing the contest to one category, French against California sparkling, instead of judging them separately."

Chris's heart fell. That would be disastrous.

Philippe gestured with his hands. "If so, we'd probably expand to two winners for that one category. We'd still cite how the others placed."

At least that would give us two chances. Still, an uphill battle among the five California sparkling and six French champagnes in contention.

"We're kicking it around and our board will meet next week to hammer it out," Philippe said.

Even though they declined dessert, they were offered a delectable plate of small pastries and gourmet chocolates. Catherine ordered a decaf espresso, as did Philippe. Chris passed on the coffee, but he did devour a few creamy chocolates.

When the time came, Chris made sure he was handed the tab. Philippe was their guest.

The hostess offered to call them a taxi. While they waited by the entrance, Guy Savoy came out from the kitchen. Still attired in his white chef's jacket and gray pants, Guy was a good-looking older Frenchman with close-cut gray hair and matching beard. He greeted Philippe with a slap on the back, gave Catherine a warm hug and asked about her parents, and warmly shook Chris's hand when Catherine made the introduction.

"I hope you enjoyed your meal," Guy said.

"*Oui, tout était parfait*," Catherine said.

"Thank you for a memorable evening," Chris added.

"My pleasure, you're welcome back any time," Guy said.

Philippe walked them down the stairs when their taxi arrived and saw them off with a wave. Traffic was minimal, and they were back at the hotel suite ten minutes later.

"How about a nightcap," Chris suggested, "to wind down and hopefully knock us out."

"Mmm, sounds good." Catherine kicked off her heels and curled up on the couch.

Chris poured small amounts of an aged Hennessy cognac into snifters the hotel had the foresight to provide. He knew he was playing with fire, and it wasn't coming from the amber liquid.

He joined her on the couch. They clinked glasses and sipped. Then he moved closer and pulled her toward him.

"Taking advantage of a woman in a vulnerable state," Catherine teased as she leaned into him.

"Whatever it takes," he whispered, and he wrapped his arm around her shoulders. "I know we made a deal to hold off until after the launch, but I'd like to make an amendment." He gazed into her eyes. "How about—what happens in Paris, stays in Paris."

She paused and tilted her head. "Okay, but let's take it slow."

That was all the permission he needed. He tipped her chin up while slowly lowering his lips to hers. She reached up and wrapped her arms around his neck, and he let out a low groan.

Her response sent him over the edge. While the kiss deepened, he massaged her back, moving his hands down to her waist and pulling her even closer in his embrace. She fit perfectly.

Chris was stunned at the intensity of his feelings for her. It ignited a simmering passion that threatened to engulf him.

Chapter Seventeen

Paris—52 Days to Celebration launch

Catherine admired Chris through the viewfinder of her camera as he gazed intently at *Le Penseur* near the entrance to the Rodin Museum. He'd insisted they make the most of their last day in France. Up and out early, he'd urged. Auguste Rodin's famous *Thinker*—seated, bent over in thought, chin resting on hand—depicted a perfect male nude. Chris seemed to hold his own in that department.

He melted her barriers more than any guy she'd ever known. Talk about sexy—last night they'd had a passionate make-out session after dinner, like teenagers who couldn't get enough of each other. She was in deep.

When she'd suggested a morning stroll on the Left Bank, Chris jumped at the idea and said he'd always wanted to visit the Rodin Museum.

"Have you two finished your conversation yet?" She put her camera away. Rodin's skill at making the bronze sculpture come alive was so strong one expected the figure to look up and acknowledge their presence.

"Let's go inside and learn more about Rodin's muse, Camille Claudel," Chris said. "She had quite an influence on him, from what I've read."

"And she was an artist in her own right," Catherine said.

"Very true."

Catherine had downloaded a guide to the museum on her phone. They read together about Claudel's relationship with Rodin. In her teens, she'd persuaded her parents to let her study with renowned sculptor Alfred Boucher. A couple of years later, Boucher sent her to Rodin's workshop. Rodin was forty-three at the time. Although there was a big age gap, sparks flew, and a torrid affair commenced that lasted ten years. Claudel was credited with being Rodin's muse and lover; their professional and personal lives became entwined.

They stepped into a room devoted to Claudel's work and viewed *Bust of Rodin,* which she created during their time together. She sculpted a more controversial piece, *The Mature Age*, depicting an older man and younger woman, after their affair ended. Reportedly, it angered Rodin when he saw it.

Chris grabbed Catherine's hand. "Let's think about their relationship in happier times." He led her into a room dominated by a larger-than-life marble rendering of a man and woman embracing; their nude bodies were breathtaking. Rodin worked on this first large-scale marble version of *The Kiss* (*Le Baiser*) when he and Claudel were lovers. Chris read aloud: "'The eroticism in the sculpture made it controversial for its time . . . was considered unsuitable for general display.'"

Catherine was mesmerized by Rodin's exquisite rendering of the male and female bodies and how absorbed they were in each other. She could relate. "Rodin is a master at portraying mood in his sculpture."

"Couldn't agree more," Chris said. He held out his arm. "Let's head outside. *The Kiss* gave me some ideas."

They walked hand in hand into the back garden where other Rodin sculptures were displayed. After glancing at the monumental *Burghers of Calais*, Chris pulled Catherine behind a nearby box hedge and into his embrace.

"Been wanting to do this all morning," he said, before lowering his lips to hers. Catherine melted into his arms and kissed him back. When they came up for air, he murmured in her ear, "So what's for lunch?"

"How about Mariage Frères tearoom. Up for a walk?"

He smiled. "I think I can handle whatever you throw at me."

Catherine enjoyed showing Chris *her* Paris. She led him down narrow streets lined with designer clothing boutiques, gourmet chocolate shops, and colorful neighborhood florists toward the Seine River. They arrived at Église Saint-Germain, a centuries-old church across from famed café Deux Magots. The area bustled with street performers and sidewalk artists working at their easels. Undeterred, Catherine continued farther into the Left Bank area of art galleries and chic home decor stores until they reached their destination.

The window display at Mariage Frères showcased their latest premium tea from far-flung exotic locales. They passed through the boutique on the ground floor to the stairs leading up to an intimate tearoom with windows facing the street, one wall taken up by shelves of metal canisters holding hundreds of varieties of fresh loose tea.

Over lunch they glanced at the photos Catherine had taken and marveled at all the sights they'd covered in a few short days: Champagne region highlights, Paris historical sights, lots of gourmet dining, and some world-class art thrown in.

As they walked out, Chris asked, "What's on the agenda for this afternoon?"

Catherine's eyes lit up. "Shopping, of course, though I'm on a tight budget. Mind if we stop at my favorite lingerie boutique?"

Chris draped his arm around her shoulders. "Far from it. Consider it my duty to assist in your choices—after you've modeled the contenders."

"Sounds like an athletic event," she said.

"Might very well be after you're done." Chris's arm around her tightened as they found a nearby cab.

"What's so special about this place?" he asked during their ride over to the Right Bank.

"Family tradition. My French grandma used to take me there. Herminie Cadolle is credited with inventing the bra in the late 1800s. She cut a corset in half and voilà." Catherine made a cutting gesture across her chest. "Every garment was handmade, called *sur mesure*, to fit each woman's body. Now much of their lingerie is ready to wear, prêt à porter."

"Don't they sell stuff like this in New York?"

She shook her head. "Not really. Cadolle is still run by Herminie's descendants—same high standards, top silk and black French lace, quality craftsmanship."

Ten minutes later, they walked into the boutique on Rue Cambon. A young saleslady welcomed them and directed Chris to a sitting area. Catherine perused ensembles hanging artfully on a partition while Chris was served coffee. Then the ladies got to work.

Catherine had a gift card from her French grandma; she hoped the amount would cover a matching bra and panty set and a silk cami. In her modeling days, she and Vanessa had worn camisoles as an undergarment for an extra layer to stay warm or as a sexy top under a fitted suit jacket, buttoned up partway with the lace peeking out.

The saleslady understood exactly what Catherine preferred and they had a good selection in Catherine's small size. Catherine playfully dangled a few lacy nothings in front of Chris on her way to the dressing room. She'd never been to a lingerie store with a man waiting nearby. She found it incredibly sexy. As she tried on each delicate bra and panties set, she envisioned modeling them for him.

Catherine knew she was playing with fire and had some trepidation. Chris had made his intentions crystal clear. No holds barred while they were in Paris. After the trip, they'd go back to their agreement to wait until the launch.

She was intensely attracted to him. Her quandary: She had difficulty letting her guard down when it came to intimacy. She might freeze up. That could nix this love affair before it started. She liked him so much she was willing to take the gamble.

There's something to this French stuff, Chris mused, while waiting on a velvet settee with a cup of strong coffee. The French didn't hide their appreciation for sexy lingerie. He'd passed more boutiques displaying lacy bras and barely-there undies on the streets of Paris than in any other city. Of course, the woman who'd captured his interest was all in on this enticing game.

In a dressing room nearby, she was in the process of selecting an ensemble that he hoped to get her to model for him in private, post haste. Fortunately, their hotel was a few blocks away.

Catherine emerged with her purchases in a decorative gold bag and looked pleased with the results. *This woman really does like to shop.*

They got back to the hotel in record time. Chris suggested a stop at the Costes bar for a late-afternoon cocktail. He managed to find a dark corner where they could sit side by side in a secluded leather booth with no distractions. After ordering the house specialty—a pitcher of Caipirinha, sugar cane, liquor, and lime—Chris reached for Catherine's hand.

I'm head over heels for this woman. He hoped she felt the same and it wasn't a dalliance on her part.

In any case, they were in the most romantic city in the world having a wonderful time together, and he wanted to take advantage of the opportunity to enjoy each other's company to the fullest—body on body. They were both adults. He felt they could handle his suggestion to give in to their temptations in Paris, then go back to their strictly-business relationship until the launch. It would make their coming together in June that much sweeter.

The high alcohol content in their cocktails was kicking in, giving Chris a nice buzz. He assumed Catherine was feeling it too because she kicked off her sandals and curled into him.

"Glad this place is dark," he murmured before leaning in for a kiss. Her response nearly set him over the edge. She kissed him back and wrapped her arms around his neck to pull him closer. She tasted of sugar and lime and was wearing that French perfume he liked. He reached down with his free hand to caress her thigh and realized she wore a skirt that buttoned up the front. *Uh oh.* While plunging his tongue into her sweet mouth, he unfastened the skirt up past her knee and placed his palm on her warm skin, massaging her upper thigh. Her quick intake of breath revealed her arousal. He needed to feel all of her.

"Let's take this upstairs." He threw back the rest of his cocktail. "We can order room service later."

They kissed while they waited for the check. They kissed riding in the elevator. They kissed while he opened the door to their suite. At last, they were alone. He dropped the keys and his jacket and pulled her back into his arms. "Let's try that again." She melted into him. His body responded like a randy teenager's.

"We need to get out of these clothes," he said.

"Good idea. Let me run into my room for one sec. Be right back."

Chris went to the bar cabinet and pulled out a bottle of champagne. He poured two flutes and took a sip from his. The glass almost slipped from his hand when Catherine reappeared.

"Thought I'd model my new purchases," she said.

"I can see that."

She wore a lacy bra with matching panties and high heels. That was it.

"Good thing you didn't model this at the store," he said. "I'd have dragged you into the dressing room and shocked the staff."

"Oh, we might try that some time," she teased.

This woman is full of surprises. He'd better hang on. "Let's take a closer look." He stalked over and ran his hands up her body, checking out the panties and bra as he caressed and kissed every inch on the way.

"I want to feel your body against mine," he said. He quickly pulled off his shirt and lay a throw on top of the couch before sitting down and pulling her onto his lap.

"This is better." He leaned over and removed her heels, admiring her delicate feet and the soft pink nail polish on her toes. "You have a thing for this color," he said. "Your new lingerie matches this color. Reminds me of rosé champagne."

"Matches my pale skin," she said.

"And what beautiful skin it is," he said as he wrapped her legs around his waist, pulled her against him—bare chest to bare chest—and kissed her deeply. She sighed and matched his kisses in intensity.

"I love your lips, but there are other enticing areas to explore." He wanted to bring her to his level of extreme arousal. He started by slowly planting warm, wet kisses around her lacy bra while using his large hands to knead her back. Then they glided around to her rib cage and started caressing the bottom of her breasts. Chris ran his tongue on the top of her breasts as he caressed them through the lacy fabric.

She made purring noises and ran her fingers through his hair.

"Yes, sweetheart, now you know how it feels." He reached between her breasts and unhooked the clasp between them. "I like this French invention."

He had to taste her, pushing the fabric aside, not waiting to pull off the straps. "Mmm," he groaned as he suckled one nipple while firmly caressing the other. "You are perfect. You have no idea what you do to me."

Yet he knew that was becoming evident, his manhood jutting up in his jeans. No doubts there.

Chris pulled her back to him for a hot, passionate kiss and wrapped his arms around her. "Don't think we're going to make it to the bed." He pulled a condom from his back pocket and threw it on the table.

"We have to get these panties off you," he moaned. He reached down and thanked god for French ingenuity. The skimpy fabric was held together by side ties that he quickly undid; the bikini fell against his lap, allowing him to feast his eyes. Catherine was breathtakingly beautiful, her hair tumbling down around her shoulders, her perfect body open to him, her arms reaching for him . . .

We may be up all night.

Chapter Eighteen

New York—50 days to Celebration launch

"Hey, sleepyhead." Vanessa knocked for the third time on her roommate's door. Catherine didn't want to come out of her dreamlike state. The loud knocking intruded on her reverie. She opened her eyes slowly, trying to separate fact from fiction. Was the trip to France with Chris a dream? No. Did they really make unbelievable love? Yes. Definitely the most intense experience she'd ever had on the first night. Double yes.

"It's past nine on a beautiful morning," Vanessa persisted. "Let's run over to Sant Ambroeus. Want to hear all about your trip."

"Okay," Catherine called out. "Let me take a quick bath and wake up my weary body." She wasn't referring to the seven-hour flight back yesterday. Her marathon lovemaking session with Chris had introduced her to muscles she didn't know existed. Mineral salts should rejuvenate her.

It felt decadent to be home on a Monday morning, not at the office bright and early. Chris had made the executive decision they'd earned a work-from-home day to recover from the trip. Thank goodness.

An hour later, revived by her mocha cappuccino, Catherine faced her friend across a small bistro table at their neighborhood hangout.

"*D'accord*, time to start dishing," Vanessa prompted. "Been waitin' patiently, now I'm dying of curiosity."

Catherine took her time, cradling the warm mug in both hands. *Where to start.* "It was pretty incredible. I underestimated my attraction to Chris McDermott, especially in close quarters."

"Thought so." Vanessa looked smug.

"He was so fun to be with. Not like a stuffy business-type at all. We took a run through the vineyards, spent a day sightseeing in Paris. He even tagged along when I went to Cadolle"—Vanessa's eyebrows shot up—"and Mariage Frères."

Catherine pulled a neatly wrapped gift from her purse and handed it to Vanessa. "A thank you for pet-sitting Soleil while I was gone."

"Yum, French Breakfast black tea, my fave. At least I know how to properly brew loose leaf tea. Haven't mastered the espresso machine yet." Vanessa opened the lid to sniff the fragrant tea.

Across town, the man in question finished a steaming shower. He'd risen early for a long run in Central Park. Chris felt exhilarated. He couldn't believe what a great trip he'd had with Catherine.

The phone rang. Thinking it was her, he made a mad, dripping dash and grabbed it on the third ring. "Bonjour," he answered in his deepest, sexiest voice.

"Good morning, son."

Chris paused to catch a breath. "Oh, hi Dad."

"Sounds like you were expecting a woman. Sorry to disappoint."

"Just practicing my French," Chris said.

"Wasn't that attractive woman from work traveling with you? How did it go?"

"Gee, Dad," Chris said. "Why don't you cut right to the chase?"

"It's about time one of you boys settled down. You're the eldest. You need to set an example for your younger—"

Chris cut him off midstream, sensing a lecture coming on. "You'll be happy to hear I'm making progress."

"Good. I like her. Don't blow it, son. She's probably used to being courted in grand style."

"You can say that again." Chris pulled the towel tighter around his waist.

"How did he do in France?" Vanessa asked. "He strikes me as so all-American."

"He's not like guys I'm used to—sophisticated Europeans—he's more like a cleaned-up cowboy, honorable, wanted to be clear about his intentions. It was refreshing. He's genuinely nice and smart."

"Not bad on the eyes either. Okay, I want the gory details."

Catherine blushed and took a sip of her cappuccino.

"That good, huh?"

"Mmm, better. You know it's hard for me to relax with a guy. Chris melts my barriers," she admitted. "We agreed Paris was a one-time occurrence until the launch. Now it's back to business as usual."

"Can you compartmentalize like that?"

"I hope so."

"So how serious are you two about each other?" Chris's father asked.

"I'm crazy about her, Dad. Seems she feels the same way,

though we're from different backgrounds. Guess that McDermott charm kicked in."

"Glad to hear you two hit it off."

"She's warm and feminine, full of surprises." Chris paused. "I can't remember feeling this way before. It's a little scary."

"I'm happy for you, son. Just take your time getting to know each other." His dad cleared his throat. "I'll let you get to your day. See you in a few weeks. Maybe I can join you and your lady for dinner."

Chris liked the sound of that. "I'll have a driver pick you up at JFK."

"Did you get into any of your family drama?" Vanessa asked.

"Not yet." Catherine shook her head. "Too soon for that. He did handle one incident like a pro."

Vanessa looked concerned.

"I had a nightmare," Catherine said, "and he comforted me." She didn't reveal that he'd climbed into bed and held her all night. That was their private affair.

"Eventually, if things get serious, you'll have to confide in him," Vanessa said. "I know that's hard for you."

Catherine dipped the last piece of almond biscotti in her mug to capture the leftover chocolate on the bottom. "Let's head back. I've got to prepare a trip report for James."

"Be careful until you're sure he's the real deal," Vanessa said.

"You're right." Catherine stood up. "As we've learned the hard way, men can be annoyingly unpredictable."

James called a meeting first thing Tuesday morning for Chris and Catherine to give him a debrief on their trip. Chris arrived ten minutes early and noticed James had a copy of *New York News* displayed on his desk.

"Have you seen this?" James thumped the paper with his hand.

"No, what's up?" Chris said.

"Take a look."

Chris sat down and skimmed the page James handed him. Jacqueline Collart's column "All About Wine" claimed there were irregularities at the Plaza Blind Tasting. Chris read out loud: "'Numerous sources claim the results of the Plaza Blind Tasting are suspect. Some of the winners appear to have benefited from insider help.'" No details, just innuendo.

"This is wacko," Chris said. "She's just throwing accusations around."

"Read on to the last section," James said.

As an example, Collart cited Winston & Wright's California sparkling entry, saying it had been disgorged three months earlier when it was common practice to allow six months for the wine to rest.

"She's implying our wine was not up to par!" Chris said.

"How would she know when our bottles were disgorged?" James said. "We didn't reveal that."

"I have no idea. We need to get to the bottom of this. Chamath will not be happy." Chris was livid.

Catherine walked in, and Chris had to tamp down the urge to jump up and pull out her chair. She looked stunning in a light-blue skirt with a tight jacket, hair worn loose around her shoulders.

"Good to see you, Catherine," James said.

She took the chair next to Chris and put her files down.

"This meeting was to go over your trip, but first I want to address this column."

"I've seen it," Catherine said. "I thought we were getting a positive write-up from her. This is a total surprise."

"Do you know her?" James said.

"Not well. We have mutual acquaintances in Paris. She usually has an agenda, have no idea what in this case. I'll try back channels—"

"Good idea," James interrupted.

"Saw her dancing with Patrick Tournelle at the gala," Chris said. "He complained about the tasting results. Wouldn't be surprised if he put her up to it."

"Wherever it's coming from, I want to nip it in the bud," James said. "Chamath specifically stipulated no drama." He leaned forward in his chair. "Let's have our attorney contact *Decanter* and offer to help suss this out."

"Will do," Chris said.

The rest of the meeting, Chris and Catherine updated James on their work in France. Chris shared Philippe Pozzo's revelation that Relais & Châteaux might combine their contest into one big category: French versus Californian.

"That's not good news," James said. "Let's hope that doesn't happen."

As they wrapped up, James asked Catherine to stay back.

Catherine was glad to have an opportunity to speak to James privately. In front of Chris, she'd downplayed Patrick's possible involvement in Jacqui's column. No need to poke the bear. In reality, she knew Patrick and Jacqueline were close friends.

Since her breakfast meeting with James, Catherine had been torn about sharing confidential information she'd received from Patrick. But Jacqui's column was going too far. They were playing dirty. Her parents would be apoplectic if they learned she'd taken sides against their best friends. But she had a new allegiance now—to Chris McDermott. He'd won her over—heart and body—and that's where her loyalties lay.

She took a sip of water. "I didn't want to discuss this in front of Chris," Catherine said. "Patrick could be behind Jacqueline's column. They're close friends."

"That's why I asked you to stay," James said. "I wondered if you'd picked up anything about the Tournelles."

"I spoke with Patrick recently." She decided to leave out the circumstances: what Patrick had assumed was a cozy dinner among friends. "He said Tournelle has big expansion plans overseas and they've lined up a financial backer. I got the impression the money is contingent on the expansion."

James finished her thought. "And maybe he sees our expansion as some kind of threat. Thank you for sharing this with me. Let me know if you learn anything else."

Catherine sincerely hoped that would be it. She didn't want to go out on a limb any more than she already had.

She returned to her office. Her top priority was landing a national hit for April to replace the coverage Jacqui had promised her. In two short weeks.

Chapter Nineteen

New York—47 days to Celebration launch

"You look awfully chipper this early on a cold Friday morning," Will said, greeting Chris at the entrance to the racquet club. "Wonder if a certain green-eyed blonde is heating things up."

"Yeah, Catherine and I are unofficially an item." Chris ran a hand through his hair. "We're waiting until after the launch to see each other. She reports to me, don't want to jeopardize her job."

"Got the impression something was up when you made a big show of outbidding us other chaps at the auction." Will slapped him on the back. "Could have given me a heads-up—saved yourself some money."

"Was still figuring it out at that point." Chris grabbed his gear. "Let's hit some balls."

Chris needed the exercise to work out stress from pressures at the office. The "All About Wine" hit piece was one big headache. Then Relais & Châteaux announced they were combining their contest into one mega-category, making Winston compete against top French champagnes for two coveted slots.

The guys started playing, and Chris focused on his strokes. Will was a tough competitor—in it to win it, he liked to say. Chris tried to keep his head in the game.

During a water break, Will asked about the launch prep. Checking to make sure they weren't being overheard, Chris filled him in.

"Aside from the obvious hurdles we know about, I'm feeling paranoid someone is trying to sabotage us." Chris ticked off on his fingers: bottle top snafu at Spago, a moldy cork at the Relais & Châteaux tasting in Épernay, and the unfounded Collart column.

"That's a lot of coincidences," Will said. "We need to be vigilant."

Forty-five minutes later, Will had given Chris a sound beating. Not surprising. Chris was preoccupied and it affected his game. On their way to the showers, they saw John Warner getting ready to play and gave him a wave.

Chris had an idea. John Warner was known for his disparagement of certain New York newspapers' tabloid mentality. "When our attorney is done gathering evidence to rebut the 'All About Wine' column, we'll be looking for a publication to run it," he said. "*Warner Business* would be a perfect fit for the rebuttal."

"Good idea," Will said. "I'll speak to him. I'm sure John will be interested."

"Great. I'll let Joel know."

"When do you leave for South America?" Will asked.

"Tomorrow."

"That soon? You are jet-setting around. By the way," Will said as they parted, "make sure to let James know what is going on with you and Catherine, even if it's on hold for now."

"We're being circumspect, keeping it professional," Chris said. "So far, no one has a clue."

Although Chris thought their secret was safe, people in the office were starting to gossip. Across the street, Sean arrived early at the Seagram Building and stopped by Delores's desk on the way to his office.

"Is something going on between Chris and Catherine?" he asked. "They're acting differently around each other since the Paris trip."

"You're just catching on?" Delores shuffled some papers. "I think this has been brewing for a while."

"What about all the lecturing on not fraternizing? Or don't the rules apply to him?"

"She must have him bamboozled," Delores said. "I can't believe his change of heart from when he hired her."

"Me either." Sean walked away in a huff.

Friday ladies' lunch was one of Catherine's favorite pastimes. On this occasion, she was meeting Sue Hamilton at Tiffany on Fifth Avenue.

Ever since the Blue Box Café opened, women flocked to the flagship jewelry store in homage to the Audrey Hepburn movie *Breakfast at Tiffany's*. Hepburn, as Holly Golightly, was the epitome of cool—in her sleek black Givenchy dress, pearls, and black opera gloves—munching on a Danish pastry while gazing at the dazzling jewelry displays.

Catherine arrived a half hour early. Though ostensibly a business lunch, if she carved out time to admire the latest glittery gems beforehand, that was clever multitasking on her part.

She started daydreaming about Chris putting a ring on another finger. *So this is what it means when people say you'll fall in love when you least expect it.* Chris seduced her in every way. They'd spent six days together nonstop. She'd enjoyed every moment, especially their last night of intense lovemaking in Paris. She was going to miss him the next two weeks. When he returned from South America, she'd be in Napa.

Sue waved and they met at the café entrance. "This is my treat," Sue said. "I wanted to thank you for getting me the documentary gig. If it hadn't been for my *Newsline* piece on Winston, they wouldn't have considered me for the narration."

The hostess recognized Sue and seated them immediately. In keeping with its name, the café featured the patented "Tiffany Blue" color in the decor and on the walls, as if each guest was a jewel inside a large blue Tiffany box.

The server placed their iced teas on the table. "Saw that snarky piece in Jacqui's column," Sue said. "Can't imagine why she'd go out on a limb like that. What's your take?"

"Off the record?" Catherine said. Sue was a friend, but she was also a reporter.

"Sure. Sounds like someone's sour grapes. I'm not getting into that."

"The brass at Winston are taking it seriously, viewing it as a personal attack." She twisted her ring. "I'm kind of feeling the same way. Jacqui led me to believe she'd give Winston a good write-up. I was counting on it."

Catherine speared a bite of her salmon salad with mango and redirected the conversation. "This is good. Haven't been here before. Glad you suggested it."

"One of my go-to places when I'm in New York. Can't beat a lovely lunch surrounded by mouthwatering jewels."

Since this was technically a business lunch, Catherine figured she'd better cover the shoot details. The documentary crew was slated to film Napa sparkling wineries week after next.

Catherine would be there and suggested they film at Winston that Wednesday, so she could help scout visuals and coordinate with Tom.

Sue pulled out her phone to check the schedule and inked it in. "If you have time, we can go over the gala footage then, too."

"Good idea," Catherine said. "Let's do that Wednesday afternoon." She had assured all the gala hosts they'd have the right of refusal on any untoward episodes caught on camera, so that was a priority.

"Speaking of the gala," Sue said, "you and Chris seemed pretty cozy on the dance floor. Anything going on there?" She took a forkful of her Waldorf salad.

"You mean romantically?" Catherine took a sip of tea to stall. *Now she asks me.* She and Chris weren't going public yet, so she couldn't reveal their status. "No time for that these days, working twenty-four-seven until the launch in Bordeaux."

Catherine asked about Sue's younger sister, Emma, and they caught up on news about the other friends in Les Femmes. Sue wasn't technically a member of the girls' club, but she was privy to their escapades.

Their espressos with chocolate wafers were placed on the table. Sue added a cube of sugar and stirred. "Been meaning to ask you"—she looked hesitant—"Sean has called a few times asking me out. He seemed to be with Vanessa at the gala, but he said that was casual, not exclusive. Do you know what their situation is?"

Catherine was stunned. She didn't want to answer until she cleared it with her friend. "I'm not sure. Let me look into it."

"Thanks, appreciate it."

To lighten up the situation, Catherine said, "Maybe he's angling to get on your 'Most Eligible Bachelors' list." Sue laughed and shook her head.

After signing the receipt, Sue picked up her credit card from the blue leather billfold. "Looks like this new job fits you well," she said. "Let's get together in Bordeaux after Vinexpo."

"I'd like that."

They walked out of the café arm in arm.

"Can't believe Sean thought he'd get away with it," Vanessa said. "It's so brazen. He knows we're all friends."

"Men are clueless." Catherine touched her friend's arm in comfort. "You deserve better." They were having Saturday breakfast at Sant Ambroeus to cheer Vanessa up.

Immediately after leaving Tiffany, Catherine had called Vanessa and relayed Sue's message. As it so happened, Vanessa had a drinks date with Sean a few hours later. It had been a disaster. Vanessa replayed the whole scenario to Catherine when she returned home that night.

Once confronted, Sean had said, "Who told you that?" Things went downhill from there. He'd started ranting about Catherine, claimed she cooked it up to meddle. Then he'd said, "What's the big deal if we're not exclusive?" He even went so far as to say he'd heard Catherine was throwing herself at Chris. At that point, Vanessa told him she was out, grabbed her purse, and left. His attempt at deflection and preoccupation with Catherine surprised both women.

Vanessa took a bite of her buttermilk pancake—topped with maple syrup, whipped cream, and fresh blueberries—and sighed. "Comfort food. Just what I need. Can't believe he'd ask for exclusivity in the beginning then say later it's no big deal. That's an asshole move."

Catherine felt for her friend. If a similar betrayal happened to her, she'd probably go to bed for a week. This reminder of the precariousness of relationships scared her.

"You're handling this admirably," Catherine said.

"Could be I'm in a state of shock." Vanessa shrugged. "Maybe I'll have a delayed reaction and feel like cutting off some of his body parts later."

"He deserves nothing less." Catherine nibbled on her toast. "What should I tell Sue?"

"Warn her," Vanessa said, "and tell her she's encouraged to rake him over the coals."

"Will do." Catherine didn't know how she was going to face Sean at the office. She wasn't that good an actress. Fortunately, he was leaving on a sales trip, and she'd be in Napa the week after that. She took a last sip of her coffee and raised her arm for the check. This morning called for treating her friend, even if she was flat broke.

"Want to head over to the Frick for some uplifting art?" she said.

"Sure." Vanessa stood up and swiveled her back in a dancer's stretch. "You're doing a good job of keeping me distracted and occupied."

One of the best things about New York—and Paris—was the world-class culture within walking distance. The Frick Collection, a few blocks over near Fifth Avenue and Central Park, was their preferred museum to spend a couple hours in the company of timeless paintings and sculpture.

The friends had both studied European art at Our Lady of Grace and developed an appreciation for the nuances in portraits and landscapes by artists like Vermeer and Turner; those artists' paintings were also favorites of Henry Clay Frick, who purchased them for his collection.

Catherine pointed to a sign by the entrance announcing that Jean-Honoré Fragonard's *The Progress of Love* gallery had reopened after renovation. "Are you up for Fragonard's take on love? Or is it too soon?"

"On the contrary. Maybe the idealized version will be inspiring. We can compare it to your love story with Chris," Vanessa teased.

"That's a stretch, but I haven't seen these paintings in years. Curious to check it out."

Frick had spent part of his fortune building the Fragonard Room to house the series, recreating the paintings' Rococo style down to the furnishings. Catherine and Vanessa read the descriptions together. The placards described four wall-size paintings Fragonard created for Madame du Barry, mistress of King Louis XV, that followed two lovers on their romantic path. The paintings depict the couple's evolution from *The Pursuit* (the man offers the lady a rose in a symbol of courtship), *The Meeting* (the couple in a garden tryst), *The Lover Crowned* (the woman places a floral wreath on her lover's head), and *The Love Letters* (the couple reminisces through their love letters).

Moved by Fragonard's skill with a paintbrush, Catherine felt the emotion and excitement of the young woman pursued by an ardent lover. She could relate. The final depiction of the older couple reminiscing about their courtship over love letters was the happy ending she hoped for—friendship, love, and fidelity—the statue of *Amitié* signifying friendship and a dog representing fidelity.

"That should have been depressing, but I found it uplifting," Vanessa said. "That perfect love is out there waiting . . ."

"And you deserve it." Catherine looped her arm through her friend's as they walked into the Frick courtyard. "We'll be on the lookout for your perfect guy—when the time is right."

"Do you think that might be you and Chris?" Vanessa asked.

Catherine hoped so but didn't want to admit how hard she'd fallen, even to Vanessa. "It's early, but I'm crazy about him. Will miss seeing him next week, that's for sure." She put her sunglasses on. "At least I'll have time to work on landing my national media hit for this month. And we can spend time together."

"Sounds like a plan," Vanessa said.

Chapter Twenty

New York—35 days to Celebration launch

Tuesday morning, Chris faced the bathroom mirror and ran the electric razor over his face. His chin felt scruffy and required attention. He hadn't bothered to shave yesterday before flying back to New York from Rio de Janeiro. That task completed, he pulled on his Stanford t-shirt. It still smelled of Catherine's perfume. She'd worn it as a nightshirt in Paris; it had looked adorable on her.

This was the first business trip where he'd missed being away from the office. He liked seeing Catherine on a regular basis, guessing what delectable outfit she'd wear that day, enjoying her contributions and occasional surprises in meetings, and imagining their life as a couple. He had it bad.

On the way to the office, Chris's phone started blowing up. A new article by wine columnist Ron Parker appeared on the *Wall Street Journal* website announcing a scoop: SEC investigating Winston & Wright on an insider tip that company showed potential investors inflated numbers. Comments on the site responding to the article called out the anonymous source and questioned the motive, but the damage was done. Chris swore loudly.

He got off the elevator and headed straight for James's corner office. James's partner, Alan, and their attorney, Joel Levine, had already arrived and were helping themselves to coffee on a silver tray on the side table.

"Glad you're back," James said to Chris. "It's all hands on deck. We need to find the source of these attacks. Someone is out to get us."

The men took their seats. "Obviously, someone has a beef, and they're playing hardball," James said. "Joel, please take us through how this kind of investigation could even be triggered."

Joel set down his coffee cup. "Normally, the Securities and Exchange Commission regulates public companies. On rare occasions, they investigate what private companies are telling potential investors"—he paused and regarded the men—"if prompted by a complaint. Otherwise, they don't get involved."

James stated the obvious. "This is not good." Then, "Joel, please contact the SEC immediately to see if that claim is even accurate. We also need to prepare a press statement to explain this is a bunch of hogwash." James chopped the air with his hand. "The million-dollar question is, who would submit a phony tip to the SEC? They'd require some knowledge of our financials."

Racking his brain to discern a motive, Chris supposed it was someone trying to sabotage the pending venture capital deal with Chamath.

"I'm guessing someone who has an ax to grind," Chris said. "Think we should reach out to all current investors and reassure them." He knew there were grumblings due to the company's commitment to overseas expansion. Chamath's cash infusion would alter everyone's ownership percentage.

"Good idea," James agreed. "It's us three, Trianon, and a half-dozen smaller investors, some of whom are on the board."

"Can't imagine there's an issue with that latter group, but we should look into it," Alan said. "They receive financial statements."

"It could be someone who has access to the financials who is not an investor," Joel reminded them. "That widens the pool considerably."

"We need to get to the bottom of this," James said. "We've always been aboveboard in our accounting, which should make it easy to disprove."

"We have another complication," Chris said. "When I met with the winery in Chile, they told me Tournelle made a competitive offer to buy them, undercutting our deal."

The other three men erupted in groans. Chris held up his hand to continue. "Luckily, it smelled fishy to them—the timing with our deal—and they said some of the paperwork Tournelle presented didn't add up. So they didn't even consider it."

"Their name keeps coming up," James said. "Our partners at Trianon said they play dirty. We must assume Tournelle is a direct competitor and act accordingly." He gave Joel a meaningful glance, then turned to Chris. "What about Chamath?"

"He's in SF," Chris said. "We're going to speak in an hour. I wanted to map out our response before I filled him in."

"Okay." James leaned back in his chair. "In the meantime, see if you can work out our legal avenues with Joel and prepare a press statement."

Chris nodded. "I'll give Chamath a heads-up on the press statement before we release it to keep him in the loop."

"Any other ideas?" James asked the group.

"I spoke to Will," Chris said. "He's reaching out to John Warner to find out if the same source who gave the story to the *Wall Street Journal* approached anyone at *Warner Business.* Maybe Warner felt the story didn't have legs and could clue us in, on background of course." Chris took a gulp of his black coffee. Now that they had a game plan, his nerves were starting to calm down.

"In light of what's going on, I'm moving up my trip to France," James said. "Leaving tonight. I want to meet with our partners at Trianon right away to assuage any misgivings they may be having. A quick turnaround. Two days in Épernay and back on Friday."

The men stood up to adjourn. Chris pulled out his phone before Joel turned to him. "I'll come by your office in a few minutes, after I've reached the SEC," Joel said.

Chris had hoped to reach Catherine in Napa this morning. He missed hearing her voice. He'd been so tied up with travel they hadn't connected. Now he'd have to wait.

Coffee in hand, Catherine walked into the Winston Resort office suite at 8:30 a.m., surprised to find people in at that hour. Tom waved her into his office and filled her in on the *Wall Street Journal* story.

Wonder who's behind this. Chris must be livid. She felt for him.

"Do you have any contacts there?" he asked. "We're trying to determine who the source is."

"Sorry." Catherine shook her head. "I haven't worked with business press."

"No problem," Tom said. "We've got the attorneys delving into it."

Catherine went to work at her guest cubicle near the receptionist. She set down her coffee, pulled out her laptop, and checked her schedule. Sue Hamilton was bringing the documentary crew over tomorrow morning. Looked like the weather was cooperating, so they could film in the vineyards.

Catherine started making calls. She still needed to secure a national placement by the end of the month. She didn't want Chris to think she was slacking off since they became involved.

Two hours later, Catherine called Claire to check in. "How's it going?"

"Crazy, due to that *Wall Street Journal* article. People coming and going from James's office looking anxious," Claire said. "James moved up his trip to France and is leaving tonight."

"Can't imagine why this is happening." Catherine tapped her pen on the desk. She knew James and Chris would be beside themselves. "Hope they get to the bottom of it soon."

The women went over pending items for the mid-June launch of Celebration at the resort. "Don't forget, I'm off Thursday and Friday," Claire reminded her. "I'm taking a four-day trip with my sister."

"Have fun. I'll send you the final version of my report, so you can turn it in before you leave." Catherine glanced at her watch. "I've got to scoot. I'm meeting Ken Barnett in a half hour."

Twenty minutes later, Catherine pulled her rental car into a parking space in front of Bistro Jeanty in nearby Yountville. Weekday traffic was minimal. Weekends were another story, when Napa's appeal as a major tourist destination clogged the highways.

Bistro Jeanty was bustling with the chic lunch crowd who frequented the popular spot. Acclaimed chef Philippe Jeanty had founded the bistro years ago when Yountville was a sleepy town. His French sensibility informed the hearty cuisine and Provençal decor: a fireplace in one corner, mustard-colored walls, bistro chairs at linen-draped tables, and a well-stocked bar along the back wall.

Ken arrived wearing his signature bow tie, a sandy-tan color that matched his slacks.

"You're looking very dapper." Catherine gave him air kisses. "Glad we could meet."

"I brought my appetite"—he paused—"for the food and the gossip." He raised his eyebrows.

They were seated and shown the specials of the day on a chalkboard. After they ordered, Ken began. "So, what do you know about the *Wall Street Journal* exposé?"

"Not a thing, have no contacts there." Catherine waved her hand for emphasis. "Assume this whole conversation is off the record."

"Sure."

"I wouldn't call it an exposé," she said. "I'd call it a hit piece, with no basis in fact."

Before she became more wound up, they were interrupted by a server who brought their flutes of champagne. They'd each ordered a glass of Schramsberg Blanc de Blancs. Bistro Jeanty's extensive wine list went on for pages and had a good selection of quality wines by the glass.

"Looks like someone's got it in for your company," Ken said. "First 'All About Wine' and now this."

"What's your take on Jacqui's piece about the Plaza Blind Tasting?" Catherine lifted her flute and took a sip.

"All I can say is my bosses at *Wine Spectator* were glad we didn't host the tasting. It's *Decanter's* mess to deal with." Ken passed Catherine the breadbasket before breaking off a piece of baguette for himself. "I do have one morsel for you." He finished a bite of bread. "Turns out, Jacqui has been spending time in France. Rumor has it she's angling for a job in the industry."

Catherine put her glass down. "I know she likes to stir stuff up, guessing she slammed the tasting to promote someone else's agenda. It's beyond my pay grade to figure out her financial motive. I can't even work out my own budget."

"I hear you," Ken said with a laugh. "I'm always catching heck from our accounting for my sloppy expense reports."

Their plates were served, piping hot and smelling delicious. Catherine chose the sole meunière with mashed potatoes and Ken opted for the coq au vin. They clicked their glasses in a silent toast.

The main reason Catherine had invited Ken to lunch was to discuss his feature profile on Winston, set to run in *Wine Spectator* in late June. Between bites, she reiterated talking points she'd sent earlier. In view of the *Wall Street Journal* bombshell this morning, she voiced her concern about its effect on his story. Ken assured her everything was on track for a positive piece, assuming the recent negative stories were sorted out. She fervently wished that would be the case.

While they were finishing after-lunch espressos, Patrick Tournelle entered the bistro. He spotted Catherine and walked over.

"*Bonjour ma chérie.*" He took a long appraising look. "I didn't know you were in town." Catherine noticed Ken wincing. *Patrick sure tends to annoy some guys.*

"You know Ken Barnett from *Wine Spectator*," Catherine said.

"Yes, hello Ken," Patrick said. "I'm meeting my distributor here for a late lunch." He looked around. "He's not here yet." He addressed Catherine: "You've been busy, glad to catch you. Let's meet for dinner tonight."

Catherine hesitated. She'd planned to work through the evening. However, James had tasked her with investigating Tournelle's plans.

"*D'accord. Dîner ce soir,*" she said. "Can we make it early? I'm still on New York time."

"How about six thirty at the Winston Resort?"

"*Oui, à bientôt*," Catherine answered.

After Patrick walked away, Ken leaned in toward her. "Sure you're not playing with fire? I was at that New York gala when Patrick and Chris were bidding against each other . . ."—he grinned—"and I don't think it was just for the cause."

Little did Ken know that Chris had won the battle for her heart. Still, Chris wouldn't be happy to learn she was "consorting with the enemy" by having dinner with Patrick. She hoped he didn't find out. Chris had not been clued in that James directed her to learn Patrick's agenda. She had a sinking feeling Patrick was involved in the smear campaign against Winston.

Catherine signaled the waiter for their bill. This was a Winston expense.

When Catherine returned to the resort, she had a pile of messages to plow through. The pastry chef, Anna, stopped by the office and asked if she had a minute to talk. Catherine assumed it was to go over one of the recipes she'd given her.

Anna held her hands together, twisting them back and forth, and blurted out that her boyfriend, Javier, was worried about getting fired, because a few bottles were missing. He swore to Anna that it wasn't him; he did spot Robert by the bottling area, where he had no reason to be. *Figures*, Catherine thought. She could see Robert pilfering bottles and blaming it on the workers. What a heel. She assured Anna she'd look into it.

Time flew by, and Catherine dashed upstairs to get ready for dinner.

After executing one of her quick-change feats, Catherine returned to the resort lobby and walked into Étoile, the fine-dining restaurant. She waved to Tom and Doug, who were also having an early dinner, and took a stool at the bar counter to wait for Patrick. He joined her a few minutes later, which prompted questioning stares from Tom and Doug.

"You're causing a stir," she teased Patrick as he leaned in for a peck on both cheeks.

"I hope so," he said. "I'm taking a beautiful woman to dinner."

Oh boy, she groaned to herself, *this evening is getting more complicated by the moment*. They were seated on the opposite side of the restaurant from Tom and Doug, next to long windows facing the terrace. Catherine worried the romantic ambiance might give Patrick the wrong idea. Votive candles cast a warm glow on linen-draped tables and strategically placed potted palms offered privacy.

Like most Napa restaurants, Étoile had a well-curated list of wines by the glass. Catherine needed to keep her wits about her, so only one glass for her tonight. Their waiter came over and explained the specials. She ordered the catch of the day, Tomales Bay mussels with vermicelli pasta, and a glass of Mondavi pinot grigio, and Patrick chose the filet mignon and a Bordeaux wine she didn't recognize.

"A champagne aperitif, *chérie*?" he asked.

"*Merci*, not tonight. Need to wrap up a few things after," Catherine said.

"*Mon dieu*, they're working you too hard." He frowned. "American companies put too much emphasis on long hours." He shook his head. "And only two weeks' vacation. Uncivilized. As you know, in France we have at least four weeks."

She saw his point but wouldn't voice that out loud; she was loyal to her American employer.

An assortment of small appetizer bites was placed on the table, compliments of the chef. Grateful for a distraction,

Catherine tried a tart topped with briny black olives and avocado, salty and creamy.

After a few sips of wine, Patrick brought up Winston's recent bad press. He appeared gleeful at the hit to the company's reputation and railed about the ineptitude of the Plaza Blind Tasting. Catherine couldn't resist asking, "Did you put Jacqui up to her column?"

"What if I did?" he said. "There's no way Tournelle champagne from France would have lost to two California sparkling wines unless it was rigged."

"How did she learn when Winston's *cuvée de prestige* was disgorged?"

"I don't know about that," he said. "There aren't many secrets in Napa."

Their main plates arrived. Patrick cut into his steak. "This is good," he said between bites. Then he went on a rant about the zoning laws making it very difficult for his company to add a gourmet restaurant to their sparkling winery in Sonoma.

Tom kept looking over at their table, which made Catherine feel conspicuous. Obviously, if she had something to hide, they wouldn't be dining in plain view. She twirled the pasta around her fork and dipped it in the butter sauce.

Patrick polished off his first glass of wine quickly and ordered another one. "My parents said they ran into you and Chris at Les Crayères—" He left the implied question hanging in the air.

"Yes, a quick business trip," Catherine said. "We had a meeting there with Yves." She wondered if his parents told him she looked pretty cozy with Chris; thank goodness they hadn't been dining alone.

"They mentioned how stunning you are now, all grown up, and they're right." Patrick's second glass of wine was served, and he loosened up. "You know our parents are hoping for a merger between our families. I'll be taking over the company soon. We could be very happy together."

It sounded coolly analytical to her, nothing like the passion Chris showed. Who would have thought she'd prefer a wholesome, intelligent, and super-sexy California country boy to a debonair Frenchman?

He reached across the table to hold her hand, but she deftly raised her wineglass to circumvent the gesture.

"Patrick, I can't even think about dating right now," she demurred. "Totally swamped with work until the launch."

"About that," he lowered his voice. "You should consider jumping ship before Vinexpo. I foresee major fireworks for Winston. You'd be better off as far away as possible."

Catherine knew Patrick tended to be dramatic, but this sounded over-the-top, even for him. What could he possibly mean? It sounded ominous. The only explanation she could come up with was that he might try to coerce Relais & Châteaux members into voting for Tournelle champagne in the contest. He'd half-admitted to influencing Jacqui for her negative column.

She set her fork down. "Don't suppose you'd clue me in on what you mean," she said.

"Can't do that right now," he said. "Just don't want to see you caught in the crossfire."

A waiter served their decaf espressos. Catherine stirred sugar into hers. "Speaking of our parents," she said, "mine are celebrating their thirty-fifth wedding anniversary in Bordeaux during Vinexpo. You might want to tell your folks."

"Thanks. I'll pass it on." Patrick popped one of the complimentary chocolates in his mouth.

When they parted at the elevator, Patrick leaned in for a real kiss. Catherine turned her cheek and gave him a light hug. *This sleuthing stuff is stressful.*

The next morning went by in a blur. Catherine met Sue and Kevin for a quick coffee in the Soleil Café before joining the rest of the documentary crew. They shot B-roll on the property for an hour then joined Tom in the winery for a tour.

The rough script had been predetermined and focused on the industry as a whole, so Tom was spared questioning about Winston's recent bad press. Wrapping up, Tom reiterated the importance of quality grapes, expert winemaking, and placing the blended wine in bottles for the second fermentation.

While Tom spoke, Catherine replayed in her mind the conversation with Patrick. It might have been an attempt to sway her to leave Winston and join Tournelle, a nonstarter as far as she was concerned. In any event, she needed to pass the intel on to James. She decided to relay the news in person, when they were both back in New York.

On the break, Catherine stopped by the office to check messages and send Claire the final version of her ninety-day report with instructions to print copies and deliver one to Chris's office.

After they grabbed a quick lunch, Kevin and the crew took off and Sue offered to stay and help Catherine review the rough video from the gala. Permission for the documentary makers to film the event had stipulated host companies could have unflattering footage withheld. Catherine's task was to log what was captured and tag any negative references. She figured it would be a snoozefest and was happy to have Sue's company while they slogged through it.

Tom gave them the conference room, which had a connection to watch on a large screen. Catherine brought a lined pad to make notes. Both women had iced tea, figuring they'd need an afternoon caffeine boost.

The first reel covered the Plaza Blind Tasting. The camera focused on the panel of experts at the long table sipping and judging each sparkling wine. Catherine had been at the back of the room, so she hadn't seen the process up close.

"Kevin authorized a copy of this first reel to be sent to the Winston attorney for his investigation into the blind tasting," Sue said. "But he won't be looking for unflattering footage, so that's our job." The end of the first reel showed the tasting results being announced at the reception and winners accepting the ribboned awards. Everything looked aboveboard.

The second reel commenced with the gala speeches and covered the auction, panning the room for audience reaction.

"We shot discreetly at the gala," Sue said, "to blend in. People didn't realize the small mic on the camera picked up audio—not broadcast quality, of course." For sound purposes, they pulled a separate feed from the mic on the stage.

On the final bidding for Trianon's valuable bottle, the camera caught Chris looking intense, Sean looking disgruntled, and Patrick looking unhappy.

"Gotta tell ya," Sue observed, "a lot of women in the room were a bit jealous at the attention from that lineup of sexy guys—like a firefighters' calendar—to lead off the first dance with you."

Catherine tried to deflect the compliment. "I think it was for the prize. Les Crayères in Reims is amazing. Went there a few weeks ago on a business dinner when I was in Champagne."

"Think I'm in the wrong line of work." Sue grinned and took a sip of her iced tea. "That's a nice perk—trips to France, gourmet meals."

Catherine didn't reveal the additional perk—being seduced by her sexy boss.

"By the way, thanks for giving me the skinny on Sean," Sue said. "Certainly wouldn't want to get in the middle of that."

"Yeah, Van was pretty upset. She appreciated your warning."

The women turned their attention back to the next section of video. In a corner, the camera picked up two men in conversation. "Did you finalize that investment?" the older man asked.

The younger man nodded. "We should make a killing when the Winston venture capital deal with Chamath crashes and burns."

"Good," the older man said. "Let's not discuss this further now."

"Oh my God," Catherine said. "That's David Saunders, a Winston board member, and his son. What a traitor!" She was stunned.

"Wow," Sue said, "that looks damaging. I'd call that unflattering footage for those two." She stopped the tape to jot down the time and note what they heard.

"I think this explains the leak to the *Wall Street Journal*," Catherine said. "He and James are close friends. He's privy to confidential financial information." Catherine felt James should be notified first. His friend. His company. "I'll notify James," she said. "Can you have the editor pull this footage and send me a Dropbox link?" She couldn't call now—it was too late in France—so she'd send an email to his private account.

"Sure. Will have that done tomorrow."

The women finished up, and Catherine persuaded Sue to join her for dinner. They could both use a strong drink, and Winston owed Sue for helping uncover this clue.

Finally, some good news. Chris hung up the phone, leaned back in his chair, and propped his feet on the desk, expelling a sigh of relief. He rubbed his eyes, 9:30 p.m., still at the office.

He'd finished a long call with Joel, who reported his investigation into the Plaza Blind Tasting was almost complete. Joel's legal team had interviewed every judge and the *Decanter* magazine staff who ran the tasting. They all swore to impartiality and full compliance with blind tasting guidelines and were signing affidavits to that effect.

Joel also reviewed the documentary footage from the blind tasting, which gave additional ammunition to their case. He was preparing a rebuttal letter to the *New York News* demanding a full retraction and apology or the legal hammer would fall, including a demand for monetary compensation for damages.

Chris needed to reach Tom to fill him in. He called his direct line and Tom answered immediately.

"Glad I caught you," Chris said.

"Good timing, heading out to dinner in a half hour," Tom said. "You're working late."

"Wanted to bring you up to speed on developments." Chris recapped his conversation with Joel.

"That's a relief. Can I loop Doug in?" Tom asked. "Met with him last night. He's concerned if someone gets away with this drip-by-drip innuendo campaign, it could damage the industry."

"Think he's right. Let me check with Joel before we make this public," Chris said. "One other thing. James learned through our French partners a rumor that Tournelle is having cash-flow problems. Yves thinks Patrick put Jacqueline up to her column criticizing the blind tasting to justify Tournelle's poor showing."

"If that's the case," Tom said, "their Sonoma subsidiary would be in violation of the California Sparking Wine Producers' bylaws."

"You're not kidding," Chris said.

"Wish we'd known that yesterday." Tom cleared his throat.

"Catherine had dinner with Patrick Tournelle last night. Could have given her a heads-up to check it out."

"She did?" Chris's voice got louder. "Are you sure?"

"Since it was here in our restaurant and I saw them, yes, I'm sure."

Chris's feet hit the ground with a loud thud. When he replied, he tried to sound cool, but he was running very hot. "Let's keep this Tournelle angle under wraps for the moment, until our investigators are able to learn more."

Thursday morning in New York was overcast and dreary. Chris arrived at the Seagram Building at ten, later than usual. He hadn't gotten to bed until after midnight and needed at least six hours of sleep to function.

He'd tossed and turned in a quandary over his relationship with Catherine. What was her deal with Patrick? Chris knew their families were friends, but meeting for intimate dinners? Quite possibly, Patrick was interested in pursuing her romantically. And what if she accidentally spilled company secrets to him? It had disaster written all over it.

He grabbed a coffee in the break room and noticed a large bouquet of flowers on Catherine's desk when he passed by. That piqued his curiosity.

Shortly after he sat down at his desk, Delores entered with his messages and mail. "HR called," she said. "They need Catherine Reynolds's ninety-day report, due yesterday, but we haven't received it yet. Maybe her assistant left a copy on her desk."

Not needing any prodding, Chris said, "I'll go look." He wanted to check out those flowers. He felt guilty using this feeble excuse for snooping in Catherine's office, but the door was open.

The lavish bouquet of white freesias—her favorite, he knew—was mixed with long-stemmed white roses, a white satin ribbon artfully tied around the tall crystal vase. He pulled the gift card off the plastic holder and unfolded the envelope. The card read: "Ma chère Cat, merci for the tip about Vinexpo. Yours, Patrick."

What the heck? What tip?

He walked around to the hutch behind Catherine's desk where she kept a wooden tray for her color-coded files. Sitting on top was the ninety-day report. He picked that up to take back to his office. Below it lay a manila file, no label. He thought she color-coded all her files. He'd never seen her with a plain manila file. He flipped it open. According to the documents inside, Catherine was the leak to the *Wall Street Journal.*

Wondering if there were any other incriminating papers, he thumbed through the rest of the files. They all looked innocuous until the final folder at the bottom of the pile. A purple file he'd never seen in meetings, labeled "Tournelle." Chris swore softly. There were a few pages of handwritten notes. One dated MARCH 30, the day he'd seen her at the Seagram Grill with Patrick, mentioned Tournelle expansion plans. No details. This had occurred before he went to South America and learned Tournelle tried to poach the winery in Chile. Why hadn't she shared this intel with him at the time? Or when they spent the following week together in France?

He needed to move quickly. Chris went back to his office, shut the door, and glanced at his watch: seven-thirty in the morning in Napa. He dialed Catherine's number.

"Hey," she sounded sleepy. "Glad you called. We keep missing each other."

He tried to tamp down his momentary joy at hearing her voice. This was a serious call. "Catherine, I was just in your office and found incriminating documents pointing to you as the leak to the *Wall Street Journal.* This looks very damaging. What's going on?" he asked in a stern voice.

Before he could continue, there was a muffled sound on the other end of the line, and he thought they might have been disconnected.

Then Catherine squeaked out, "I can't talk," and hung up.

He looked at the phone. *What just happened?* She wasn't denying or explaining. His heart sank.

The next call Chris placed was to Tom Banbury. Tom picked up on the second ring. "Morning, what's up?"

"I have some bad news," Chris said. "Looks like Catherine is the source for the *Wall Street Journal* hit piece."

"That's not possible," Tom said. "When I told her about the story, she looked genuinely surprised and said she doesn't have any contacts there."

"I'm afraid she's a better actress than we realized. When I confronted her just now, she didn't deny it."

"Oh jeez. What do you want me to do?"

"Tell her she's formally suspended, pending termination, as of now. Confiscate her company laptop and have her escorted off the property."

"Okay, you're the boss. But I want to go on record as objecting.."

Chapter Twenty-One

Napa—32 days to Celebration launch

In a cab on her way to the airport, Catherine was reeling from the last couple hours. Chris had accused her of being a traitor. It sent her into a fierce panic attack, her worst yet. She'd barely managed to hang up the phone before she'd slumped over on the bed and passed out. Tom's knock on the door twenty minutes later roused her.

She'd splashed cold water on her face, taken two aspirin for a raging headache, and forced herself to get dressed and meet Tom downstairs. He apologetically said she was suspended and he needed to take her laptop. *Might as well say "fired,"* she thought. She was devastated.

Tom didn't ask for an explanation. She didn't know what Chris had seen in her office, so she couldn't refute the claims. *What was he doing in her office anyway? And how could he have so little trust in her?* It was heartbreaking.

She wished she could turn back the clock, decline the job, and save her pride—and her heart. No bonus. Flat broke. She couldn't afford the tuition to Cornell. It would be very hard, if not impossible, to find a PR job once word got out about the accusations. She didn't have the energy to battle Chris to clear her name. Maybe James could sort it out when he got back.

Time to reach out to her refuge.

"Hello, sweetheart." Elizabeth Reynolds's voice calmed Catherine's anxiety a bit.

"Hi Gran. Hope I'm not calling at a bad time."

"Not at all. I just came in from the garden. What's the matter, honey? You sound upset."

"Things aren't going so well." A sob escaped Catherine's mouth. "I just got suspended."

"My poor dear." Elizabeth took an audible breath. "I can't imagine how that could have happened. Why don't you come out here for a few days and get spoiled by your grandma?"

"That's the best offer I've had in a while." Catherine sniffled. "Can I bring Vanessa and Soleil? I could use some female solidarity right now."

"Of course, dear. I'd be happy to see Vanessa, and my grandcat is always welcome." That put a short-lived smile on Catherine's face.

"I'll have Estelle prepare the guest rooms," Elizabeth said. "Let me know when you want Sam to pick you up."

"Thanks Gran," Catherine said. "See you this weekend."

That afternoon, Chris met with Winston attorney Joel Levine in the conference room. Chris had Catherine's file folders on the table in front of him. Joel was poised to take notes on a lined legal pad.

"These are strong allegations you're throwing around," Joel said. "We'll need concrete proof."

"Not sure how we'll get that," Chris said. "Unless we get a confession."

"I'm concerned it looks circumstantial at the moment. I don't want Winston to have exposure to a lawsuit for unfair suspension and damage to reputation."

Chris slapped the manila folder in front of him. "I found copies of confidential board minutes and documents listing our private investors. These minutes detail the accounting report we gave to Chamath, the same report the *Wall Street Journal* claims is misleading."

Joel held up his hand. "Hold on. Don't handle that anymore. I want to have my PI try to pull fingerprints." He paused. "For all we know—or Catherine could say—the minutes were placed there by a disgruntled employee. Hasn't she been out of town?"

"Yes," Chris acknowledged.

"What about her assistant?" Joel asked. "Have you spoken to her?"

"Not yet. Claire took a few days off. I assume Catherine will get to her first. For all we know, she's in on this too."

"How would Catherine have gotten these documents if they're so confidential?"

"She has a key to enter the office after hours." Chris didn't add he was afraid she might have snooped on his laptop when they were traveling in France. He wasn't careful about keeping his password protection on. She could have accessed his files and emailed them to herself. The thought made him shudder.

"We only have part of the puzzle at this point," Joel said.

"I assume we'll find more evidence when we get her laptop," Chris said.

Joel jotted down a few notes.

"In addition, Patrick sends her a thank-you note for info on Vinexpo where we're having our crucial launch, and I find this file with notes on Tournelle company plans." Chris slumped in his chair. "Catherine has known that family since she was a child."

"Again, circumstantial." Joel took a sip of coffee. "Don't you watch *Law & Order*? I'll have my associate start going through both their offices. When is James due back from France?"

"Tomorrow," Chris said. "Honestly, I hope I'm wrong. But in the moment, I didn't want to take any chance of further harm to the company's reputation."

"Okay. In the meantime, we need to do damage control," Joel said. "We still don't know the endgame and all the players involved."

Late Friday morning, James Sterling's plane touched down on the tarmac at JFK and taxied to the gate. His fellow passengers in first class turned on their phones and started scrolling. He checked his voicemail and shook his head—twenty messages. What a mess. He needed to speak with the attorney before dealing with Chris.

"Hi Joel," James said, no preliminaries. "Fill me in on what you've learned so far."

Joel described the papers Chris found in Catherine's office—confidential board minutes about Winston's finances.

"Did anyone ask Catherine about this?" James asked.

"Chris said when he confronted her on the phone she hung up."

"Okay, that's not a denial. I'll grant you, it looks suspicious, but perhaps something else was at play." James felt sure Catherine was set up; he didn't know how or by whom yet.

"Could be someone planted those papers, possibly to deflect blame," James said. "We need to figure out how they ended up in her office. Did you check for fingerprints?"

"We're working on that. We did a sweep of both offices—"

"Two offices?"

"Catherine's and her assistant Claire's. One more thing," Joel said. "Chris found another file in Catherine's office with notes about the Tournelle winery. Why would she have that?"

"Dammit," James said. "I asked her to snoop on Tournelle since she knows the family. That was a confidential job for me. What was Chris doing in her office anyway?"

"Said he went there to look for her ninety-day report that was overdue."

"Seems like a slim excuse to me," James said.

"Are you sure she's not leaking to the press?" Joel asked.

"I've known her all her life," James said. "I don't think it's something she would do."

The plane pulled up to the gate and people were unbuckling seatbelts and putting on jackets. "Let me know as soon as you find anything concrete," James said.

"Sure thing. I'll have an initial report on your desk by Monday morning."

"Thanks, Joel."

Catherine looked out the window and waved at her grandma as Sam pulled the white Lexus SUV up to Elizabeth Reynolds's sprawling home in Southampton Village on Saturday morning. Wearing a wide-brimmed straw hat, Elizabeth set a watering can down near a row of white hydrangeas and walked over to greet her guests.

Catherine grabbed her purse and Soleil's carrier, on the seat between her and Vanessa, while Sam opened the trunk and took out their luggage. The friends traveled light, casual clothes for a few days. Catherine hoped that would be enough time to get her mojo back before she started looking for a job to pay the bills. Mending her broken heart would take much longer.

"Hello dears," Elizabeth said. "Happy to see you both."

"Thanks, Gran," Catherine said. "I'm relieved to be here." They all shared hugs.

"We're having nice weather, so you can spend time by the pool, walk on the beach," Elizabeth said. "Estelle and I prepared lunch to enjoy alfresco on the patio after you've gotten settled."

The living room boasted an unobstructed view of the water; large windows facing the ocean were framed by cream-colored wooden shutters to block the sun when it became too intense. Over the years, Elizabeth had purchased large seascapes painted by local artists for the walls. A glass bowl designed in the color and shape of a sand dollar held seashells collected by Catherine and her friends. It sat on a glass coffee table in front of a sage overstuffed sofa.

The ladies dropped off their bags in adjoining rooms, and Catherine set up Soleil's litter box and water bowl. They met Elizabeth on the patio in a tropical setting near the pool. Palms in large yellow ceramic pots provided shade.

"This is quite a spread," Vanessa said, pointing to the table. "Looks delicious."

"We went to the farmers market this morning," Elizabeth said. "Found locally sourced asparagus, artichokes, and strawberries. Let's take a seat." The patio table was covered by an umbrella and set with linen placemats and floral-patterned melamine plates.

Elizabeth described the ingredients in each dish: salmon salad with organic greens; steamed asparagus and lemon dressing; cold pasta salad with artichoke hearts and black olives; and strawberry shortcake with whipped cream for dessert. To drink she offered wine, fresh-pressed grapefruit juice, and mineral water.

"Gran, you outdid yourself," Catherine said. She indulged in a glass of chardonnay to calm her nerves. Vanessa joined her. Near Catherine's feet, Soleil dug into a morsel of salmon. The women passed the platters around and started eating.

"Now Cat, can you tell me what happened?" Elizabeth asked. "Or is it too painful to discuss?"

"I'm not really sure where to begin." Catherine broke off a piece of baguette. "Chris called me early Thursday morning. Said he found confidential financial papers in my office indicating I was the source for a defamatory story about Winston in the *Wall Street Journal*." Catherine paused and twisted her ring. "I felt a panic attack coming on—and hung up right before I passed out."

"Oh, you poor dear," Elizabeth said.

"When I recovered, I went downstairs and spoke with Tom. He told me I was suspended." Catherine wiped tears from her eyes and took a sip of water.

"Did you talk to Chris later?" Elizabeth asked.

Catherine shook her head. "If he doesn't trust me, it feels pointless. I'll try to see James next week. I owe him that."

"Good idea," Elizabeth said. "James will straighten this out." Elizabeth put her fork down. "I feel partially responsible since I asked James to hire you."

"Don't say that." Catherine reached out and placed her hand on Elizabeth's arm. "You know how grateful I was for the job. Either it's a misunderstanding, or I made some enemy I'm unaware of . . ."

"Sounds like someone set you up," Vanessa said, "and Chris overreacted."

Catherine took a small bite of pasta salad, silently agreeing with Vanessa.

"Don't know what set him off," Vanessa continued, "but I saw him almost lose it when we were having drinks with Patrick."

When Catherine had handed Tom her laptop as she was leaving, he'd mentioned Chris was stunned to learn she had dinner with Patrick at Étoile.

After Claire got the news, she'd called a friend at the office Friday and was told Chris saw a large bouquet of flowers Patrick sent Catherine. Maybe that was a tipping point.

Elizabeth cut into the strawberry shortcake and put slices on dessert plates with a generous dollop of whipped cream. She even put a smidgen of whipped cream in Soleil's dish under the table, which the cat started lapping up.

"Now Vanessa, tell me about your new singing gig," Elizabeth said. When they were teenagers, Catherine had brought Vanessa to stay with her grandma on many occasions, so Vanessa was practically family.

"I bragged to all my friends when you appeared at the Academy Awards," Elizabeth said.

Vanessa regaled them with stories about crazy patrons at her club: unusual song requests, wild birthday celebrations, and the numerous marriage proposals that Vanessa received from inebriated patrons.

Amid the laughter, Catherine's mood improved. She bit into a piece of shortcake smothered in whipped cream. The comfort food cheered her up. Thank goodness she had grandma and Vanessa in her life.

After lunch, Vanessa chose to take a nap by the pool. Catherine wanted to clear her head, so she set off for the beach, her camera strap wrapped around her neck. She walked briskly and breathed in the salty air. A light breeze blew her skirt, and clouds rolled in providing respite from the sun.

Taking advantage of the solitude, Catherine reflected on the past few days. She'd felt such a deep connection with Chris, unlike any other guy she'd dated—and there hadn't been many, only a handful. It hurt so much because she was falling in love with him.

The nightmare with Chris had Catherine rethinking her beliefs. She'd always held out for a grand love story while many of her girlfriends from school were more practical and goal-oriented. They had a timetable and they stuck to it—married by twenty-five, pregnant by twenty-seven. If that meant they "settled" for a guy who didn't knock their socks off, so be it. Maybe they had it right.

Choosing a good provider was also part of her friends' equation. Up until now, her parents had filled that financial gap, but Catherine realized it had prevented her from committing to her own path. She didn't know what the future held, but she was determined to figure out a way to take control of her life.

She took off her sandals and waded into the water. It felt cool and refreshing. A seagull swooped nearby. The clouds were disbursing, just the right light for filming. Grateful for the distraction, Catherine pulled out her camera and focused on capturing the shots.

Vanessa woke up from her nap and found Soleil curled up beside her on the chaise lounge. They both stretched. "I can see why Cat is so devoted to you. You're loyal and loving, no disappointments." She gave the calico a scratch behind the ears, put on her flip-flops, and went to the kitchen, led by the scent of Elizabeth's baking.

"Mmm, smells good," Vanessa said. She noticed a yellow Limoges plate piled high with scones.

"Hi dear," Elizabeth said. "Just took cranberry-orange scones out of the oven." She pointed to a pitcher on the counter. "Thought you might like some English Breakfast tea, sun-brewed this morning."

"Sounds refreshing." Vanessa poured the tea over ice cubes in a glass tumbler and took a sip. "Is Cat back from her walk?"

"Not yet. Poor thing," Elizabeth sighed. "Hope being in nature will help. She always liked our outings to the beach."

"This trip was a good idea. Thanks for inviting us." Vanessa took another sip of her iced tea. "Catherine fell hard for Chris. It's going to take time for her to recover."

"She told me her mother wants her to marry a successful Frenchman," Elizabeth said. "I know her parents are close friends with the Tournelles and would be happy if Catherine became serious with Patrick. He's cultured, from the same world, due to inherit his family wine business." She put the pitcher of tea in the refrigerator. "I think she dated the younger son when she was a teenager."

Vanessa looked dumbfounded. "Didn't she tell you what happened with Édouard?"

"She just said it didn't work out. I figured it was young love, her first infatuation. You know she's a very private person. I didn't want to pry."

Vanessa couldn't believe Catherine hadn't confided in her grandmother after the devastating experience with Édouard. At the time, she had said her mother could have been more supportive, but not that her family members didn't know about the trauma she endured.

"Think I'll catch up with her on the beach," Vanessa said. "See if she wants company."

"That's a good idea."

Vanessa found Catherine sitting on a bluff overlooking the ocean, snapping photos of sailboats bobbing on the water. A seagull perched on a rock nearby gazed at her expectantly, as if waiting for a peanut to be thrown its way.

"Hey." Catherine smiled. "How was your nap?"

"Restful. Woke up to find Soleil curled up next to me." Vanessa sat down next to her friend. "Heck, Cat, why doesn't your grandma know what an asshole Édouard is? She mentioned he was your first boyfriend but didn't know why you stopped seeing him."

"It's not that simple." Catherine frowned.

"I don't know, date rape seems pretty clear-cut to me—and you were a virgin, on your sixteenth birthday." Vanessa was incensed just thinking about it.

"Oh Van, it's so complicated with my family." Catherine looked crushed.

"I'm sorry, I don't mean to be so blunt. We never talked about how they reacted." Vanessa knew the story intimately because Catherine had confided in her the next day. After her birthday party, Édouard had taken Catherine out dancing. He'd been plying her with strong drinks all night. When they got back to his car, he'd said he had a present and asked her to join him in the back seat. They started kissing. Then he pulled up her minidress and forced himself on her—even though she screamed out in pain and cried for him to stop. Vanessa thought he should have been sent to jail.

"Since Édouard and I were dating, my mother said he must have thought it was consensual." Catherine shook her head. "It clearly wasn't."

"What did your father do?" Vanessa asked.

"I didn't discuss it with him. It was so humiliating. Patrick found out, and he was furious with his brother. I got the impression he did something about it, but I don't know what."

Vanessa wrapped her arm around Catherine's shoulders. "Sorry to bring up the past."

"That's okay. It's been holding me back." Catherine winced. "I saw a therapist for the panic attacks. She said the more I come to terms with the assault, the easier it will be to move on."

"I'm here for you. Whenever you want to talk about it," Vanessa said.

"I appreciate it." Catherine put her camera in the case. "I've been thinking . . . maybe I should hock my ring." She twisted it in her fingers. "It's a one-of-a-kind vintage piece. I should be able to get enough to cover my Cornell tuition and expenses for the next few months."

"That's a last resort," Vanessa said. "Isn't it a family heirloom from your French grandma?"

"Yes. I confided in her after the rape. She gave it to me the day after my birthday, said she wanted me to have the ring as a symbol of resilience. She admitted she was raped at fifteen—by a German soldier during the World War Two occupation in France."

"How terrible. You didn't tell me that story."

"She passed away last year, so I don't need to keep it secret any longer. The ring was created by Cartier for her mother. They said it represented strength and endurance. So it's been a talisman in my family."

"You must keep the ring," Vanessa said. "We'll figure out another solution."

"I hope so." Catherine stood up and brushed off her skirt.

"The tide is going out," Vanessa said. "Let's look for seashells to add to our collection at Gran's. Race you to the water."

The friends took off. Vanessa counted on the diversion to clear Catherine's mind of harsh memories, for a few hours at least.

Chapter Twenty-Two

New York—29 days to Celebration launch

The video stopped playing, and the men looked at each other in amazement. It had ended with David Saunders Jr. saying to his father, "We should make a killing when the Winston venture capital deal with Chamath crashes and burns."

James and Chris were meeting with Joel Levine at his law office in the Woolworth Building near City Hall on Monday afternoon. They'd been reviewing the Plaza gala footage filmed by the documentary crew. Chris couldn't believe his eyes. Looked like he had it all wrong about Catherine, which was gratifying to learn on one hand. On the other hand, boy had he blown it.

"That's damning evidence," Joel said. "It indicates Saunders, a board member, was abetting the failure of Winston & Wright's expansion plans." He closed the laptop screen. "It's not a smoking gun, but it shows motive for him to be the tipster to the SEC and the *Wall Street Journal*."

"If he was the source," James said, "he would have needed to alter the financial statements to show a discrepancy from what we provided to Chamath."

"His son could have doctored them," Chris said. "He's an accountant."

"What about those financial papers Chris found in Catherine's office?" James asked.

"We may have a lead on that." Joel gestured to the two files on the conference table that Chris had found in Catherine's office—each in its own plastic sleeve for protection. "My PI has been investigating, and there are some distinct markings on the document that indicate it came from Chris's office."

Chris reacted vehemently to that news. "Well, I didn't put it there."

"Of course not," Joel said. "But your secretary, Delores, might have. We brushed for fingerprints and found some that match hers." He held up his hand. "Don't ask—my guy figured out a way to isolate her prints."

"Do you think she's working with Saunders?" James asked.

Joel shook his head. "We don't know yet. We're gathering more evidence before we interview both of them."

It gets worse and worse, Chris thought. Not only had he prematurely accused Catherine, but it also appeared his secretary was involved. He glanced at the manila file. If his blood pressure hadn't been elevated by seeing the flowers from Patrick, he might have realized the manila folder was out of character. He'd only seen Catherine use color-coded files.

"Then there's the question of Tournelle's involvement," James said. He filled the others in on his conversations with Yves at Trianon. From what Yves could gather, it appeared Patrick had nothing to do with the SEC predicament. Earlier, James had expressed regret to Chris for not cluing him in on Catherine's assignment to snoop on Tournelle. Chris still harbored resentment that he was left out of the loop. That had contributed to his mistrusting Catherine.

While Joel jotted notes on his lined pad, James reiterated their marching orders. He asked Chris to run interference with Chamath. Joel would pursue their legal remedies with the SEC.

"I'll speak with Catherine," James said, "and apologize on behalf of the company for the turmoil she's been put through."

Chris wished he were the one seeing Catherine. He wanted to beg her forgiveness but feared she'd rebuff his overture.

Catherine arrived at Sant Ambroeus a few minutes early on Wednesday morning to grab a quiet table, glad this meeting was on her home turf. She ordered coffee and pondered her next move. She'd gotten word from the Winston attorney they were in the process of clearing her name, but he didn't go into any detail.

James strode in right on time. "Good morning, Catherine. Thanks for seeing me." He pulled out a chair and sat down.

"Sure," Catherine said. She held her mocha mug tightly.

"First, let me apologize for all the distress you've been put through this past week." He paused to give the waiter his order for black coffee with cream. "It appears Chris's secretary, Delores, vindictively put those confidential financial papers in your office to set you up. We haven't determined a motive yet. She may have been put up to it by someone else."

Catherine was stunned. She hadn't had any meaningful interaction with the woman. She couldn't imagine what caused her to be so malicious. "Are you positive?" she asked. "Can't conceive what brought that on."

James nodded. "Looks that way. She even lied to Chris, said she didn't receive your ninety-day report and suggested he look for it in your office so he'd see the papers she planted."

Her mind was reeling. She'd heard about corporate intrigue but she'd never been a target before.

James put his hands on the table. "Also, the gala documentary video points to David Saunders as the SEC source. He's lawyered up, so that will take a while to unpack." James furrowed his brow. "I thought he was a friend."

Catherine knew how it felt to be let down.

"I understand this is a lot to absorb," James said. "Again, I'm sorry about all this." He looked hesitant. "I'd very much like for you to continue your work on the launch . . . if you're willing." Before she could object, he rushed to finish his pitch. "You would be reporting to me, not Chris, and you could work from home."

To stall for time, Catherine took a sip of her mocha. She was flat broke and needed that bonus for Cornell. She wanted to accept the lifeline. But if she'd learned anything from this experience it was to consider the ramifications before diving in. "Can I get back to you on that?" she asked.

"Of course. Take all the time you need." James took a gulp of coffee. "By the way, Chris feels remorseful. Please consider accepting his apology. He said he's tried to reach you."

"I'm not ready to face him yet. Not sure when that will be."

"I understand." James glanced at his watch. "I'd better head to the office."

"Thanks for coming to speak with me." She pushed her chair away from the table. They parted with a light hug on the sidewalk.

Catherine walked back to her apartment deep in thought. As she walked up the steps to her front door, a florist van pulled up. The driver took out a large bouquet and met her on the porch.

"Miss Reynolds?" he asked.

"Yes."

"These are for you." He handed her a tall green vase wrapped with a gold ribbon.

She took it inside and set it down on the foyer table. It was a beautiful arrangement of white tulips mixed with white freesias and a sprinkling of white edelweiss.

The card read: "White tulips represent forgiveness. I hope you'll find it in your heart to forgive me. They're also a symbol of renewal and hope. Catherine, I haven't given up hope for us. Yours, Chris."

She smiled inwardly. He'd paid attention to what she shared with him about flowers on their France trip: their meanings, her love of freesias, and her forays for edelweiss on Swiss Alps hikes with friends from her girls' school.

He was trying to make amends, but Catherine was scared to open her heart to him again. He'd nearly undone her the last time she did.

Two nights later, Chris met his father for dinner at the neighborhood Italian restaurant near his apartment.

"This was a good idea," his dad said. "I'm famished after my long flight."

The waitress brought their drink order—two beers—and an antipasti platter of cheese, salami, and thinly sliced vegetables. His dad picked up a piece of salami and took a bite. "This beats airplane food."

"I'm afraid I'm not very good company," Chris said. "Seems I've made a mess of things at work."

"I'm sure it's something that can be fixed, son." His dad's phone rang and he glanced at the screen. "I've got to take this, it's my supplier. Be back in a minute." He picked up the phone and started walking to the door.

Chris appreciated his dad's optimism but knew he'd blown it. His heart ached. Catherine wasn't taking his calls, and James was mad at him for pulling the trigger too quickly. It was one big mess.

His dad returned to the table, and a server placed piping-hot plates of chicken Bolognese in front of them, offering to grate more parmesan on top.

"So, what's the problem at work?" his dad asked as he twirled his fork into the spaghetti.

Chris set his beer down. "I reacted to circumstantial evidence indicating Catherine was giving misleading company financials to a journalist and suspended her. Since then, other information has come to light pointing to someone else." He grimaced. "And it looks like my secretary is the culprit who set Catherine up."

"I'd say that's more than a work problem."

"You're right. It's a debacle. We were falling for each other and agreed to start dating after the launch." Chris couldn't believe he'd blown it so spectacularly.

"Have you spoken to Catherine?" His dad took a roll out of the basket and broke off a piece.

"She's not taking my calls. I care for her, Dad. But I doubt she'll forgive me."

"You know, your mother and I got off to a rocky start." His dad looked dreamy for a moment. "We never told you boys because she was embarrassed." He relayed the story of their first date. She'd just moved to Napa and didn't know many people. Mutual friends matched them up on a blind date. He'd recently graduated college and was putting in long hours on the ranch. He became so caught up in work he mixed up the dates. She'd gotten all dressed up, even had her hair done, went to the fancy restaurant he booked, and waited for an hour. When he didn't show up, she became convinced he'd looked in the window, seen her, and decided to leave.

"Gotta tell you, it took me months to convince her to agree to a second date, and you can be sure I pulled out all the stops on that one." His dad put his fork down. "Not a day goes by that I don't miss your mom."

"Me too," Chris said. "It still hurts. Don't think I'll ever find what you two had."

His dad pursed his lips. "I've worried losing your mom would stop you from getting close to another woman."

"Believe me, Dad, I don't ever want to feel that pain again," Chris said.

"I'm afraid we don't have a choice. That's what love's all about. We take the highs with the lows." His dad rolled the beer pint glass in his hands. "Have you considered maybe you sabotage relationships so you won't get hurt?"

Chris looked skeptical and took a bite of chicken.

"I've watched you throw up roadblocks with women," his dad said. "This one with Catherine is a doozy—you must like her a lot."

"That part is true. I can't remember falling so hard." Chris put a hand on his heart. "Other women I've met seem interested in my money and position, not the real me."

"And Catherine?"

"That's the thing. She was raised in influential circles, doesn't need it from me. Even though we come from different backgrounds"—he paused—"we just fit together. Felt so natural."

"That's something to hang onto, son."

Chapter Twenty-Three

Paris—5 days to Celebration launch

"*Les Nymphéas renvoient à une nature élémentaire et intemporelle . . . Un rêve d'harmonie hante l'espace baigné de lumière de l'Orangerie.*" Catherine translated the plaque in front of her: "The *Nymphéas* refer to an elementary and timeless nature . . . A dream of harmony haunts the space bathed in the light of the Orangerie."

The "dream of harmony" in the description aptly conveyed Catherine's desire of the moment: She dreamed of the harmony to make it through the next week. She was back in Paris at Musée de l'Orangerie, near Place de la Concorde, visiting Claude Monet's final masterpieces, *Les Nymphéas*—immense wall-size paintings of abstract water lilies. She sat down on a bench in the first room and let Monet's explosion of blues, greens, and whites in a splash of color representing sunrise wash over her while she reflected on the past few weeks.

Catherine had accepted James's request to work through the launch. She didn't want to let him down, and she needed that bonus—contingent on there being no hiccups in Bordeaux. She'd even started tackling her finances, logging every expense in an app on her phone and plotting her monthly budget. No extravagances. *Baby steps*, she told herself.

A large tourist group came in. Catherine stood to stretch her legs and went into the second room of paintings, evoking dusk, before the crowd materialized there. The two large oval rooms in Musée de l'Orangerie were built for Monet's paintings; each *Nymphéas* landscape of water and reflection stretched six feet high and more than thirty feet wide. She slowly walked the room.

Catherine had made time for today's respite with Monet before the big countdown began. The Winston staff was gathering in Bordeaux this weekend to prep for Vinexpo. Then she'd see Chris for the first time since he suspended her. She hadn't responded to his calls; the rejection still hurt too much. In his defense, she'd learned the "evidence" he found in her office was compelling. Since she hadn't told him about her panic attacks, he had no clue why she didn't defend herself when he called.

Leaving the museum, Catherine walked into the Tuileries Garden, one of her favorite parks in Paris, extending from Place de la Concorde to the Louvre along the Seine River. Young parents were out pushing baby carriages; older couples held hands while sitting on benches near large fountains. She envied their contentment being together. She'd started to feel that possibility with Chris and felt devastated to lose it.

Crossing Rue de Rivoli, Catherine reached her destination, Hôtel de Crillon, for a lunch date with her parents. Their driver pulled up in a new model Audi sedan, one of the perks of her dad's job at the consulate.

They greeted each other with proper hugs and kisses. "Hi honey, it's good to see you," her father said.

John and Marie-Christine Reynolds were an attractive couple. Marie's dark hair was cut in a chic bob, and she wore a knee-length Chanel dress with matching jacket and high heels that brought her height up to five-six. Catherine's dad stayed in shape, tall and fit, with piercing blue eyes and shortly cut salt-and-pepper hair. She thought he looked like an aging movie star; George Clooney came to mind, and she smiled.

The hotel's lobby resembled a modern-day palace with arched doorways, sparkling chandeliers, gold accents, plush seating, and artistic touches. They stepped into the hotel's brasserie and were seated on the patio.

After they ordered and the wine was served, her dad lifted his glass to propose a toast. "Catherine, we're very proud of how you've conducted yourself at Jim's company. Here's to a successful event in Bordeaux next week." They clinked glasses and sipped the French cabernet sauvignon he'd chosen.

"Thanks, Dad," Catherine said. "It's been a roller coaster." When they spoke on the phone after she'd been rehired, she'd given them her version of events, omitting her personal involvement with Chris. Over appetizers, Catherine filled them in on her plans to attend Cornell's program in resort management. "Assuming we pull off the launch and I get the pledged bonus to pay for my tuition."

"About that." Her father set down his glass. "One of the reasons we stopped your draw was to spur you to get your money matters in order."

"I understand," Catherine said. "It's been a hard—and scary—lesson, but I've started the process." She showed them the app on her phone where she logged all her expenditures, big and small, including cups of coffee. "The job was a godsend, thanks to Grandma Reynolds."

"She thought you'd be a good fit at Jim's company." He cleared his throat. "There's another reason we took the tough-love approach." Then he dropped a bombshell. "Your trust from Grandpa Reynolds is more than we led you to believe."

Catherine knew her trust vested when she turned thirty in two years and understood it initially held $250,000 but was down to approximately $150,000 due to her spending over the last few years. She figured it would go toward buying a condo or taking a small stake in a resort she hoped to manage.

"The true amount is $2.5 million," he said.

"My goodness!" Catherine said. "Makes a big difference when you add a zero."

"Yes, it does," he said. "We want you to be prepared, and I'm sorry we didn't emphasize training in fiscal matters earlier."

"Obviously, I'll need some coaching," Catherine said. "Think I'll start by rehiring my accountant, Curt."

"That's a good idea. And we'll be here to guide you through the challenges and pitfalls." He put down his steak knife. "You've made a strong start by focusing your career goals."

Catherine felt gratified at the compliment and overwhelmed at the implications for how the money might change her circumstances. "Does anyone else know about this?"

"Your Grandma Reynolds, of course." He looked pensive. "We also confided in the Tournelles. In retrospect, we should have kept the information private."

"Why? What happened?"

"Our relationship with them is strained at the moment." He winced and glanced at his wife. "Édouard Tournelle was accused of date rape by a young woman in our circle. It's rumored that the police are talking to other female acquaintances."

Catherine was not surprised at the news. Édouard was a sexual predator—who had very nearly ruined her life. Due to her recent talk with Vanessa, she was ready to address the trauma with her parents.

"After Édouard assaulted me, I started having panic attacks. It's prevented me from having meaningful relationships with men." Catherine twisted her ring. "There are long-term consequences to his brutal behavior."

"Honey, I'm so sorry about what you endured," her father said. "That man is a monster. We should have been there for you."

Her mom wrung her hands. "*Je suis desolée, chérie.* It's my fault. Your father didn't know. I should have understood the seriousness. When my mother gave you her ring, I realized I hadn't handled the situation properly, but you were already leaving for school." She looked chagrined. "I should have brought it up later."

Catherine fought off tears. She knew her family wasn't good at communicating. She'd adopted the same shortcoming, and it had affected her relationship with Chris.

"Needless to say, we're very upset, and the Tournelles know it," her dad said. "They claim they're disgusted with Édouard but want to make sure he has decent legal representation. They're complaining about the costly legal fees—"

"We heard from friends they're having money problems," her mom interrupted.

"And Patrick?" Catherine asked.

"I don't know where he stands on this," her dad said. "Honey, we're here for you, whatever you need."

"Thanks, Dad."

A busboy cleared their plates, and the waiter placed dessert menus on the table. They declined dessert and ordered espressos.

"Jim asked us to come to your launch," her dad said.

"I'm glad we'll be in Bordeaux," her mom said. "We're looking forward to your big event, and it will be good to see Vanessa. You said she's singing."

That put a smile on Catherine's face. "Yes, she's performing at the party. We're pulling out all the stops."

The next morning, the gal pals were on their way to Bordeaux. "I'm so glad you were able to come on this trip," Catherine said.

"Wouldn't miss it. Reminds me of the travel adventures during our modeling days," Vanessa said.

They were on the TGV, France's high-speed train, after rising early and having a light breakfast at their hotel. In search of a caffeine boost, Vanessa set off for the dining car to get two strong coffees with cream.

Catherine looked out the window as they passed the outskirts of Paris on their way south. This was an industrial area: mainly warehouses, factories, and clumps of high-rise apartment buildings. The less glamorous side of Paris—the one not shown in brochures.

When Vanessa returned with their coffees, Catherine filled her in on the news about Édouard.

"I'm not surprised." Vanessa frowned. "What an asshole. I'm glad your parents are finally acknowledging your ordeal."

"I'm relieved it's out in the open. Thanks for pushing me," Catherine said. "I felt violated and humiliated—and powerless. Never told anyone." She crossed her arms. "I'm facing up to how it's been affecting my relationships. The misunderstanding with Chris is partly my fault. I didn't communicate with him, share my past, that I get panic attacks."

Vanessa wrapped her arm around her friend's shoulders. "You deserve a great guy. Not sure if Chris is the one, but he's passionate and seems to care about you, a lot."

Catherine shrugged. "I don't know." She took a sip of coffee before broaching her next topic. "Turns out there's something else my parents and I haven't been discussing—money."

Catherine relayed the conversation about her trust. "That could explain why Patrick started pursuing me," she said. "Mom heard the Tournelles are having financial problems."

"It is suspect," Vanessa agreed. "Hey, look on the bright side—you're rich!"

"Yeah, silver lining, but I don't want anyone else to know."

"Won't breathe a word," Vanessa said.

The conductor came by to check their tickets. After he finished, Vanessa asked, "Ready for your first travel lesson?"

"Sure." Catherine knew her friend liked to do research before a trip.

"I've been reading up on Bordeaux." Vanessa pulled out her guidebook. "This fast train increased the number of visitors, because people can get from central Paris to the heart of Bordeaux in two hours."

A civilized way to travel, Catherine thought. French TGV trains (*train à grande vitesse*, with an emphasis on *vitesse*, meaning fast) were a marvel. They were whizzing past green pastureland at two hundred miles per hour.

"Before the TGV was inaugurated, the slower train to Bordeaux took almost a day," Vanessa said. "Now, Parisians can go for a quick weekend trip. The renovated city center, where we're staying, has lots of restaurants, wine bars, shops, plenty to do, especially if you're a wine aficionado."

That cheered Catherine up. They'd have a fun twenty-four hours exploring the city before she reported to work.

Their train arrived on time at half past noon. The quai where the train stopped was two tracks over from the main station, so they dragged their luggage down a flight of stairs to the underground passageway that ran below the tracks, then up the stairs on the other side to enter the station. That part hadn't been modernized yet.

They hailed a cab for the ten-minute ride to their hotel, tucked away on a small side street off Place de la Comédie, which boasted a Bordeaux landmark, the Grand Théâtre.

"Great location, V," Catherine said.

"Notice our Best Western is next to the Intercontinental. We can grab a drink there later, if you want."

Since it was too early for check-in, they dropped off their bags and headed out to have lunch. "Where to, boss?" Catherine let her friend take the lead.

They walked in the opposite direction of the plaza to discover a quieter neighborhood and arrived at a peaceful open space at the end of the street. Place du Chapelet featured a beautiful church facing the square.

"Always good to get off the beaten track to find the gems," Vanessa said.

A nearby tearoom in the adjacent *passage*, a covered shopping arcade, had outside tables. They took advantage of the perfect weather and ordered gourmet sandwiches and fresh-brewed iced tea.

As they polished off cookies for dessert, they plotted their next move. Vanessa wanted to go window-shopping. Catherine persuaded her friend to visit the nearby church first. She picked up Vanessa's guidebook and found the entry for Église Notre-Dame de Bordeaux. They skimmed the history together: built by the Dominicans in the early 1700s; dramatic carved stone facade in the Baroque Jesuit style; great proportion of columns and statues.

They walked over and looked up in awe. "No wonder it's been designated an historical monument. It's amazing," Catherine said. "Love the proportion and the intricacy of the sculpture." The interior was just as impressive: vaulted ceiling, stained-glass windows, and beautiful wall murals. The organist began a practice session as they were admiring the paintings.

The haunting music rolled off the walls and instilled a feeling of tranquility. Just the minibreak Catherine sought before her work commenced tomorrow.

Twenty minutes later, they met in front of the church and went through the *passage* to Cours de l'Indépendance, an upscale shopping boulevard. "Saw this in the guide," Vanessa said. "It's part of the Golden Triangle, three intersecting streets known for high-end shops." The ladies set off on a mission.

After two hours of browsing, Vanessa had purchased a couple of sexy tops, and Catherine needed a break to recharge. "Let's see if our room is ready," she said.

The route back took them past the entrance to the Intercontinental Hotel, facing the Grand Théâtre. Fancy cars drove up to drop off well-heeled guests. One of them looked very familiar. Will Frost got out of a limo, pulled on his jacket, and walked to the trunk to instruct the bellhop retrieving his bags. When he saw Catherine and Vanessa approach, his eyes lit up.

"Hello ladies." Will smiled in greeting. "Are you my welcoming committee? Definitely a sight for sore eyes after a long flight. You two look awfully fresh. Not jet-lagged?"

"We got to France a couple of days ago," Vanessa said, "stopped in Paris."

"Where are you staying?" Will asked.

"Around the corner at the Best Western." Catherine pointed in the direction.

"If you don't have dinner plans, I'd love to take you two out."

Catherine and Vanessa exchanged glances. "Sure, we'd love to," Vanessa said.

Of all the gourmet dining in Bordeaux, Will chose an atmospheric crab restaurant a few blocks from their hotel on the

Garonne River. The riverbank was bustling with tourists on this warm night; the sun wouldn't set until after nine. Catherine was struck by the width of the river; it was difficult to see the other side, unlike the narrower Seine in Paris, where you could easily walk across on one of the pedestrian bridges.

Le Crabe Marteau had a seaside vibe, adorned with fishing nets and large apron-sized bibs for patrons to wear while cracking their fresh crab with mallets and wooden boards conveniently placed on each table. They all ordered crab dishes, and Will chose a local Bordeaux wine. From the pounding noise coming from the kitchen, it sounded like they were doing much of the crab cracking back there, at least for dishes that called for it, like Catherine's crab risotto.

A long bar counter by the door did a brisk happy-hour business. If this were LA, the handsome bartender would also be an aspiring actor.

"I'm glad your hotel happened to be so close," Will said. "My good fortune running into you two. Love the location across from the theater."

"Van's our travel agent," Catherine said. "She's good at sussing out boutique hotels in the center of the action."

"The Best Western where we're staying, called Bayonne Etche Ona, is beautifully decorated and less than half the price of the Intercontinental." Vanessa took a sip of wine.

"I'll have to make you my travel agent as well," Will said.

A server brought their plates, and the pounding commenced.

Will asked Catherine and Vanessa how they became friends. They answered in unison, "Our Lady of Grace, L'École des Femmes," and laughed. While they ate, Vanessa divulged escapades from their high school days, and Will looked captivated. Catherine was glad to see her friend enjoying his company after the debacle with Sean. Will was an attractive, eligible bachelor, as Sue would say, but he didn't interest Catherine. *I'm not as over Chris as I'd like to tell myself.*

With prompting, Will shared the story of his proper English upbringing, including lessons in ballroom dancing and fencing, and his own formal prep school education. "Dealing with the hazing and competition there equipped me for the ruthless world of Wall Street," he said.

That was an eye-opener for Catherine. She knew Will mentored Chris during his time on Wall Street but hadn't understood how cutthroat it could be.

Will insisted on picking up the check and walked them back to Place de la Comédie. Many couples were out strolling, and the Grand Théâtre looked beautiful lit up against the night sky.

When they reached the Intercontinental, Will pulled Catherine aside. "You know, Chris is totally broken up over what happened between you two," he said. "He has a big heart. I've never seen him fall for a woman like he did for you. Think about giving him a second chance. He's worth it."

If she allowed herself to be honest, Catherine did harbor a dream that she and Chris could rekindle what they started. She was afraid it was only a dream.

Then he addressed both ladies. "Why don't you join me for a drink at the hotel bar? The night is still young."

Catherine covered a yawn. "I've got some emails to handle, and I'm pretty tired. You two go ahead."

"*D'accord*," Vanessa said as she hooked her arm through Will's. "Let's see what girly cocktails they're pouring."

Chapter Twenty-Four

Bordeaux—3 days to Celebration launch

Chris arrived at Bordeaux's Mérignac Airport late Friday morning in need of a good night's sleep and went out to hail a cab. He'd taken the red-eye from New York to Paris, then changed planes at CDG for his final leg.

The long flight had given him plenty of time to brood. He'd made the worst mistake of his life suspending Catherine before all the facts were in. Relieved that she'd been exonerated, he'd spent the last three weeks agonizing over how to win her back. He'd tried to reach her by phone. He'd tried to reach her by text. He'd send smoke signals if that would help. She ignored all his entreaties.

He now knew deep down that Catherine had everything he desired in a woman—from her beauty inside and out; to her warm, playful nature; to how naturally she fit with him and his lifestyle. Their time at his family ranch and on the trip to France had been the happiest moments in his life since his mom passed away. After the talk with his dad, he realized he hadn't trusted Catherine's attraction to him. A mistake he vowed to correct this week.

He instructed the cab to drop him off at Place de la Comédie for his lunch appointment with Will, who was out front to meet him at the entrance to the Intercontinental. "This is some setup you've got," Chris said.

"I wanted to decompress before Vinexpo, and this hotel is perfect, right in the middle of the action." Will instructed the bellhop to hold Chris's luggage, and they walked over to the outdoor restaurant facing the plaza.

"It's such a central location I ran into Catherine and Vanessa yesterday," Will said. "Ended up taking them to dinner last night."

Chris's gut clenched. He hoped Will hadn't developed a romantic interest in his girl. He put on his game face. "So, how are they?"

"They wisely arrived in France a few days ago," Will said. "They were fresh as daisies and good company at dinner."

After the men were seated and had ordered, Will asked, "How is it with you and Catherine? She seemed subdued last night."

"She's avoiding me. Not that I blame her. I should have trusted her." Chris sipped his iced coffee, figuring it might hold off jet lag for a few hours.

"In your defense, who knew Delores would leverage the *Wall Street Journal* piece to sabotage Catherine?" Will said. "Good thing Joel figured it out."

"I should have fired her sooner, after the first incident of gossip," Chris said. "I didn't realize Delores harbored feelings for me that caused her to be vindictive."

Will picked up his burger. "At least the SEC cleared us, and the deal with Chamath is on track."

"Assuming the launch goes off without a hitch," Chris said, "and we manage to get a decent showing in the Relais & Châteaux contest." This was going to be one stressful week.

"Well, Trianon is campaigning for both labels, theirs and ours. That should help," Will said.

"You're right. I'm just paranoid after all the snafus." If he was honest with himself, Chris knew he wouldn't breathe a sigh of relief until they successfully launched Celebration.

During the meal, the men went over final numbers for the presentation to Chamath. The new winery partners from Australia and South America were attending the launch party and would seal their agreements after the venture capital deal was inked. Chris prayed everything ran smoothly, no more hiccups.

"Anything I can do?" Will asked.

Chris put his fork down. "Yes, but it's not business. I want to win Catherine back."

"Actually, I put in a word on your behalf last night, figured it couldn't hurt."

"Thanks, man," Chris said.

"Heck," Will added, "I really hit it off with Vanessa. We went to the hotel bar for drinks after dinner and talked for hours. I find her appealing. If it works out, the four of us might be spending a lot of time together."

Chris liked the sound of that.

While the guys were plotting their pursuit, the ladies in question explored Bordeaux on a bicycle tour. Catherine welcomed the exercise to clear her head before seeing Chris. The last time they'd been together a month ago, she'd envisioned a future together. She hoped she could hold it together.

The guide pointed out the Miroir d'Eau as they rode past along the river. Beyond the reflecting pool, the majestically proportioned Place de la Bourse reminded Catherine of similar squares in Paris. Bordeaux's city center held interesting historic sites at every turn.

Vanessa had arranged a late checkout, so they returned to the hotel by early afternoon and were out in front an hour later for their ride to the château Trianon had reserved for the week. When the driver pulled onto a private road and approached the entrance, the ladies oohed and aahed.

"It's like a fairy-tale castle!" Vanessa said.

The centuries-old, two-story structure, in the Châteauesque style, had been restored by a French luxury company to use for exclusive events. The surrounding park had been modeled after the Luxembourg Garden in Paris and appeared beautifully maintained.

Catherine and Vanessa went to the reception desk and were given keys to their shared room upstairs. All sixteen rooms and suites were reserved for guests from Winston and Trianon, including Chamath and their new winery partners, who were arriving tomorrow. Tonight, James had arranged a strategy dinner for staff to finalize the week's assignments.

A bellman carried their luggage up the grand staircase to their room and pointed out the amenities before he left. Two double beds were adorned with Porthault linens and matching throw pillows. The sumptuous bathroom had all the modern conveniences and Dior toiletries.

Catherine pushed open large windows overlooking the manicured grounds in back. "Let's tour the property," she said. "We can unpack later."

They viewed the main floor first. On the left side of the entrance was a clubby bar with leather chairs and oil landscapes on the walls. Adjacent to the bar, a small office for guests was equipped with desks and a copier. On the other side of the entrance, a salon led into the formal dining room.

As they walked on a gravel path around the château to access the back gardens, Catherine noticed a sign indicating steps leading to an underground cellar. She knew many Bordeaux properties had large cellars for their extensive wine collections. In this climate, they naturally maintained the proper temperature and humidity without needing special refrigeration. Luckily for Winston, the château cellar had room to store their *cuvée de prestige* jeroboams, so they could ensure proper control before the launch.

A fountain gurgled nearby. They sought it out and came upon a mini-oasis—a large circular pond with a three-tier fountain in the middle, surrounded by fragrant white roses. A wrought-iron bench sat alongside.

"Let's soak up the sun," Catherine said. "I'll be stuck inside the convention hall for five days starting on Sunday."

"*Bonne idée*," Vanessa said.

They leaned back on the bench, kicked their feet up on the edge of the fountain, and closed their eyes. Fifteen minutes later, a groundskeeper blowing leaves nearby interrupted their reverie.

"This is relaxing," Vanessa said. "Not to burst our buzz . . . are you up to seeing Chris tonight?"

"I'm apprehensive," Catherine said. "I still care for him." Privately, she hoped the stress wouldn't bring on another panic attack. She had so many emotions swirling around.

"I'm worried about running into Sean." Vanessa put her sunglasses on. "Haven't seen him since I walked out on him at the restaurant. The château is an intimate space, not like a big hotel."

"True. At least you have a dashing distraction."

"Yeah, isn't Will wonderful? That British accent melts me. We're meeting for drinks in the bar, and probably supper, while you guys have a working dinner."

"Speaking of, I've got to unpack and get changed," Catherine said. "Let's head back."

Dressing for the evening, Catherine opted for a masculine Armani pantsuit and pulled her hair back in a ponytail. No need to glam it up. She didn't want to give Chris the impression she was trying to win him back. She kept her makeup minimal, added a spritz of Chanel perfume, and went downstairs.

The moment she stepped into the salon, Chris came up to her. "Can we speak privately?" he asked. He looked dangerously handsome, and her heart skipped a beat.

She didn't want to expose herself to more turmoil, but they had to work together. "Okay," she said.

He led her onto the terrace, and she noticed how well he wore the dark-blue suit and white dress shirt, no tie. The night was warm; a linen-covered table outside offered bottles of white and red wine and a plate of munchies with small napkins.

"What would you like to drink?" Chris asked.

"Chardonnay is fine."

He poured two glasses and handed one to her. They stepped over to the balustrade overlooking the gardens behind the château.

"I'm so sorry I didn't trust you," Chris said. "I shouldn't have jumped to conclusions." He took a sip of wine and gazed out in the distance. "Can you possibly forgive me?" He turned to face her.

At a loss for words, Catherine clutched her glass. Chris McDermott still had a powerful hold on her emotions, and her heart. "I'll try," she finally said.

"I know we'll be busy the next few days, but I'm hoping we can grab some time to talk further."

James called everyone in for dinner, cutting their conversation short.

The formal dining room could accommodate up to thirty guests at a grand oak table. Tonight, it was set for eight people at one end: James at the head; Yves, Jean, Agnès, and Frédéric on one side; and the Winston staff on the other, which put

Catherine between Chris and Sean—exactly where she didn't want to be.

Large tapestries of hunting scenes hung on the walls. Two wooden sideboards held French porcelain dinnerware and crystal glasses. The table was adorned with two large bouquets of flowers and sterling silver flatware.

A waiter set filled champagne flutes at each place. Yves picked his up. "I'd like to propose a toast." Everyone raised their glasses. "Welcome to Bordeaux. We at Trianon are happy to share our latest vintage champagne with you"—he indicated the glass in his hand—"and to partner with such an exciting US firm. To a successful week and a stellar launch."

Everyone clinked glasses, and the meal began. To move things along, James had arranged for the kitchen to prepare large platters passed around family-style. After the first course was served, he began the meeting. "Let's review our timeline for the week," he said. "Tomorrow is an off day. Sunday, we set up our booth, and Vinexpo starts on Monday. Our launch party is that night."

Catherine looked forward to seeing the party venue at Cité du Vin. Agnès had booked the top observation floor and told Catherine it was an ideal setting to enhance the drama. Talk about drama; the jeroboams were so large they would require two skilled operators for the sabering.

After taking a sip of champagne, James continued. "People who visit the booth on Monday may ask why we're not offering tastings of Celebration the first day. We decided to build suspense and introduce it at the splashy event that night, before pouring it at the booth the rest of the expo."

The main course commenced, and James paused to take a few bites. Catherine focused on her French bouillabaisse to avoid speaking with the guys on either side. She dipped her spoon in the seafood broth and chewed on a tender shrimp. Tasted delicious.

James asked Jean to recap his process creating Celebration so they could glean talking points for their discussions with buyers. Jean ticked off the intricate steps and concluded, "*à la fin*, the dosage to top off the bottle before the final cork."

"Thanks Jean," James said. "Of course, some of this is in the press materials. A reminder, Agnès and Catherine are the point people on media coverage. Agnès, do you have anything to add?"

"*Oui, merci*," Agnès said. "We'd like to get a read on what other houses are featuring. Please let us know what you see at other booths and pick up their materials, if you get a chance."

"Good idea," James said. "Many thanks to Yves for finding this beautiful château to use as our home base. Also, keep in mind that Chamath and the new winery partners arrive tomorrow. Let's all reach out to give them a warm welcome."

While people lingered over coffee and dessert, James stood up and pulled Chris and Catherine aside in a corner. "Glad we've righted the ship," James said. "You two work well together."

Catherine was skeptical of that assessment but kept her thoughts to herself.

"I know I said tomorrow is an off day," James continued, "but I'd like you to do one task. Yves told me about a Relais & Châteaux property in Saint-Émilion, not far from here. I'd like to have it checked out as a venue for our closing-night event for friends and backers. This château won't accommodate the size of the crowd. Can you run over tomorrow for lunch and see if it fits our needs?"

"Sure, boss," Chris said, smiling broadly.

"Okay, Jim," Catherine said. Chris seemed overly enthusiastic about their excursion. She worried he'd get the wrong impression. This was not a date.

Chris had an extra bounce in his step Saturday morning. James had thrown him a lifeline when he assigned them the task of going to Saint-Émilion. If he were a betting man, he'd wager James did it intentionally. Chris intended to take full advantage of the gift James bestowed.

He grabbed the keys to one of Winston's rental cars and waited for Catherine in the entrance area. He'd dressed down in jeans and cowboy boots, figuring the boots would coax a smile out of her. To adhere to the Relais & Châteaux dress code, he wore a tailored shirt and brought a blue blazer.

Catherine came down the stairs looking scrumptious in a slim sundress and a short-brimmed straw hat, her long hair flowing instead of pulled back severely, the way she'd worn it last night. He hoped this indicated a slight thawing in her feelings toward him.

"Good morning," he said. "All set for our field trip?"

Catherine pulled her ubiquitous lined pad out of a large tote. "Yep, ready to take notes and report back. I read up on the restaurant. The chef has good write-ups and two Michelin stars."

"Looking forward to lunch," Chris said. "I booked our table for one o'clock. That should give us time to look around beforehand."

The drive to Saint-Émilion was dotted with signs indicating turnoffs to various local wineries offering tastings. Tourism was big business in the Bordeaux region. Family-run operations sold wines out of small shops adjacent to their winery operations.

"I don't know much about Bordeaux wine," Catherine said.

"I'm not an expert either," Chris said. He checked his rearview mirror before changing lanes. "All I know is it gets really complicated. Leave it to the French." He recapped what he'd gleaned.

The Bordeaux region encompassed more than fifty separate appellations. The AOC (*appellation d'origine contrôlée*) designation regulated how the wines were made—starting with the type of grape, how it was grown, and the winemaking method.

Bordeaux wine was normally a combination of three to five different grape varietals; there were red and white blends, and the highest-standard Bordeaux wines were classified as *Châteaux*. "In contrast," he concluded, "bottles that have the more generic label of Bordeaux AOC are generally wines of lower quality, still drinkable, of course."

"That is complicated," Catherine said. "Glad I only had to learn the champagne process for my job."

They approached a sign for Saint-Émilion, and Chris turned onto a smaller road leading up the hillside.

"This region is known for its cool climate, with moisture from nearby rivers," Chris said. "In Napa, we're having all kinds of problems due to the hot, dry conditions."

Catherine pulled out her camera and started taking photos as Chris drove into the picturesque medieval village. Parking was practically nonexistent amid the narrow streets and swarms of tourists, so he pulled into the convenient valet parking provided by Hôtel de Pavie, their destination for lunch.

"This is spectacular," Catherine said. "What a location. Right out of a movie. And look at that beautiful church a few steps away."

Chris smiled. He'd learned from experience Catherine liked checking out churches, so he'd done some research before they left. The Saint-Émilion Église Monolithe was very old and fragile; you could only enter with a tour guide, which he'd arranged in advance. Yes, he was treating this outing like a date.

He gave the car key to the attendant and walked around to open Catherine's door. Chris held out his hand to assist her.

"Miss Reynolds, we have an hour to check out the church before lunch." Her eyes lit up, and she held his hand a moment longer than necessary. *Baby steps*, he told himself.

Their guide, Valerie, met them at the entrance. Like many guides in France, she spoke five languages. As they stepped into the aboveground portion of the church, Valerie began. "This is called the Saint-Émilion Monolithic Church. Monolithic is a specific designation for churches that are made from a single block of stone, cut into the side of a mountain, or underground."

Valerie handed them a one-page description with photos. In the eighth century, a monk from northern France, named Émilion, traveled south seeking refuge and contemplation. He chose to establish a hermitage in a limestone cave on the hillside. Émilion's reputation for piety and performing miracles drew other monks to this remote spot.

Over the next few centuries, more worshippers came and expanded Émilion's original sanctuary, cutting into the hillside to create a large underground church, which eventually included three naves and a catacomb. Their painstaking labor built the largest monolithic church in Europe.

"Now, I will show you around," Valerie said. She led them down steep, narrow steps into the underground portion. It was dark and damp and unlike any church Chris had ever experienced. Catherine seemed to be enjoying herself, which was all that mattered.

It reminded Chris of the underground cellars in Champagne: miles of carved-out caves converted to store bottles as they aged. *The French are masters at hidden depths below the surface.*

When they climbed back up, Valerie led them outside to the hilltop square near fragments of the church's original walls. She pointed to the tall church tower. "The Saint-Émilion bell tower is fifty-three meters high. You can climb up the circular staircase for an awesome view of the town."

"Unfortunately, we won't have time for that today," Chris said. "We have a lunch reservation." He thanked Valerie for the tour and give her a generous tip. Chris wondered what monk Émilion would think of his town now. Cafés, wine bars, and shops were the main draw. Right in the heart of the action sat Hôtel de Pavie.

Chris put on his jacket. Catherine retrieved a lightweight cardigan from her tote, which appeared to have limitless room for whatever she needed, and they entered the restaurant. He'd requested a quiet table; they were seated side by side at a curved banquette in a corner near floor-to-ceiling windows. The perfect ambience for pressing his pursuit.

They each ordered one main plate and a glass of Saint-Émilion local wine. There were no salads on the menu. When Catherine requested a small green salad to accompany her Dublin Bay prawns, they accommodated her off-menu request—*like any good restaurant*, Chris noted.

After their wine was placed on the table, Chris twirled the glass stem in his hands. He decided to get right to the point. "Catherine, I'm glad we could have this time together today. I plan to do everything in my power to demonstrate my desire to rekindle our romantic relationship." He took a sip of wine, giving her time to digest what he'd said.

While he was speaking, Catherine blushed, her cheeks matching the color of the Saint-Émilion wine in her glass. "I never stopped caring for you," she said. "But you closed the door. The suspension felt like a total rejection." She paused. "It hurt, a lot."

"I can only imagine, and I'm so sorry." Chris contemplated his next words. "This caused me to do some soul-searching, and with some prodding from my dad"—Catherine smiled at his last phrase—"I realized losing my mother to cancer so young held me back from fully committing myself to a woman. I didn't want to risk my heart again."

He continued, "I didn't know if I could trust your feelings for me. It's why the attention from Patrick made me jealous." He shook his head. "I totally screwed up."

The server brought their plates, interrupting him for a moment.

"You're one in a million, Cat Reynolds. I don't ever want to lose you again," he finished.

Catherine clasped her arms in front of her stomach. "We both did some soul-searching this past month," she said.

That scared Chris. Was she turning him down?

"I don't know if you heard—Édouard Tournelle was recently accused of rape." Chris wasn't expecting this turn in the conversation.

"Édouard was my first boyfriend. It was young love, infatuation, I thought"—she paused, looking down at her lap—"until he raped me on my sixteenth birthday." Chris was stunned—and angered. No one should be subject to that pain.

She took a sip of wine. "I haven't had success in relationships, not surprising after that bad start. Kept ending up with flashy guys who didn't treat me very well." She set her wine down and faced him. "I thought we had something special, but I didn't share my past with you." She blew out a breath. "Since the rape, I get panic attacks. That's why I didn't respond when you called about the papers in my office. I hung up because the accusation triggered an attack; I was on the verge of collapse."

Now Chris really felt like a heel. His transgression was much worse than his dad forgetting the first date with his mom. He vowed to do whatever it took to win her back.

"Thank you for revealing this to me," Chris said. He was dismayed at what she'd been through.

After he paid the bill, they walked into the garden, and he pulled Catherine into a tender hug. He ran his hands up and down her back in a caress and pulled her closer before murmuring in her ear, "I care for you deeply, Cat Reynolds. I'll always take your side, and protect you, from now on." He moved his mouth closer to her lips and gave her a tender kiss, which she returned, making his heart sing.

Chapter Twenty-Five

Bordeaux—1 day to Celebration launch

Bright and early Sunday morning, Catherine and Vanessa took a "power walk" around the château grounds to work off some of the calories they'd consumed on the trip. Catherine was lost in thought as they walked briskly.

Chris McDermott was very persuasive when he set his mind on a goal, and she was it. Spending time with him one on one, she felt the magnetic pull reignite between them and acknowledged the obvious—he was the love of her life. He had a way of breaking down her defenses so they could be their real selves with each other. It was liberating.

She couldn't wait to share the news with Vanessa and her parents; they planned to go public right after the launch. She subconsciously rubbed a finger along her lower lip, reimagining the toe-curling kiss they shared in the garden at Hôtel de Pavie.

Vanessa decided to walk another lap, but Catherine had to get to work. After a quick shower and continental breakfast in the room, Catherine went to the château office to meet Agnès. They spent the morning on last-minute tasks for the week. Press releases to proof. Guest lists to confirm. Venue details to verify.

After lunch, James popped in and pulled Catherine aside. "I'm glad the Hôtel de Pavie suggestion paid off," he said.

"Yes, it's a beautiful space, big enough for our group. Agnès and I will hammer out the details."

"One other thing," James said. "Yves heard Patrick Tournelle might try to bribe Relais & Châteaux members for their vote in the contest." He shook his head. "Odd, since he was the one calling foul play on the Plaza Blind Tasting. Maybe that was projection."

"With the widespread news about Édouard's indictment, I'm surprised they'd be risking more trouble," Catherine said. "I'll see what I can pick up."

"Thanks. We have enough hurdles to surmount without a rigged contest."

An hour later, Catherine caught a ride with Frédéric to the expo site. She needed to drop off materials in the pressroom and check on the Winston booth. The hall bustled with activity. Attendees pushed rolling carts piled high with boxes of supplies and signs for their booths. Today, most people wore jeans. Tomorrow, they'd be dressed and pressed in suits and ties, even heels for some of the ladies undaunted by the large space.

While Catherine was laying out Winston fliers in the pressroom, Ken Barnett came over and read the sign out loud. "'Celebrate: You Deserve It!'" He added, "Clever tagline."

"Ken, good to see you." Catherine gave him a quick hug. "What do you think of our display?"

"Impressive. I'm hoping to win the drawing for a three-night stay at one of your company properties in Napa or Épernay. Bet that was your idea."

"You know I love giveaways," Catherine said, smiling, "and this is a dreamy prize."

"Glad the brass at Winston came to their senses and reinstated you."

"Thanks. What are people saying about that?"

"That it was some sort of misunderstanding. People weren't surprised to hear David Saunders was double-dealing to enrich himself—plays into people's distrust of Wall Street types."

Relieved to hear the suspension hadn't damaged her career, Catherine said, "I'm headed over to our booth. Want to check out the hall with me?"

"Good idea." Ken opened the door for her. "A beautiful woman by my side will cause tongues to wag."

"You flatterer. Don't want to make your boyfriend jealous." Catherine laughed.

"No worries, he thinks you're beautiful too."

Catherine had attended a few conventions, but nothing like this huge gathering at the Parc des Expositions, which included two thousand wineries exhibiting for forty thousand industry visitors from one hundred and fifty countries. One needed stamina to navigate the million square feet of space.

On the way, Catherine asked Ken, "Any buzz about this week?"

He leaned in and spoke softly. "A source tells me Tournelle is forming an alliance with a Saudi company for an infusion of cash."

"That is news," Catherine said. "Assume you heard about Édouard Tournelle's arrest for rape."

He shook his head in disapproval. "Oh yeah. Don't think it'll deter the Saudis though." They passed a sign indicating they were entering the Champagne section of the hall. "On a happier note, lots of anticipation about your bash tomorrow night." Catherine was gratified to hear that.

Ken's phone buzzed and he glanced at the screen. "I've got to scoot for an interview. See you tomorrow night." He leaned in and gave her an air kiss on one cheek then strode off toward the food court.

After they parted, Catherine continued down the aisle and saw the Tournelle booth ahead. Patrick arrived from the other direction, carrying a box.

"*Chérie*, I was hoping to run into you," Patrick said. "Heard there was a dustup at Winston. They don't deserve you."

"Misunderstanding. That's resolved," Catherine said.

"I'm going to a private reception tonight. Why don't you accompany me for a quick glass?" he said as he put the box down.

She'd planned to crash early to rest up before tomorrow but figured she might be able to learn something about Patrick's contest scheme. "Sure. I can go for a short time."

Patrick opened the box and took out a stack of pamphlets. "How's your launch going?"

"On track for tomorrow night," she said.

"You're not featuring it at the booth tomorrow for opening day?" He looked perplexed.

"No, we're building suspense, going for the drama, saber and all."

"Be careful with that." Patrick inclined his head. "You know the big bottles are difficult to saber safely."

An older gentleman interrupted them to ask Patrick a question. They spoke rapid French for a minute, then he turned back to Catherine. "Why don't I pick you up at six-thirty?"

Catherine gave him the address and they agreed to meet in front of the château.

In a cab on her way back, something nagged at Catherine. What was off? Then she figured it out. Patrick had talked about the danger of sabering big bottles. *He can't mean magnums; everyone knows they're okay to saber.* How did he learn they were using jeroboams? That information was closely held. Only a handful of people at the company knew about the jeroboams and were told to keep it in strictest confidence.

She remembered Anna's concern about her boyfriend being blamed for theft when he saw Robert near the bottling area. What if the launch jeroboams were sabotaged so the corks flew off early, like the fiasco at the Spago party? She envisioned corks popping off uncontrollably—it would be a disaster that could hurt people, crash the pyramid of glasses, and cause spillage. She needed to reach James and Chris right away.

Sean Dunlavy walked into the château office at 5:45 p.m. Everyone else had gone. He sat at one of the desks, picked up his cell phone, and hit a saved number. The other person picked up on the first ring.

"Patrick, Catherine is all wound up about the bottles for the launch," Sean said.

"What do you mean?"

"She said they need to be checked out. There may be sabotage."

"Where would she get that?"

"She said a hunch. Did you say anything?"

"Only that large bottles are hard to saber."

"You fool," Sean hissed, "showing off your expertise. You're not supposed to know we're using jeroboams. I told you that's strictly confidential. You're always lax around her, letting your guard down. How do we fix this?"

"Simple. I'm coming by to take her for a cocktail. I'll work into the conversation I thought it was magnums . . . never specified what size large bottle," Patrick said.

"Everyone knows magnums are fine to saber. It's the jeroboam quadruple-size bottles that get dicey. You'd better remedy this, without her getting any more suspicious." Sean hung up the phone.

Catherine had forty minutes until Patrick arrived. First, she sent a text to James and Chris sharing what she'd learned from Ken and mentioning her plans to join Patrick at a reception. She added that, from something Patrick said, she had a bad feeling about the jeroboams; they might be tainted.

She dressed quickly in a conservative button-down dress, almost schoolmarmish, she conceded. With fifteen minutes to spare, she decided to go to the cellar and check out the bottles herself. Sean was in the office when she grabbed the key off the hook. She told him she'd return it in a few minutes.

Catherine took the same gravel path she and Vanessa had strolled, past the parking area to the cellar entrance. She unlocked the door and left it propped open. A light switch turned on one lone bulb, enough visibility to make it down the steep, slippery steps—barely.

The cellar was cool and damp from the thick stone walls and had a dusty old wine smell—*very atmospheric, if you're into horror flicks*, she thought. Wooden racks and boxes piled high crowded the narrow aisles. Handwritten signs indicated the ancient treasure within.

At the end of the center aisle, Catherine found tall shelving stacked with the jeroboams, placed horizontally to keep the corks moist. A large saber hung nearby, to be taken to the venue at the same time.

The bottles were heavy and unwieldy, so she carefully pulled each one out partway to check the foil around the wire cap. None had signs of damage or tampering, and the corks didn't pop off while she handled them. Everything appeared to be in order, which eased her worries. She'd still ask Chris to check later.

"*Chérie, j'arrive.*" She heard rapping on the open door, and Patrick descended into the cellar. "Sean said I could find you here. Hope everything is okay."

"Seems to be," Catherine said. "Let's head out." She wasn't comfortable being in a dark, confined space with him.

"What's the rush? Let's take advantage of the privacy." Patrick caressed her arm. "You're very enticing." He leaned in for a kiss.

She turned her head, causing his lips to brush her cheek. "Patrick, I care for you as a friend."

"*D'accord, amis proches*," he said. "After this launch business is over, think about joining Tournelle. We're expanding. You're half French. It's a good fit."

"I could never work in the same company with Édouard," she said.

"*Merde*, he's so stupid. We're in the middle of a big deal and he loses control. If he weren't my brother, I'd cut him out."

She gave him a strange look. He caught himself. "I don't want to bore you with family problems," he said. "I thought your childhood spat with Édouard was past history."

"Childhood spat!" Catherine was incensed. "He raped me. You know that. You took my side at the time."

"Figured if I calmed you down it would blow over," he said.

Seeing his true colors, she asked, "Why are you really pursuing me? Is it because of my inheritance?"

"So, you finally learned about that. Thought it was odd your parents kept that from you." Undeterred, he continued. "We could make a strong alliance." He grabbed her arm to pull her closer.

"Are you kidding?" Catherine raised her voice. "Take your hands off me!"

"Forget the money. You're not worth the aggravation," Patrick growled. "There is something I will take, though . . ." He grabbed her dress and ripped the buttons all the way down, exposing her bra and thong.

Struggling to cover herself, Catherine yelled, "Knock it off! You can't get away with this." Then she kicked him in the shins, hard.

He winced and slapped her. "You little bitch. No one will believe you. I'll say we're lovers and you like it rough—and kinky." He grabbed a piece of rope hanging nearby. She tried to fight him off, but he managed to bind her hands.

Catherine started screaming as loud as she could. She was terrified. Patrick moved closer, looking murderous. He gripped her body and fumbled with his pants zipper.

Chris sped up. He'd received Catherine's text on his way back to the château. If there was foul play, she could be in danger, especially if she went to the cellar by herself. That fear multiplied tenfold when he pulled into the circular drive and heard her screams coming from the side of the building.

He opened the car door, raced to the cellar entrance, and rushed down the stairs. When he saw Patrick assaulting Catherine, her dress ripped wide open, he went into a blind rage.

"You beast!" Chris shouted. "Let her go!" He ran down the narrow aisle, jerked Patrick off Catherine, and started pummeling him with his fists. Not an even fight—Chris was much stronger and livid. He landed a flurry of blows to Patrick's upper body and face, bloodying his nose.

Patrick grabbed the saber off the wall. It made an eerie metallic scraping sound as he pulled it out of its sheaf. Chris stepped back, away from the blade.

Circling the saber closer to Chris, Patrick taunted, "Now let's see how brave you are."

"You can't get away with this," Chris snarled. "Put that down."

"Can't I? Everyone knows you fly off the handle. I'll say you were upset to see me and Catherine enjoying each other's company."

Catherine strained to free herself. "Stop it, Patrick," she said. "It's over."

He looked in her direction. "I'm not done yet. Your boyfriend broke my nose. He has to pay," Patrick said.

While Catherine diverted Patrick's attention, Chris observed freestanding shelves in the aisle. When Patrick lunged forward with the sword, Chris pulled the heavy shelving down, knocking Patrick to the ground and burying him in wooden slats and heavy bottles. Patrick flailed and cursed in French but couldn't extricate himself.

The groundskeeper yelled down from the open door, "Is everything okay?"

"There was an assault!" Chris shouted. "Call the cops and bring some zip ties." Chris freed Catherine's hands and wrapped his jacket around her. He carried her up the steps, avoiding the broken glass and spilled wine.

The police arrived quickly and secured the scene, taking Patrick into custody. Catherine gave a preliminary statement to the officer and agreed to be interviewed at the station the following day.

"I'm taking you to my suite," Chris said. "I don't want you to be alone right now."

After they stepped into his room, he closed the door and gazed at her tenderly. "Did he hurt you?"

Catherine clasped her hands. "My hands are scraped." She had a look of panic on her face. "My ring is missing."

"I'll find your ring," he said. Chris enveloped her in a warm hug and caressed her hair. "I'm so sorry this happened to you."

She rubbed her arms. "I was scared, couldn't fight him off. Thank goodness you showed up. I shudder to think what would have happened." She started to shiver.

"I'm going to draw you a bath," Chris said. "Looks like your body is going into shock." He pulled out a fluffy white bathrobe from the closet and wrapped it around her. "I'll have Vanessa bring your clothes over."

While Catherine soaked in the tub, Chris reached James, who rushed back to the château. They met in a corner of the salon downstairs.

"He won't get away with this," James said. "Catherine is like a daughter to me."

"We spoke to the police briefly and have an appointment to meet tomorrow to give a full statement, under oath," Chris said.

"I want a good French attorney there to represent you both," James said. "No funny stuff. I'll get Yves on it."

"God knows what Patrick will say to get out of this." Chris agreed they shouldn't take any chances. "One other thing. Catherine thinks Patrick knew about the jeroboams for the launch. We might have a traitor in our midst. She smelled something off when a few bottles shattered."

"I'll look into it. We need to keep this quiet until we figure out what's going on." James pulled out his phone. "Do you think Catherine will be okay tonight?"

"I plan to make sure of it."

"Good. We'll speak first thing in the morning." James got to work on his calls and Chris went into the dining room to order a meal for two brought up to his suite.

Then he returned to the château cellar. Yellow police tape crossed the doorway. He crawled under it and searched for Catherine's ring, using the flashlight on his phone. It was eerie to imagine what could have happened to her. It gave him chills.

He found her ring under broken shelving. A small victory for the evening.

Two hours later, Catherine nestled into Chris's arms in his bed. It was all he could do to stop himself from taking things further. He reminded himself that she'd been through a terrible ordeal and needed rest. She wore the same sexy rose silk pjs he'd admired when he saw her on that balcony in Napa five months ago. Before she changed his life completely.

Chapter Twenty-Six

Bordeaux—Celebration launch day

Catherine woke slowly. Sun streamed in through parted drapes framing French doors that led out to a small balcony. She glanced around. This wasn't her room. And it wasn't her bed. Then she remembered.

Patrick had assaulted her last night, and Chris came to her rescue. If he hadn't arrived in time, she would have been raped. Again. By another Tournelle brother!

She couldn't recall much after that except Chris being very solicitous and protective, insisting she stay with him. She must have taken a sleeping pill because she felt rested.

Chris walked into the bedroom, a towel draped around his waist, and gave her a concerned look. "I'm going to have breakfast brought to the room. What would you like?"

What she wanted was him. "Think I'll take a shower," Catherine said. "Wanna join me?"

"Are you sure?" He looked hesitant.

"Positive," she said.

"Oh yeah. Breakfast can wait."

The suite had a luxurious bathroom. A large walk-in shower resembled a spa, complete with steam function, water jets to massage the back, rain showerhead, and built-in stone bench.

Chris picked up a soft mitt, poured scented bath gel on it, and slowly caressed Catherine's body. Then he pulled her closer, devouring her mouth with deep kisses.

She figured he might be reluctant to take things further after her trauma yesterday, so she seized the initiative—soaping his bare chest and moving her hands down his stomach, past his waist, and around his large erection, an unmistakable sign of his desire.

"Are you sure about this?" Chris asked for the second time. She answered by nibbling his ear.

Not waiting for another invitation, he groaned, "Let's take this to the bed." They toweled each other off quickly, and he swooped her up in his arms.

Chris cherished her body, taking his time and bringing her arousal to a tormenting state. She reveled in the closeness and urged him on. After screaming their orgasms, they lay wrapped around each other. Catherine never felt more complete. This was where she belonged. In Chris's arms, in his life.

She wished they could linger, but Chris needed to be at a meeting downstairs in an hour, and she had work to do. This was it: Launch Day.

Breakfast arrived, and Chris placed the room service cart in front of the opened French doors, facing the garden. Wearing robes, they ate in companionable silence. Everything tasted better: her strong coffee, flaky pastries, and fresh berries. Chris smiled tenderly and reached over to hold her hand.

"I don't ever want to lose you again," he said.

"You won't," she said, feeling overjoyed.

Chris entered the château dining room a few minutes before his ten o'clock meeting. He didn't want to be far from Catherine until they knew what they were dealing with in the aftermath of Patrick's attack. Patrick was in custody with Bordeaux police but was scheduled to be released later in the day.

James arrived with Yves. The three men ordered coffee and went to work. Yves gave them a status report on the legal situation. Trianon had hired a French attorney to represent Catherine—and Chris, if needed—and deal with the Bordeaux authorities. The attorney rescheduled their appearance at the police station to the following day so they could meet with him first.

"I'd like to set up protection for Catherine this week," Chris said. "God knows what Patrick will try." Now that he'd found the woman of his dreams, he was making damn sure she was safe.

After looking at Yves for confirmation, James said, "We'll work something out when one of us isn't with her. We have other problems with Patrick. Looks like he's behind the attempts to sabotage our launch."

Chris was livid. He knew he'd smelled a rat with this guy.

James detailed what they'd learned last night after Catherine's attack. Jean had tested the jeroboams and confirmed they were tainted. He detected a slight change in the taste and suspected whatever was added could cause stomach distress and vomiting. It would have been devastating to Winston's reputation.

Yves interjected, "Fortunately, we're replacing them with a shipment of Celebration magnums we received at Trianon for the Relais & Châteaux contest. Our trucker is bringing them here this morning."

We dodged a bullet. Catherine was the heroine in this drama. She suspected foul play when Patrick revealed he knew they were using jeroboams.

James took a sip of water and continued his recap. He'd reached Tom in Napa last night, which was midday California time. Tom immediately called in the authorities. An FBI agent from San Francisco questioned the staff, and a winery worker caved quickly, admitting Robert paid him to add a solution to the jeroboams during disgorgement before they were capped.

"I wouldn't be surprised if Robert intentionally caused the bottle fiasco at Spago, too," Chris said.

James said Robert had lawyered up, but Joel's team had done a forensic examination of his emails and texts and found suspicious communications between Robert, Sean, and Patrick Tournelle. Joel recommended Sean be suspended, pending termination.

"I agreed and sent him back to New York on an early flight this morning," James said. "I'm very disheartened to learn my sales director is in cahoots with our competitor."

"What's the motivation?" Chris asked. "Money?"

"I have a partial answer," Yves said. "According to my sources, Tournelle is having financial problems. They found a Saudi backer who is stipulating that they must expand to overseas wineries."

James completed the thought. "If our launch is a bust and Chamath pulls his funding, Tournelle could swoop in and pick up our contracts in South America and Australia. That's incentive for Patrick to enlist Sean and Robert . . . and pay them off."

"They already tried to poach the Chile winery," Chris said.

James dragged a hand through his hair. "We'll need to keep these findings to ourselves for now."

Yves nodded and put down his espresso cup. "Are we still

on for lunch with Chamath and the new winery partners?" he asked.

"Yes, of course," James said.

Another day. Another party. Catherine and Vanessa were in their room going through a preparty routine perfected over many years.

This day felt different though. For the first time in her life, Catherine was madly, deeply in love—and felt loved back. Even the distress from Patrick's assault didn't dampen her mood.

When her parents learned the news, they were furious and said they'd cut all ties with the Tournelles. Catherine asked them not to bring it up at the party. She wanted to avoid that distraction, if possible.

Vanessa finished blow-drying Catherine's hair and smoothed it down. "You were off in never-never land. Dreaming about your beau?" she asked.

"Caught me." Catherine smiled. "You've got a dreamy date yourself."

"Yep, and Will's picking us up soon. We've got to scoot. He rented a Jaguar Classic. Wanted to take us in style."

"Too bad there's no red carpet to show it off."

They'd packed dressy outfits specifically for tonight. Catherine wore a powder-blue Alberta Ferretti Grecian-goddess gown, and Vanessa shimmied into a skin-tight Dior minidress with high, spiky heels.

After a final makeup check and spritz of perfume, they put their phones and lipsticks in small-beaded clutches and went downstairs to meet Will.

Showtime, Catherine told herself.

They arrived at Cité du Vin at five, ninety minutes before the event kicked off. Recently constructed and already a Bordeaux landmark, the modern architectural wonder was designed to evoke "the very soul of wine" and stood out among the more traditional buildings on the Garonne River shoreline.

During normal hours, visitors to this international wine museum were taken through an immersive, interactive experience demonstrating the creation and culture of wine, culminating in a tasting on the top (eighth) floor, boasting an unobstructed view of Bordeaux from all sides.

Tonight, the Belvedere space was transformed for the Winston launch party. Wait staff bustled to prepare serving stations. Frédéric supervised workers constructing a five-foot-high pyramid of champagne flutes under a monumental chandelier made up of thousands of wine bottles.

"I need to do my final check with the band," Vanessa said. Will gave her a warm embrace and went to find a quiet spot to handle calls.

Catherine headed over to assist Agnès and her team at sign-in tables nearby. A full press contingent had RSVP'd, including television crews and all the major wine reporters. Once word got out about Patrick's assault on Catherine and Chris coming to her rescue, it became the most tantalizing news of the week; everyone wanted to show up in case there were fireworks—of the human variety.

Immersed in conversation with Agnès a half hour before start time, Catherine didn't know Chris had arrived until he appeared next to her, looking devastatingly handsome in a midnight-blue suit. Unmindful of stares directed their way, he gave her a bone-crushing embrace. "I love you, Cat Reynolds," he whispered in her ear.

He's letting his guard down and trusting me. She'd never felt so cherished.

"Love you back," she said.

"I spoke with James about us, and he couldn't be more supportive," Chris said. "You won't be reporting to me, but you will always have a job at Winston if you want it, full- or part-time while you're taking classes."

Beyond thrilled, Catherine could pinch herself. All her wishes were coming true. From over Chris's shoulder, she saw her parents approaching with James. *We're public now.*

"Hi honey," her mom said. "I know we're early. We wanted to be here first thing to share this moment with you."

Catherine gave them hugs and motioned to Chris. "Mom and Dad, I'd like you to meet Chris McDermott, president of Winston . . . and my boyfriend." She added to Chris, "My parents, Marie-Christine and John Reynolds."

"Very nice to meet you," Chris said and reached to shake their hands while keeping his other arm wrapped possessively around Catherine's waist.

"We're thankful to you both for giving Catherine this job opportunity," her dad said.

"One of the best hires I've ever made," James chimed in. "Have to give Elizabeth most of the credit. She's very astute."

"Mom is a real chess master—five moves ahead of everyone else," Catherine's dad said.

The band began playing background jazz music, reminding Catherine of a different party five months ago, when she'd first met Chris in Napa. What a whirlwind. So much had transpired since then.

Invitees streamed in, and the space filled up quickly. The festive mood was contagious as people partook in hors d'oeuvres and mineral water until the unveiling. James pulled Chris over to speak with Chamath and the new winery partners from South America and Australia. Sue Hamilton and the documentary crew set up and rolled tape while she interviewed Doug Barr.

Ken Barnett approached Catherine. "Quite a bash. You doin' okay?"

"Very well, thanks." Catherine looped her arm through his. "Let's circulate. You can be my protection against unwelcome questions."

"Happy to," he said. Ken lived up to his promise and ran interference when reporters tried to get a statement from Catherine about what they referred to as her "incident" with Patrick.

A loud bell rang, indicating the ceremony was about to commence. The crowd gathered around the glass pyramid in the center of the room.

James turned on a standing mic. "Welcome everyone. I see we have a big turnout. The team at Winston & Wright is very excited about the next phase in our company's growth, starting with today's launch of our first prestige sparkling, aptly named Celebration," he said and smiled at Catherine.

"I want to thank my cofounder, Alan Wright"—James pointed to Alan, who waved to the guests—"and our French partners at Trianon for getting us to this point. With that, I'll turn it over to Jean Boyer, the masterful winemaker responsible for this blend."

"*Bienvenue mes amis*," Jean said. "I will open the first magnum the old-fashioned way, with a saber." Jean pulled the saber out of its sheath, Yves handed him the magnum, and Jean swung the saber in an upward motion against the lip of the bottle, causing the cork to fly off.

Jean immediately righted the bottle and handed it to Yves, who poured the sparkling wine into the top glass in the pyramid. That glass filled and the wine trickled into the glasses below.

The crowd reacted instantly with oohs and aahs. Cameras flashed. Television crews filmed. It was quite a sight.

Frédéric opened other magnums and helped Yves pour the sparkling wine into the rest of the glasses. Waiters circulated with trays of champagne flutes, streams of tiny effervescent bubbles floating to the surface of each glass.

The band struck up the intro bars to "Celebration" by Kool & the Gang. Vanessa winked at Catherine and started singing. The music was so contagious that guests began to dance and sing along to the lyrics. Catherine knew it was the perfect song; it truly was a Celebration. The party mood was infectious; the evening was a hit!

Chris joined Catherine and Ken. "Hello, Ken," he said. "Thanks for guarding my girl."

"No worries," Ken said. He lifted his flute, "This is good stuff. Warrants a top rating in my piece on Winston."

"We appreciate that," Chris said.

The next oldie began, Vanessa's signature Stevie Wonder tune, "Knocks Me Off My Feet."

"Miss Reynolds." Chris held out his hand. "I believe they're playing our song."

She placed her hand in his and they walked onto the dance floor. Chris pulled her tight in his embrace and swung her around the floor in time to the music. She let herself get swept up in the music and apt lyrics—*this man makes me weak and knocks me off my feet.*

He whispered in her ear, "I booked Hôtel de Pavie in Saint-Émilion for tonight. Figured we'd get away from the crowd. If the lady is willing."

Yes, she was. Catherine held him even closer and lay her head on his shoulder in response. She could hear shutters clicking as photographers snapped pics of them. *Never a dull moment with this man.*

It wouldn't be dark until after nine, so people congregated on the outdoor terrace to enjoy the soft breeze and striking views of Bordeaux and the river below.

Catherine had a moment to herself. She took a sip of Celebration and was immensely proud they'd pulled it off. She looked around at her loved ones and her heart was full. Vanessa and Will conversing intimately in a corner. Chris and James, heads bent together, hatching some plan. Her parents speaking rapid French in a group with Yves, Jean, and Chamath. They caught her eye and came over to join her.

"We're very proud of you, honey," her dad said.

Her mom nodded in agreement. "Your new beau seems very devoted. He's quite handsome—you two would make beautiful babies." Leave it to her mom to cut to the chase.

This time, Catherine agreed with her wholeheartedly. "Thanks, Mom. He's a special guy. I'm very happy."

At that moment, a firework display started bursting off from a nearby boat on the river. Chris came up behind Catherine and wrapped his arms around her so they could watch together. "This is a surprise," he said. "Didn't know you planned this."

"Hope I'll always keep you on your toes," she said.

"I'm sure you will," he said and nuzzled her neck.

Vibrantly colored fireworks, designed to be seen in daylight, created quite a show. Partygoers sipped the prestige sparkling and pointed to the streaks and pops in the sky. A word appeared to be forming. All at once it flashed before them—CELEBRATION—unveiled by tiny drones.

A dazzling spectacle. A true celebration.

Epilogue

Napa—eleven months later

Their wedding day! Chris marveled at his luck finding the woman of his dreams. Catherine captivated him. Thank goodness their paths crossed and they'd surmounted the hurdles thrown in their way.

"Almost ready?" Will asked as he rapped on the door.

"Am I ever," Chris said. He couldn't wait to start the next chapter of his life. "I'll meet you downstairs."

Chris adjusted the bow tie on his black tuxedo. The wedding ceremony was taking place in the local church where his mom and dad were married. He and Catherine had decided to keep it intimate: only fifty guests, close family and friends. Of course, James was attending. He'd practically matched them up.

Since Vinexpo in Bordeaux, James had increased Chris's responsibilities and salary. The Winston expansion was booming, helped along by great reviews for Celebration. Their French partner, Trianon, won first prize in the Relais & Châteaux contest and Winston's Celebration *cuvée* placed second, a great accomplishment competing against quality French champagnes. Naysayers groused that Winston was pulled along by Trianon's good showing. No matter, it gave them bragging rights and ammunition in the California sparking versus French champagne debate.

Chris met Will in the lobby of the Winston Resort where they'd booked rooms for most of the wedding guests. Maura insisted on hosting Catherine and her close friends at the McDermott ranch so she could pamper them, and make sure Chris didn't see the bride beforehand.

The congregation stood as the priest recited a final prayer and blessed their union as man and wife. The couple shared a steamy kiss, and Catherine's eyes teared up as they faced their family and friends. This was the happiest moment of her life.

The wedding party followed the newlyweds down the aisle as they proceeded outside. Maid of honor Vanessa and best man Will had become a couple, which thrilled Catherine and Chris. His brothers were groomsmen. The bridesmaids were Catherine's other friends from Les Femmes, the club formed at her Swiss girls' school—a truly international group: Emma Hamilton from Australia, Erin McCartney from Ireland, and Isabella Orsini from Italy.

For this occasion, the ladies wore matching ankle charm bracelets they'd made in Gstaad before their graduation. Each anklet held six charms: the edelweiss flower and the five club members' names etched on silver hearts. Catherine wore it on her wrist so it wouldn't be obscured by the train on her finely beaded white wedding dress, the same gown her mother had worn thirty-three years ago.

Her parents and Chris's family had hit it off immediately, so there was no friction when Chris and Catherine revealed they planned to settle down in Napa in a few years. In the meantime,

James tasked them with overseeing the transition of a new Winston winery in Tuscany. Catherine would get a chance to put her recent Cornell training to use designing the adjacent resort; an added plus, she could visit her parents in Paris on a regular basis.

The after-ceremony festivities were kicking off with a champagne reception in the church garden before a sit-down dinner at Winston Resort.

Catherine and her friends gathered at a tall round table sheltered by a eucalyptus tree, champagne flutes in hand.

Vanessa lifted her glass aloft. "To the first member of Les Femmes to get hitched. Congrats Cat."

They all clinked glasses and began chattering at once.

"About that," Emma's voice carried the loudest. "Can't believe you're the first. You never talked about wanting to get married."

"Surprised me too," Catherine said. "What can I say,"—she gazed off dreamily—"he swept me off my feet."

"Any guy would win me over with that amazing ring," Erin said.

Catherine held out her left hand so the women could admire her engagement ring. "He got it at Cartier in Place Vendôme to match the trinity ring from my grandma," she said. The platinum band was set with a dazzling emerald surrounded by brilliant-cut diamonds.

"Speaking of weddings,"—Catherine got a gleam in her eye—"let's decide who should catch my bouquet." They all believed in the magical power of certain traditions; this one needed to be taken advantage of.

"Well, it's certainly not going to be me," Isabella huffed.

"Why not?" Vanessa asked.

"The only man in my life is a very annoying Brit who owns the Tuscan estate where I'm renting a guesthouse."

"Is he devastatingly handsome?" Catherine asked.

Isabella shook her head. "I suppose, if you like that type, which I don't."

Vanessa picked up the ball. "We'll be in Florence in a few months. Think we should check him out."

Catherine grinned. "Or find a handsome Italian for Isabella. Hear they grow on trees over there."

All the friends, except Isabella, were laughing now. She looked steamed as the conversation circulated around her.

"Not so fast." Isabella made a time-out gesture with her hands. "I'm focused on my career right now."

"That's what I said," Catherine retorted, "and look where it got me."

On cue, Chris and Will joined the group.

"Hello ladies," Chris said. "I've come to claim my wife."

Author's Note

The Champagne Crush is a work of fiction set in the time period right before the Covid pandemic. Many of the restaurants and hotels in the story are real places, all of which I highly recommend for a visit.

Vinexpo, a trade show for the wine industry, features prominently in the story. It was held in June in Bordeaux for decades but has recently moved to Paris and is held there earlier in the year. Bordeaux is still a center for wine appreciation and well worth a trip.

Relais & Châteaux is a real association of charming accommodations and gourmet restaurants. They had no participation in the creation of this book, and I received no remuneration from them.

I hope you enjoyed reading *The Champagne Crush* and would be very grateful for a rating or short review on Amazon.

Let's stay in touch. You can sign up for my monthly newsletter at https://www.CarolineOC.com to receive giveaways, travel tips, and updates on the next book in the Les Femmes Series.

Merci beaucoup,

Caroline O'Connell

Acknowledgments

In France

Composing this story would not have been possible without Yves Bénard and Jean Berchon—dear friends and former executives at a major French Champagne house—who introduced me to the inside world of champagne. In addition to extending invitations to elegant Parisian soirées featuring top French chefs, they shared their expertise on the business of champagne: how it's made, how it's marketed, and how it's enjoyed. *Merci milles fois.*

While living in Paris, I met Sue Cameron Cosser, who took me on my first visit to the Champagne region and an unforgettable lunch at Royal Champagne in Épernay, and Carole Darnat Bricout, who shared an insider's view of Frenchwomen's femininity.

I am also indebted to two other close friends in France: Frédéric Reglain, my Paris photographer, for providing insights on all things Parisian; and Guy Verda, my French teacher.

Writing and Publishing Support

Many thanks to two fellow writers instrumental in reaching this goal: longtime friend Roger DiSilvestro, a brilliant novelist and environmental writer (and former PR client); and my sister, Katie

Sweeting, who recently published her first novel, *Remnant*. Roger's words of wisdom helped carry me through the many (and I mean many) drafts to tighten the story and polish my prose. Katie and Roger shared support and advice amid the angst and rejections that are part of the process of getting a book published.

John Truby's teachings provided a roadmap to plot my story. He is also a former PR client and friend, and the author of two excellent books on writing—*The Anatomy of Story* and *The Anatomy of Genres*.

In a writing workshop in Ojai, California, led by literary agent Toni Lopopola, I learned about Renni Browne's excellent book, *Self-Editing for Fiction Writers* (with Dave King). That book led me to Renni's firm, The Editorial Department (TED), run by her son Ross Browne. Through TED, I hired Lindsay Guzzardo for an excellent developmental edit that was key to refining my story and upping the stakes.

My publisher referred Anne Durette, who did a meticulous job on the final copy edit and proofread.

I'm thrilled to be working with Brooke Warner and the team at SparkPress and am grateful for their efforts to give *The Champagne Crush* the best launch an author could hope for.

Friends and Family

My "Art Group" partners Ginny Davis and Andrea Levine have been great company on numerous research trips to Paris and other European locales.

Close friends Liza Garfield, Elke Owens, and Christine McClure accompanied me on earlier trips to France when the initial concept was conceived.

Kristin Mattes is my fashion guru and go-to consultant for research on the jewelry mentioned in the book.

Curt de Crinis lent his expertise on financial matters in the story and urged me on: "Is your novel done yet?" he asked on a regular basis. Admittedly, it was long process.

I won the lotto when it comes to supportive parents. Claire and Richard O'Connell demonstrated continual learning, curiosity, and love of reading. There were bookshelves in every room of our house—from Shakespeare to Ian Fleming to Jane Austen to Ralph Waldo Emerson. Miss you both every day.

Finally, writing is a solitary pursuit, but not a lonely one when you have a passel of fab felines to keep you company. Special shout-out to white fluffball Belle-Peony for being my intrepid companion on recent trips to Paris and Tuscany, in preparation for my next novel set in Italy.

About the Author

Photo credit: Jill Salmi

Caroline O'Connell is the author of six travel guidebooks, including *Every Woman's Guide to Romance in Paris* (Square One Publishers) and *Affordable Paris Hotels* (Travel Smart Press). She has written numerous travel articles for magazines and websites, appeared on national TV, including *The Oprah Winfrey Show*, and been featured in the *Los Angeles Times*.

O'Connell helmed a successful public relations firm for twenty years that specialized in national author tours. She is a member of the Authors Guild and lives in Los Angeles, California.